THE THINGS WE LEARN WHEN WE'RE DEAD

CHARLIE LAIDLAW

ISBN 9781786150356

Copyright © Charlie Laidlaw 2016

Printed by Accent Press Ltd 2017

For Neil Johnson, teacher

Single is the race, single
Of men and gods;
From a single mother we both draw breath.
But a difference of power in everything
Keeps us apart;
For one is as nothing, but the brazen sky
Stays a fixed habituation for ever.
Yet we can in greatness of mind
Or of body be like the Immortals

On the Olympics: Pindar of Thebes,
Ancient Greek lyric poet

The universe is change; our life is what our thoughts make it.

Meditations: Marcus Aurelius Antoninus
121AD – 180AD

END

At the end of her Edinburgh street, where it joined a busier road, was a security camera perched high on a metal pole. If anyone had been watching they would have seen a slim young woman in a red dress illuminated under a streetlight. They would have seen that she seemed agitated, her feet fluttering on the pavement's edge, her hands raised to her face, turning this way and that, and then stepping into the road. She seemed to be crying, unsure what she was doing. They would have seen the approaching car and that the young woman was looking in the wrong direction. When she did hear it, turning in mesmerised surprise, it was too late. But perhaps nobody had been watching the CCTV screen because it was the driver of the car who called for the ambulance as a small crowd gathered, and who then tried to make the young woman comfortable – talking to her, even pushing his jacket under her head – and waited beside her until the ambulance arrived and the paramedic said he couldn't detect a pulse.

* * *

On the morning of her death, suicide bombers blew themselves up on London's transport network. Three on the Tube and one on a bus. Dozens were killed, many more maimed. She watched, appalled, as the news unfolded, curled on the sofa, making cups of coffee that she didn't drink, while the sun traversed the rooftops and

1

patterned her in shadows. It seemed a rerun of 9/11 or Bali or Madrid; random and senseless. That was what angered her the most: it was carnage without fathomable purpose. She was alone in her flat; she'd had an argument with her flatmate who had flounced off, muttering darkly and swearing loudly. But she was used to being alone; she welcomed the silence and solitude because it didn't allow for distraction: it gave her the space to frown over her law books, sucking on a pencil or tapping on her keyboard. But today she wanted company, someone to share her outrage with, and she didn't know who to phone. Instead, she'd make another cup of coffee, set it on the table beside the sofa, and throw it away when it was stone cold.

She'd been invited to a dinner party in the evening but didn't want to go. However, invitations to a Redmarsh soiree did not arrive lightly and, as Toby Redmarsh was senior partner at the law firm for which Lorna would soon be working, it wasn't an invitation that could easily be refused.

That didn't mean that she was looking forward to it. Born and bred in modest circumstances, she still felt socially uncertain in the company of the more gilded. It was stupid of her, and she knew it; she had overcome disadvantages of class and schooling to arrive at the hallowed portals of Wilson, MacGraw & Hamilton. It had been always been her ambition to be a lawyer but now, on the verge of attainment, she had become increasingly uncomfortable. She would be the office's sacrificial socialist – she knew *that* as well – the example held up as living proof that talent could reap its reward in the rarefied world of corporate and commercial law.

'Casual, of course,' Toby's wife Tessa had commanded. In Edinburgh's New Town there was a bohemian tradition to live up to. 'We'll see you at eight. 'You know our address, don't you?' The voice was contralto, and it was not really meant as a question: everyone should know where Tessa and Toby Redmarsh lived. If not, they had no business being invited.

In the morning, after the bombs had gone off, Lorna phoned Toby, who spoke to his wife, who told him that the dinner was of course still on. 'We can't give into them,' he then told Lorna, having been given the party line. 'We have to keep going as normal. Tessa thinks that we're doing the right thing,' he said.

She dressed, watching the evening news, marvelling at the simplicity of mass murder. It made no sense to her; she'd never wanted to hurt anybody in her life. Then she cried and had to put her make-up on again.

The Redmarshes' house, Lorna discovered, was on an imposing square close to the city's West End; near enough to allow its residents to feel themselves in close proximity to real people, but far enough away to be insulated from them. It was Georgian and on four floors, and lit from top to toe like a cruise liner.

A Filipino maid dressed in black, down to her jet earrings, opened the door to Lorna and, without speaking, took her coat and ushered her to the drawing room. Tessa was holding out both hands as Lorna waded through thick carpet, and although they had never met, beckoning Lorna like an old friend.

'My dear girl! How nice to finally meet you!'

Tessa allowed her cheek to be kissed; offering Lorna its flat surface as if to a supplicant, then took her arm and led her towards the unlit fireplace, and the group of other guests around it. On the walls hung large and impressive canvases, each lit from above by a downward-slanting brass lamp. No art expert, even Lorna recognised two sets of tortured faces as Howsons; in another, matchstick men streamed from a factory gate that just had to be by Lowry. Lorna gazed around the room with a mixture of awe and contempt, as Tessa took her arm and they negotiated the baby grand piano on which sat family photographs in silver frames and what might have been a small and abstract Paolozzi.

'This, everyone, is Lorna Love,' trilled Tessa, pushing her towards several pairs of devouring eyes. 'She's also a lawyer, aren't you?' Her hands plucked and tugged Lorna to an ornate gilt settee and prodded her down into one upholstered corner. The unspeaking maid offered Lorna a flute of pink champagne on a silver tray.

'I'm not really a lawyer,' Lorna replied.

'But you will be. Soon. Toby says great things about you.' Tessa beamed, displaying whiter-than-white teeth. 'Anyway, it's great fun, don't you agree?' she said, moving in beside her. 'Pink champagne, I mean.' Her long fingers, wrapped around the stem of her glass, had blue fingernails, the same colour as her dress. 'But how remiss, I haven't done the honours, have I? I don't suppose you know anybody here.'

Tessa's bracelet in the half-light was a golden rattle as she thrust her hand towards the nearest couple: a balding bespectacled man in his late fifties, and a flaccid woman in a purple tracksuit and double string of pearls.

'This is Geoffrey Crumb – or should I say Lord Geoffrey Crumb – and his Lady wife, Monica.' Lorna solemnly shook their hands, recognising the man as a High Court judge.

'– and this is Marcia Apsley, whose husband Walter is such a *darling* man.' Marcia, dyed-blonde hair to her shoulders, and too old to be wearing the shortest of short black dresses, gave her a broad smile; Walter, in a sober blue suit, barely touched her fingers and looked away. Tessa indicated her husband with a sweeping motion of her hand. 'And you know old Toby, don't you.' Toby Redmarsh, propped against the mantelpiece, raised his glass in welcome.

'Right then,' said Tessa and tinkled a small silver bell. 'We can eat.'

Lorna was placed between the tracksuit of Lady Crumb and, on her left, Marcia Apsley who, without ceremony, immediately poured herself a glass of white wine. No girl-boy-girl seating arrangements at the Redmarsh table. There was avocado to start, carefully scooped from its shell, mashed up with cream, herbs, and chopped bacon, and served back hot in its skin. 'We got the recipe from a friend in Cape Town,' explained Tessa, although it was clear the Filipino maid did all the cooking. 'Out there, of course, avocados are almost weeds.'

'Makes you think,' said Marcia, poking at her avocado with a fork. 'I don't think I've ever eaten weeds before.'

Walter snatched a quick glance at his wife and guffawed to signal that Marcia, already pouring herself a second glass of wine, had made a joke.

* * *

In a lull in the conversation, as they were finishing the hot avocado, and as the Filipino maid began to clear plates, Marcia asked Lorna if she really was a lawyer. It was clear that, in Marcia's circle of acquaintances, lawyers spoke the Queen's English.

'I'm going to be working with Toby,' replied Lorna, making no effort to disguise her provincial accent, 'although I still have exams to pass.'

'How exciting!' said Marcia. 'At least, I suppose, it must be somewhat exciting. Being a lawyer, and all that. Actually, that's a strange word if you think about it,' she added after a pause. 'Somewhat.' She pronounced it *sum-wot*. 'Like a fruit.'

'That's kumquat,' said Toby.

Marcia looked up from her plate, shrugged, then handed her plate to the Filipino who was circling the table replenishing empty glasses. She held the bottle in a white napkin that obscured the label, and her face was pitted with the pockmarks of some childhood affliction.

'She's from Manila,' said Tessa when the door had closed and their empty dishes were rattling down the hallway. 'Nowadays we wouldn't know what to do without her.'

'I went there once. In the Army,' said the High Court judge, and tilted back his head. 'Extended leave. Ate dog once. Not very nice, but did have a bite to it.' He paused to see if anyone thought this funny, which nobody did. 'Thought I should see a bit of the world. Long time ago, of course.'

'We call her Gertie,' said Tessa, ignoring him. 'Her real name is unpronounceable.'

Let others invent a name for you, Lorna thought, and hide behind their generosity. She shouldn't have drunk the pink champagne or the wine with dinner. The doctor had said her medication was incompatible with alcohol. Lorna felt light-headed, suddenly tearful, thinking about the bombings.

London, of course, dominated the conversation, punctuated by appearances from the unpronounceable Filipino who circled their laden table, balancing salvers and empty plates in her sensible hands. Lorna watched the maid's studious anonymity, feeling hot, and then shivering; a pool of tears had gathered behind her eyes. She dabbed at them with her serviette, or napkin, or whatever they were called in a house like this.

'It's an obscenity,' Toby was saying, 'but the real danger lies in getting our response wrong. It's a question of choice. Either we continue to uphold the sanctity of human rights or we now make national security paramount. The two are incompatible. The government will bring in new terror laws, no doubt about it.'

The High Court judge agreed. 'It's also a question of rights and responsibilities,' he said, enunciating clearly as if giving a judgement. 'Everyone has the right to disagree with what the government is doing. In Iraq or about anything else. That doesn't give them the right to kill people.'

It was a blindingly obvious point but, since he was a High Court judge, nobody could disagree.

'Anyway,' said Tessa, keeping a close eye on the Filipino who was circulating once more with wine and replenishing glasses. 'I just think we should shoot them.'

Toby cut a slice of gristle from his beef and slid it to the side of his plate where it bled like a sacrifice. 'All very well, of course, if you manage to shoot the right people. We can only hope that the intelligence services know who the bad guys are.' Toby's confident tone suggested he had a rare faith in the intelligence community, nodding and smiling over his heaped plate.

But Tessa felt that he had missed the point and waved her fork alarmingly at him. 'Meanwhile, don't you see, more people get blown up. Bugger their human rights! What about *our* human rights?' She made it seem like a personal affront and sawed at her meat with hunched shoulders.

Marcia had been listening to this exchange like a tennis spectator, moving her head back and forth, a dimpled smile playing on her lips. 'Actually, Tessa's quite right. All you lawyers do is pontificate, which is worse than useless. If suicide bombers want to take radical action against us, we should take radical action against them. The more radical the better, if you ask me.' She laughed across the table and tapped her empty wineglass in hospitable rebuke.

After dinner they sat over coffee and mints in the drawing room, with the curtains open and garden lights on the lawn conjuring daylight from the darkness. Lorna was standing with her back to the unlit fire, feeling light-headed. The doctor had been right; small white pills and wine was not a sensible combination. She sat down heavily on the settee and put a hand to her forehead.

Toby sat beside her and put a fatherly hand on her knee. 'Are you OK?' he asked. 'I have to say, you don't look terribly well.'

'Just tired,' said Lorna.

'You've been ill,' said Toby, 'and coming here tonight was probably not a good idea. Do you want me to call you a cab?'

Lorna nodded, wanting to cry.

'She's not well,' said Toby to nobody in particular, and helped her into the spacious hallway where he lowered Lorna into an upright chair. A grandfather clock ticked in one corner, and a staircase, thickly carpeted in green, led to a shadowed landing. The Filipino maid brought her a glass of water in a crystal glass. Lorna smiled her gratitude. The maid's eyes were black and impenetrable.

The taxi arrived and Toby helped her inside. Tessa fussed in the background, in a pool of light from the open doorway, her hands threaded together, smiling uncertainly. She unfurled her hands to wave goodbye.

'Just pass those bloody exams!' shouted Toby as the taxi door closed.

With her life fast diminishing, Lorna sat in the back of the cab with her eyes closed, squeezing tears inside her eyelids. Her veins were filled with a heady cocktail of regret. When the cab stopped, she stepped from the kerb to cross the street to her flat. But alcohol and conflicting thoughts had pressed in and deafened her.

* * *

For a few moments she didn't know where she was, except that she was lying in the road. She knew she was wearing a red dress – she was lying on one side with her head tucked down and could see it. With an effort she could remember she'd bought it in an Oxfam shop, and been worried by a red stain down one side that could have been tomato ketchup or blood from a previous murdered owner. She simply hadn't heard the approaching car or the screech of brakes until it was too late, feeling the push of air as it advanced and its bright and predatory eyes.

Then she was aware of a paramedic in a green uniform gently turning her onto her back and as she lay there, gazing at the stars, all she could feel was great sadness and a void that might not now be filled. Then, her eyesight fading, she heard a child crying, muffled sobs from nearby. The child seemed to be crying into a pillow, the feathers pressed against its mouth and nose. Lorna knew that the child didn't want to be heard or wake anybody up. It didn't want to make a fuss and, more than anything, it didn't want anybody to ask what was wrong. The child's sobs sounded familiar, but it still took Lorna some moments to realise the child was her. By then she was in darkness and becoming frightened. A part of her understood that something bad had happened, but she couldn't remember what. The child's sobs faded to silence.

LIFE

Her first recollection after the accident was of a dream, fragmented memories of a distant childhood; of reciting catechism on a Sunday with her nostrils full of incense; of soft words and kind hands upon her shoulder, propelling her towards an aged aunt who held a ribboned package in her hands. She felt water close around her, enfolding her in silence, while sunlight blazed on the water's surface. The water was cool; it soothed her. She opened her mouth and breathed it in. Aunt Meg had opened her package for Lorna to see: inside were the cut-up remains of a child's T-shirt. Aunt Meg was looking down through water and smiling. Lorna smiled back; bubbles floating to the surface. And then she was running barefoot on a summer meadow, gathering speed as she broached a hill and careened down the other side; wildflowers were spread at her feet, long grass billowed at her legs. She saw her mother; a picnic was scattered around her. Lorna peered through sunshine. Amid the cake and piles of sandwiches, her mother was buttering bread. Above, high in the sky, hung a single star and her mother was motioning for Lorna to sit beside her and close her eyes. She ran toward her mother, gaining speed, the wind bruising her face, watering her eyes. Then she stopped to catch her breath, blinking through tears. She was in a different place now: a deep valley. On both sides rose jagged hills, coal-black; broken bottles glittered, newspapers turned and tumbled. Sharp stones bit at her bare feet but there was no pain. A stream ran through the valley, black with coal-dust; birds, like pieces of tissue, wheeled high above. She fell effortlessly in slow motion, like a football replay, turning and tumbling down the valley wall while, on different peaks, she saw her parents watching her. Distant thunder echoed and raindrops patterned her upturned face.

Then, slowly, she seemed to rise upwards, like a diver leaving the bottom of the ocean. As she drew closer to the light, she also became aware of her breathing, of blinking, of wriggling her nose. She couldn't yet make out where she was, but could see shapes of people bending over her. She supposed that they were doctors or nurses, checking her pulse, changing drips, as she rose upwards towards the light, and finally awoke in an unfamiliar bed in a white room. One minute, she'd been asleep; the next, awake, blinking rapidly like a nocturnal animal. It took her some minutes to readjust to the light. She lay and blinked, giddy with relief. Above her head was a ventilation grille and she was wearing, as far as she could tell, a white nightgown. She felt drained of all energy. She slowly moved her head, looking around. I'm in a high-dependency ward, she concluded, with my own room. But she was puzzled by the lack of any visible medical apparatus. No oxygen tubes or feeding drips; no cabinets with painted crosses; not even a pedal-bin in which to deposit swabs or old bandages; just her bed, a bedside table, and on the far wall, tantalisingly, a full-length mirror.

For the next few hours or days, she kept her arms under the bedclothes; lifting them out would have been too much of an effort. In any case, they didn't feel like her arms. She tried to move them, to move just a finger, but they stubbornly disobeyed her. In between the relief of wakefulness, she also experienced waves of panic, of wondering if this was all she had left, but mostly she slept and it was when she slept that she seemed to see the

12

shadowy figures bending over her.

After a while she was able to wiggle her fingers and toes, small triumphs that were exhausting yet wonderful. Through it all, she thought constantly about her accident, cursing her stupidity; feeling the onrush of air and the sound of a car skidding. Then stars spinning and falling in her eyes; a blue light with paramedics rushing. She'd tried to speak to them but, then as now, it was too much effort. She supposed her random memories and lassitude was something to do with the healing process; her mind making sense of physical assault, her brain relearning how to order her limbs to move.

Then, hours or days later, she extracted her right arm from under her blankets and lay looking down its length to her hand. One by one she commanded her fingers to move; reluctantly they obeyed. Buoyed by this small success, she did the same with her left hand. Once more, her fingers responded.

She frowned, sensing dislocation. Everything looked normal, but nothing felt right. She supposed it was the accident; being broken against a car bonnet and then bounced on the road: a porcelain vase painfully damaged and stuck back together again. Probably her own bloody fault, she told herself, raising her right hand from the bed and marvelling at how her brain could once more command such respect from her limbs.

Afterwards, she slept without dreams. She could have slept for ten minutes or ten hours; without a watch she had no way of telling since her room had no exterior window. When she woke, she felt strong enough to conduct an inch-by-inch inspection of her body. She had feared lost limbs, broken bones encased in plaster. At the very least, lacerations and bruising. Tentatively she eased down her blankets and withdrew her legs. She could now see that she was indeed wearing a white nightgown that stretched to her toes, all ten of which looked remarkably intact. Tugging up the nightgown she saw only the pink flesh of two undamaged legs.

It took only a few more minutes to ascertain that, as far as she could tell, there wasn't a mark on her. Elated, she slowly swung her legs off the bed and kneaded her toes against the warm flooring. The room seemed to be heated from below. The only sound was a distant hum. Breathing deeply, she tried to stand, using the metal bed-head for support. Her first attempt wasn't successful; her legs buckled and she fell back on the mattress. She took a deep breath, gritted her teeth, and tried again. This second attempt fared better; she gained the vertical for a few seconds before her legs again decided that enough was enough. She sat on the side of her bed, willing strength into her thighs and knees.

This time, success, and a dizzying sense of achievement. She stood by her bed, leaning against the white wall, feeling new strength course through her. She seemed to be reclaiming her right to her own body's functions. Becoming whole again. On the far side of the small room was the full-length mirror and she slowly edged along the wall towards it, feeling more confident with each hesitant step. At the mirror, she halted; once more kneading the floor with her toes. Then she pushed herself clear from the supporting wall and stood upright on her own two feet. Once more, a rush of elation, a small Everest conquered and new strength flooding into her limbs. Almost afraid, she turned to the mirror.

She didn't know what to expect, what horrors might have befallen her face. Instead, her reflection was much as she remembered: strawberry auburn shoulder-length hair, blue eyes, high cheekbones. Her mouth, a little too wide for her liking, was puckered with the effort of standing. Freckles dappled her cheeks. She ran her tongue round her mouth; her teeth all seemed OK. Then she tugged her nightgown from her shoulders and let it fall with a faint rustle to the floor. Underneath, she was naked. Tall and angular, small-breasted, with long legs. She turned in a full circle, looking at her back over her shoulder.

It wasn't right. It couldn't be right. She was unblemished. Not even the faintest of bruises.

She frowned, then ran a hand through her hair, and stared dumbly at her reflection, elated but disquieted. How could she be so untouched? The only explanation was that she must have been in a coma for months. But how many? Or, God forbid, *years*. Having reached this conclusion, she didn't now know what to feel, still staring at herself in the mirror and wondering how many days, weeks, or months had been taken from her. But at least I'm OK, she kept telling herself over and over, like a mantra.

She imagined her parents at her bedside. Her mother, hopelessly emotional, would have been in tears at each visit but trying to put a brave face on things. In contrast, her father would have hovered at the end of the bed, not entirely sure what to do; being in hospitals had always made him uneasy. She imagined him, his hands bunched, puffing out his florid cheeks. Not unloving, but incapable of dealing with difficult situations. Her friends would also have come. Suzie, her best friend since ... well ... forever, with whom she shared all her secrets; other friends too, perhaps colleagues from the HappyMart where she worked to make ends meet, all holding her hands and talking to her. Isn't that what you do to coma victims? Play them favourite pieces of music? Play them tapes of TV shows? Tell them what's going on in the world? Read them newspaper stories? So that, in time, the conscious makes contact with the subconscious, and all the broken bits in your head are put back together.

'Oh Lord, I'm so sorry.'

Lorna turned sharply from the mirror to see an old man in a cream tracksuit standing in her doorway. Her room, she now saw, had a pneumatic sliding door that opened and closed with only a faint hiss.

The man had long white hair tied back loosely in a ponytail and an impressive white beard. His piercing blue eyes were now gallantly turned upwards to the ceiling as Lorna scrambled for her discarded nightgown and clutched it in front of her.

The old man looked faintly embarrassed. 'I should have knocked first,' he shrugged.

'Who the hell are you?' demanded Lorna, surprised by the strength of her newfound voice. 'Are you a doctor?'

The old man didn't look much like a doctor; for a start, he seemed well beyond pensionable age. Also, not many doctors she knew of wore strings of brightly coloured beads around their neck and open-toed sandals.

'Not exactly,' he conceded. 'Look, perhaps I should come back another time.' He nodded for a moment, weighing up this course of action. 'Yes, that's probably the best idea,' he said, suddenly offering her a warm smile which cracked open deep lines on his face. 'I sincerely apologise once again, young Lorna.'

'But who are you?' Lorna, now fully awake, wanted some answers – from anybody, even old men in tracksuits.

'For now, that can wait,' he replied. 'But I'm glad you obviously feel so much better. It takes time, you know,' he added with a small wink of one blue eye. 'Anyway, after all this time, you must be hungry. I'll make sure that some food is brought to you.' The old man fingered his beard for some moments, perhaps undecided whether food was a good idea. 'You must eat, Lorna, get your strength back. But please,' he said, removing a hand from his beard and wagging a finger, 'you mustn't feed the little brutes, all right?'

* * *

The old man was as good as his word and a tray was swiftly brought by a male nurse in white clinical overalls who looked spookily like a young Sean Connery. On it was a plate of grilled lamb cutlets, string beans, and sautéed potatoes. There was also a warm bread roll with a knob of butter and, under a silver dome, a bowl of chocolate profiteroles with cream. In short, exactly what she would have ordered in an expensive restaurant, given the choice, and if she'd ever been able to afford to eat in one. Also on the tray was a small metal jug of white wine, which made no sense. During her coma, had it become health service policy to keep patients inebriated? And why the metal jug?

'The boss says you're up and about now,' the nurse remarked, placing the tray down and making sure it was well balanced on Lorna's knees. The jug of wine and glass he placed on her bedside table. Why wasn't there a bunch of flowers in a vase? That's the first thing her mother would have brought. It was the first thing she always took to friends and relatives in hospital, even the ones who suffered from hay fever.

'Who was the old man? The one who was here a minute ago?' she asked, as if there might be several old men in her wing of the hospital. 'Grey hair. Beard. Beads,' she added.

The nurse gave a small shrug. 'He'll tell you himself the next time you meet. Anyway,' he added, making for the door and looking uncomfortable, 'if there's anything else I can do, just ask.'

'I'd like to know how long I've been asleep.'

'Asleep?' The nurse raised one eyebrow.

'Yes, asleep. I mean, how long have I been here?'

He didn't reply for a few moments, hands clasped behind his back. 'Not long, as far as I know.'

'And how long is not long?' she asked. 'Look, if you don't know, could I please speak to someone who does?' Lorna, running out of patience, had raised her voice. The nurse took a step backwards towards the door.

'All in good time,' he assured her and indicated the tray. 'For now, you need to eat. Get your strength back.'

'Look, I really *need* to know how long I've been here. Can I see a doctor? Actually, I shouldn't have to bloody ask that, should I? What kind of useless hospital is this?'

The nurse, perhaps unused to being shouted at, had backed himself to the door. 'Anything you need, just ask, OK?'

Lorna wanted to scream at him. 'But how?' she asked instead, looking around the blank walls for a call button. 'And what did he mean by not feeding the little brutes?'

'Just ask, that's all. Your room is sound-activated so don't worry, I'll hear.' He touched a blank place on the wall that somehow made the pneumatic door hiss open. 'But he's right about not feeding them,' he added as the white door closed again, leaving Lorna utterly exasperated.

* * *

As she ate, she considered the circumstances in which she found herself. No doubt she was in a specialist unit for the brain-injured; in other rooms would be the lucky survivors of other car accidents, all of them suffering the aftermath of head trauma. Strangely, it was a comforting conclusion. I have emerged on the other side of mental assault to

18

reclaim my life, she thought, recalling the kerb under her heels, teetering slightly on its stepped edge, feeling the chill of a still night; looking up, a canopy of stars. In that moment, a sense of the infinite and of being a minute speck in a great universe. The huge sky above the city, lit with stars and galaxies, had made her momentarily insignificant: a small cog in a universe that was overwhelming. Thinking back, she could dimly remember the outline of the driver, both of his arms at full stretch on the steering wheel, his face in a grimace as he tried to stop the car. He looked young, had slicked back hair; like an actor she knew she should recognise. Then she was on the road looking up, watching as a shooting star crossed the night sky.

The driver had pushed something soft under her head. A pillow? Jacket? She'd tried to focus on him, but couldn't even remember what films he had appeared in. A spy, she finally recalled. He was frantically speaking into a mobile, summoning help. Around the puddle of light within which she lay, other shadows were forming; lights in adjoining houses were being switched on, a woman in a blue dressing gown, emblazoned with a hamster motif, had a hand to her mouth. Lorna felt cold, but relaxed, without pain; she could only lie and wait. In the distance, a siren was getting louder and closer. Above, another shooting star. She saw its burning path and made a wish. I just want to live, to touch the stars. Is that too much to ask? Or too little? Not like this, she thought, her head now strapped tight in a brace. Her only view was of the heavens; a vista of light from a billion other worlds. They looked so beautiful; a panorama so perfect that she tried to reach up, to touch them, but a restraining strap was being tightened across her chest.

No pulse, one of the medics had said. Lorna knew this to be nonsense. She was keeping a close eye on the pneumatic door, before it hissed open to reveal friends and family. She might be in a strange hospital but her ordeal seemed to be coming to an end; she had recovered. She had wished upon a star and her wish had been granted. She looked at the tray on her lap and, despite what she had heard about hospital food, decided to have a small taste. The lamb was perfection, likewise the profiteroles. It was one of the best meals she had ever tasted, taking her mind off her strange surroundings and transporting her back to a Norfolk holiday with her parents and brother, with river-boats pottering past and a riverside pub on the other side of the water at which yachts and pleasure cruisers would tie up.

* * *

She must have been about ten, her brother Tom a couple of years older, and the holiday had been her idea. She'd seen a story about the Norfolk Broads on a travel programme on TV and badgered her parents into submission. They lived in a three-bedroom flat in North Berwick, a small town on Scotland's east coast, from which her father would depart each morning for the railway station and, so he said, a relatively lowly job with an insurance company in Edinburgh. Her mother worked in the town's bakery shop, and sometimes brought home cakes and sticky buns that, with a muttered *don't ask*, she would present to her children. Each morning she'd put on a garish red smock with STAFF written across the back. Lorna never understood the need for this. In every shop she'd been into, staff stood on one side of the counter, customers on the other. The difference between the two was obvious. She sometimes wanted to pin a piece of paper to her back with CUSTOMER written on it, but never did.

Her father came home with brochures of river boats, the family gathered round the small kitchen table, and Lorna had her way.

'I've never driven a boat,' said her father, flipping pages, already seeming rather enchanted with the idea of being a ship's captain. The boats all had pictures of happy families on them, and girls in bikinis and dark glasses. The sky was uniformly blue. Lorna looked surreptitiously at her mother and hoped she wasn't going to do anything as gross as wear a bikini. Then she glanced at her dad who was also looking surreptitiously at her mum and no doubt thinking the same thing.

Her mother was also looking at the girls in their thongs and dark glasses and had probably (hopefully) reached the same conclusion. 'But you, young lady, must wear a life-jacket,' she commanded, nodding solemnly at Lorna. 'You'll have to promise me that.' Lorna looked at the pictures in the brochure. Nobody seemed to wearing very much of anything, and certainly not a stupid life-jacket.

'I promise!' she said, reluctantly, knowing the battle of the holiday was already won.

The week on the Broads was fun, as she'd imagined it would be: gliding up meandering rivers, eating evening meals in the motorboat's small living-room-cum-virtually-everything-else. There was a cabin up front in which she and Tom slept; a steering area in the middle where they grouped themselves during the day and, aft, the living area which doubled as a bedroom for her parents, with a small loo and shower room off it. Lorna kept away from the loo when her father was inside. The noises were frightening and, after each performance, every window on the boat had to be opened, letting in the rain. They hadn't said anything about rain in the brochures.

There was even a TV with a selection of videos,

including several episodes of *Star Trek* and the first *Star Wars* film. She'd never seen it before and watched, mesmerised, as Luke Skywalker saved the universe. She took to endlessly repeating 'May the Force be with you' to Tom until, thoroughly irritated, he pushed her off the side of the boat. Not wearing her lifejacket, as promised, Lorna had to be rescued with a lifebelt thrown by her father. But even then she could swim, so it wasn't a life-threatening experience. However, her parents didn't see it that way and Tom was sent to his cabin to ponder his stupid behaviour, emerging sheepishly some hours later when supper was ready. The incident was quickly forgotten; her mother, despite the tiny cooking area, had cooked a special meal of lamb cutlets with beans and potatoes. At the stern of the boat, open to the elements, was a miniscule sitting area, from where Lorna fed the ducks and moorhens with scraps of bread.

In the last days of the holiday, Lorna discovered that her mother was a little odd. They'd moored beside a hotel which advertised that it had a swimming pool, free to patrons. Her dad figured that if they had a sandwich in the hotel bar, that would qualify them as patrons. Lorna would much rather have swum in the oil-coated rivers, but her mum said it was unhygienic and she would still have to wear a stupid life-jacket. However, the algae-infested swimming pool in the hotel garden was considered OK, even though they were its only patrons; everybody else having presumably decided it was a genuine health hazard. Her mum said that she was going for a lie-down on the boat. Tom said he was feeling sick and also went back to the boat, unusually holding his mother's hand.

The swimming pool was completely round, with a diving board at one end. Lorna jumped up and down on the board, testing its bendiness, then dived onto the bright green surface of the water. It was like diving into pea and ham soup, but more tasty.

At the far end of the swimming pool was a red inflatable dolphin (not theirs) and she swam round the pool and climbed onto it, then lay on her back and stared upwards through shuttered eyes. Unusually, in that week of monsoon rains, the sun was warm, the sky cloudless. There was a faint breeze that shook branches on the trees surrounding the hotel, stirring up the green surface of the water into swirls. Half-dead insects buzzed feebly on the water's surface. Suddenly she was being heaved upwards by a tidal wave, then falling through water. Lorna struggled to the surface and emerged spluttering. Her father had dive bombed her. He was now on the other side of the pool, wiping slime from his face and laughing.

'Gotcha!' he said and pushed himself backwards from the side wall, then floated, his toes pointing at the sky. His eyes were closed.

'Dad, can I ask you something?'

'Yes, Lorna,' he replied, eyes still closed.

'Why doesn't Mum ever go swimming?' It was something that had always bothered her because Lorna would have liked to live in the sea, or a swimming pool. If she died and was reincarnated, she'd choose to be a fish. Not a small fish, she'd reasoned, because they get eaten. But a large fish; a large, *pretty* fish, that doesn't taste nice. Or a mermaid, that would be really cool. She would live in a sunken galleon and talk to dolphins. Not in a sunken galleon anywhere near Scotland, of course: somewhere with a warm sea, without sharks. Lorna didn't know if sharks ate mermaids.

He didn't say anything for a few moments, and she wondered if he'd heard her. Then his eyes opened and his toes sank to the bottom of the pool. He waded through the water and planted his forearms on the side of the pool. 'Because she can't swim.'

In Lorna's experience, everyone could swim. Even fat people who weigh a ton and can't walk properly. Like seals, they transform in water. Her mum even made Lorna take swimming lessons. Her father heaved himself out of the pool and sat on the side, his feet in the water. 'Actually, I think she's a little frightened of water,' he said. 'But don't tell her I said that,' he added, wagging a finger.

Lorna remembered how her mother never went walking in the rain, which was a bit of a problem in Scotland. She always looked at the sky before they ventured out. She said that she didn't like getting her hair wet. 'Frightened of water?' Lorna echoed, not sure what he was telling her. They were on a boating holiday. Who would go on a boating holiday if they were frightened of water?

'Anyway, she can't swim,' he said, flopping back into the water. He had a lazy but effective breaststroke and swum round and round the pool, emerging from the primeval ooze with a bright green wizard's cloak hanging from him in lacy tendrils.

'God Almighty!' he said, looking down at himself. 'Lorry, I think you'd better get out.'

'You look scary!' she laughed, climbing out as well and marvelling at her new green scales. Her wish was coming true. She was turning into a fish. Soon she'd be able to breathe underwater, like a real mermaid, and wouldn't have to wear a stupid life-jacket.

'Dad?'

'Yes, Lorna.'

'Can I ask you something else?'

'Of course you can,' he replied, picking off a large bit of slime and dropping it by the side of the pool.

'What does redundant mean?'

He paused. 'It's complicated,' he offered.

'Does it mean we don't have any money?'

'Enough to buy you a new bike for your birthday,' he said, knowing it was what Lorna absolutely wanted, but also looking a little sad, as if he was doing mental sums in his head, despite being almost as bad as her at arithmetic, which always made Lorna wonder why he worked in a financial institution, whatever that was.

It was then that one of the hotel managers rushed out and shouted at them, gesticulating at one of several absolutely huge signs saying that, because of technical difficulties, the pool was closed until further notice.

* * *

She woke with a start to find that the tray had been taken away, so too the empty jug of wine. She sat up and looked around. The light, as always, was turned down low. There was no way of telling whether it was morning, afternoon, or the middle of the night. She debated trying the voice-activated call system, then decided against. Perhaps the old man would see her again tomorrow. Perhaps, eventually, a doctor would see her. Maybe tomorrow she would have tests done, assessments made on her recovery. Maybe tomorrow she could go home, although she rather doubted it. She had so many questions to ask. Most immediately, how long had she been asleep? Why no visitors? And why waste taxpayers' money on lamb cutlets and white wine?

Behind her eyes was a stab of tears and a glimmer of panic. Where the *hell* was she? Only the white walls of her room, and an aftertaste of the best meal she'd eaten in years. She rolled her tongue around her mouth, tasting chocolate and old memories and then heard a small scrabbling noise apparently coming from the ventilation shaft above her head. Come to think of it, she'd heard the noise before. She thought back to the old man's entreaty and, squinting more closely at the recessed grille, saw two unblinking eyes looking back.

BIRTH

Lorna Jennifer Love was born accidentally not far from the family home in North Berwick. The town, famous for its golf course, is picturesque and quaint. Tourists take photographs along its beaches; the sandstone and granite buildings stand grandly on the shoreline. It has small streets filled with craft and coffee shops and the air tastes of salt, the sky filled with seabirds whose shadows weave patterns across the streets and fairways. She once saw some old pictures of North Berwick that were taken at the dawn of photography, and was surprised at how little had changed.

They had always lived in the same flat on the High Street. At the front was noise and bustle from the street below; at the back were views up the town to North Berwick Law, the conical plug of an extinct volcano. Below the Law, washing was pegged in small patches of grass.

Her father was away at work and her mother had taken sandwiches and a flask of tea to spend a quiet lunchtime on a headland overlooking the Firth of Forth. Her mother later put Lorna's birth down to a dodgy prawn sandwich. All she recalled was lying on her back and watching the clouds wash in, when almost immediately, stabbing pain, gut-wrenching and nauseous, paralysed her to the spot. She was unable to walk or crawl, marooned like a beached sea creature, open to the elements and churning clouds. Despite the intense pain and solitude, it was a straightforward birth. Once it was over, mother and new daughter were found by an American couple, Jack and Alice Brotherstone, on holiday from Ohio. He ran back to North Berwick to raise the alarm and an ambulance was called. They were taken to hospital in Edinburgh and pronounced well.

The local newspaper got to hear what had happened and took a photograph of the Brotherstones standing on the spot where Lorna was born, Jack Brotherstone with his chest puffed out, one arm around his wife, and looking pleased with himself, as if he had performed a heroic deed, like charging into gunfire or a burning building, rather than taking a short jog into town. The newspaper put the picture on the front page so that by the time Lorna was three days old she was already a minor local celebrity.

* * *

Her mother was Catholic and it was from her knee that Lorna first learned about Abraham and Moses. Fascinated by God's appearance as a burning bush, but less happy about plagues of frogs and locusts, it seemed to her that God could be both nice and nasty; if you didn't believe in him, he might not like you and, if so, the consequences could be pretty dire. From an early age, her mother would read Lorna stories from the Bible; how Jesus fed the masses with a few loaves and fishes, about the good Samaritan who didn't pass by on the other side, the escape from Egypt with the pursuing soldiers obliterated in engulfing water. The stories seemed inconsistent, fragmentary. At school, one of her first projects was on the ancient Egyptians. About how they worshipped cats; about Anthony and Cleopatra; how their civilisation eclipsed the rest of the known world. Why then could God plague them with so much misery? They're just old stories, her mum would say. It doesn't mean that God doesn't exist.

'He sounds like a real bastard,' Lorna said.

'Lorna!' said her mother, shocked.

She didn't really know what *bastard* meant. She'd just heard some of the boys at school say it. However, judging by the look on her mother's face, it was a word she'd definitely store away for future use. It was then that she also stopped believing in God.

* * *

Her father, in contrast, was an affirmed agnostic. He didn't believe in anything very much except getting out of bed, going to work, coming back on the train, and having supper, the four of them sitting around the small table while her mum said grace. Her dad would pretend to lace his hands but, sometimes, he'd wink across the table at Lorna or Tom. Also sometimes he'd have a pint at the Auld Hoose before watching the news on TV, after which he'd get up from his chair, yawn, declare himself tired, and go to bed. Every day the same, week after week, until the weeks became years and Lorna could no longer fathom his purpose. Like the gannets on the Bass Rock, indistinguishable one from another, her dad's life seemed insignificant, perhaps even to him. Sometimes, she'd catch him by the window, looking out over the High Street, listening to the distant thud of waves on the beach. At those moments, he'd look pensive but lost. He was a big and solid man who wore a suit but said little. He didn't accompany them to church on Sunday mornings; that was his golf day.

His one discernible gift was being able to conjure coins from Lorna's ear. He'd come up behind her, twiddle with an ear lobe, then present her with a five-pence piece.

Lorna thought it enchanting and an easy way to earn pocket money. Sometimes his breath smelled beery when he did this; his eyes sparkling with unusual mischief.

'I'm a wizard, you know,' he would tell her, and Lorna utterly believed him although, disappointingly, it was the only trick he could do. His height and shock of black hair made it easy to imagine him in a long wizard's cloak emblazoned with stars and suns and moons and other magical symbols. Always a good wizard in her eyes, someone who could undo a witch's spell or turn frogs into princes, except when he smacked her bottom for poking a knitting needle into an electrical socket. That was when she learned that even wizards have a dark side.

* * *

Her primary school lay in the shadow of North Berwick Law. From her school desk she would marvel at its symmetry, its bulk filling the classroom window. It seemed to her to be as big as Everest, although it was easy enough to climb without the need for Sherpas. During break time, she could outrun the boys – if she tried – making friends and enemies in equal measure. She was forever scraping knees or elbows, or once, memorably, her forehead. She'd been running flat-out, tripped, and woken in the sanatorium; her head was bandaged and her mother was fluttering nervously at the end of her bed. The experience frightened her; she'd never been knocked out before. It felt like a temporary death, although the scrape on her forehead, sore and unsightly, was also a badge of honour, a reminder that girls could beat the boys. But the absence of consciousness, of being unnaturally asleep while a doctor and her mother were summoned: that was unnerving. From then on, she let the boys win their races; instead, she turned her attention to her classwork. She was too young to understand about jobs and careers, but she did sense that everything had a price.

When she was nine, her parents gave her a hamster for Christmas. She hadn't particularly wanted one, but didn't know what she did want. If pressed for a pet, she'd have much preferred a cat or a dog, however, living in an upstairs flat with both parents working imposed limitations. The hamster arrived with a cage, a plastic wheel around which it ran, sawdust, feeding bowl, and a water bottle that clipped to the outside of its cage. She called the hamster Tonto and allowed it free rein down her school shirts, where it would crawl and chew her clothes, much to her mother's dismay. Sometimes it would wake her in the night, galloping on its little plastic wheel. She'd lie in the darkness, snug and warm, just able to discern its small shadow against the wall. When it died a year later, they buried Tonto in a favourite picnic spot: a headland to the east of the town, with rolling waves stretching across the Firth of Forth. Her mother placed the cardboard box in the deep hole they'd dug and said a prayer. Lorna didn't know whether hamsters went to Heaven, and neither did her mother. Close to the place where Lorna had been born, they laid her first and only pet to rest. After that, no more hamsters. The pain of final parting overshadowed what had been before.

But she still remembered little Tonto: a small bundle of cream and brown fluff, front paws holding a tasty morsel to be nibbled and stored inside cavernous cheek pouches, and its small, dark, and unblinking eyes. From across the years, Lorna immediately knew what was looking back at her from the other side of the latticed grille.

* * *

31

Her small shriek quickly brought the good-looking male nurse to her room. He stood at the end of her bed, hands laced behind his back, rocking on the balls of his feet. He seemed concerned, a small frown creasing the corners of his eyes.

Lorna pointed upwards with one finger. 'I may be mistaken,' she said, feeling suddenly foolish, 'but I could have sworn I saw a hamster.'

The nurse peered at the grille. The hamster, if that's what it was, had already scampered off, scared into flight by Lorna's yell. It hadn't been a shriek of terror; rather, a yelp of absolute surprise. Lorna had heard its swift progress down the ventilation shaft, speeding paws reminding her of Tonto, just as her door had whooshed open to reveal the nurse.

Instead he sighed and shook his head. He didn't seem in the least disbelieving. 'I'm afraid this facility does have a small problem with them,' he explained, rocking on his feet and now dangling his arms at his side. 'I will of course inform Maintenance at once,' he added more brightly. 'I'm only sorry that it gave you a fright.'

'Not a fright exactly,' replied Lorna. 'Actually, they're rather cute. I used to have one. As a pet,' she added, rather unnecessarily. 'Look, could I please see a doctor? I need to know what's happened to me.' He'd said *this facility*. Did hospital employees call their place of work *facilities*? The nurse said nothing; pursed his lips. Once again, she felt a wave of panic.

'OK, then why can't I see a doctor?' Lorna was aware of a rising timbre to her voice. This was no ordinary hospital, with orderlies and cleaners bustling about, doctors with stethoscopes hanging over their shoulders; the crash and din of trolleys down corridors. Nor did it smell medical – it smelled distantly of roses and lavender. 'Look,' she said in a lower tone, catching her breath,

'Why can't you answer me? I just need to know what's going on.'

The nurse found trouser pockets in which to deposit his hands. 'I realise you must have a lot of questions, young Lorna,' he said, not quite meeting her eye. 'Only understandable, given the circumstances.'

'Circumstances? What circumstances?' There was real fear in her voice.

The damnable man even had Sean Connery's Scottish burr and slicked-back hair. The only thing missing was a dinner jacket and bow tie although, Lorna thought unkindly, he probably puts them on at night to perfect his act in front of the mirror. 'I *know* that all this has been a bit of a shock,' he continued, staring intently at the grille to avoid looking at her. 'However, it's best that you talk to Irene. Believe me, she has the answers. From now on, she'll be looking after you.'

'Is Irene a doctor?' Lorna's tone was almost pleading. Why all the bloody secrecy, as if she was a child again? 'And has anybody thought to phone my parents?' She felt suddenly alone; she wanted to be small again and feel comforting arms around her shoulders. Or the HappyMart; she had a job to go to. Or the university. Did her professors know? 'People will have been worried,' she said, a catch in her throat.

'If you don't mind, I think that I'd better fetch Irene. She'll know more than me, believe me.' Given he'd answered none of her questions, Lorna did believe him. 'Anyway, Irene's been designated to look after you,' he concluded, looking genuinely upset.

'Designated? What the hell does *designated* mean?'

'It means that she's been assigned to you.'

'I *know* what designated means!' shouted Lorna, now at her wit's end. 'I just want some straightforward answers to some straightforward questions. Why in God's name is that too much to ask for?'

The nurse was again rocking on the balls of his feet, hands clasped behind his back. 'It's not quite that simple,' he offered, frowning.

'I'm not a child!' she retorted, utterly exasperated by the man's evasiveness. For Heaven's sake, what was there not to understand? 'OK, I've had an accident. But I'm better now. What's so fucking complicated about that!' Lorna bit her lip. 'I'm also a lawyer,' she added, hoping that this might alter his view of simplicity.

'Were,' he said.

'I beg your pardon?' Lorna couldn't have heard him properly.

'Past tense, I regret, Lorna, although I shouldn't really say so. Everything is in the past tense now.' He too was biting his lip, perhaps having said too much. He took a deep breath and exhaled slowly. 'I'd better go and find Irene. She's been …'

'Designated, I know,' sighed Lorna, burying her face in her pillow and breathing in its alpine freshness. In my short lifespan, she thought, I have been in hospital as a patient three times. I have had stitches put in a gashed leg (horse-riding accident), an appendectomy … and now, this. I have also visited friends and relatives in hospital; I have seen and heard the mundane rituals of hospital life. Surely a neurological ward wouldn't be that different? OK, she hadn't been awake very long, but why no specialist in a white coat to examine her? Why no flowers on her bedside table? For God's sake, not even a window! She frowned into her pillow. All hospitals had windows. It was therapeutic, even if the view and the weather outside was dismal, which it usually was. She sensed, rather than heard, the male nurse leave and waited for the hiss of enclosure.

And waited.

Lorna sat up, pushing hair back from her eyes. The door to her room had been left tantalisingly open. In his haste to find Irene, Sean had forgotten to close it. She swung her feet to the floor and took a deep breath. To escape or not to escape, that was her question. Well, not *properly* escape, there wouldn't be much sense in that – and she had no outdoor clothes to wear – but if she couldn't get straight answers to straight questions, she'd find someone who would help. In the process, she'd also discover where she was. She supposed Edinburgh but, who knows, maybe she'd been transferred to some highly specialised unit. Perhaps her injuries had been so unusual or complex that she'd been moved to another city. That might explain the absence of flowers or visiting loved ones. The quality of the food, judging by her one meal, suggested a private hospital. Hospital or facility. He'd also said *past tense. Everything in the past tense.* She looked at the open door and listened, heard nothing. No clattering trolleys, no chatter, no squeak of feet on lino; just the faintest hum from the overhead ventilation system.

It was time, she concluded, to get some answers.

She peered cautiously round the door, like a kitten using a cat-flap for the first time, anxious to avoid discovery before making her own discoveries. She wrinkled her nose, smelling meadow flowers. To her left, the dimly lit passageway stretched for perhaps fifty yards. Like her room, it was white-painted and featureless. She was able to stand at its centre and touch both walls with her hands. As she did so, her bedroom door hissed shut.

Lorna controlled her breathing and looked hard at the spot that she'd inadvertently touched. Like the rest of the corridor, the wall on which her fingers rested seemed utterly blank. She touched the spot again and her door opened. Bending her face close to her trembling fingers, she could just discern a small bluish circle against the white wall. She tapped the circle again and her door sighed shut.

To her right, the corridor extended for some twenty yards then inclined upwards. This was the direction that Lorna immediately took, reasoning that, without windows in her room or the corridor, she must be at basement level. Having experienced no natural light for … well, long enough, she craved sunlight. She wanted nothing more than to feel moving air, even the wet sting of rain. She'd been knocked down in early summer; for all she knew, it might now be autumn or winter … or, God forbid, summer again. A year torn from her life's book and ripped up. She shuddered, suddenly chilled, although the corridor, like her room, was comfortably heated. She padded soundlessly on the warm floor, fervently hoping that nobody would chance the other way. Irene, perhaps, designated to look after her, now hurrying to her bedside. Halfway towards the incline, she stopped and listened. Once more, only a faint and reassuring hum from the ceiling air-conditioning. No hospital bustle; more importantly, no self-important 007-lookalike in hot pursuit. It took her only a handful of seconds to reach the bottom of the incline and look up. Once again, a featureless rising corridor leading to the next level. Pressing her back to one wall, Lorna slowly inched up the incline, listening intently. She stopped again as she broached the next level, chest hammering, and almost had to laugh. Here she was, a grown woman, creeping around a hospital like a mad person.

She emerged from the inclined corridor into a large rectangular room. Like everywhere else, it was dimly lit from above with the same flat and featureless walls. Ahead, another thin corridor, like the one below, stretched away into the distance. Then she became aware of a light glimmering on the floor; it pulsed alternately red and green. A thin light, a strip of changing colour. Lorna stared at it for a few moments; the first primary colours she had seen in this place of medicinal white. Then she realised the light was coming from outside. On the left side of the rectangular room was a floor to ceiling window.

She edged closer. At first all she could see were stars. That would explain the lack of hospital activity, she thought, reassured. It was the middle of the night and only she was out and about, creeping around like a deranged person. Then she reached the glass; she pressed her face against it, seeing only her reflection. Gradually, her eyes focussed on what was beyond.

At a distance of about a hundred metres was a huge white structure. It stretched far to her left and right, almost as far as she could see, like an impossibly large ocean liner, but without recognisable ship's superstructure. The sides of its hull were gently rounded, although other smaller structures protruded, seemingly at random. On top of its upper deck were arrays of backward-facing communication dishes and, on extended antennae, red and green lights that winked in sequence down its great length. Surrounded by stars, the hull of the structure was bathed in white light; in places, its creamy exterior was blank, elsewhere, other lights glowed from inside. One hand to her forehead, Lorna counted thirty storeys. She didn't know what to think. Her mind had fused: credulity and disbelief melded together.

She put her hand to her mouth.

Suddenly she wanted Irene or James Bond to find her. Facing the impossibility of what lay beyond, she didn't want to be alone.

An intricate latticework joined the structure she was in to the one beyond the glass; a bridgework of diamond lights from one to the other. Squinting, it looked as if the two structures were connected with ice or crystal walkways; rainbows of lights at different deck levels. And all around, another latticework of stars and flaming suns that reflected off the gleaming hull and bridgework and made the whole structure glow with celestial fire.

On the side of the structure, painted in lustrous gold letters twenty storeys high, were three letters.

HVN

It was the last thing that Lorna saw as she collapsed to the floor, her assailed mind finally attaining critical overload and switching itself off.

HEAVEN

She woke to find herself in a book-lined room, a blazing log fire throwing out heat and shadows. She was in an easy chair, with plump cushions supporting her back, her feet propped on a circular wooden coffee table. She was still in her nightgown, she noticed, warily looking around the room. The room was crammed with an assortment of furniture. Bookcases jostled against chests of drawers, an oak sideboard entirely covered with empty flower vases had been pushed against a cupboard door. Sepia prints of a city she didn't recognise covered what wall space wasn't devoted to books. The room had a high ceiling from which hung a simple chandelier and two large windows across which were drawn red velvet curtains. It was warm and cosy and on the coffee table beside her bare feet was a bottle of malt whisky, a bottle of white wine, and two crystal glasses.

As she blinked her eyes open, a Kate Winslet lookalike appeared suddenly and soundlessly at her side, throwing her a quick smile and holding out a manicured hand.

'I'm Irene,' she said. Her handshake was cool and firm. 'I thought you might need a drink,' she continued and, without waiting for an answer, poured liquid into two glasses. Wine for Lorna, whisky for herself.

Lorna removed her feet from the table and placed them on the carpeted floor. She no longer knew where the boundaries of reality lay. She existed, that much was clear from the warmth on her face and the taste of wine in her mouth, raised there by a shaking hand, but how much else was in her imagination? The near-empty hospital bedroom, the windowless corridor without any obvious doors, a giant white superstructure bathed in starlight? Lorna sipped from her glass and laid it shakily on the table.

Irene was dressed in a knee-length black skirt with matching blouse, a silver belt at her waist. 'You must have a lot of questions,' she remarked, fetching cigarettes, a lighter, and an ashtray from the mantelpiece, setting them down on the table, and taking a seat in an armchair opposite. Irene regarded Lorna evenly. The log fire hissed, throwing shadows across her face.

Lorna cleared her throat. 'Are you the person designated to answer them?' She tried, and failed, to smile.

Irene nodded, lighting her cigarette. Unlike Kate Winslet, Irene exuded authority. Where Kate Winslet's mouth was framed in a smile, Irene seemed slightly disdainful. They were identical, or so it seemed to Lorna, but quite different.

'Then what the hell is going on?' she asked. 'For a start, what is this place?'

Irene looked at her through smoke. 'Which question would you like me to answer first?'

'Frankly, I don't much care,' said Lorna. 'I just want the truth, the whole truth, and nothing but the truth.'

'You really were a lawyer, weren't you?'

'Am a lawyer. Or shortly to be a lawyer. Present tense! I want some answers, Irene.'

Irene, puffing on her cigarette, inclined her head and nodded again. 'You must first understand that you are among friends. You might not believe it, not immediately, but it's true. Friends, Lorna, who mean you no harm. All of us want the very best for you and to do everything we can to make you welcome.' Abruptly, Irene stubbed out her cigarette. Her mouth was curled down; her sharp eyes flashed. 'But first you must come to terms with what's happened.'

'I have come to terms with what's happened. I had an accident, I've been in a coma, and now I find I'm in a lunatic asylum.' Lorna put a hand to her mouth. 'Christ, this isn't some kind of mental home, is it?'

'It does sometimes resemble one, but no, it isn't. I'm only sorry that your arrival has caused you so much distress.'

'Then what has happened to me?'

Irene picked up her glass and tapped the rim with a manicured hand. 'OK, here goes. The difficult bit, Lorna.' She exhaled slowly then laid her glass on the table. 'Sadly, your injuries were quite severe. You suffered internal damage, a fractured spine, and extensive trauma to your skull. The car, I regret, was travelling quite fast. Legally, I assure you, but quickly. Frankly, I'm rather surprised you didn't hear it.'

Lorna listened, as if to someone else's life. She should have heard the car, of course; looked right and left and right again. Irene's unblinking eyes were appraising; she was biting her lip. Lorna sensed a threshold, a boundary about to be crossed.

'The medics on the scene did what they could, which wasn't much, and you were then taken by ambulance to the Edinburgh Royal Infirmary. They also did everything possible, Lorna, that's the main thing. Everything that could have been done, was done. But your injuries were too extensive, that's the truth of it. You didn't suffer. You never regained consciousness.'

Lorna had a panicky desire to laugh. Here she was in a nightdress in a book-lined room drinking white wine. While it didn't quite add up to normality, equally it wasn't the alternative that Irene seemed to be suggesting. She drank the contents of her glass and felt tears prickle her eyes.

'That means I'm dead,' said Lorna flatly, feeling warmth from the fire and finding everything preposterous. At the same time, a gulf was opening. Through a chink in the curtains, she could see blazing starlight and the white outline of the gleaming hull.

Irene now adopted a businesslike-tone, the bringer of bad news having run out of evasions. Her voice wasn't Kate Winslet's either. Irene had a voice that demanded compliance. 'There's actually no easy way of saying this. You died in hospital from your injuries and you are now, I'm afraid, dead and gone. Oh, God, sweetie, I'm so sorry.'

Lorna had been staring at Irene open-mouthed. She really was in a lunatic asylum, except she was the only sane one. This can't be happening, she thought. Maybe I'll wake up any moment. Maybe it's April Fool's Day. 'This is a joke, right?'

But Irene wasn't smiling. She had picked up her glass again, tapping its rim with one finger. 'Then where do you think you are?' she asked eventually and gestured round the room. 'Doesn't exactly look like a hospital, does it?'

'Irene, you're scaring me,' said Lorna. But at the back of her mind she also had to concede that Irene's words, however absurd, did hold some sense. When all avenues of logic had expired, curiously even the ridiculous now seemed possible.

* * *

Lorna had not inherited her mother's steadfast faith. Her belief in God and life eternal was tempered with doubt. As a small child, she had accepted the wisdoms of her mother without question, particularly since God could be distinctly homicidal at times. She didn't want locusts or plagues of frogs, thank you very much. If the price of escaping his wrath was simply to believe in him, then the young Lorna was happy to oblige. But as the years passed and her visits to church became less frequent, she came to realise that, in matters of faith, she was neither an agnostic nor an unbeliever. She no longer believed in the God of the Bible: its ancient stories held no resonance for her when people were dying of hunger in Africa and God didn't seem to care very much. Ever since that *Star Wars* video, she'd believed in the nothingness of the universe; a God of the mere Earth seemed meagre set against a million billion galaxies. Growing up, she had been caught between the unquestioning devotions of her mother and the disinterest of her father. Church or golf. While neither appealed to Lorna very much, her parents' choices offered her options: she chose neither to believe nor disbelieve, and instead found a temporary home in radical politics. If God wants me to see things otherwise then, she thought, he knows where I live.

'I'm sorry to have scared you,' Irene was saying. 'But it's not easy telling people that they're dead. Not something anyone wants to hear, is it? And for some reason it's usually me that has to say it. Not that I'm complaining, of course. Not easy for the person being told, either. Anyway,' Irene continued, after a small pause to refill their glasses. 'I have absolutely seen it all. Tears, tantrums, throwing stuff.' She looked at Lorna over the rim of her glass. 'Do you want to throw something? Feel free if you do.'

'But I can't be dead,' said Lorna, although there was some doubt in her mind. Her clear memory of the accident suggested that her injuries had been serious, and the bizarre surroundings in which she had woken up seemed to indicate changed circumstances. She held out one hand for Irene's inspection, seeing each vein and artery. Then she was angry; angry at Irene, and at the joke being played on her. Now she did want to throw something. Abruptly she stood up. 'I'm not dead,' she declared loudly. 'How the hell can I be dead?'

It was something in Irene's eyes that stilled her. They were the eyes of someone who had seen it all, eyes that could see over horizons.

'But it does make a curious kind of sense, doesn't it?' Irene said softly.

Lorna sat down, her anger melding into a kind of acceptance. But in the middle of the mind-numbing reality in which she now found herself Lorna felt only that she was alive. The fire crackled and shadows chased across the wood-panelled walls. 'But I don't feel dead,' offered Lorna.

'And what does being dead feel like? Actually, sweetie, don't bother to answer that. Rhetorical question. Maybe,' she leaned across the table, 'it feels a lot like this?' She paused to light another cigarette and sat back in her chair, neatly crossing her legs. 'Your mother and father scattered your ashes on North Berwick Law.' Irene's voice was precise and clipped; it didn't hold sentiment. 'You used to go there as a child, remember? You used to think it was Mount Everest.' Lorna did remember, wondering how Irene knew. Another birthday, another picnic, this time on the top of the world, the small town laid out towards the sea. On its conical peak, a whale's jaw. On the water, white waves across the Firth to Fife. From the peak of the Law you could see the whole world – and eat a ham sandwich at the same time. Her world. At the age of six, her only world: a panorama of houses, water, and fields. Everything she knew could be seen from the volcanic tip of the Law. She tried to imagine the scene: a scattering of dust to mark the end of everything, her mother with a tissue to her nose, her father not quite knowing what to do with his hands. A priest, almost certainly, reading a prayer and sounding hopeful for her soul's progress to a better place. Yes, it was where she would have chosen to be scattered. A haunting place where others could remember her, her child's world painted at their feet.

'I know it's difficult, Lorna, but try not to worry about those you've left behind,' Irene was saying. 'They're far, far away and there's nothing you can do for them. You're in a different place now.'

Lorna believed it. 'Where am I?' she asked. It was the question she had dreaded asking, but she now knew what Irene's answer was going to be. She'd seen the giant hull of the other structure and read the three gold letters on its flank.

'You're in Heaven, sweetie,' said Irene.

* * *

But it felt more like life than death, although she'd never really given it much thought. Death had always seemed the ultimate full stop and, if an afterlife existed, it would be a place beyond understanding; a spirit domain of ascended souls, where nothing would resemble the mortal world. Instead, everything here seemed to point to a continued mortality. She was still breathing, eating, thinking. She had ascended intact to a place that, while odd, was filled with the familiar.

'I'm in Heaven,' echoed Lorna, taking a deep breath and pinching herself hard on the palm of one hand with fingers from the other. Her lungs worked, she could experience pain. 'Then that presumably means I was a good girl.' All good girls go to Heaven, everyone knew that.

'Were you?' asked Irene.

'I don't know.'

Irene lit yet another cigarette and offered Lorna the packet. Strangely, she couldn't remember whether she smoked or not. Irene appraised her for a moment. 'Anyway, you won't find many of us who are judgemental. As far as we're concerned, it doesn't really matter whether you were good, bad, or indifferent. Believe me, we've all been here too bloody long for that kind of crap. But we are, I assure you, rather interested in *why* you're here.'

'Why *shouldn't* I be here? After all, I'm dead.'

'Technically, yes.' Irene blew smoke at the ceiling and refilled their glasses. Lorna stared intently at the floor. 'True, you were involved in a road accident. You remember that. True, you're dead. I think you now believe that, don't you?' Irene peered closely through another exhalation of smoke. 'Also true, your ashes were scattered on North Berwick Law. But none of that gets closer to explaining *why* you're here.'

'I don't understand.'

'Well, frankly, neither do I. It is rather a puzzle, you see. Are you absolutely sure?'

'I'm dead. Dead people go to Heaven. Or did I miss something in Bible class?'

Irene was scaring her again. Why was she suggesting that Lorna had arrived in Heaven on false pretences? And why the hell couldn't she remember more about her former life? All she could remember were fragments; spinning shards that didn't fit together.

'I wouldn't worry about Bible lessons, Lorna, because they are somewhat irrelevant in Heaven. Irrelevant *and* inaccurate. Not, of course, that I'm blaming scholars or prophets, but all your great religious texts don't quite describe Heaven as it actually *is*. They describe how ancient scholars thought how it might look. All complete bollocks, of course. You really don't have the smallest inkling why you're here, do you?'

Lorna shook her head warily.

'Everyone who comes here is here for a reason.' Irene let this sink in before continuing. 'Although the realities of Heaven and eternal life are not exactly what you learned in Bible class. Actually, persuading you of your death was the easy bit,' Irene said with a sigh. 'Believe me, explaining the next will be a little harder and may require … how should I put it? … A certain suspension of disbelief. It might be best if I left that until tomorrow.'

'Irene, I really do believe I might be dead,' countered Lorna. 'Believe *me*, that has already taken quite a lot of suspended disbelief.' Didn't everyone go to Heaven? Or just everyone with a spotless soul? I've never done anyone any harm, she wanted to say, just in case it made a difference. But she simply couldn't remember. Maybe she'd been a mass murderer.

Irene stubbed out her cigarette, her lips curled downwards. Lorna was again struck by incongruity; Irene *was* Kate Winslet, but wasn't. Her voice was all wrong; it held an edge of harshness, and her eyes were again hard and appraising. 'To be blunt, this facility isn't quite the Heaven you might have imagined.'

That word again. *Facility*. 'Until a few moments ago, I wasn't certain that Heaven existed.'

'Well, clearly it does or you wouldn't be here.' Irene drew her to her feet and motioned Lorna to follow her to the closed curtains. 'Don't worry, young Lorna. But perhaps I should show you what your new home looks like.'

Irene drew back the heavy curtains to reveal a large observation window, through which Lorna looked out on the vastness of space. A hundred metres away, the same giant hull she had seen earlier, crystal walkways leading between there and here. On its flank in burning gold letters, HVN. It shone in a celestial fire, bathed in starlight from surrounding galaxies, the most breathtaking, impossibly large, and beautiful thing that Lorna had ever seen. Earlier, thinking herself alive, it had caused her to faint; a final impossible fact on top of too many other improbabilities. Now, dead and scattered, Lorna saw it through different eyes, the eyes of the child who had watched a *Star Wars* video and been transformed. If there was a Heaven, it had to be among the stars. She had known it, *always* known it. She pressed her fingers to the cold glass. The other hull was simply enormous: it stretched far to her left and right, its great length illuminated by a universe she didn't recognise while, inside, Heaven's newest occupant stood awestruck and incredulous. In that transfixing moment, Lorna truly believed. Nothing on Earth could have conceived or constructed a thing of such immense beauty and placed it among the stars for nobody to see.

'I really am dead,' she said finally.

'Afraid so, petal.'

'There is a God, isn't there?'

Irene nodded. 'We all need someone to look after us, Lorna. Of course, there's a God.'

'Will he tell me why I'm here?'

Irene cleared her throat. 'Well, yes, I suppose that he will,' Irene replied, sounding uncertain and avoiding eye contact. 'But to be blunt, God isn't the person you think he is either.'

'Will I get to meet him?' she asked.

Irene looked slightly embarrassed. 'Actually, you already have.'

Lorna let this pass, still looking outwards. 'Then does it matter what we've done on Earth?' she asked. The cold, white lines of the giant hull now seemed almost antiseptic. 'All those sins that we've committed. The really *big* ones, Irene. I mean, is God a forgiving kind of God?'

Irene put a hand on her arm. 'There's nothing to forgive, sweetie. We all make mistakes.'

'Even God?'

'Believe me, petal, *mostly* God.'

Then Lorna found herself on her knees, her forehead pressed against the glass. Her legs must have buckled from under her and she struggled to stand up again, utterly exhausted. It was as if a huge weight had been loaded on her shoulders. 'But I don't want to be dead,' she said, finding it hard to speak.

'No, I don't suppose you do, sweetie.'

'And my memory seems to have gone haywire. I can't remember stuff.' She put her hands to her head. 'Christ, I can't remember anything!'

'Your memories will come back, Lorna. It might take a few days but they will. They always do.'

There was a bedroom next door to the wood-panelled living room and Irene half carried her to a giant four-poster bed. It had snug cotton sheets and a grandmother clock in one corner that gently counted out the seconds. There was also an en-suite bathroom, with a large cast-iron bath with lion's feet. They'd had one at home in North Berwick, nearly the same, except that this one was in pristine condition, without chips and cracks in the enamel. She'd played with her brother in that bath, floating battleships to one another and then sinking them with soap. Toothpaste and a toothbrush had been laid out.

'I'll get some other stuff tomorrow,' said Irene. 'A girl can't survive without lippie, can she?'

The dead weight was still on Lorna's shoulders and she was too tired to think. She tried to stay awake, to think back, to find a point of singularity that would explain what had happened to her, but the only person she could remember was Joe, the heartless bastard.

SCARECROW

She was alone in the flat and had just settled down to a Clint Eastwood film and reheated pizza when the doorbell rang. He was on the doorstep, carrying flowers and cognac, with a look of divine remorse on his chiselled features. Her heart fluttered. She should have shut the door in his face – and would have done just that if he'd phoned in advance. She would have had time to say no, to tell him exactly what she thought of him, to build her defences. But he hadn't phoned, so she had no defences against his charmer's smile. She knew he must have planned it this way, to catch her off-guard. Instead, almost without conscious thought, she held him tight, her eyes squeezed shut.

He put his hands upon her and she felt the warmth of his fingers. He kissed her forehead, drawing her face to his with both hands. His fingers felt rough against her cheeks and musty, like mothballs. She knew what was coming next, as his hands now traversed her back, her spine arching. He was whispering endearments, pressed against her on the sofa, empty platitudes meaning nothing. One part of her resisted, the good girl jilted who feels an explanation is in order. That part of her knew Joe best: his heavenly good looks providing easy and practised access to the bedroom. She tried to resist, pushing against his chest to ward him off, turning her face away from his. But there was another part of her that was more accommodating; this part of her suspected his motivation, but didn't mind. And so she allowed herself to be undressed, turning her face to his, succumbing to him, tasting the familiarity of him and, eventually, tugging at his belt, pressing his face to her breasts, pulling him to the floor.

Afterwards there was an unexpected ache, like an unscratched itch. She looked down at him cradled in her arms; a lost boy up to no good but who had, at least, returned to mama. But, try as she might, the clock wouldn't run backwards. This wasn't Joe – just someone who looked like him.

He kissed her. 'How've you been? Still doing the lawyer thing?'

She shrugged, not entirely sure. Those were the kind of questions that should have preceded sex, not followed it.

'I got myself another job,' he was saying. 'Not much of one, but it's better than working in the bar.'

'That's good,' she replied without conviction. She realised in the silence of the living room that she no longer knew this man. Joe, who had briefly been at the epicentre of her firmament, the bright star towards whom she had journeyed, was a stranger to her. He had come again into her life without explanation or invitation. Her equilibrium had been shifted.

'Don't you want to know what it is?' Joe seemed crestfallen, one hand fluttering.

She probably didn't, but asked anyway.

'Radio DJ,' he said with some pride. 'Edinburgh FM. I sent them those demo tapes from back home.' Joe, ever the dreamer, had always wanted to make it big. He'd often talked about doing radio. Back in Melbourne he'd cut his teeth on a hospital station, charming old ladies with hip replacements. 'It's not much of a radio station, to be honest, but it's a start.'

'Yeah, I suppose. It's a start.' She felt weary, not wanting to share his excitement. She'd never heard of

Edinburgh FM.

'I do the early show,' he was explaining, hand fluttering again – a new gesture, one she didn't remember. She watched his hand warily, fingers now bunched against his palm. 'Six til eight, Monday to Friday. You should listen in. Maybe I'll play you something. Would you like that?'

'Whatever, Joe.' But what could he play? Something sad? Remorseful? Tender?

His eye had been caught by a placard propped against a wall. 'Still marching for the whales, I see.'

'Someone has to, Joe. They can't do it themselves.' Joe wasn't a demonstrator, although Lorna had never blamed him. She'd been happy to march for both of them. It was something that she was compelled to do, to turn conviction into action, rather than stand on the sidelines and do nothing. It was her way of being more than a useless student, her way of saying she cared, and not just about whales, standing shivering outside the Japanese consulate in Edinburgh and waving her placard, the one he now seemed to be poking fun at.

'Don't you ever care about stuff, Joe?' Without meaning to, she laid her head on his shoulder, smelling the mustiness of him. He smelled of someone she might once have loved. Then she frowned, realising she'd framed this thought in the past tense.

'Not like you, I guess. Maybe when I'm a bit more settled, with a career … all that shit. Right now, that's what's important.' He laid a hand on her hip, then slipped it round her waist. 'I'll leave saving the world to you.'

She removed her head from his shoulder to look at him. His eyes were closed, his lashes fluttering. Was he still poking fun? With Joe it was sometimes difficult to tell: something in his Aussie accent, the unfamiliar intonations. His hand was now caressing her back, the way she remembered. She knew what was on his mind.

'I'm not sure it's about saving the world, Joe.'

'Just whales.'

'And other things. People, for a start. People without voices, Joe. Don't people matter?'

But Joe was no longer listening, his lips forming moist kisses across her shoulder, and she would once have rolled towards him and held him tightly, willing him to become part of her. Now she found herself resisting, still angry at the way he had belittled her. This time there were no whispered endearments, merely his urgency as if she might change her mind. His body gave her no pleasure: the carpet rubbed against her back. He felt heavy and clumsy.

Afterwards, they lay on their backs, not touching. 'There's something wrong, isn't there?' he asked eventually.

'It's been fucking *weeks*, Joe. You could have phoned.'

She saw that he was unnerved. He had expected gratitude; he had expected forgiveness, to be making plans, to be asked to her bed. She realised that Joe had assumed that all he had to do was walk through the door and she would rush to his arms. Which she had done, holding him tight with her eyes squeezed shut. Now at least, he had the good grace to look uncomfortable.

She felt a tremble in her voice, a black box opening in her mind. 'Why are you here, Joe? I mean, *really* – why are you here?'

'To see you, of course.' The question seemed to offend him.

'It's been weeks!' she repeated, the lawyer making sure that the defendant understood the charge. 'You could have got in touch before now. Anyway, what happened to your trollop?'

'Sarah-Ann? Look, Lorna, it was a stupid mistake. I

shouldn't have done what I did. I'm sorry. I apologise. Fact is, I'd like us to get back together.'

'A mistake,' echoed Lorna.

'We all make them.'

'You especially, Joe.'

He poured brandy into a glass and handed it to Lorna, who refused it. Rising from the floor, she searched for her clothes. She had made herself available, but cheaply, for old time's sake. It didn't feel right; it felt like an ending. Through the window, she could see Edinburgh Castle. It was lit up and seemed to float above its rock.

'Suzie will be back soon.' She felt tired, at a turning point. 'I don't want you here.'

'Lorna, I know what I did was stupid. OK, I *know* I should have got in touch. I just didn't know what to say,' he added, pulling on boxer shorts and jeans, watching her carefully. He reached a hand to her; she brushed it away.

'Just go, will you, Joe.' She was aware that her voice had risen, reaching that dangerous level beyond which self-control might slip. Her mind lurched, a giddying emptiness rushed upwards. She put a hand to her head.

Joe sulked. 'I said I'm sorry.'

Lorna rounded on him, her voice still rising. 'No! That's just it! You didn't say you were sorry. You just fucked me on the floor. Twice!' she added for good measure, her back still tender from carpet abrasions.

'But you let me.' He seemed genuinely affronted. 'Anyway,' he continued, trying to be conciliatory, 'I prefer the term making love.'

'It's not a term I ever remember you using.'

Lorna's mind had lurched: this time a sharp stab of pain in her forehead. She put a hand to her face and was surprised to find her cheeks wet with tears. Joe looked on, as if from a great distance, his fine features encasing someone who had become someone else. Moonlight played across his face, a reflection from the TV caught in his eyes. He looked uncomfortable.

'You'd better go,' she said.

His face was flushed, hair tousled. He bent to tie the laces of his trainers. But he kept watch on her, frowning. At the door he paused, jacket casually across one shoulder, a lock of brown hair over one eye. It was his classic pose, his James Dean, the one she remembered best.

'Well, um, so long,' he said, looking unsure of himself.

Lorna thought for a minute, savouring the moment and his patent discomfort. She had longed for this man; now, at the end of longing, she simply wanted finality.

'It's goodbye, Joe.'

'You make it sound like a line from a film.' He tried to laugh, to regain the situation, to win over her affection.

She nodded towards the television, the sound turned down low, as Clint Eastwood, gun in hand, dashed from doorway to doorway. 'All the world's a play, Joe. You should know that. After all, you got what you came for, didn't you?'

'No, I'm not sure I did.'

A weight pressed on her forehead, but from inside. She felt her head balloon out, the skin on her face taut. 'Just get the fuck out,' she said.

'Lorna –'

'Now!'

The word emerged high and shrill, unsettling the dust under his shoes as he turned for the door. He appeared on the point of protesting, but thought better of it.

The door closed, with Joe safely on the other side, his footsteps receding into distant silence. Whatever she had done, she had done it. Instinctively she looked from the window. She saw him appear in the street, saw him hesitate. Her Adonis, her burning star: he didn't know what to do! She frowned through the glass, shielding her face with one hand as a shaft of light pierced her eyes. Her mind raced. She ran to the bathroom and was copiously sick. Happier memories of Joe were intermingled with darker thoughts. She ran a bath and soaked in it. Then she was sick again, cursing Joe and her cheap availability. The shadows at the back of her mind jostled in. She saw his face forming and dissolving in the steam. She had cast him adrift. Later, she found the one photo of the bastard she hadn't already torn up and hurled it from the bedroom window. It caught the breeze, turning and tumbling, rising high above the rooftops until it was lost from sight.

* * *

In the morning, despite being dead, Lorna felt oddly refreshed. Sleep seemed to have rearranged the jigsaw of her new existence. She knew other revelations would lie ahead, but she now accepted the biggest revelation of them all. A cream polo shirt, blue jeans, sensible underwear, and red trainers had been laid out for her.

As she brushed her teeth, she noticed that small things had changed. The faint scar on her forehead, her one permanent reminder of North Berwick primary school, had disappeared, ironed flat like a shirt's wrinkle. She searched in vain for her appendectomy scar. All of life's imperfections had been carefully removed.

Lorna revisited the book-lined room next door. Close up, the antique furniture was moulded from what seemed to be plastic. No more real were the books on the shelves. They seemed to have been painted onto the wall. A room designed for solace, to please her, to offer a version of home. Then she stood for some time at the observation window, watching a new galaxy and the other giant hull of Heaven. Its array of communications dishes still all faced backwards, small lights flashing in sequence.

Irene breezed in, smoking a cigarette.

'Feeling a bit cheerier, petal?'

Lorna nodded.

'Excellent! Actually, most people find being dead quite an easy adjustment. Surprising, really, but that's generally the way it works.' Irene poured herself a cup of coffee from a silver pot that Lorna hadn't noticed before. 'Actually, sweetie, it's something that gets pumped into the air supply. Don't ask me what. Diazepam, or something. Fact is, in Heaven nobody is allowed to be unhappy. Against the rules, Lorna. Fun, fun, fun, that's what this place is about. Can't have the dead moping about, can we?'

Lorna stared at her. 'Actually, there's quite a lot I need to know.'

Irene held up a manicured hand. 'Let's not go jumping in, Lorna, there's a good girl. I guarantee that everything you want to know will become clear. There are no secrets in Heaven, sweetie, I can absolutely promise you that. Look, I know how weird everything must seem at the moment. Not quite the Heaven you were expecting, is it? No, don't answer that, petal, it's written all over your face.' Irene put down her coffee cup, stubbed out her cigarette, and joined Lorna by the observation window.

'I keep having strange thoughts,' said Lorna. 'Memories, maybe.' Joe's hands, *that* carpet.

'Only to be expected, petal. You've been through quite a trauma, haven't you? Memory dislocation is only to be expected.'

Lorna stared out to Heaven's other hull. Memory dislocation? She had no idea what Irene was talking about.

'So, what do you think of your new home?'

'Big.'

'Well, yes, I suppose it is,' Irene replied, already reaching for a new cigarette and patting her pockets for a lighter, 'although *big* is a little vague, don't you think? Being precise, Heaven comprises two hulls, each one measuring exactly one kilometre in length. At their widest point, each hull is one quarter of a kilometre wide.'

'As I said, big,' repeated Lorna, seeing only the handiwork of celestial endeavour.

Irene had lit up and was shrouded again in smoke. Lorna cast an envious eye to the mantelpiece where Irene had deposited her cigarette packet. 'My first task was to convince you of your demise, Lorna. A task, I think, that is now complete.' Lorna nodded reluctantly. 'OK, now that you accept that you're dead, my job is to help you make sense of this place. To do that, Lorna, it's best if we take things one step at a time. Oh, and God was asking after you. I told him you were coming along fine.'

'Where am I?' Lorna asked. Heaven, yes, but a Heaven she couldn't comprehend. A place of sublime beauty where life's scars could be erased. 'Heaven is a spaceship, isn't it?'

'More precisely, Lorna, a *facility*.'

That word again, a rather ugly word that hardly did justice to the impossibly large superstructure beyond the observation window.

'A facility,' she echoed.

'A facility for the search for extra-terrestrial life. I told you we had to take this one step at a time.'

Lorna had a sudden urge to laugh. 'And did you find any?'

'Well,' said Irene, not smiling, 'we found you, didn't we?'

HOLIDAY

On the day before they went on holiday to the Norfolk Broads, Lorna's father was made redundant. Lorna didn't know this at the time, and wouldn't have known what such a long and unfamiliar word meant. He'd worked for the same financial institution in Edinburgh as man and boy and, now on the wrong side of fifty, was deemed surplus to requirements. After all those years, he was given the news in a phone call. Him and dozens of others: new technology meant that rationalisations could be made, departments were being downsized, human casualties were inevitable. Redundant: of no use anymore. Although she only found out later, her dad was being replaced by a machine.

They drove south in virtual silence, which in itself was odd. Although her father wasn't normally chatty, her mother wasn't good with silence. She made up for the both of them with constant monologues about the scenery, the sky, the clouds, other drivers: she didn't like to give others too much time to think.

They passed a road accident on the M6 and her mother said nothing.

There was a sudden downpour, with raindrops the size of golf balls, and still she said nothing.

They stopped at a dreary service station and ate burgers and chips, which normally her mother would have forbidden. Working in a bakery, she knew how things were prepared and had an understandable distrust of cheap food. But not a word of protest, and she even helped herself to one of Lorna's chips.

By the time they reached their destination, pulling up outside the boatyard, Lorna knew that *something* was wrong. It might not be a big something, but not all was as it should be. They were on holiday, her mother had been looking forward to it for weeks. Not only that, but the sun was shining and they had their very own gin palace to float down the waterways. Her father's expression, not hers, which had made her mother laugh when the holiday was booked.

That first night, laughter wasn't on the menu either.

They had been going to go out for a meal, but her mother protested at the cost and rushed off to a local supermarket to buy bread and ham. Instead of a first-night feast, they ate sandwiches and an apple while her parents sat on deck and drank wine.

'It's not the end of the world,' she heard her dad say. By then she was tucked up in an unfamiliar bed and being soothed to sleep by wavelets against the hull.

'No, but it feels like it. All those bloody years! All that time and effort and loyalty, and what do they do? One *fucking* phone call, Jack!'

Despite her eyelids closing, Lorna fought hard to stay awake. This was not the mother she knew. In one short speech, she had used not one but *two* banned words, one being the worst possible swearword of them all. Something was up.

She kept listening, but her mother and father had lowered their voices, perhaps fearful of being overheard. Lorna could make out that her dad was making placatory noises, his low voice discernible, but not the words.

* * *

Irene was speaking through smoke, and still not smiling. Lorna had the strangest feeling that her thoughts had been stripped bare and Irene was able to read them. Irene lips were curled down, sharp eyes on Lorna's face.

'A research facility, yes, but you are also in Heaven. Physically and metaphorically, Lorna, you have my word on it. It is, however, a place of spiritual and temporal contradictions. Its realities may at first seem like impossibilities. My task is to help you understand, to help you put yourself together. OK, babe?'

To *petal* and *sweetie* had been added a new term of endearment. Lorna nodded, while Irene dragged on her cigarette.

'You are now in a place where you can wish for almost anything, within reason, and have those wishes granted,' Irene continued, exhaling. 'It's perfectly permissible, by the way. We all have our little fantasies and foibles, don't we?' Irene at last smiled and winked. Lorna had no idea what to wish for, except for what she couldn't have.

'But to understand Heaven as it is, you must also understand that Heaven has always been more than just a place. It's a concept of veneration, for which we are responsible. As far as we're able, it's a responsibility we take seriously. You see, Lorna, where you are now is an ideal of perfection for millions and millions of people. To them, the ultimate goal of coming to Heaven is eternal solace, a personal reward for believing in whatever god they chose to believe in.' Irene crushed out her cigarette, seemingly angry, but about what Lorna couldn't tell. 'However, Heaven does exist and, although it's not what you expected, it continues to play a small part in Earth's story. It could, perhaps, have played a better part but that, thankfully, is God's domain. Ours not to reason why, Lorna,' said Irene, offering her a wan smile and a small clue as to the source of her irritation.

'For you, Heaven now offers all of life's pleasures, given unconditionally and quite possibly for all eternity. But that doesn't make it a final resting place, don't think that for a minute. In time, you will learn that as, no doubt, you will also find out why you were brought here. Everyone who comes to Heaven is here for a reason. Or, perhaps, it will be revealed to you, I can't say.'

Lorna listened, stars burning on Heaven's other celestial hull. Irene had called it a facility, a research facility.

'In Greek, the original translation of the Kingdom of Heaven was *he basileia tou ouranou*. It means, literally, the rule of the skies. The Bible places Heaven among the stars or in the region of the clouds that pass along the sky. In the Islamic faith, Heaven is synonymous with the Gardens of Paradise and is a place to which you ascend. In Buddhism, there are several heavens. The Jews call it *olam ha-ba*, the world to come. But always in the skies or among the stars, Lorna, in a place hidden from mortal eyes.'

'Here, in other words.'

Irene nodded, wrapped in smoke from a new cigarette. Lorna suddenly experienced a nicotine pang and realised to her dismay that she badly wanted to smoke. 'Don't forget, the theological texts of all the main religions were written long before the invention of the electric kettle. Hardly surprising that ancient scholars imagined Heaven to be in the one place they couldn't see or get to.'

'In the sky,' said Lorna.

'It made sense, I suppose, because virtually every religion adopted the idea,' Irene continued, raising both hands, fingers spread, and counting along them. 'Baha'i, Sikhism, Buddhism, Christianity, Lukumi, Confucianism, Hinduism, Macumba, Islam, Jainism, Judaism, Druse, Shinto, Taoism. The list goes on and on, but I won't bore you with it.' Irene brushed ash from her dress and shook her head. Behind her head, the observation window, curtains open: a blaze of stars across an empty sky. 'It was God's one monumental mistake and one, Lorna, he fervently regrets. Damn fool, he was warned, but didn't pay attention. All those gods, Lorna, all those different heavens. All those lives lived in the shadow of a personal creator and each believing that they're right and that they alone will find immortality.'

Despite its great size, Heaven now seemed too small for all those countless billions of souls. 'God chooses only a very few, Lorna, and you were one of them.'

Lorna opened and closed her mouth. 'But why? Irene, it makes no sense.' From all the countless bodies on Earth, why pluck a trainee lawyer off an Edinburgh street? Why not someone more deserving?

Irene paused, phrasing words before speaking them. 'His really big mistake was to give you faith, petal. For now, we can overlook his other little experiments. It was his one, big inadvertent gift, deeply regretted, but which has been your curse ever since. Still, what's done cannot be undone, even here.'

'But why am I here?'

Irene shrugged. 'I've told you, I don't have the slightest idea.'

'Then can I ask God?'

'Of course.' Irene abruptly pushed herself upright, motioning Lorna to do likewise. 'Let's go and see the geriatric old fool, shall we?'

Lorna gulped. 'God?'

'Of *course*, God,' replied Irene before adding, 'but this time, my love, try to keep your clothes on.'

Irene had mentioned that she'd met him, but in the sweep of revelations, Lorna had let it pass. She would have remembered a physical encounter with a deity.

Lorna had assumed that he'd visited her while she'd been asleep, perhaps spreading his arms in a divine blessing at the foot of her bed. Now she was faced with another memory: an old man in a cream tracksuit and strings of beads, his long hair in a ponytail tied with an elastic band.

Lorna again swallowed uncomfortably, transported back to the antiseptic room in which she'd awoken before finding out she'd died.

Who the hell are you?

Her first words to her God, her nightdress around her ankles, and God looking chivalrously at anything but her.

* * *

Her parents were up on deck somewhere, sharing a bottle of red wine. Lorna's mum had been crying, not for the first time that week.

'Lorna, I don't feel very well.'

'You said that yesterday, Tom.' And the day before, Lorna thought, not taking her eyes off the TV screen. 'I'm watching the film. So shut up, will you?'

'But I don't feel very well.'

'So what do you want *me* to do about it? Go and tell Mum or something.'

'She'll just give me disgusting medicine.'

The rebel X-wings were taking off, streaking towards destiny, the black orb of the Death Star manoeuvring into firing position and charging up its ray gun. Darth Vader strode menacingly across the screen. 'Medicine is supposed to be disgusting,' said Lorna.

'Why?' asked Tom. 'That's stupid.'

'Tom! I'm watching the film.'

'Only for about the zillionth time, Lorry.' Red lorry, yellow lorry. When he was very small, he couldn't pronounce Lorna. At times of stress, Lorry sometimes re-emerged.

'Anyway, you *know* how it ends.'

'I'm still watching it, Tom.'

'Anyway, it's a stupid film.'

'It's *not* stupid.'

'It is stupid.'

'Just fuck off, will you!'

She'd heard her father say that same thing, on the phone, the night before they'd left North Berwick, Mum unusually silent. She'd never heard her father use the dreaded word before, all swearing, profane or otherwise, being strictly taboo. And then, in the space of a day, her mother had used *two* swear words, including the absolutely-beyond-redemption f-word.

'I'll tell on you,' he warned.

'Just do that, see if I care.'

'I will, you know. I'm not joking.'

'Tom, *please*! I just want to see the end.'

'Mum!' shouted Tom. 'I don't feel well!'

He got up and headed for the middle section of the boat, the steering area, where their parents were propped up on cushions. She could hear raised voices, her mother laying down the law about something. Her dad was protesting, but without real zeal.

'Oh, and Tom,' Lorna called after him, her eyes on the small screen. 'May the Force be with you,' and ducked a cushion coming the other way.

* * *

Irene motioned Lorna to follow her, leading her into a featureless labyrinth of corridors that resembled a budget hotel. Each corridor was lined with doors, all designated with a complex number. Irene explained that the numbers related to which hull they were in, the section of the hull, and the deck level, underlining in Lorna's mind the similarity between Heaven and a Travelodge, but with better facilities. She had a hard task keeping up with Irene, who knew where she was going and would suddenly stride off down a bisecting corridor without warning. Walls, ceilings, and floors were spotlessly white, making everything two-dimensional and visually confusing. There were no visible markings to indicate what might lie behind each door.

As they walked, Irene explained that at the moment of Lorna's death, a DNA and brain-scan had been undertaken and the contents within her cerebral cortex uploaded to Heaven for regeneration. Irene stopped to light a cigarette, reminding Lorna that the cloning of human beings was already technically possible on Earth. 'So don't look so surprised, sweetie! All we do is speed up the process by activating cells to grow and multiply at a much faster rate. Memory integration,' she went on, pacing ahead, 'is accomplished by chemical and electrical analysis at a cellular level. Once regeneration was complete, we simply downloaded those chemical imprints back into your new brain.'

Irene stopped to deposit her cigarette into a small white receptacle that had soundlessly and mysteriously slid out from the wall. Lorna, already reeling from the advanced technologies of regeneration, stared at it blankly.

'We call them ashtrays,' said Irene, and set off again at high speed, Lorna scampering in her wake. 'In Heaven, Lorna, you will only find things that are either functional or which we find beautiful, or preferably both. As a rule, we don't value useless or aesthetically displeasing objects. Integrated wall-mounted ashtrays provide a good example of that philosophy.'

'But aren't cigarettes displeasing objects?' was all she

could think to ask, thinking back to Joe and making love on the floor. Hadn't she lit a cigarette afterwards? Lorna frowned, still not quite sure whether she smoked or not or if, now being dead, she should start again.

'Well, they may not be very good for you but, as we enjoy both perfect health and eternal life, we have eliminated the paradox between unhealthy living and pleasure. As I said, Lorna, you can enjoy all of life's foibles and fantasies to your heart's content. From now on, what you choose to enjoy is entirely your affair.'

They ascended a broad staircase and emerged into a broader corridor that had observation windows set at intervals down one side. They were now on Heaven's other flank, with vistas only of distant galaxies set among the empty blackness of space.

Then she heard voices and a woman's laugh.

Rounding a bend, Lorna saw a group of about a dozen people standing and chatting in what looked to be a lounge area. All appeared to be wearing loose-fitting tracksuits in either blue or light green. Apart from the young Sean Connery, Irene, and God, this was Lorna's first encounter with Heaven's other inhabitants. As she and Irene approached, the others stopped talking and turned towards them.

Irene waved airily and sailed past, not pausing in her stride. Lorna raised a hand at the group before rushing back into Irene's wake. A few smiled and waved back without speaking. Among them, Lorna recognised a Brad Pitt, a George Clooney, two Sean Penns, and a Claudia Schiffer.

Pacing on, Lorna heard a symphony of whispers behind her back.

'They are,' said Irene, 'as curious about you as you must be about them. Hardly surprising, really. We don't get many visitors and as your arrival had not been predicted it has, understandably, given rise to speculation. In time, you'll get to meet everyone. Right now, that's not important.'

Lorna glanced over her shoulder, but they had turned a gradual corner and the small group was lost to sight.

'We reproduced your body at the moment of your death,' Irene continued, marching onwards. 'We thought it best if you woke up in your old skin, as it were. Less traumatic, don't you agree?' Lorna said nothing, panting with effort. 'However, as you may have guessed, in Heaven you can also be anybody you'd like to be. A character from history, perhaps? A person plucked from your imagination? Your choice, Lorna. Although you can, of course, remain as you are.'

Irene looked her up and down, making it unpleasantly clear that she thought a makeover might be appropriate. Until now, her looks had never much bothered Lorna. She was who she was, end of story.

'Rock and film stars are very popular, as you will have noticed. Hollywood provides a great deal of our entertainment and Earth's film stars are therefore also quite big here, although they do go in and out of fashion. For example, after *Four Weddings and a Funeral*, the Hugh Grant was quite a popular look. Then it went out of favour until *Notting Hill* and *Love Actually*. Somewhere in Personnel, there's a Charlton Heston, I believe, who continues to watch reruns of *Ben-Hur*.' Irene shook her head, clearly mystified at this absurdity. 'Personally, along with a number of others on this facility, I found *Titanic* extremely moving. For now, I have adopted the persona of its star.'

She paced on. 'The film did, I suppose, strike a chord.'

'Actually, an iceberg,' said Lorna from behind.

Irene stopped and turned, looking suddenly pleased. Lorna was being granted a rare smile. 'A joke, Lorna!'

She clasped Lorna's shoulders in both hands. 'Not a very good joke, but a joke nevertheless. That indicates progress, by the way. Humour is generally the last faculty to integrate. Actually, you will find that Heaven and *Titanic* have rather a lot in common.'

Irene dropped her hands to her sides but didn't elaborate. 'Any thoughts, Lorna? I mean, about who you'd like to be? Who among all womankind is your ideal of physical perfection?' Irene was daring her, playing a game.

Lorna didn't know; everything was too new and confusing. She had been Lorna Love for too long to suddenly desert her familiar self. To do so would feel like betrayal. She had died and been reborn and she owed it to herself to remain herself, at least for the time being. Then she might think about it, although she rather doubted it. She wouldn't know how to be an actress or a supermodel, even a pretend one.

'Maybe in time, Irene. But not now, not yet.'

Irene nodded, the smile fading from Kate Winslet's face. Lorna wondered if she might have inadvertently offended her. 'Biologically,' Irene informed her, 'you are now therefore at the precise age at which you killed yourself.'

Lorna, affronted and shocked, felt her hands tremble.

A silence, Irene looking at her evenly. The smile was gone.

'But I didn't,' said Lorna, her mouth dry and cold perspiration wetting her hairline. 'It was an accident.'

Irene was frowning. 'If that's what you want to believe then, young Lorna, it was an accident.'

Irene was muddling things up, a trick of chemistry and electrical discharge.

'Of course I'm sure!'

'Then I apologise, Lorna. If you say so, I must have

71

been mistaken. An accident, of course it was.'

For no real reason, Lorna felt chilled. It came from inside, but was reflected in Irene's eyes, now hard and glassy. 'The transference of memory can only be accomplished in its entirety,' said Irene. 'It wouldn't be right for us to pick and choose your memories, would it? What you did in life is your affair entirely. In Heaven, sweetie, we don't make judgements on others, and we don't expect them to make judgements about us. It's up to you, not us, to choose which bits to forget.'

'It's not something I would have forgotten.'

Irene raised an eyebrow. 'Regeneration takes time, Lorna, and memories can at first be jumbled. The integration of brain and body is a complex process and doesn't happen overnight.'

'I didn't kill myself!' shouted Lorna.

'I have apologised, petal. For now, let's leave it at that, shall we? Anyway, we're there.' Irene touched a small blue panel on the wall beside her, a white door soundlessly opening, and pushed her gently through the doorway.

Lorna found herself in the same book-lined room that they'd left a minute or an hour before; the same view from the observation window, the same fireplace crackling and throwing shadows, the grandmother clock ticking away the seconds; everything the same except for the old man in a cream tracksuit standing by the fire, hands clasped behind His back.

'We went for a walk,' explained Irene with a small but unapologetic shrug, and lit a cigarette.

* * *

I didn't kill myself, she told herself over and over. It was something she positively, instinctively knew, but it didn't explain the clamminess on her forehead or her shaking hands. She could recall the pavement slipping from her shoes, the panic as she stumbled into the road. She hadn't wanted it to happen, but it had – so Irene was horribly wrong. Now, in the presence of God, confused and angry, she felt like a child again. Too many years on her knees in church had left her unprepared to meet God standing up. To be loved by God you had to worship him, not shake his hand and allow him to take your arm and settle you on a high-backed chair by the window.

'I'm God,' said God, sitting on a chair opposite. Between them was a small table on which lay plates of sandwiches. 'I hope you don't mind.' He indicated the table. 'I thought you might be hungry.'

Lorna bit her lip, her mind temporarily blank. She had no idea what to say to him, or why Irene had been so disparaging. In Heaven, were you allowed to be rude about God? Strangely, he looked familiar, but Lorna couldn't place where she'd seen him before. His grey hair was still tied in a ponytail, and he was wearing the same cream tracksuit. She could have sworn that, like the male nurse, he was speaking in a gentle Scottish accent.

'I realise, young Lorna, that everything must seem strange to you. For a start, *this* place.' He indicated the wood-panelled room with one hand. 'We just thought that it might be nice if you woke up somewhere familiar, didn't we, Irene?'

Irene had kicked off her shoes and was sitting by the fire, flicking ash into the flames. She imperceptivity shrugged, the merest rise of her shoulders.

Lorna found her voice, although it was no more than a whisper. 'God, Irene says I killed myself. But I didn't. It was an accident!'

'Are you sure?' God leaned back in his chair and cast a sideways glance at Irene, who was staring moodily into

73

the fire and not seeming to pay any attention. He looked about eighty, with a deeply-lined face and a straggly beard that he endlessly stroked. Above his nose were blue eyes that twinkled mischievously.

Lorna nodded.

'But you can't really remember, can you?'

Lorna took a deep breath and exhaled raggedly. 'It's not something I would do. I couldn't!' She wanted to cry, despite whatever chemicals were being pumped into the air supply.

'OK, then maybe Irene was wrong,' said God, to a loud snort from the fireplace. God cast an irritated glance at Irene, who was still staring fixedly into the fireplace. 'She often is, you know,' he confided, leaning across the table, to a louder snort from Irene.

'So you believe me?' asked Lorna.

He spread out his hands. 'I have absolutely no reason *not* to believe you, young Lorna.' He smiled and leaned back in his chair. 'Does that make you feel better?'

After a few moments and another deep breath, she nodded.

'In which case,' said God, 'let's leave the subject of your untimely demise, shall we?' His voice was definitely Scottish, and he *did* remind her of someone. 'Sandwich?' He held out a plate. 'Tuna and cucumber, I think. And what about a cup of tea? Or something stronger? A bit early for me, but don't let me stop you. In Heaven, we don't have many rules, do we, Irene?'

Again the sideways tilt of his head, looking to the fireplace for support. Irene merely flicked her cigarette butt into the flames. Lorna's mouth was too dry for food; her hands, bunched tight in her lap, were shaking too violently to hold a teacup. She didn't know what to say or how to behave. In his baggy tracksuit and beads, God might not seem like God, but apparently he was.

'You are on a research facility, young Lorna,' said God, popping a dainty triangle of tuna and cucumber sandwich into his mouth. It took him some moments to masticate, swallow, and dab his mouth with a serviette. 'That much Irene will have told you. A HVN-class facility, to be precise, and a marvel of technology when she was launched. A bit long in the tooth now, I suppose, although she still functions perfectly well. It stands for Hyperspace Vehicular Navigator, by the way.'

'Not a very snappy name,' said Irene, 'but that's committees for you.'

'Our mission,' God continued, 'was to chart a particular quadrant of the galaxy and search for signs of life.' Lorna, sitting still in her chair, hands still shaking, felt a groundswell of panic. 'Just like yours, we are also a curious race. We wanted to find out if we were alone in the universe.' God smiled. 'We decided to find out.'

This much Lorna could understand, panic rising further. Heaven isn't Heaven, Heaven is a badly-named alien spaceship.

God again, eyes twinkling. 'Normally, Lorna, a spacecraft can only fly across lightspeed in a straight line. Did you know that?'

Irene, lighting up, coughed gently. 'I *really* don't think that Lorna wants a flying lesson, God.'

'No? Well, perhaps you're right.' Agitated, he stroked his beard, looking thoughtful. 'Anyway, in hyperspace you can't just dodge things … not like in one of your aeroplanes. Travelling in a straight line means you can't avoid what lies ahead. Of course, we have all sorts of fail-safe systems on board that should, in theory, have protected us. Alas, for reasons that I don't understand, they didn't.'

'God flew us too close to a black hole,' said Irene, flicking ash.

'I most certainly did not!' God glared at her.

'The harmonics along our flight path …'

'… did *not* indicate a gravitational anomaly.'

Lorna decided that she was keeping it together rather well considering she was not only dead but on an alien spaceship, with God having an argument with one of his crew.

'God,' she asked, 'who are you?'

'God is God,' said Irene, firelight playing on her hair, 'although that absolutely *doesn't* make him infallible.'

'I am the ship's captain,' said God, ignoring Irene. 'It's my rank, Lorna.'

'What, like a sergeant or a general?'

God smiled, displaying perfect teeth. 'More exalted than the former, but not quite as important as the latter. But I am the commanding officer of everything that you survey.'

'Then you're not a real God,' said Lorna, struck by contradictions. If he wasn't God, then where was the real God?

'Alas, he is,' said Irene, standing, and seemed to press a hidden button on the book-lined wall. A portion of the bookcase slid silently open to reveal a small back-lit compartment roughly the same dimensions as a microwave oven. Irene extracted two long glasses of pale liquid. 'White wine and soda,' she informed Lorna, handing over a glass. 'It's what I told God you'd prefer, but would he listen?' She shook her head in exasperation.

Strangely, it was exactly what Lorna wanted, although she had no idea how Irene knew, or how she had ordered it or what pair of unseen hands had prepared it. She had met God only to find that he was the wrong God. She had ended up in a Heaven, but the wrong one.

God was rubbing his hands together and examining the plate of sandwiches. Choosing beef and horseradish, he popped the small triangle into his mouth and chewed thoughtfully. 'They are rather good,' he informed Lorna, dabbing his mouth, then looked outwards to the sea of stars beyond the glass.

Lorna waited for him to continue. Her hands had stopped shaking. 'Two weeks into our mission, and while on a routine flight *nowhere near* a black hole, we encountered a large gravitational well.'

'A worm-hole,' said Irene, 'and you were warned about it! The science officer warned you about it! The navigation officer warned you about it! I warned you about it!'

'A worm-hole, Lorna,' said God loudly, speaking over Irene, 'is a temporary phenomenon that joins a black hole to a white star. The huge forces that it generates are capable of creating a shift in the very fabric of the time-space matrix.' God saw that his explanation was falling on scientifically deaf ears, while casting a bleak glance at Irene who was again pretending not to be listening.

Lorna had understood every tenth word.

'We were caught in a temporal fluctuation.' He again glanced at Irene, seemingly daring her to contradict him. 'A highly unusual occurrence, even in *relative* proximity to a black hole.' He sighed, raised his arms, and then let them drop to the table where they made the plates rattle. 'One minute we knew where we were, the next we had been transported through time and space to a completely unfamiliar part of the universe.'

Lorna sipped at her glass, seeing her reflection in clinking ice.

God continued in a softer voice. 'Our mission, Lorna, should only have lasted a few months. Instead, we have been here for many thousands of years.'

'But this is a spaceship.' In her experience, gleaned from TV and the cinema, spaceships could fly across any universe, however large, and still be home for tea.

'The gravitational forces that close to a black hole are quite considerable,' said Irene with some emphasis, her feet now up on the coffee table, wine-and-soda glass balanced on her knee. 'We suffered some structural damage.'

'And catastrophic damage to our main engines,' added God. 'No hope of repair, so no chance of getting home – not under our own steam, anyway. All we could do was sit and wait for rescue, which we've been doing ever since. Our distress signals have gone unanswered.'

Lorna waited for God to say more, but he seemed content merely to stare outwards at star systems that Heaven could presumably once have reached in the blink of an eye.

'And wait, and wait, and wait,' said Irene. 'It's what we do best, Lorna. Doing fuck-all.'

TRINITY

It was what Lorna was accused of doing, or not doing, by her flatmate, finding Lorna curled in a ball on the sofa and a small sea of tissues eddying across the floor. It was late afternoon and a chill wind was blowing from the north. Suzie unwrapped a woollen scarf and hung it on a peg beside the door, then her coat, all the while looking at her foetal friend, her mouth in a thin line. Lorna had her hands over her face, looking at Suzie through chinks between fingers. She didn't want a lecture. She didn't even want to talk to her.

'Lorna, you've got to snap out of it.'

'I can't, Suze. Not yet, anyway.'

'Can't or won't? Christ, it's stuffy in here.' Suzie opened a window, letting in an arctic blast. 'Have you eaten anything?'

Lorna couldn't remember. 'Probably not.'

'What, all day?'

'Suze, I'm not hungry.'

'Then why don't we go out for a pizza? Lorna, you can't stay stuck in here forever.' Luigi's, just down the street, was a favourite haunt. In it they had celebrated birthdays, whispered secrets, shared notes about prospective boyfriends. It held memories, mostly good ones.

But it was warm inside the flat. She didn't want to go outside. She didn't want to see other faces. She might bump into *him*, and that would be a disaster. At the same time, thinking about him, it seemed to her as if he was filling up less of her mind's eye. She supposed that was a good sign, reaching for another tissue.

'You can't stay like this, Lorna. Crying your eyes out, doing fuck-all.' Suzie's patience was wearing thin.

'I'm not doing fuck-all.'

'Then what are you doing? Studying? I don't think so.'

'I'm having a holiday,' said Lorna, feeling persecuted.

'That's just crap.'

'It's not crap. It's how I *feel*.'

'Then why not see someone at the health centre? Listen, Lorna, I'm going to make an appointment for you. If you feel this bad, you've got to *speak* to someone!'

'And be given a bucketful of pills? No thank you.'

'I'll make the appointment anyway.'

'I don't *need* to see a bloody doctor!'

Suzie sighed, at her wits end, but running out of cheery suggestions. 'I'm. Still. Making. You. An. Appointment.' When Suzie started talking in disjointed words, it was time to surrender.

Lorna sighed, stretching her feet out on the sofa.

'I'll make you a sandwich,' suggested Suzie.

'Suzie, really, I'm not hungry.'

'You've got to eat, babe.'

'Suze, this is just a temporary blip. I know I'm not handling things very well, but I'll be fine. Just give me a few days, OK?'

'Whatever, Lorna. Look, can I get you anything?'

Lorna shook her head. 'I'm going to my room,' she said. 'Suzie, I'm tired and I'm sorry.'

'For what?'

'For everything,' said Lorna, and closed her eyes.

* * *

Lorna had no problem with the *concept* of God. Although she'd doubted his existence, she had always conceded in his possibility; a being so far removed from human experience or recognition to be meaningless from a living perspective on Earth. By separating concept from belief, Lorna had in time reconciled her early upbringing: if God existed, then he would be ruler of a very different kind of place. But now, opposite her on a straight-back chair and thoughtfully chewing another sandwich, was another version of God. A God who was palpably flesh and blood, who wasn't even a *general*, and whose kingdom only encompassed a broken-down spaceship. This wasn't a God to inspire terror or devotion, leading his people out of Egypt or smiting the Philistines. This was a God who wore strings of beads and, despite Heaven's advanced technology, didn't appear to own a beard trimmer.

A God, therefore, who wasn't her God, because the idea was absurd, except that Irene had said he was.

'To our surprise,' God continued, stroking his beard, 'we found your planet to be in close proximity. Naturally, we were all very excited, because it's not every day you come across a planet with life on it. Oh, yes, Lorna, life does exist elsewhere in the universe. Mostly pretty primitive, I grant you, but life nevertheless.' He exhaled slowly. 'Planet Earth isn't unique, Lorna, and I've always found it odd that your people believe it is. Nevertheless,' God said in a more commanding voice, 'the life forms we found on Earth were amazing because they very closely resembled those on our planet. It would seem that the same coincidences of galactic positioning had manifested themselves on Earth. We had, in a very real sense, found a mirror-image of our own planet on the other side of the universe.'

Lorna said nothing, having nothing to say.

'At the time, we believed that rescue would happen

pretty quickly. We therefore set about conducting as much science as we could on this new-found planet, in the certainty that another spacecraft would soon reach us. We catalogued as much flora and fauna as we could. Earth, truly, was a source of scientific treasures, a glimpse back in time to a point where evolution was happening at a whirlwind pace. A hugely exciting time, Lorna! Many of Heaven's crew are scientists, you see. For them it was like finding a living, breathing laboratory. But, as the years passed, the certainty of rescue diminished. Then, as the years became decades and then centuries, we had to come to terms with the reality that Heaven *was* our new home and would be forever.'

Out of everything she had been told, Lorna latched onto one fact. 'You were able to travel to Earth?'

'Heaven is what you would call a mothership, Lorna. We do carry other space vehicles able to travel short distances. From here, Earth is approximately half a light year away. In space, that isn't very far.'

From being speechless, Lorna now found that her brain was able to phrase questions and transport them to her mouth. 'So why didn't you just move to Earth?'

God smiled, again revealing His perfect teeth. 'We may appear the same as you, Lorna, but we are psychologically very different. You see, we have had the benefit of thousands of years of additional evolution. Our bodies haven't changed, but our intellectual perceptions have. In Heaven we have eternal life; on Earth we would live and die like anything else.'

Irene was still brooding by the fire, her legs propped on the coffee table, and now she spoke. 'Everyone in Heaven carries an isotope that is activated by the regeneration process. On arrival, Lorna, that same isotope was inserted into your system. It was another fail-safe mechanism, just in case of long-term emergency in deep space. Our High Command felt that, if we were marooned for a lengthy period, the least they could do was make sure we returned home at the same age we left. Good for morale, Lorna, if anything went wrong. Which it did,' she added, looking pointedly at God.

God shuffled in his seat, again casting an irritated glance. 'It meant we had a choice, Lorna. To stay here and live forever, or colonise Earth and choose mortality. We chose life,' he said, spreading his arms wide.

'Can I choose mortality?' asked Lorna.

'Mortality was chosen for you,' said God, eyeing another beef sandwich. 'Your parents made that choice when they chose to have you. Mortality, I regret, has one final price, young Lorna.'

'You died, remember?' said Irene, who had extracted two more clinking glasses from the hole-in-the-wall drinks cabinet and handed one glass to Lorna without smiling. 'The ultimate process governing the cessation of life cannot be undone. Once you die, you're dead.'

Lorna stared at the table, traced a whorl in the wood with one finger. Like everything else, the table seemed made from plastic. 'But are you the *real* God?'

'There's only me,' said God, smiling sadly. 'I wish it were otherwise, but it's not, I'm afraid.' He laid a hand on her shoulder and gave it a fatherly squeeze. 'However, in your hour of need, I didn't ignore you, Lorna.'

'But are you *my* God?' Her voice had risen, white wine giving her the courage to demand an answer.

'I made you in my likeness,' said God simply, his hand still on her shoulder. 'So, yes, I suppose I am your God.' He looked at her kindly for a moment. Once more, she absolutely *knew* she'd seen him somewhere before. 'I do admit, however, that you are rather better looking than I am.'

Again, a blankness; she didn't know what to ask, or

whether she wanted to hear any more answers.

'Tomorrow, Lorna, we will speak some more. For now, it's better if you rest. Regeneration, as Irene will have told you, takes time. You are also in a new place, with much to learn. One day at a time, Lorna. Save some questions until tomorrow, OK?'

Lorna nodded. A nagging headache had emerged from behind her temples.

'If you like, I could also show you the flight deck. Only if you want to, of course. Show off our little fleet of space vehicles. If you wish, I could tell you how they fly.'

Despite herself, Lorna had to smile. God, it appeared, wasn't that much different from any other man she'd known, always keen to show off their new computer, car, or spaceship.

'I'd like that,' she said.

* * *

She didn't immediately go to bed having no means of knowing whether it was late morning, afternoon, or night and whether, therefore, she *should* go to bed. All she'd done was get up, had breakfast, been for a walk, and had a chat with God. Had that taken a whole day? She was used to time's tick-tock: alarm calls, deadlines for dissertations, the mundane shift of a clock's dial. But time had collapsed inwards, rendering it meaningless. Did anyone here wear a watch? Or was time simply an unnecessary encumbrance that superior technology had rendered obsolete, like her father? On closer inspection, the grandmother clock in the bedroom was only a dial with painted hands: its only function was to tick. She sat on her bed for a while, wondering if God or Irene saw the clock any differently from her. To Lorna, it was a thing of charm. Her grandmother had one just like it so, she supposed, she was biased towards it. But did it have the form and functionality necessary for Heaven's approved list? Lorna doubted it. Most things in Heaven were either white or off-white. The only part of Heaven with colour and clutter was her bedroom and living area, and neither room was real. She walked around her small quarters. The fake bookshelves framed a view of the stars that was both mesmerising and completely incongruous. She stopped beside the portion of wall from which Irene had plucked two glasses of wine and soda. She knocked her knuckles against the wall but it sounded solid and she couldn't see any buttons. Lorna stood back and looked intently at the wood panelling.

If you want something, you just have to ask.

Lorna nearly jumped out of her skin. A woman's voice, soft and sensual, speaking out of nowhere.

Lorna looked around wildly. But the voice seemed to come from the walls themselves, without a visible source.

Is there something I can get for you?

Lorna regained some composure. 'Who are you?' she asked.

My name is Trinity. It's a pleasure to meet you, Lorna.

Trinity? 'Then *who* are you?'

I am responsible for the smooth running of this space facility and, of course, for all the requirements of the ship's crew.

'You're a computer?'

This time a short silence before Trinity replied, her voice still lisping and sensual. *I hardly think that is a fair judgement, Lorna. Please don't underestimate my intellectual capabilities, as I certainly won't underestimate yours.*

Oh God, she thought: a computer with attitude.

Would you like another white wine and soda?

'God says I should rest.' Now she was answering back

to the bloody thing.

God is often right, said Trinity, *although not always.*

To Irene's disrespect could now be added Trinity's. 'In which case,' said Lorna, 'that would be very nice, thank you. But only if it's not too much trouble,' she added, feeling she might inadvertently have insulted Trinity, whoever Trinity was.

Nothing is too much trouble. Ice?

'Yes, please, Trinity.'

Hardly had she finished speaking than the bookshelf opened and Lorna was presented with a filled crystal glass. Beside the glass was a packet of Marlboro Lights and a lighter. Lorna hesitated before picking them up, now remembering that she'd been meaning to give up smoking for years.

Irene thought that you might want them, said Trinity.

* * *

She sat in the same chair as she had earlier and ate a beef and horseradish sandwich. As he'd promised, they were rather good, so she ate another. She still had no idea of the time and supposed she could ask Trinity, but in the etiquette of Heaven asking a computer for the time might seem undignified, for both of them.

The view, spectacular and spellbinding, no longer held the terrors it had the night before. The day before, she had been alive and in a curious hospital; then she was dead and beyond retrieval. Now she was in Heaven, except she wasn't. The only real fact she could cling to was that she'd died in a road accident, the car driven by a look-alike British spy who did what he could to make her comfortable. I didn't kill myself deliberately, she told herself, whatever Irene thinks.

Without consciously deciding, Lorna tore open the

packet, removed a cigarette, and lit it. She expected her lungs to burn, her head to burst with white light, or to double up coughing. Instead, she drew the smoke down and exhaled with a satisfied sigh. Then, after she'd finished her drink and stubbed out her cigarette, she washed, brushed her teeth, and lay down on her bed. She didn't bother to draw the curtains. The night sky, if it was night, was dark and offered reassurance; it could almost have been the same sky she'd looked at from her bedroom window in North Berwick or from her bunk on the Norfolk riverboat. But that's all so long so, she told herself firmly. Now I'm dead, it's time to grow up.

MACHINES

As soon as Lorna closed her eyes she had a nightmare. She dreamed that she was alone and in darkness. She felt sick and there was a pain in her arm – and the pain could mean that more pain would follow, pain over which she might have no control. She tried to move her arm, but nothing was connected. Her brain didn't know where her arm was. She tried to concentrate, forcing neurons and synapses to talk to one another. And then her screen flickered. At first, all she could see were shadows. Then she realised that one of the larger shadows was coming towards her. The shadow seemed to be carrying a large stick. She watched as he materialised out of smoke. Behind him was a village of broken mud houses. Smoke was billowing from a window. A woman in black Arabic robes was holding a child. She was wheeling around, crying hysterically. The child was also crying, but softly, as if it didn't want to be heard. The man continued to walk towards her, his boots throwing up puffs of sand. He was wearing a khaki uniform. On his arm was emblazoned the Stars and Stripes. A steel helmet sat lopsided on his head; his eyes hidden behind dark glasses. He was chewing gum and his face was expressionless. He was cradling an automatic rifle and pointing it at Lorna. She was able to look down the sightless barrel of his gun.

* * *

One minute Lorna was asleep, the next she was wide awake, the same cascade of stars beyond her window. Once more she had no way of knowing if she had been asleep for minutes or hours. She lay on her back and stared out at the stars, remembering her dream, the fear of it, and the desperate cries of the mother. She didn't know what it meant, or if it meant anything: a random dream seeping in from another dimension about which she could recollect virtually nothing. Regeneration. Memory integration. She could remember bits about North Berwick, her parents, Suzie, Joe. She could remember having been a law student, and swimming in the North Sea and, chilled but exultant, jumping from the harbour wall. She could remember marching down Princes Street in support of whales and that she had a part-time job in a grocery-cum-everything-else shop. But most of her memory was blank. It was discomfiting only to know bits but not all the bits: to have only an incomplete jigsaw. She would have to relearn who she was and discover what she'd become.

In the living room, all trace of sandwiches and used ashtray had been removed and in their place had been set a pot of hot coffee and chocolate croissants. She poured herself coffee, not hungry, then relented and nibbled on a croissant.

'Morning, sweetie.' Irene had waltzed in unannounced and poured herself a cup of coffee, helping herself to one of Lorna's cigarettes. 'Sleep well?'

'Not particularly.'

'Bad dreams?' Irene settled into a chair and crossed one immaculate leg over the other.

Lorna was by the observation window, her breath forming and dissolving in condensation on the glass. 'Nothing seems normal,' was all she could muster.

Irene cast one arm around the room. 'Does anything

here strike you as normal?' she asked, a flintiness to her voice. 'The fact that you're dead, for example? The fact that you're on a deep-space research facility? Where's the normal in that, Lorna?' She paused to tap ash into an ashtray. 'I see you've started smoking again.'

'No thanks to you.'

Irene held up one hand, nails perfectly painted in lustrous red. 'I merely suggested to Trinity that you might be in need of them. Smoking can be such a comfort in times of stress and, I suppose, this must be a stressful time for you.'

'Trinity told me the cigarettes were your idea. Actually, I think I may have offended her.'

Irene dragged deeply and sighed out smoke. 'I'm sure you didn't, sweetie. Trinity doesn't easily take offence, so I wouldn't worry about it. She exists for our well-being, and her pleasure is to satisfy our every whim.' Lorna waited for Irene to continue, dabbing croissant crumbs from her plate with a wetted finger.

'A spaceship needs only to perform three things,' said Irene. 'One, to keep its crew safe and healthy. That involves a raft of things from artificial gravity to making sure the toilets flush properly. Two, propulsion. OK, we don't have any, but we did. God will maybe explain how our propulsion systems used to work. He's a career pilot, by the way, or was. Started out on the Oberon system, ferrying miners about the place. Usually, although I simply can't believe it, to the *right* place. That was before some stupid *fucking* selection panel promoted him to God, of course. Believe me, you won't be any the wiser if he does try to explain anything scientific. Absolutely bloody hopeless! Three, telemetry and navigation: the ability to plot a course through hyperspace which, without propulsion, we also don't need.' Irene dragged again on her cigarette.

'Put those three things together in a space facility the size and complexity of Heaven and you have an absolute requirement for a bit of intelligent help about the place.' Irene leaned conspiratorially across the table, 'God may think he runs things around here but it's actually Trinity.'

The three things to run a spaceship. Trinity. It made a kind of sense.

'You can ask her for anything,' Irene continued, 'even if it's just to ask the time.' How the hell did she know *that*? thought Lorna. 'More importantly, sweetie, Trinity may be only a collection of bits and bytes but she is, in every sense, a sentient being. Don't forget that, and the two of you will get along just fine. OK?'

'OK, Irene.'

'That's the spirit!'

* * *

Somebody else had said that to her, but not here. She could remember a beach and water. It had bubbled with fluorescence, each like tiny stars trapped between her fingers. The water was warm, the same temperature as the air; insects burped from surrounding trees. A hidden cruise liner or cargo ship must have passed unseen; suddenly, larger waves had fallen on the shore. She'd been sitting in the water's margins, her chin resting on her knees. The force of water had toppled her over, making her shriek with laughter.

Then she was diving into the sea, the water closing over her head. Under the water there was silence; she remembered being happy. From the corner of her eye she could see a lithe man with long hair. He was laughing, chasing her. She couldn't immediately recognise who he was. *That's the spirit*, he had said, she was sure of it. He wasn't Joe, she knew that. Joe had shorter hair and wasn't

92

so tall. Her brother? But the beach didn't look like North Berwick and the only other place she could remember going as a family was Norfolk. The sea seemed different, the sky too big, the water too warm.

Irene was looking at her quizzically, having announced that God was waiting for them on the flight deck. They were walking along a featureless corridor, Lorna quickening her pace to keep up.

'Sorry, I was just thinking about something,' said Lorna. 'A place I once visited … or at least I think I did. It's not far, is it?' she asked, remembering their mammoth trek the day before, before ending back where they'd started. At the back of her mind was shifting water and sand moving under her feet.

Irene put a hand on her shoulder. 'The process of regeneration involves memories becoming untangled, Lorna. It's your mind's way of rearranging things. Think of it like this, petal. Your old brain has moved into a new home and it's trying to shift the furniture about.' Irene exhaled smoke. 'If it matters, then perhaps you will remember. If it doesn't matter, then perhaps you won't. Memories aren't always important, young Lorna, and sometimes it's better to forget than to remember.' Irene arched her eyebrows. 'None of that make any sense, does it?'

'Not really, no.'

Irene turned on her heel, motioning for Lorna to follow. 'In which case, to answer your earlier question, the flight deck is twelve floors down and at the other end of Heaven. However, young Lorna, the good news is that in Heaven we never walk anywhere. Yesterday was all about testing your new musculature, to make sure everything had regenerated properly.' Irene stopped by a door with a small green triangle on it, which she pressed. 'Today, we travel in more style.'

93

Seconds later, a door slid open to reveal what looked like a lift.

'After you,' said Irene, motioning her inside.

It also felt like a lift, but without buttons.

'Flight deck, please.'

Of course, Irene.

Trinity, soft and sensual and omnipresent, her voice oozing from every portion of the walls, ceiling, and floor.

'Best hold onto the rail,' Irene advised. 'This thing goes sideways as well as up and down.'

The transporter first moved to the left, which made Lorna flinch, having never been in a lift that did anything except travel vertically. Lorna had the impression that it was attaining high speed before it slowed and stopped, then travelled downwards. Another stop, sideways again, and then down.

The door slid open.

Flight deck.

'Thank you, Trinity.'

Irene set off down a wide corridor that, unlike anything Lorna had yet seen, was painted dark grey. 'Trinity does like to hear please and thank you,' Irene advised over her shoulder. 'It's not compulsory to be nice but, as you'll find, if you're nice to her, she'll be especially helpful to you. Whenever you see a wall panel with a green triangle on it, you know you're beside a transporter stop. If you can't find one, ask Trinity. Wherever you are on this facility, you just have to ask. Usually, Trinity will respond.'

'But not always?'

'No, not always.'

Irene had reached what looked like a blank wall. Lorna, following behind, heard internal locks slipping and unlocking, then saw that the wall was slowly cranking open. It was double-leafed, each plate fully six inches thick. A few feet further on, another blank wall and the sound of more locks unfastening. A screech of metal as this wall inched open. This time, a triple-leaf door of six-inch plates.

'Blast doors, sweetie, in case of unforeseen accidents.' Irene tapped her foot impatiently as the heavy doors edged open. 'Actually, Trinity does have a teeny-weeny problem, Lorna, attributable to yet another of God's little mistakes. You've already seen one of the little bastards, haven't you? Come on, you used to own one! As a pet, or so I've been led to understand.'

The little face in the latticed grille, small back eyes looking at her unblinkingly, her shriek bringing the young James Bond at a canter.

'They're bloody everywhere!' said Irene with some venom. 'Thousands of the little fuckers! But does he do anything about it? No, he bloody well doesn't! They eat through wires, and Trinity's peripheral subsystems are particularly vulnerable to their little rodent teeth. Trinity sometimes won't answer, because she's been rendered temporarily deaf.' Irene sighed and shook her head. 'The old fool's over there,' she said and turned on her heel. 'I'll see you later, petal.'

STARBRIGHT

Lorna found herself in a place the size of several dozen cathedrals. The ceiling, somewhere above, was lost in darkness. It took her some moments to acclimatise herself to the twilight. The rest of Heaven was filled with light; here it was sepulchral gloom, save only for small lights down the flight deck wall, stretching almost as far as she could see.

'Over here, young Lorna.'

God's voice from underneath a giant shadow.

She tiptoed across the metal floor.

'You want me to show you one of our spaceships?'

'It's awfully dark, God, but yes.'

With a snap of his fingers, celestial light poured down on the area in which they stood. Lorna gasped. Above her loomed a cream-coloured flying machine the length of a football field. It had a snub nose, square body, and stubby wings. Looking up, Lorna saw a darkened cockpit window. A couple of inspection hatches on its flank were open, cables attached to the flight deck floor. Stencilled to its side was HVN-2 in gold lettering. Edging backwards from it, she saw that its stern fluted into six giant exhaust nozzles. She could have fitted comfortably into any one of them and not been able to touch the sides.

'I apologise for being theatrical,' said God with a small shrug. 'But, sometimes, a little drama is a good thing. This,' he said, laying a hand on one arm of the spaceship's hydraulic landing gear, 'is an Adelphi class freighter. We use it to transport personnel and material around. It's a sublight craft, so it isn't very fast, but it is reliable and robust.'

Lorna simply stared at it in wonderment.

'It's huge,' she said eventually, reverentially.

'Well, it has to be,' replied God, 'otherwise it wouldn't be fit for purpose, now would it? Like all spaceships, even Heaven itself, the Adelphi is powered by anti-matter annihilation reactors. These can take the craft to near lightspeed, but not beyond. Close enough to cause a ripple in the space-time matrix, but not into hyperspace.'

God, warming to his subject, was lapsing into gibberish. 'However, Lorna, if you think this is large, follow me.'

God walked straight under the Adelphi. Lorna reached up but couldn't touch the craft's under-belly. It smelled damply of oil and neglect.

Another snap of his fingers and more lights.

In front of her, another spaceship, but this one was double the size of the freighter. At its prow, a long tapering nose, rising and thickening in a perfect wedge to its tail which had the same configuration of exhaust nozzles as the Adelphi. In the circle of light, Lorna could imagine its potency.

'This is a Gemini,' said God. 'One of our greyhounds.'

For a few moments Lorna was unable to speak. The Gemini was perfection; the absolute image of what she might have imagined a spaceship to look like. Like the Adelphi, its cockpit window was in darkness.

'It certainly looks fast,' said Lorna, adding mischievously: 'But can it do the Kessel run in less than twelve parsecs?'

God looked at her blankly. 'Do you want me to tell you how it flies?'

She didn't really need to reply. God was going to tell her anyway.

* * *

'Proper spaceflight involves the ability to pass safely and repeatedly from realspace to hyperspace and back again, crossing and re-crossing the speed of light. Without that capability, Lorna, you don't get anywhere very fast. In fact, given the dimensions of space, you don't get anywhere at all.' He paused, looking mournful, and stroked his beard. 'Anyway, to cross from realspace to hyperspace requires a hyperdrive. However, to understand how a hyperdrive works, you must *first* understand the resonance between pulsed electromagnetic and gravitational wave forms, which together make up space-time metrics. Is that clear so far?'

Lorna coughed. 'Not really, God, no.'

God, one-time space-pilot, wasn't listening. 'Tell me, Lorna, how much do you know about magnetic-field line merging?'

'Absolutely nothing,' conceded Lorna, miserably realising that the principles of spaceflight might be more complicated than she had first thought.

'Hydromagnetic wave effects?'

'No.'

'Free-electron lasers?'

'No.'

'Containment fields? Artificial gravity? Inertial dampeners? Lorna, to understand how a hyperdrive works, you have to first know *something* about elementary science.'

'Which I don't, obviously.'

'In which case,' said God with an exasperated sigh, 'I can see I'll have to keep it simple. You did ask.'

Lorna's eyes traversed the great wedge of the Gemini, from its elegant nose to the six giant exhaust nozzles at its rear. It towered over them both, technology beyond imagination, reduced to useless metal.

God had clasped his hands behind his back and addressed her as might a schoolteacher. 'Try not to think of hyperspace in terms of speed, young Lorna. In hyperspace, speed is irrelevant. Try to think of it as a dimensional crossing point because, in the realspace dimension that we occupy, objects can only travel below or above the speed of light. Never precisely *on* the speed of light. Your Einstein was quite correct, you know. His second law of motion rightly postulated that nothing can cross lightspeed because the energy to do so becomes infinite.'

God bit his lip and frowned. 'Nice chap, if I remember. Well, anyway, the point is that every space-time location is unique. Gravitational and electromagnetic fields, you see.'

He paused to see if Lorna was following him, which she wasn't.

'The next bit is more tricky, Lorna. When a supralight spacecraft like this Gemini reaches the threshold of lightspeed, it generates a configuration of electromagnetic and hydromagnetic fields that have a perfect resonance with the distant space-time point that it wants to travel to. To achieve that, the Gemini's lasers are capable of generating many times more energy than all of Earth's power stations put together. Quite simply, by changing those lasers' wavelengths and frequencies, the hyperdrive can tune into even quite faraway harmonics.'

To Lorna, the Gemini looked frozen to the deck; an obsolete museum piece that could never again regain the power of flight. It seemed desolate or stranded, a marvel without discernible purpose.

God looked at it sadly, as if reading her thoughts, and continued in a softer voice. 'The harmonics that it

100

generates create an imbalance in the space-time matrix that allows it to pass from realspace to hyperspace in a fraction of time so small that time itself is meaningless.'

'Thus getting round Einstein's second law,' said Lorna, feeling momentarily that she was catching on.

'Bravo!' said God, and clapped his hands, setting up an echo. 'After crossing into hyperspace, the secret of its flight then lies in the basic projection laws that govern all dimensional travel. That too was postulated by Einstein, by the way, although nobody took much notice at the time. Only now are your scientists, rather belatedly in my view, beginning to pay attention.'

Lorna was looking at him blankly.

God sighed again. 'Projection laws, like all physical laws, are there to re-establish order and balance. Think of space as a place filled with TV stations, each broadcasting on a different frequency. What Gemini does is dial into a particular frequency, which may just happen to be thousands of light years away. Because the laws of physics don't allow one object to be in two places at the same time, the simple laws of projection takes Gemini to where it wants to go. We call that process *transition* and, frankly, Lorna, even a child should be able to understand something so simple.'

'Unfortunately,' said Lorna, 'I'm not a child.'

* * *

Tom would understand what God was talking about, and for a moment Lorna wished that her brother was there with her. Growing up, she never got to know him, not really. Despite being close in age, they were separated by gender. Her brother smelled of sweat and rugby, alien and male; he might have been her flesh and blood but, to Lorna, there were no obvious similarities. He had fair hair to her brunette; he possessed square features and short, fast legs. Lorna was slender, so slim that she sometimes seemed to bend against the wind. There were few points of similarity, at least few that she could see. Relatives had concluded that Tom took after his father, and that Lorna took after her mum. But her father didn't have short, fast legs; her mum was forever grumbling how long it took him to complete a round of golf. Nor did he have Tom's pugnacious features or his shock of unruly hair, always needing a cut; Lorna looked in vain from father to son hoping to find echoes of herself.

They were different in other ways. Lorna liked to read. She was happy in her own company, aware even then that North Berwick offered only entrapment and believing that books might offer an escape. Tom, twirling a rugby ball on one finger, lived only for the company of others. It didn't matter to Tom where he was so long as he had friends around him. The solitary daughter and gregarious son grew up like boxers, warily circling. Only once, however, did it come to blows. Tom had said something, on top of a lot of other things, and Lorna had snapped, a red mist descending. She'd punched him quite hard, on the nose, and was surprised to see blood on his face. Tom put a hand to his nose and examined the blood that had been transferred to his fingers, gleaming red under the living room light. But he didn't react as she thought he would, already cringing and backing away. All he did was stand there, looking like a large puppy, startled and inert, until Lorna had to laugh and he joined in.

But if Tom didn't share her love of books, he was good with his hands. As a child, his Lego creations were works of art that drew gasps of admiration from their mother. He built robots that actually walked; he painstakingly glued together replicas of the Titanic and B-52 bombers. Lorna would marvel at his sausage fingers and their clever dexterity. She couldn't make things. The instruction booklets that came with his scale models could have been written in Greek or Latin (neither of which were on the syllabus of North Berwick High School). The logic gene that could make sense of assembling lots of little bits into one big thing had only been inherited by Tom. He would huff and puff and shake his head at her stupidity, but it was no good. She took solace in her mother's shared inability to build flat-pack furniture. When they bought Lorna a new wardrobe, it was Tom who assembled it, their mother holding the instruction sheet upside down and scratching her head.

Tom would understand how a spaceship could defy the laws of the universe. With a bit of encouragement, thought Lorna, he might one day build one. For Lorna, it was enough that the TV worked when you switched it on. It was enough that the car worked when you turned the ignition. She didn't want to know how they worked; merely that the technologies she encountered *did* work. Lorna preferred books. For her they conjured up worlds beyond her own, mental pictures of how things could be in a place and time beyond her here and now, where her father once more reached for the bottle he kept under the sink and looked guiltily over his shoulder to see if anybody noticed. Lorna, curled on a chair, would raise her book to cover her face. There were other things she didn't understand, and didn't want to.

She smiled sadly at God, who was once more stroking his beard. Above them loomed the impossibly large hull of the Gemini, crammed full of wonders that Lorna now realised would forever remain far beyond her understanding.

God, sensing this, offered a small shrug. 'The intricacies of spaceflight are rather complicated,' he said, one hand gesturing towards the spaceship's flank. 'I'm sorry if I sounded condescending.'

Lorna smiled. 'I was never very good at science.'

'I know,' said God.

Lorna was startled by his certainty. 'You do?' she asked, trying not to sound disbelieving.

'Lorna, I chose you.'

Another absurdity: God had a whole world of humanity to choose from. What muddled thinking had led him to choose her? Even if he was a real God, which he wasn't.

'Why?' Only a few are chosen, she reminded herself, once more feeling like an intruder. She didn't belong in Heaven; her new skin felt tight and unused. In her world, her old world, unexpected guests were eventually asked to leave.

'I felt sorry for you.'

'That's hardly an answer,' said Lorna, more forcibly. God seemed to be playing a game with her and she didn't know why.

'I chose you, Lorna, but I'm not yet at liberty to explain why. That may sound contrary but, in Heaven, there is a reason for everything.' He looked uncertain for a moment, as if he didn't quite believe himself. 'However, I do appreciate what you must be thinking. Why me? Why have I, among so many others, been gifted eternity? I wish,' he conceded, looking downcast, 'that I could be the God you imagined I would be. Believe me, it would be so much easier.'

He sighed and slowly took a deep breath. 'I have granted you an afterlife, Lorna, and for now let's leave it at that. It might not make any sense at the moment but it will.' God's head was tilted back so his words rose softly towards the distant flight deck roof. His eyes were twinkling; in their azure depths, under the overhead lights, were reflected trapped galaxies. 'However, in making my choice, I did find out everything about you, including your lack of scientific aptitude.'

'Not everything,' she said.

'Oh?'

'I didn't kill myself,' said Lorna, as if it now made any difference.

* * *

With the merest flick of God's hand, a panel on Gemini's side soundlessly opened and a crystal walkway unrolled to their feet. Lorna now saw that the interior of the ship was illuminated, a greenish glow emanating from the cockpit window far above. God seemed pleased with his theatrical trickery and, lacing one arm through hers, led her up the glass-like ramp. Questions burned on the tip of her tongue, but she knew better than to ask them. Eternity gave her limitless time; she'd find out why she was here eventually. God's certainties and patent fallibility had unsettled her: he wasn't *her* God, yet he had chosen her and brought her to Heaven. For a purpose, she reminded herself. But what purpose could a lawyer serve in Heaven? On Earth, her purpose had been defined by aptitude and training; here she was defined only by death. The interior of the spaceship smelled damply of wet blankets.

They were in an open cargo area and their footsteps echoed across what sounded like a metal floor. God led her to one end of the cargo bay, where a glass partition opened, and ushered her inside a rather cramped lift that also seemed made from glass.

'Flight deck,' said God.

Of course.

Trinity, her dulcet tones no different from the voice she used in Heaven.

The lift ascended through several floors of living quarters. On one floor, luxurious seats laid out aeroplane-style; on another, easy chairs set around coffee tables. The lift slowed then came to a halt. The glass door soundlessly opened.

Flight deck.

'Thank you, Trinity.'

The inside of the cockpit at first seemed spartan, with two seats for the pilot and co-pilot and a third seat set behind and to one side. In front of the pilots' position was a flat pyramid that rose from the floor, its tip just extending above the bottom line of the cockpit window. However, unlike a conventional aeroplane, there didn't seem to be any controls. The flat pyramid was devoid of obvious gauges or buttons.

Lorna peered out into Heaven, careful not to touch anything. Although she couldn't *see* any controls, she was pretty sure they were around somewhere. Looking up from the outside, the Gemini had seemed huge; looking down from the inside, it was *massively* huge.

God had settled himself in the left-hand seat and motioned her to the one on his right. In the greenish light, his face looked sickly, like an old man on a turbulent sea crossing. 'Unlike you, we think in colours,' he said, and gestured to the base of the pyramid, 'and when this space vehicle is readied for flight the control panel begins to light up in different shades of blue, green, and red. Down here are the ship's more basic functions. Oxygen supply, hull integrity, that kind of thing.' To Lorna, those seemed anything but basic, but she didn't say anything. She hadn't said anything since her feet had left Heaven's floor. She had questions, but not words.

'Further up the control panel, subsystems become integrated,' continued God, his hand moving up the pyramid. 'Propulsion becomes integrated with navigation, telemetry with environmental protection. The safety of the ship's crew,' said God forcibly, 'is of paramount concern.' His hand now moved down one side of the pyramid. He frowned. 'I suppose I could tell you how everything works, but I doubt if you'd understand.' He looked at her sideways, a small smile playing at the edges of his mouth. 'Actually, when it comes to details, I'm pretty hopeless myself. I suppose I did once know how everything worked, but I must have forgotten. It's been a long time, Lorna.' He sat quietly for a few moments, seemingly lost in thought, then added, 'When it comes to things like environmental protection systems, all that matters is that they do work.'

Lorna coughed but still couldn't find any words. They had become frozen at the back of her mouth.

'The top of the control panel represents the most important of the ship's functions,' continued God, leaning back in his seat, 'the point at which every sub-system has integrated with all the others. Only then will one last light become visible.' He leaned forward and tapped the top of the pyramid. 'This one, last light is the only light on the control panel that is pure white.' He sounded wistful, having perhaps sat in that same seat watching stars unfold across space and time. 'It means that we have hyperdrive integration. Without *that*, you get absolutely nowhere. That last light is the very best thing a space-pilot ever sees, Lorna. It means that we're safe and can go places. Or get home,' he added quietly.

Lorna stared at the blank spot at the top of the pyramid, trying to imagine it lit up like a Christmas tree.

'Us old-timers used to call it *starbright*, I don't remember why.'

Lorna immediately felt the tickle of a memory, too distant for retrieval. Small and indistinct memories kept seeping back, some welcome, others less so. But, despite being anchors to her past, they were also encumbrances; they were what she had been, not what she had become.

Lorna found voice. 'Starbright,' she echoed.

'In space, Lorna, you absolutely require a hyperdrive. Without it …'

'I think, God, you've already told me that.'

God folded his hands in his lap and smiled. 'You know, I do rather believe that I have. Anyway,' he said, one hand gesturing to the cockpit window, 'we have company.'

Far below and advancing towards the Gemini at a brisk pace was Irene, a plume of smoke behind her. God sighed and shook his head. 'Smoking is *specifically* forbidden on the flight deck,' he said, an exasperated tug to his voice. 'I don't know, I really don't.'

* * *

Back on Heaven's flight deck floor, Irene seemed oblivious to God's displeasure. Although she had now discarded her cigarette, wisps of smoke still eddied overhead, disappearing into the darkness above. God looked at the smoke, once more shaking his head but saying nothing. Irene, Lorna had concluded, was probably unmanageable. Prohibiting Irene from smoking on the flight deck would have been like commanding the tide to turn. 'I thought that you might be hungry, sweetie,' she said to Lorna. 'God, I hope you weren't boring her?'

Behind them, the crystal walkway had furled up back into the Gemini and the outer door had slid shut. Looking up, Lorna saw that the cockpit was once more in darkness, the giant space vessel returned once more to redundant metal. The smell of Irene's cigarette lingered in the air.

In Irene's presence, God seemed less divine, less sure of himself. 'I don't think so. At least I hope not, was I,

Lorna?' Instinctively he fiddled with the beads around his neck, the fingers of one bony hand slickly lacing themselves between each brightly-coloured string.

'No, of course not, God. Thank you. I didn't understand very much but, well ...' She trailed off, words again becoming stuck at the back of her throat.

'In which case, young Lorna, I'll leave you in Irene's most *capable* hands.' He said this while looking upwards at the last faint traces of cigarette smoke that were circling upwards in a hidden current. Irene pointedly ignored Him. 'I would prefer,' said God, 'to remain here just a little longer. It's been a while since I was last on the flight deck. Memories, Lorna, lots of memories.' He bowed slightly, trying to be gentlemanly, which made Irene snort loudly.

'Come on, petal,' she hissed in Lorna's ear. 'When God gets maudlin, it's time to go.' In a louder voice she asked: 'So, what's it to be, Lorna? More lamb cutlets? Can't abide them myself, but everyone to their own, that's what I say. Or something French, perhaps? Coq au vin, or some-such muck. In Heaven you can have whatever food you want, sweetie, and whenever you want it. Night or day, isn't that right, God?' she asked. God, after a moment's pause, nodded. 'Or what about a plate of spaghetti?' Irene continued quickly, just in case God chose to reply. 'Pasta, pizza, and hamburgers are very popular here. Advertising, I suppose. Anyway, your choice, Lorna. What would you like to eat more than anything else in the whole world?' Irene was teasing her.

But she was still in a world without obvious clocks, or a sun or a moon to rise and traverse the sky. 'Should I be hungry?' she asked.

TIN MAN

Many of her memories were defined by food. Her mother's gargantuan picnics, lamb cutlets on the riverboat, a birthday picnic on North Berwick Law, the town laid out like a tapestry beneath them. Potted shrimp, tuna and cucumber, beef and horseradish. She could remember other meals: Sunday lunch after church, her eighteenth birthday in an extortionate Italian restaurant in Edinburgh. She had become an adult yet knew only to order the cheapest things on the menu, even though she'd never much liked pasta. By then, her father was only working intermittently and her mother's job in the bakery wasn't making up the difference. They couldn't really afford to treat her, but it was a special birthday. Lorna would have preferred something homemade, something they could afford and which she wouldn't have felt guilty eating. By then, her dad wasn't eating much. Food no longer interested him. He looked at his plate or the wine bottle. He was creeping further into the cupboard under the sink. He didn't say much either.

Indian food was her least favourite. She didn't like spicy food. It burned her mouth and lay heavily in her stomach, making her feel bloated. She preferred homely food, bland and unpretentious: ordinary food that had some connection to where she lived. The further away the cuisine came from, the less that she liked it. It wasn't just that she was unadventurous – although she'd often been accused of it. Perhaps it was something to do with living by the sea, smelling the tang of saltwater on the breeze, hearing the rush and pull of waves on the beach. At night, the hush of water lulled Lorna to sleep; in the morning, she would wake to the raucous call of seagulls.

Her father knew a fisherman and from him they'd receive lobsters and crabs, mackerel and cod. In return, her dad helped with the fisherman's accounts. Most of the catch, Dad explained, is simply put onto refrigerated lorries and sent to Spain. That seemed especially odd to Lorna: why couldn't people, like her, eat what their surroundings provided?

Lorna realised she knew nothing of her Heavenly benefactors. Her concerns had all been about herself. 'What do you people eat?' she asked Irene as they once more negotiated the sets of blast doors, giant locks grinding.

'The same as you, sweetie,' said Irene, a cigarette to her lips. 'I suppose we must once have eaten something else but I guess we've forgotten. You have to remember we've been here for rather a long time. Now we just eat whatever you eat.'

'But how can you forget something as basic as food?'

Irene smiled, the last of the blast doors grinding open. 'Our brains can't remember everything, that's the truth of it. A lifetime of memories, that's what you get, and then you die. At least, that's how it's supposed to be. Instead, we've been here for many, many lifetimes. Too many memories for one brain, sweetie. So, old memories get erased to make way for new ones.' She stopped to deposit her cigarette into another white receptacle that had soundlessly appeared from the wall, then continued in a quieter voice: 'Few of us remember much about our home planet or the people we left behind. Some of us keep photographs, but it's sometimes difficult to know who they were. Brother? Sister? Husband or wife? You see, Lorna, it's all but a distant dream now – a long, long way away and a long, long time ago. Earth now provides our inspiration.' Irene coughed and took a deep breath. 'As I said, pizza and hamburger are popular, although there are a number of gastronomes among the crew who insist only on fine dining. Maybe,' she concluded brightly, 'our own food was crap.'

'What was the name of your planet?'

'Arthuria,' replied Irene, sounding wistful, and coming to an unexpected halt. 'It was beautiful, I think. It had mountains and seas, rivers and valleys. Big cities, small villages. Forests and deserts. Even now, I can remember blue skies and cold rain.'

'You make it sound just like Earth.'

'We are much the same, you and I,' replied Irene, looking Lorna up and down. 'The same weight and mass. The same internal organs. The same hopes, fears, and dreams. Given our striking similarities, it stands to reason, Lorna, that our planets should also be similar.'

They had stopped at a transporter. The corridor wall slid soundlessly open. 'Entertainment complex, please.'

Of course, Irene.

As the transporter set off horizontally, Lorna asked: 'Do you miss your home?' Even as the words came out, they sounded inane.

Irene glanced at her sharply. 'This *is* my home, Lorna. And yours, although it may take a while for that to sink in. In any case, and like everyone else, I've pretty much forgotten everything about home, and you can't miss something you've forgotten about. I only know Heaven.'

But memories are what shape us, Lorna thought, wondering whether the same thing would happen to her. I am what I am because of what I was, she thought, and if we learn from experience, surely it's only the memories of those experiences that are the teachers. If we forget that it's bad to put a knitting needle in an electrical socket, aren't we doomed to make the same mistake twice? Like celestial dementia, would her old memories be silently erased, even the good ones? Would she wake one day and not know where she came from? Would the push and suck of the North Sea be forgotten? Already Lorna could see amnesia and boredom ahead, with nothing to look forward to, not even death.

Irene sensed her thoughts. 'Don't look so glum,' she chided, the transporter rushing upwards. 'As with anywhere, Heaven is what you make of it. Use your time wisely and you'll be happy. Believe me, sweetie, I should know. I've been here long enough!'

But Lorna was still thinking about home and how long it would take to forget about it, crystal memories becoming sepia then fading altogether. 'Am I allowed to talk to people on Earth? Can I do that?'

'It is forbidden.'

Lorna took a deep breath. 'God told me that smoking was forbidden on the flight deck.'

'So?'

'So, you chose to disobey that particular rule.' She removed a hand from the handrail and waved it for emphasis. 'Oh, come on, Irene, please! All I want to do is let people know I'm OK. Surely that's not too much to ask?' Grief had always unsettled her, particularly other people's grief, and she was reminded again of the Arab women with the baby, its angry eyes piercing hers. She didn't like to think of friends and relatives grieving over something that hadn't really happened.

'You're dead, petal. You're therefore not OK.'

Lorna tried again. 'But you were smoking on the flight deck, Irene. That's forbidden.' If Irene could do what was forbidden, then surely she could too.

'Unless a spaceship is actually about to go somewhere, it's perfectly safe to smoke on the flight deck. There's nothing to catch fire, so there's nothing to worry about. Therefore, God's stupid edict can be safely ignored.' Irene's eyes met hers; the flinty edge was back, her lips unsmiling. 'However, there is a higher law of space and time we must all obey. The law of projection, Lorna, surely God explained *that* to you? Without that universal law, we wouldn't have the secret of space flight. It's what allows us to make transitions across space and time. But it also governs everything in the universe. The simple fact,' concluded Irene, finally realising that simplicity was the best course, 'is that no one object can exist in two places at the same time.'

'But I'm not an object,' sulked Lorna.

'Maybe not, sweetie, but you are a temporal anomaly. You're dead in one place and alive in another. What that means is that the dead can't talk to the living.'

Entertainment complex.

'Thank you, Trinity. Come along, petal.' Irene was smiling again, and reaching into a pocket for a long-overdue cigarette. She found time to squeeze Lorna's shoulder before lighting up. 'Time for lunch and, afterwards, a spot of retail therapy.'

* * *

In her short stay in Heaven, Lorna had become accustomed to surprises, yet at first glance the entertainment complex looked no different from the kind of shopping centre she was used to on Earth, but without the crying babies or litter. For a moment Lorna could have been in a town centre anywhere in Scotland, Britain, or the world, and was disorientated by finding herself in familiar surroundings.

'We've even got a McDonalds,' whispered Irene, and pointed with the tip of her cigarette. Sure enough, across the circular atrium over which they were now walking, were the familiar golden arches. 'It's a bit naff,' conceded Irene, 'but the crew like it.'

From the centre of the atrium Lorna could see everything around and above her. The level they were on seemed filled with a variety of sandwich and fast-food outlets. Apart from McDonalds, there was a Burger King, Costa, and Pizza Express. As her eyes travelled upwards, Lorna's sense of wonderment was restored. The next level, reached by an escalator that looked sculpted from glass, contained retail outlets. She exhaled slowly, not knowing whether the likes of Armani, Versace, Dior, Jimmy Choo, and Prada could be described as mere outlets.

The third level, reached by another crystal walkway, offered Dolce & Gabbana, Jean Paul Gaultier, Chanel, Rolex, Fendi, Valentino … the list went on and on – all of the world's greatest and most luxurious brands gathered in a place where nobody on Earth could possibly buy them. She slowly turned, open mouthed, her gaze flitting from one shop to the next, her eyes ascending towards the upper galleries, and to the panorama above. The ceiling, three levels away, comprised one vast expanse of glass. Beyond the glass, the blackness of space and boiling light from surrounding galaxies. Inside, from behind display cases, fiery diamonds on watches, bracelets, necklaces, and rings twinkled back at the stars.

'We also have a Marks & Spencer,' Irene told her, as if this might make Heaven seem more civilised. She pointed upwards with her greatly-diminished cigarette. 'They do *such* nice underwear, don't you think?'

* * *

For no reason, Lorna remembered she had been wearing Marks & Spencer knickers the evening she lost her virginity.

She was seventeen. Her boyfriend, Austin Bird, was deputy head boy and captain of the school First XV. Like her brother, rugby was in his blood. It was their names, of course, that had drawn them together. Wouldn't it be silly, they'd joke, if we went out together. What would people say! They joked about it so often they eventually did go out, just to see what people *would* say. They got on well and, almost without thinking, he morphed from friend to *boy*friend. Sometimes they went to the cinema in Edinburgh, usually to friends' houses for a party. The school year was drawing to a close. It would soon be the end of schooldays for both of them. Lorna had never really had a boyfriend before: the word seemed alien, new. She'd concentrated instead on passing exams, making sure she could leave North Berwick eventually. Austin was a departure; like her brother, he smelled different.

Inevitably, as they'd always known would happen, they were nicknamed the Lovebirds.

Austin was tall and sporty with a shock of dark hair. Lorna liked his boyish smile and daft enthusiasm. He had a square chin and roguish smile. He was a tiger on the rugby pitch, tackling with ferocity, his face so contorted she barely recognised him. Off the pitch, he was a pussycat, shy and unsure of himself. Lorna found this touchingly attractive; the motherly instinct in her wanted to cocoon him. Like her, he had set his sights on university, but in Bristol.

Austin was going to study engineering. He'd set his heart on building bridges, although, he conceded, he might have to start with roads and work upwards. He loved the *idea* of bridges, of land and people being joined

117

up. He couldn't really explain this to Lorna, although he did try, becoming increasingly tongue-tied. When he tried to explain things he would grow agitated, then inarticulate. He showed her a picture of the Clifton Suspension Bridge, and said that this is where modern bridge engineering really started. But the picture meant nothing to her. A bridge was simply an extension of the road on either side. While most boys of his age had pin-ups of pop stars or actresses, Austin's bedroom was festooned with pictures of great bridges of the world, mostly shot at night or early dawn for maximum effect. Lorna didn't see this as odd – although others did. Instead, she found it rather endearing. In class, he would frown and suck on his pen; nothing he was taught ever made much sense to Austin until he'd had a chance to think about it. He wasn't the brightest boy in her class, but she admired his perseverance; the way that his brows would slowly unknit, the pen leave his mouth, and he'd smile. The rest of the class might already all have solved the problem, but Austin never gave up. Lorna liked that.

Their first kiss was in the cinema, under cover of darkness. His lips were surprisingly soft for a burly rugby player and he smelled of aftershave and nerves. Emboldened, he placed a hand across her breast where it remained for the rest of the movie. Afterwards, there was a sweaty palm print on her T-shirt. Lorna knew where this was headed, and realised it was something that had to be done, although she wasn't sure whether she was looking forward to it. She didn't want the commitment that Austin seemed to want, so having sex with him didn't seem like a good idea either, although most of her friends had already lost their virginities, or so they said.

On their next visit to the cinema, to see the same film, Lorna sat on his other side. Austin said he wanted to see it again because he'd enjoyed it so much the first time, although Lorna knew precisely what he really meant, and allowed her other breast to be subjected to damp squeezing.

On the beach later that week, shielded by tall grass and the high dunes, Lorna unclasped her bra and allowed him free rein inside. She knew, however, that this was mere preparation. Other male friends had got this far (although she'd never termed them *boy*friends) – with Austin, she was being coaxed into submission. So when his hand, slowly and clammily, crept up the inside of her leg, she didn't resist. Only when his fingers came to rest against her knickers, sending shafts of light across her eyes, did she decide to hold out for a little longer. Lorna's hand settled on his and prised it loose.

'I'm sorry,' he said, pulling back from her. 'I just thought … I mean, I didn't mean …'

'It's OK, Austin.' Lorna didn't know what else to say. A light breeze had sprung up, particles of sand had caught in his eyebrows.

'Is it me?' he asked. His brows were furrowed with such intensity that she had to laugh.

A couple with two Labradors were walking towards them, taking turns to throw sticks for the dogs. Although hidden in the dunes, their privacy was being invaded. 'Of course not, silly … You're my boyfriend. But it's just a bit public, Austin,' said Lorna, realising immediately that this suggested that she might capitulate sooner rather than later.

Austin said, 'That's nice.' It seemed the first thing that had sprung to mind. Sometimes Lorna felt that she had the power to startle him, even by saying something banal.

'Nice? Is that all you can say?' she asked. She had allowed him to touch her *there*; until a moment ago, *there* had been her private place.

He looked down, drew patterns in the sand with one

hand. 'I don't know what else to say.'

'Then try telling me I'm your girlfriend.'

Austin had little experience in these matters. 'I've told you before, Lorna. You *know* what I feel about you.' Seabirds fluttered raucously on the sand, competing for some morsel that the sea had thrown to the beach.

Austin propped himself on one elbow and kissed Lorna quickly on the forehead. His lips felt welcoming; they touched her senses like electricity. 'I've never had a proper girlfriend before,' he admitted, kissing her now on the mouth. He tasted bittersweet, and small bubbles of saliva had gathered on his lips. There was an ominous bulge in his trousers. 'I like you, Lorna,' he said.

'Only like?'

'Love … like, it's the same thing.'

Lorna drew up her knees, pulling her skirt down, barring further access. '*Like* is when you have a hamster, *love* is when you have a girlfriend.' But, she thought, love is also what makes us saddest, thinking about her father and his losing battle with the cupboard. You can't have it both ways.

Lorna scrambled back to the beach. The couple with the dogs smiled at her sweetly, guessing what she'd been up to. Austin followed meekly, as she knew he would.

KNICKERS

In the week that school finally ended, there was a party at Julie and Pam's house close to the beach. Their parents had left hurriedly to visit a sick uncle, and their two children – non-identical twins in Lorna's year – had grasped the opportunity of an adult-empty house with both hands. As Austin remarked, it couldn't have been a much-loved relative, given the alacrity that the two girls displayed in organising a party at high speed.

Everybody brought cans of beer, cider, or Bacardi Breezers. There was dancing in the living room and drinking in the kitchen. Unsurprisingly, there was virtually nothing to eat. To Lorna's annoyance, Austin smelled of curry. 'A carry-out,' he explained. 'We always have a carry-out on a Friday.'

The Lovebirds were soon on the dance floor. During the smoochy dances, holding each other close, she could feel his arousal. It didn't just make her feel wanted; it made her feel powerful. She had something he wanted and she could choose to offer it or withhold it.

'We could go for a walk,' he suggested, which wasn't really what he was suggesting.

Lorna hadn't drunk enough yet. This night of all nights, if she was to go through with it, required just the right amount of alcohol. Her inhibitions needed to be subdued, but not her wits. She hadn't made up her mind yet, not completely. Lorna's senses were still too jagged and raw.

'Later,' she replied. 'Not just now, OK?'

'When later?'

'It's a party, Austin,' she reminded him. 'Just … later.'

Later turned out to be much later. Lorna had a few dances with other friends and girlfriends, swigged back a few Bacardis, and slowly mellowed. The loud music and unaccustomed alcohol had entered her bloodstream, making her tipsy and elated. She had left school and was almost a woman: She could do whatever she wanted. The future beckoned, full of big cities and bigger opportunities. The white sands and pettiness of East Lothian were already dropping from her shoulders. Lorna had outgrown the place, and soon she would be free.

Lorna found Suzie in the living room, twirling like a maniac while holding a glass of what looked like orange juice, but which probably wasn't.

'Austin wants to go for a walk,' she told Suzie over loud music.

'A *walk?*'

'Yes, a walk. You know, putting one foot in front of the other.'

Suzie flicked blonde hair and pouted. Despite it being dark, a pair of sunglasses was perched on her head. 'Yes, but he doesn't mean a walk, does he? How exciting!'

'Suze, it's not exciting. I don't know what to do.'

'Go with the flow, babe.'

'That's the best advice you can come up with?'

'OK, wait there.' Suzie disappeared into the kitchen, emerging a minute later with another glass of orange juice which she handed to Lorna, who took a sip and nearly retched.

'Suzie, it's disgusting!'

'It's Demon's Revenge. Medical, Lorna.'

'*Medicinal?* What the hell is Demon's Revenge?'

'I made it up. Mainly whisky, peach brandy, and orange juice.'

'Mainly? What do you mean *mainly*?'

'And some vodka, I think. Might have been gin.'

'You actually want me to drink this muck?'

Suzie leaned in close. 'To help you decide.'

Lorna had confided every detail of her relationship with Austin to Suzie. There were no secrets between them, although Lorna's secrets usually became common knowledge within days. 'Do you think I should?' she asked, as if Suzie had ever given useful advice.

'If you don't, I will.' Suzie smiled wickedly.

'That's not exactly the answer I was looking for.'

'Then what answer would you like me to give?'

'I don't know what to do,' Lorna said again.

Suzie swept back hair with one hand, while Lorna swallowed another mouthful. 'You don't really have to do anything, sweetie. He does the work, you get to look at the sky.'

Strangely, Demon's Revenge had begun to taste quite nice. 'That actually wasn't what I meant, Suze. It was you, remember, who told me about the birds and the bees. I just don't know if I should or not.'

Suzie sighed. 'You like him, don't you?'

Lorna swallowed more of Suzie's concoction, feeling her inhibitions begin to slip. 'Yes, of course I like him.'

'So you don't find him physically repulsive?'

'No.'

'Well, there you are.' Suzie raised her glass and winked.

Austin had spent a good part of the party in the kitchen, talking about footballers and the obscene amounts of money they earned. She found him centre-stage by the kitchen table, talking about Manchester United and ticking off names on the fingers of one hand. His forehead shone under the overhead light. His voice was loud and slightly slurred. Lorna supposed that he had been drinking more beer than was good for him. His smile seemed too wide and forced, his face slightly contorted as if about to make a tackle. Pretty soon, he might be a gibbering wreck. Lorna didn't much like football. She only recognised a couple of the players being complained about.

'Come on, Austin. Let's go.'

'Where?' Lorna saw that he was slightly swaying.

'Anywhere. I don't know. You said you wanted to go for a walk.'

He was carrying a heavy leather coat and slung it over one arm. They walked down to the beach and then away from the town. Here, the golf course meets the beach; here, sunbathers have to be careful of poor golfers. He fumbled in his jacket and produced a bottle of vodka. He held it to the moon and squinted: half empty. Lorna avoided asking whether he had drunk the rest. 'Go on, have some,' he was whispering, pressing the bottle against her chest.

'I don't like vodka.'

'You've been drinking those Bacardi things all evening.' His tone was scornful. 'That's vodka, isn't it?' He tilted the bottle to his own lips instead. Lorna could see his Adam's apple bob as he swallowed. 'Here, why not try some?' he was whispering again, demanding compliance. She shook her head, wrapping herself in her fleece, wondering if being with Austin was such a good idea. He was drunk, and Lorna wasn't yet at a point of surrender.

'Actually, give me some of that,' she then said, looking at the canopy of stars as she swallowed. The stars seemed closer immediately. Lorna swallowed another large mouthful, then another, then another. If it had to happen, didn't it always first happen under the influence of alcohol? That's what Suzie had told her. *Get yourself legless, babe*, was her advice. *You've got to lose it sometime.*

They were climbing into the dunes, swishing through long grass. Shadows moved, and turned out to be small trees. Careful not to trip in rabbit holes, they walked to the top of the dunes; the sea on one side, the golf course on the other. 'Where are we going?' she asked.

'Nowhere,' said Austin and sat down heavily.

They could hear the sea across the wide beach; stars sparkled on its surface. Austin sipped at the bottle and handed it to Lorna. Once more, she found herself swallowing and swallowing. Then an owl hooted and they looked round uneasily, expecting to see its shadow in the sky.

Lorna felt transformed. She had rarely tasted raw spirit before. The vodka was liberating her, she felt she could touch the stars. Her ears were buzzing and it took a moment to realise he was yelping, 'Don't finish it, don't finish it!'

Lorna looked at him, the bottle held from her mouth.

'Christ, I feel sick,' he said, swallowing bile. 'Finish it, Lorna. Fucking stuff.'

Lorna's head was spinning, thoughts fragmented. She stood up, putting one foot in a rabbit hole, and swore. She looked up, watching the stars whirl in silky streamers. She blinked rapidly, and the stars became fixed points once more.

'I love you,' Lorna heard him say, surprised that he seemed to mean it. But his face was in shadow, she couldn't see his eyes. The vodka was either spoiling things, or making them happen. Lorna couldn't decide. It was depriving her of her better senses, the ones she needed to relish the moment. But it was also unfastening her inhibitions, the ones that would say no.

Lorna held up the bottle, feeling warm – a mellow

calm bordering on invincibility. All of her life, all she remembered, she had been a schoolgirl. It had defined her as a child, now she could put away childish things. A few inches of liquid sloshed at the bottom of the bottle, looking as harmless as water.

'Would you mind if I was sick?' he asked, as if Lorna had any say in it. She detected a hint of defeat in his tone, or desperation.

'Maybe,' Lorna suggested, 'we should walk about a bit. It might make you feel better.' She held onto his arm and pulled him upright, held onto him tightly as they walked across the dune, as if they were lovers on a seaside promenade. North Berwick was a cluster of lights in the distance, as if a handful of stars had fallen from the sky.

'I think I feel better,' said Austin and suddenly laughed. 'In fact, I feel fucking great!' He pulled away from her and slithered half way down the sand dune on his backside. Lorna slithered down beside him, then swallowed again from the bottle.

'Hold me,' she said. Her mood had again shifted; her eyes brimmed with tears. And then it seemed as if a rolling tongue of flame had erupted from over the head of the dune, spewing towards them in a fiery burst. She blinked, but the beach was black. Above, a shooting star was falling to Earth. Lorna turned her face to Austin, waiting to be kissed, and they lay like that for what seemed like hours, under the bright stars, oblivious to the owl hooting from the second fairway.

* * *

Later still she took off her fleece and put it on the grassy dune as a pillow. Lorna felt elated, thoughts jangling – the alcohol had released her, making her bold. She tugged her jeans down, twanging her underwear on her ankles. It seemed that Austin was shaking all over. He'd probably never seen a naked woman before, except his mum, maybe. His hands were certainly shaking, as if she was a fragile gift that might break. Again Lorna felt a sense of power. She felt that her body was a weapon: she could use it to conquer. Then Lorna was guiding his hand between her legs, grimacing as his nails dug into her; taking his forefinger and showing him what to do, lights exploding across her eyes, the first time anybody had touched her *there*. She kept her hand on his until she was certain he would do it right. Her body moved, pressed against his – then she arched her back with a small cry and pressed her legs together.

'Jesus Christ,' said Lorna.

Austin said nothing. His whole body was shaking, he sat up.

Lorna lay on her back. Tears spilled from her eyes.

'I've got to pee,' said Austin, and stumbled into the darkness. Then Lorna heard him retch and went to find him, staggering naked across the dunes. He was on his hands and knees being sick into a gorse bush. 'Um, can I do anything?' Lorna offered.

'I know how to be sick, thank you,' he informed her. His voice was fogged with alcohol. Lorna had expected orgasm to bring a sense of adulthood: an elation, a heady feeling of fulfilment. She hadn't expected to enjoy it and then for him to be sick.

Afterwards, his face was sweat-streaked and his eyes shone like bright marbles. Lorna licked her lips. 'Pass me the bottle, Lorna,' he said then, seeing her expression, added, 'to wash my mouth out.' He gargled with a little of the vodka, then spat it into the sand.

Lorna took a deep breath and felt revived, seeing her life in spinning shards like a shattered mirror, the pieces tumbling. On the larger pieces she could see herself reflected: as a small child crawling up the stairs to their house; laughing at some long-forgotten joke; choosing clothes in one of North Berwick's numerous charity shops; catching a gaily-coloured beach ball from her father; finding out her ears were filled with invisible coins that only her dad, the wizard, could find. The pieces of mirror tumbled, providing other glimpses: a birthday on North Berwick Law, a picnic set before her, and her mother whispering in her ears. Then her mind lurched again, the mirror-fragments disappeared, and she felt empty inside, tenderness between her legs. There was still unfinished business to be completed.

She made Austin take off his shirt and trousers. He was drunk enough not to be too embarrassed. Lorna was fascinated by his erect penis. She touched it, intrigued and repelled, and felt it twitch like a living thing.

Austin, bless him, had remembered to bring a condom and, turning his back, rolled it on. Lorna smiled at his sudden shyness; putting on a condom didn't seem an act requiring privacy.

He said, 'I suppose we should lie down.' Lorna dutifully spread her legs and, with great care, took hold of him and guided him inside her. It was over within five seconds.

'Is that it?' she asked.

Lorna never did find that pair of knickers. They must have twanged off into the undergrowth. She had a surreptitious look for them the next day but found only an empty vodka bottle.

* * *

Coincidentally, she was also wearing Marks & Spencer underwear on the evening they drove back to North Berwick from the Norfolk riverboat holiday. She and Tom were in the back and trying to sleep. From the front seats, at least for the first couple of hours, there was silence. Their mother, usually voluble, was again being silent. It had been like that for most of the holiday.

It wasn't until they were on the M1 that she spoke. 'All those *bloody* years,' she said softly. 'Can't you say something to them?'

Another swearword. Lorna's ears pricked up. She'd only been half asleep; now she sat with her eyes closed and ears open.

'Say *what* to *whom*?' replied her dad. 'It's a done deal, that's the fact of it. All signed and sealed by some management hotshot in London. There's *nothing* to be said to anybody.'

'Then what about seeing a lawyer?'

She heard her dad's sharp intake of breath. It took him a few moments to reply. 'Lawyers cost money.'

'A good lawyer might also *get* you some money.' Lorna peeked through half-closed eyelids. Her parents were looking forwards into the gathering night. She had no idea what lawyers did, or why her dad should speak to one.

They drove on in silence, and then Tom was sick. Not badly sick, but sick enough for a stop at a service station. While her mum took him off to the loo for a clean-up, her father did what he could with the interior of the car. The rest of the journey was completed in near-total silence, the smell of Tom's vomit all-pervasive.

Eventually her mother spoke. 'I'll take him to the doc's in the morning.'

Tom snored softly, a string of saliva anchoring him to a cushion propped against the door. Lorna sensed, with the prescience of childhood, an undertone in her mother's voice.

***

The episode of her virginity should have ended on North Berwick beach but it didn't because, two years later, she was also wearing Marks & Spencer underwear when she travelled down to Bristol to see Austin Bird. They hadn't seen much of each other since … well, *it* had taken place, and they hadn't repeated the experience, at least not with each other. For the rest of the summer until they went their separate ways to university, they'd kept a distance from one another. Lorna felt embarrassed about it; no doubt he felt bad about it not lasting longer. Her friends had assured her this was normal the first few times, but it didn't stop them giggling when they saw Austin in the street. It was her fault. She shouldn't have told Suzie all the grisly details and Austin, of course, guessed wrongly that she was spreading stories and didn't find it remotely funny, particularly when he heard giggles behind his back. Losing their virginities together could have brought them together, but it hadn't. Old enough to have sex, but not old enough to understand its ramifications, Lorna had merely come to see it as a rite of passage. She was a woman, and now it was official. That brief, simple, and not unpleasant act on North Berwick beach was the proof of it. No, she should have left it there, a first and last fling before escaping to somewhere better, and putting childhood things behind her. But, although she didn't much want to remember that first time, she did want to think fondly of the person she'd done it with.

***

But of course none of it was coincidence. Random memories, plucked from nowhere, and meaning nothing. She'd always worn Marks & Spencer underwear. It was a

130

habit inherited from her mother and she'd never seen any reason to break it. Now, her face turned to the upper levels of the entertainment complex, she probably never would.

'Yes, Irene,' said Lorna. 'Very nice underwear.'

BARBEQUE

Irene led her up crystal walkways, past shimmering diamonds and designer dresses, across deeply carpeted aisles that smelled of Dior and Chanel. The entertainment complex was absolutely quiet and entirely empty. In the shops were clusters of emeralds and rubies, chains of topaz and gold. Lorna wanted to stop, to run her hands over silk. She had never seen such insane riches: diamonds that could have built wells in Africa, emeralds to feed the starving. She felt vaporous indignation coalesce in her stomach then well up inside her. These were fripperies that she'd never seen the point of owning, not when their value could be put to better use.

Irene marched on, ascending the walkways until they reached Heaven's upper floor. Here there was a discreet restaurant, walled in oak. Picassos hung on the walls, and looked real. Tables were draped in damask and set with silver cutlery. Like the rest of the entertainment complex, the restaurant was entirely empty. Irene flapped open a serviette. A bottle of red wine was already open on the table, and Irene filled their glasses. Lorna looked round for a waiter. There didn't seem to be one.

Irene sat back and appraised her. 'You were asking about God, Lorna. Is he the real God? I suppose I should fill in a few gaps.' She sipped from her glass, laid it back on the table.

'The fact is, petal, your race was dying out. It was a time of dramatic climate change: ice caps were melting, sea levels rising. There was torrential rain and heat-waves.

Your world was either flooded or parched. In the middle of all that came a new disease. But this wasn't just another pandemic that would wipe out a few million and then fade away. This was an illness against which you had no protection and no means of developing protection. A new illness that had crossed a species barrier. Within a generation the human race would have been history.' Irene sipped red wine and looked wistfully into the glass. 'We hadn't been here long and God simply didn't know what to do. Not at first, anyway. The prime directives governing our mission didn't allow us to interfere artificially with other worlds.'

Lorna understood this, having watched wildlife films. As a child, wildlife documentaries had saddened her. Why couldn't the film-makers scare away the lions? How could they allow the pride to kill the innocent zebra? Only later, watching *Star Trek*, did she realise that nature was red in tooth and claw and that Captain Kirk wasn't allowed to change things. She still didn't like it when the zebra/deer/antelope was brought down, but now she understood the ways of the world and that lions aren't vegetarians. But unlike Captain Kirk, Lorna had tried to change things. She'd marched against foxhunting in a dreary procession through Edinburgh, being pelted by tomatoes by fat agricultural men in Barbour jackets, and for whales – being photographed by bemused Japanese tourists. Lorna had always been on the side of the underdog. She could empathise with them and, placard held aloft, had trudged the city's streets to demonstrate her support.

'God, however, eventually decided that he had to do something. We were stuck far from home without any means of knowing whether our home planet still even existed. We could be in its future or its past. It seemed to God that prime directives didn't therefore now apply and that mankind was your planet's best hope of advancement. He decided to act independently, on his own authority. He therefore set about saving the human race.' Here Irene sighed and swilled her glass. The wine coiled and twisted in a whirlpool, releasing heady fragrance that Lorna could smell over Irene's cigarette. 'However, it wasn't a decision that met with universal approval, particularly when he unveiled his plans for your salvation. But he felt he had to give you immunity against the disease. That required some of our DNA being transferred into the human species.'

Lorna anticipated what Irene was going to say. 'He used his own DNA, didn't he?'

Irene looked up, her chiselled eyebrows raised. 'He made you in his likeness, Lorna. A small vanity on his part, but he was God, and it was his decision. However, the old fool decided to not only give you a specific immunity against the illness, but to give you a whole bunch of immunities. He wanted to give you the best possible chance of surviving every possible pandemic we could foresee. That, I'm sorry to say, was a mistake. *His* mistake, Lorna, and one he has come to regret. He was warned that it was risky, but even then could be a cantankerous old devil. He chose to ignore the scientific advice and proceed with his plan.'

In her short acquaintance with God, Lorna could hardly have described him as cantankerous. However, Irene had known him a lot longer and probably knew best. 'The DNA sequences that we injected into mankind contained too much of his genetic imprint. Before that, the concept of God was alien to your people. Afterwards, people started to believe in him. If it's any consolation,' said Irene, twirling her glass again, 'he's very sorry. He never meant for it to happen. However, once it became clear that it had happened, it was too late.'

Lorna thought of her own mother on bended knee, incense in her nostrils: all around, the certainty of salvation, at least for those sensible enough to go to church. 'That's utterly ridiculous,' said Lorna.

'Yes, I suppose it is,' replied Irene, glass to her lips and reaching once more for her cigarettes. 'But isn't everything here just a teeny-weeny bit ridiculous?'

Lorna's eyes were drawn to the bottle of Chateau Lafite, from which Irene was replenishing her glass. Several floors below were the golden arches of McDonalds; in between, emeralds and diamonds jostling for shelf space. She sipped her wine, not trusting herself to say anything.

'I appreciate that faith can provide solace,' said Irene, 'particularly at times of loss.' Irene wasn't looking at Lorna when she said this, her eyes concentrated on a point beyond Lorna's head. 'But think of the wars, sweetie. Think of the intolerance and bigotry. Think of all those who die every year because they believe in a different god from everyone else. Then try to imagine what your world would be like if there were no gods.'

Lorna thought about this. 'It might feel pretty lonely,' she said eventually.

'Maybe so,' said Irene, 'but without gods, you'd have only life.' Irene fixed her with steely eyes. 'After all, Lorna, without a belief in Heaven, wouldn't everyone on Earth get along just a little bit better?'

* * *

They were in a French restaurant, so Irene told her, and were drinking Irene's usual plonk. Chateau Lafite 1787, so Lorna discovered, looking at the label. Irene explained that a bottle of this muck, once owned by Thomas Jefferson, had recently sold at auction in New York for more than £100,000 – and she'd wanted to know what it tasted like, or how it would have tasted at its best. Now it had become her stable accompaniment to every meal – except breakfast, of course, said Irene, smiling thinly.

On the way up to the restaurant, Lorna had stopped. She simply couldn't resist. She'd stepped from the walkway and had a look inside Dior. All the glittering arrays were laid out on glass shelves, but not only were there no price labels, there were no tills or security.

'Why bother?' said Irene dismissively. 'Everything is free. Take what you need, take what you want.' She shrugged. 'The difference between want and need is immaterial.' Irene picked out a diamond and emerald bracelet and handed it to Lorna. 'Take it, sweetie. Suits you … goes with your eyes.'

Lorna weighed it in her hand with the usual ambiguity she felt when confronted by obscene extravagance. 'I just don't know if I want it,' she said, although her fingers were still lingering on its tightly arranged gemstones.

Irene raised an eyebrow.

'Not my style,' said Lorna, more apologetically, but still unable to quite let go of it.

'So you prefer cheap and tatty, is that it?'

'Cheap and tatty is all I've ever been able to afford.'

'Until now,' said Irene.

Without meaning to, Lorna had somehow attached the bracelet to her wrist, her eyes drawn to the clarity of its stones and its exquisite gold latticework, but also remembering how the world's wealth was concentrated in just a few hands, and how just a few of their baubles, liberated by force if necessary, could feed the masses. Reluctantly, she unclasped it and laid it back on the shop counter.

'Then if you don't want to take it, think of it as a

present. From me to you, petal.'

'I couldn't, Irene. It wouldn't feel right.'

'But you do like it, don't you?' Irene had lowered her voice to say this, as if imparting a secret and, with a shock, Lorna realised that the bracelet had once again become attached to her wrist, and she looked at it again: dark emeralds and white diamonds held in platinum and gold. It was the most beautiful thing she had ever seen. 'I don't know, Irene. Wearing this kind of stuff really isn't my thing.'

'Your *thing*? What exactly is *thing* supposed to mean?'

'I don't believe in conspicuous wealth.'

'Why?' asked Irene dismissively. 'Or is it just because you've never been able to afford good jewellery? Nothing wrong in that, Lorna. But why transfer all that understandable envy into pseudo-political claptrap?'

'I have principles,' said Lorna, drawing back her shoulders. 'They might not be your principles, or make any sense to you, but I've always lived by them'

'Oh, for fuck's sake! The graveyards are stuffed full of people with principles. None of whom are here, by the way. Anyway,' added Irene in a softer voice, 'you don't exactly have to live by them anymore, do you?'

In the restaurant, they simply told Trinity what they wanted and food appeared from the magic box beside their table. Irene explained that Heaven was largely self-sufficient because everything was recycled. 'We can't just pop out to the supermarket, petal. We grow all our own fruit and veg. Fish and meat we artificially create. What's important is that our food tastes good and is nutritionally balanced.'

Irene also explained that the crew all lived and worked in Heaven's other hull. 'That's where the *real* action takes place, petal. By comparison, this hull is pretty dull. After we get you kitted out, I'll take you over. From now on, that's where you'll be living.'

Irene let this sink in before continuing: 'This hull is mostly deserted, Lorna, as you can see,' she said with a flick of her wrist. 'Nobody has much need to come over here, so very few bother. However, we wanted to give you a bit of peace and quiet for your first few days. Allow things to settle. In your mind, I mean.'

Why, Lorna wanted to know, was Heaven so much bigger than it needed to be? Why was this hull deserted? The same thought had occurred to her before; all those corridors, one after another, soulless and white and empty. 'Will there be other dead people there?' she asked instead, realising immediately how stupid this sounded.

'Not dead people, no. Dead people don't often come to Heaven ... virtually never, in fact, although that's probably a good thing. Dead people aren't very entertaining, at least in my view. Apart from which, what would we do with them all? Heaven might be big, but it's not *that* big. Remember, Lorna, you were chosen.'

'But he won't tell me why.'

'Well, that's God for you ... so there's no point looking at me, petal! Ours not to wonder why, and all that.' Irene sighed loudly. 'Anyway, we're moving you across to the other hull to be with the rest of the crew. It's where everyone lives, so from now on you'll be alongside the rest of us. Meet people, make friends. You are, I suppose, one of us now, Lorna. They're all simply dying to meet you, by the way. Understandable, of course. It's not often we get visitors. You are a rare species.' Irene smiled and drank the rest of her wine. 'Drink up, petal. It's time to get you tarted up.'

'Irene, I'm not sure that ...'

'You're going to a party, babe. A *welcome* party,' added Irene and gave Lorna's hand a squeeze. 'An opportunity to get legless and dance the night away. A chance to meet everyone and for everyone to meet you. So,' she said, stubbing out the last of her lunchtime cigarettes and indicating the shopping centre with a small nod, 'for starters, we'll need to get you a posh frock and a bikini.'

Lorna looked at her, frowning.

'It's a beach party,' said Irene in a matter-of-fact tone, as if this could possibly make any sense.

* * *

Lorna's mother had a wonderful knack of conjuring marvellous picnics from the humblest of ingredients. It was a genius born of long practice. Her sandwiches weren't just sandwiches: they could have won prizes, or maybe it was just a trick of Lorna's memory. Back then, the sun always shone and her mum was forever buttering bread. The Loves loved their picnics.

In contrast, her mum was hopeless at barbeques – which was a pity because both Love children looked forward to them. It was the ritual more than anything, lugging the use-once barbeque across the High Street and onto the beach, setting it alight – not easy on breezy days – and then cooking sausages and burgers until they sizzled and turned black. In Lorna's experience, her mother's barbeque sausages never turned brown, the way she sometimes saw them do on films or in adverts. One minute they were raw, the next cremated. There was no halfway stage at which burger or sausage could safely be eaten. They always came with a thick layer of charcoal. Lorna had come to believe that all barbeque food tasted of ash.

It didn't stop Lorna and her brother from pestering their mother to have barbeques, and all the better if they were allowed to bring a friend. For Tom, that could be anyone from his rugby team, each arriving on the doorstep with a rugby ball balanced on one finger. For Lorna, that usually meant Suzie Bryce. Suzie also lived in North Berwick, further away from the beach than them, but in a proper house with a garden. In the garden was a swing. They would take turns and if Lorna swung really high, she could see over the garden wall and down into the town. She could just make out her bedroom window. Sometimes, from their bedrooms, they'd signal to each other with torches. The signals meant nothing, although they kept trying to invent a code. But it was fun seeing a twinkle of light and knowing it meant a friend was thinking of you.

Suzie's father was a lawyer, whatever that was, and owned a shiny Porsche. Lorna longed to grow up and to own one. She loved looking at its silver bodywork and seeing her own incredulous face looking back. More than anything, she wanted to grow up and earn lots and lots of money, and buy a car just like it.

'What about a barbeque?' suggested her mum, who had been in the kitchen. Lorna was in the living room watching TV.

This was an unusual suggestion, what with Tom being in hospital for tests. Barbeques were usually family affairs, with both of the children, although not generally including their dad. On good days, when he wasn't working, he was golfing. God gives us only a few days of sunshine, he'd say, we mustn't waste them. Her father rarely dispensed advice; this was as good as it got.

'A barbeque?' echoed Lorna and instinctively looked out the window. From that angle, it was difficult to tell if the sun was shining.

'You may not know it, young Lorna, but it's a nice day outside. I just thought it might be a nice idea to go to the beach. Is it a nice idea, Lorna?'

Her mum's repeated use of the word *nice* suggested to Lorna that she was meant to agree and normally she would have leaped at the chance. But something made her hold back. It was the novelty that was wrong. Her dad had only taken Tom to hospital that morning, and her mother was due to visit when he got back. It didn't seem right to be having a barbeque. Lorna suspected that her mother had something she wanted to tell her.

'OK, Mum,' Lorna dutifully agreed. 'That would be nice.'

Although warm, a stiff breeze was blowing off the sea, carrying grains of sand that caught in Lorna's hair. So, instead of plonking themselves down on the beach in front of the town, they walked some way along the beach to the dunes by the golf course. Lorna half expected her father to walk up the fairway. They found a reasonably sheltered spot, sufficient for her mother to light the barbeque at the third attempt. 'Phew!' she said, 'that was lucky. I only had four matches!'

'I know you've been worried,' her mother began, kneeling on the sand and drawing patterns with her fingers. 'You have, haven't you?'

Lorna shook her head. She wasn't old enough to believe that bad things could happen to her or others around her. She did, of course, watch the TV news each night – well, she had to, it was one of her dad's obligatory programmes – and she knew that bad things did happen to other people. But always to other people, although it could come close. On Friday nights on the High Street, right outside their living room window, she sometimes heard bad things. Usually only drunken singing but, once, the sound of breaking glass and a burglar alarm sounding. Someone had chucked a brick through a shop window.

'Not really, no,' replied Lorna. 'I'm fine.'

'Fine?' Her mother seemed disappointed.

'Fine.'

Her mum reached into a plastic bag and extracted burgers and sausages. In all of their many barbeques she had never attempted to cook anything else. She placed a selection on the smoking grill and prodded them with a fork. Opened rolls, already spread with butter, were laid on another plastic bag and slowly gathering blown sand.

'What Tom has isn't serious, young Lorna. It's just that his insides have got a little bit twisted. He just needs a wee operation to sort it out.'

'Will he be asleep?' Lorna didn't like to think of Tom having knives stuck into him.

Her mother laughed. 'Of course he will! Goodness, what made you think that he wouldn't be?'

Lorna looked at the sausages and hamburgers. Her mum had forgotten to turn them, as she always did. 'It's just that you said it was a wee operation. I don't know what that means.'

'It means that they open up his tummy and untangle his intestines. Do you know what intestines are?'

'I'm not stupid, Mum,' she said.

Her mother had finally remembered to turn the sausages and burgers. As always, they were black. 'Looking good,' she said hopefully, as she always did. Then she took a deep breath and laid down the fork beside the buttered rolls. 'I didn't mean to imply you *were* stupid, Lorna. I was only trying to reassure you. About Tom, I mean. It's just a silly little operation, and it's nothing to worry about.'

Lorna had finally realised that this outing to the beach wasn't for her benefit. She really hadn't been worried. Her faith in doctors, like her faith in her parents, was boundless. Until then, everything that had gone wrong with her had been cured. Chicken pox, no problem. Cut knee: it'll hurt a bit but we'll get it sorted. Twisted intestine? Lorna had no doubt that her mother was right. It wasn't serious and, in any case, nothing bad could happen to her family.

'When is his *wee* operation?'

'Tomorrow.'

'It'll be OK,' said Lorna. 'Really, it will.'

'I know, I know.' Her mother smiled, hair across her eyes. 'Anyway, how's school been this week?' Lorna thought that this was a pretty lame way to change the subject.

'We learned about space,' she replied. All week they'd been learning something different: finding out how the universe was created, and what it would be like living in a spaceship. Her class had even made papier mâché space helmets, then written their names on the front. Lorna had thought this was stupid. Surely everyone on a spaceship would know everyone else?

'My, how interesting!' replied her mum, but didn't really seem to be listening.

'We also learned about Einstein and how spaceships might someday fly across the universe.'

Her mother was looking out to sea, a frown creased on her forehead. 'And how might they do that, young Lorna?'

'It's quite hard. But first of all, you've got to find the right TV station.'

They ate their burgers in silence and stared out over the water. Lorna didn't know what her mum was thinking. She only knew that her burger, as always, tasted of charcoal.

* * *

'So, you want to be a lawyer.' Mr Sullivan, the careers-guidance teacher, didn't seem impressed. He was sitting back in his seat, his feet up on the table. Only teachers could get away with doing something like that; Lorna would have been told off. His small room was thin, book-lined, and had a partition wall. It had only recently been sectioned off from the secretarial office next door, from which could clearly be heard the tap-tap-tap of a keyboard and the slamming of a file drawer. On the wall behind his head, Mr Sullivan had hung his diplomas – presumably to remind his students that he, unlike them, was qualified.

'Yes,' said Lorna.

'And on what have you based this momentous decision?' Mr Sullivan looked bored. Raindrops dripped down his office window. It overlooked the primary school in which her schooling had begun. 'What process of logical deduction has led you to this choice?'

'I don't understand you,' she replied, feeling that it was her career and it didn't need any justification. 'It's just what I want to do, that's all.'

'It's just what I want to do,' mimicked Mr Sullivan and, grudgingly, opened a manila file. On its front, Lorna saw her name stencilled in black felt pen. 'You have achieved exemplary grades, Lorna. Your teachers speak highly of you. It's likely that you'll achieve excellent results in your Highers. So why spoil it all by becoming a lawyer?'

'What's wrong with lawyers?' she asked. Everyone else said that being a lawyer would be cool. OK, maybe a bit dull, but really quite cool as well. You get to make lots of money, do interesting things, maybe change the world. That's what Lorna wanted to do. She'd give some of her money to charity, or her parents. 'I simply believe I have the aptitude to study law. It's what I want to do,' she added stubbornly.

'I hear you, Lorna. However, my job is to make sure you've made the right choice. I have to be, if you like, a devil's advocate. Do you know what a devil's advocate is?'

'Of course,' she told him. 'I'm not stupid.'

Mr Sullivan tapped a finger against her file then closed it. 'That's not what I was implying,' he said. 'My concern is not so much with your choice of university course, but in the reasons for your choice. I don't want you to rush into this and realise, two years from now, that it was all a big mistake. Making the transition from school to university can be difficult. My job is to make it easier for you.'

'Transition?'

'From this life to the next. It'll be a big change, Lorna. University. Not like school.'

'I know what transition means, Mr Sullivan. And if I thought that university was going to be like school, I wouldn't go. No way. Look, if it proves to be a mistake, then it'll be my mistake,' she said. 'It just seems the right thing to do. With the right grades, I can get into Edinburgh.'

'I know that.' Mr Sullivan had threaded his hands together then made a steeple of his forearms. He laid his elbows on the desk and his chin on his laced fingers. 'But you have so much potential, Lorna. Too much potential to let it go to waste. For example, have you ever thought about journalism?'

'No.'

'Teaching?'

'Definitely not.' Mr Sullivan looked pained, if unsurprised.

'Business studies?'

'I want to study law, Mr Sullivan.'

'I have to tell you, Lorna, I think it's a bad choice. You're not just doing it for the money, are you? Listen, I appreciate that your family ...'

146

'My family have got nothing to do with it! I'm sorry, but I don't understand why you're not supporting me. Everyone else seems really excited. Except you,' she said.

'Is it for the money?' he repeated.

Lorna pressed her lips together in exasperation. 'No, not the money,' she said quickly, although she still secretly coveted Suzie's father's car. He'd replaced his Porsche several times over the years, but always with another one. He'd even promised her a shot in it when she passed her test. *If* she passed, she had to remind herself. Her father would be worse than useless at driving lessons, and would mostly be committing an offence, and her mother had never learned how to drive. Austin Bird, who had passed his test and who owned a cast-off Fiesta from his mother, had offered to take her out, although new drivers aren't allowed to teach learner drivers; but maybe she'd take him up on the offer, on a quiet country road.

'In which case, do you honestly believe you'll be making the world a better place?'

Lorna nodded, sure of herself. 'Yes, absolutely.'

Mr Sullivan leaned back in his chair and laced his hands behind his neck. 'Jesus wept!'

'Then perhaps you might like to tell me why you think I'd be making a mistake.' The tap-tap-tap from next door had stopped. Lorna had the impression they were now being listened to. Hardly surprising, Lorna had raised her voice.

'Please don't underestimate my intelligence, as I certainly don't underestimate yours,' said Mr Sullivan, who had also raised his voice. His cheeks had flushed, and a reflection from the rain-soaked window had patterned one side of his face and made it look as if he was melting. Lorna looked at his face, seeing molten wax. 'It's all about intellectual capability, Lorna, and what choices we make in our lives. You, I have to say, have both the aptitude and intellectual capacity to make a better choice than the one you have done.'

Lorna was at a loss of words. 'What exactly have you got against lawyers?' she finally asked. There was still an eerie silence from next door.

Mr Sullivan puffed out his cheeks. 'Until recently, nothing. Then I got divorced and, now, quite a lot, actually. *Now*, I don't get to see my kids very often. *Now*, I don't have a house to call my own. *Now*, I'm having to pay those bloodsuckers every last penny I've got.'

'I'd better go,' said Lorna.

A few days later, Mr Sullivan went on sick leave, and still hadn't returned by the end of the school year, by which time Lorna had also left. By then, with Austin's help in the dunes, she was officially a woman but still hadn't taken him up on his offer of driving lessons. Having sex with him was OK but tuition in the front seat of his car seemed too intimate an act. It would also have smacked of a relationship she didn't really want.

But the interview with Mr Sullivan had unnerved her. Before it, she'd received nothing but praise and admiration. Her mum, who hadn't advanced further than the bakery, was ecstatic. Her father seemed pleased as well, although it was harder to tell. Despite the high school having a good attainment record, being accepted for a degree course in law was an achievement: something to be proud of, not a choice to be belittled.

'Fuck Mr Sullivan,' was Suzie's advice. 'Forget it, babe.'

So Lorna tried not to think about Mr Sullivan or the reasons for his mental anguish. We all have our problems, she could have told him, but hadn't. In any case, she had decided, she was going to be a good lawyer, whatever that was.

HOME

'Welcome, Lorna, to your new home.'

A door slid open to reveal a small living room. Irene stood aside to let Lorna pass, which she did with some trepidation. On Earth, generally speaking, you had a choice about where you lived. If you didn't like it, you could always move on. Here, she was acutely aware, her property ladder had begun and ended.

'Of course, sweetie, if you don't like the furnishings you can always change them. Don't feel that you have to live with beige if you'd prefer pink. Here, I thought you might like this.' Irene picked up an IKEA catalogue from a glass coffee table. 'It might give you a few ideas on how to spruce up the place. If you see anything you want, just ask Trinity. She's *terribly* good at interior design, by the way. But you don't have to stick with IKEA, not if you don't want to.'

Her new home was filled with an eclectic mix of the familiar and unfamiliar; she was sure she recognised the glass coffee table from somewhere, but couldn't place it. However, the leather sofa in the living room was an exact replica of the one in her Edinburgh flat, even down to a cigarette burn in one of its arms. Lorna ran her fingers across it wistfully, remembering different times when she and Suzie would put the world to rights. As with her previous apartment in Heaven, it seemed a place designed to put her at ease, providing comforting reminders from her old existence. Against one wall was the set of bookshelves from North Berwick that Tom had assembled. Sure enough, in the bathroom, was the giant tub with lions' feet.

More annoyingly, in the kitchen was her old fridge, which now contained several bottles of white wine and one bottle of soda. In her old kitchen, it would have also contained milk and salad. Now, it was devoted to a dozen bottles of Chateau d'Yquem, each dated 1787. Lorna had to peer closely to confirm this, the interior light having broken, as hers had in Edinburgh.

'You don't actually have to use the damn thing,' said Irene. 'With Trinity at your beck and call, it's superfluous. You can therefore get rid of it any time you like. It does, however, add a certain primitive charm and, well, we thought you might like it.'

Lorna pulled out a bottle and looked closely at the label.

'A bottle of this stuff also came up for auction,' said Irene, 'and I couldn't resist asking Trinity for the recipe. Not my cup of tea, of course, but I thought it might be yours.' Before Lorna could say anything, Irene had turned on her heel and marched off to the bedroom. 'Excellent!' Lorna heard her call. 'Everything's been delivered. Cinderella *can* go to the ball!'

In the bedroom, laid out neatly on the bed, was the vast wardrobe that she had purchased that afternoon – each, except for the M&S underwear, with their luxurious designer labels. Well, not quite purchased. Taken.

Like the living room, the bedroom had the same mix of old and new, of things remembered well and others dimly so. The bed was from her Edinburgh flat, with a rattan headboard that was both practical and uncomfortable. The chest of drawers into which she deposited the underwear and a diamond necklace was from North Berwick. Its top was ringed from years of Coke cans, which her mother had constantly berated her for. The room also contained an empty bookcase and writing desk. Above the desk were drawn curtains; She didn't recognise the floral pattern, and made a mental note to ask Trinity to change them. Lorna drew back the curtains to reveal a blank wall.

'You can have whatever view you want,' advised Irene. 'Something inspirational, perhaps? A particular landscape you once saw and thought especially beautiful? It's up to you, sweetie. Just tell Trinity and she'll put your choice of view into the window.'

'I can choose my view?'

'Of course. But we didn't want to make that choice for you.'

Lorna thought about this. 'What choice did you make, Irene? Or,' she added, 'do you change your view depending on which famous person you happen to be?'

Irene merely shook her head. 'Just the stars, petal. I like to look at things as they are, rather than what I'd like them to be. Anyway, Lorna, I have to dash. Duty, alas, beckons. However,' she said, turning smartly and heading towards Lorna's new front door, 'I'll be here on the dot of eight to pick you up. So no dilly-dallying, young lady.'

Before Lorna could reply, the door had swished shut.

She returned to the kitchen and, without thinking, opened a drawer beside the sink and took out a corkscrew. Then she extracted a wine glass from a cupboard over the fridge. Then she stopped and thought about what she'd just done. She'd known where to find the corkscrew and where the glass would be. Lorna looked around, remembering. Above the sink were more curtains framing a blank wall. But it should have been a grimy window smeared with grease and bird droppings that looked out over rooftops with, far in the distance, and only if you looked closely, a glimpse of the Clifton Suspension Bridge.

She sat on the leather sofa and drew her legs up under

her bottom. She fingered the hole in the settee arm, then balanced her wine glass over it, covering up the burn and the memories it exuded.

Welcome, Lorna, to your new home.

Trinity's sexy voice, using the same words that Irene had spoken only minutes earlier.

'Thank you, Trinity.'

I appreciate that not everything in your apartment will be to your satisfaction. You must therefore tell me, Lorna, what alterations you'd like made. It will be my pleasure to make those alterations. My satisfaction is to ensure your satisfaction.

'I'll do that, Trinity.' For a start, the kitchen, and those ghastly bedroom curtains. 'But could I ask you something first?'

Of course.

'Who is Irene?'

Irene is the person designated to look after you.

'I know that much, Trinity. But *who* is she?'

A short silence. *Irene is the executive officer of this facility.*

'OK, then what exactly *is* an executive officer?'

It's her rank, Lorna. Irene is second in command of this space vehicle.

Lorna felt flattered. Not just anybody had been assigned to her. 'You mean, a sort of demi-god?'

There is only one God, said Trinity who, like Irene, didn't appear to have a sense of humour. *Would you like me to run you a bath?*

'Yes, please, Trinity.'

At that moment all the lights went out.

* * *

Ten things that Lorna may or may not have known about hamsters:

1. The most common names for hamsters include Daisy, Boo-Boo, Fluffy, Bilbo, Sonic, Barney, Gizmo, Zippy, Twinkle, Hammy, and Sniffles. Tonto is not a common name for a hamster.

2. Hamster babies are called puppies.

3. Hamsters can live for up to three years, not that hers did.

4. Hamsters are colour-blind and can only see six inches in front of their noses.

5. They can burrow down up to two metres.

6. Hamsters are allergic to cedar, but will eat virtually everything else, storing food in their cheek pouches. Indeed, the word hamster is derived from the German *hamstern*, meaning to hoard.

7. Once hamster babies are a week old, their parents will probably not eat them.

8. Hamsters can remember who their relatives are. However, this doesn't necessarily stop their relatives from eating them.

9. Hamsters can give birth as young as five weeks old. They can therefore breed at a phenomenal rate.

10. After God created mankind, he tried his hand at other species. However, after inventing the hamster and the kangaroo he decided that nature knew best and didn't repeat the experiment, according to Trinity. Lorna had never much liked the dark, so Trinity was keeping her company.

I regret, Lorna, that hamster infestation is a significant problem on this facility. God, however, will not allow his creation to be interfered with and we pay the price in electrical short-circuits. It is, I assure you, merely an inconvenience rather than a danger, so don't worry. God didn't much likes rats or mice and wanted to make something nicer. But what he won't now accept is that their numbers have to be controlled. Lorna detected a hint of disapproval. *Some early prototypes escaped, you see, and that's when the problem started. Now they're everywhere. You should be aware, Lorna, that God has commanded the crew not to feed them, as if anybody would. So please don't leave food lying about. It is specifically forbidden. Eventually, of course, we'll have to do something, but God simply hates bloodshed of any sort. In the meantime, we have to put up with the inconvenience. There, that should do it.*

Immediately the lights came on again.

'Well done, Trinity.'

Repairing chewed wires is not difficult, Lorna. Your bath is ready. I hope you don't mind but I've added bath salts.

* * *

Curiously, despite soaking in the bath for what seemed like hours, her wine glass remained perfectly chilled. In all the miracles that had been revealed to her, it was the small things that were the most impressive. So, for Lorna, it wasn't the fabulous diamond and emerald bracelet on her wrist that was totally surprising, nor the fact that she was in a Victorian bathtub transported from her childhood. It was the chilled glass of wine that stayed chilled.

She was enveloped in steam, lost in a private world that wasn't quite Heaven and wasn't quite Earth. She was pleased that God had invented hamsters; kangaroos had always seemed a little bizarre. Her diamond and emerald bracelet caught the light as she raised her glass. Then she became aware of someone moaning from the apartment next to hers. Lorna blinked herself back to Heaven; the noise stopped. It must have been her imagination.

* * *

Nearly two years after the episode on the beach, Lorna met up with Austin for a drink in a North Berwick bar. It was just before the start of their second year at university. Austin's bags were packed for the return trip. He'd spent the summer in North Berwick staying with his parents and had left it until the last day to phone her. He was, he explained, now living in a shared flat in Bristol and heading back the next morning. He wanted to apologise, or so he said over the phone.

'For what?' asked Lorna, truly surprised, once they had found a quiet spot in the corner of the bar. A couple of friends were also in the pub. They looked over from time to time, obviously speculating whether the Lovebirds were being rekindled.

'For, well … not being in contact.' He shrugged and clasped a hand to his pint of beer.

'You don't have to apologise, Austin. I've been just as guilty.'

'I could have phoned. I didn't.'

'So could I. Ditto, didn't.'

'Well then,' he said and lapsed into silence, which made Lorna uncomfortable. She didn't know what he was thinking, or why he'd phoned her.

'So how's the course?' she asked, trying to be jolly. 'Built any bridges yet?'

'Good, yes … um … and no. Yours?'

'Yeah, OK. Bit dull. Still …'

That unspoken defining episode was between them, stifling any chance to talk sensibly. In their different ways, they were both still embarrassed by it. In the intervening months, Lorna had moved from halls of residence into a shared flat with Suzie, and had had a brief relationship with an intense Spanish student called Emilio before realising that his ardour and passion was suffocating. He'd wanted to be with her every moment of every day, holding her hand, looking into her eyes, murmuring in Spanish in her ears, and Lorna could never decide if they were words of love or a shopping list. He might just have been saying *baked beans, bacon, toilet cleaner*. She also found out that Emilio and his father liked to shoot small migratory birds. She'd therefore ended the relationship for both personal and ethical reasons. Emilio, rather endearingly, had cried. Now here she was, looking over the table at Austin, nursing his pint and frowning. Then she remembered why she'd been so fond of him, apart from his rugby-hunky physique: there was an honesty about him. You could always trust Austin. He was dependable. You got what you saw.

'I see you're still trying to change the world.' He pointed to Lorna's lapel, on which was pinned a STOP THE WAR badge.

'Well, someone has to. It would be a pretty crap world if nobody tried.'

'It still happened though, didn't it?'

'Operation Iraqi Freedom,' she intoned like a newsreader. 'Yes, Austin, it did.' In the build-up, she'd marched through Edinburgh and would have marched through London if she'd had money for the train fare. She'd flirted with the Left then drifted towards conventional socialism, and had campaigned for the re-election of New Labour, pounding the streets with bundles of leaflets, fairly sure she was going the right thing, and supporting someone who she believed would also do the right thing, even in dim and distant parts of the world. Now, thoroughly disillusioned, she still wore her anti-war badge. It represented her allegiance to a higher moral code, a code that stood against the killing of other human beings and small migratory birds. 'Please don't tell me you supported the invasion?'

Austin looked at the table. 'They did say he had weapons of mass destruction.'

'Yeah, and they were wrong! Christ, we fucked up Afghanistan, and now we're fucking up Iraq. Where's the sense in all that?'

He fluttered a placatory hand. 'Maybe it'll get sorted. Look, Lorna, I don't know. Anyway, Saddam wasn't exactly a saint, was he?'

'No, but that didn't give us the right to invade his bloody country and kill thousands of his people.' She paused to breathe. 'Know what, Austin? Know what's going to happen next? They're going to want payback, that's what. We bomb them, they bomb us. It'll happen, believe me.'

'It's not going to happen.'

'9/11 happened and it'll happen again, because we keep waging illegal wars.' Not in my name, she reminded

157

herself, remembering the anti-war march through Edinburgh, the wall of protestors; a sea of people so large and so loud that the government couldn't possibly ignore them, which it promptly did.

He was smiling and, despite herself, she smiled back. She now also saw that there was perspiration on Austin's brow, a tremor in his fingers. He seemed on the point of asking something. He was frowning as she remembered; concentrating on some puzzle he would eventually unravel. 'Anyway, it's good to see you,' she finally said, deciding to put aside her soapbox. She'd made her point at the Edinburgh rally, waving her placard and being jeered from the pavement. She couldn't now be bothered to argue with Austin.

'Really?' He seemed genuinely pleased.

'Of course it is. After all, we did, um …' If he wasn't going to mention it, she would.

He swallowed beer and cleared his throat. 'It does get better with practice, you know.' Lorna saw with relief that he was still smiling. The taboo subject was being broached. She'd forgotten how rugged he looked when he smiled. 'Anyway,' he said, again staring at the table with a concentration it didn't deserve, '… are you … um …?'

'Um, what?'

'You know …'

'Married? Yes, Austin. To Marcel. Polish waiter, but he really wants to be a novelist. We met in a nudist camp.'

'I think I would have heard,' said Austin, still looking gravely at the table.

'Whirlwind romance, then married in secret. In Prague.'

'Prague's not in Poland.'

'… *and* we've been blessed with five kids, although we'd like more. He's from a big family, you see. Oldest

158

is Jamie, named after that irritating chef guy. Then there's Mary, Joseph, Peter, and Troy. Such a *lovely* name, we thought.'

'You can't have had five kids in a year. You should have paid more attention in biology.'

'Quins, Austin. Runs in the family. His, not mine.' Austin was still intent on the woodwork between them. 'Actually, I'm exaggerating,' she conceded, which made him look up. 'I don't know anybody called Marcel. But still, living in hope.'

Unexpectedly, across the small table, he grabbed hold of her hand. 'Look, why don't you come down to Bristol? Stay for a weekend, have some fun. Let me prove it to you,' he said throatily. He was babbling so fast she barely understood what he was saying. Her hand was still clasped in his and she had to struggle free to flex her fingers before permanent damage was inflicted. 'Please say yes,' he added, in such a little-boy-lost voice that she had to laugh.

It was a stupid idea. Prove *what,* exactly? Austin was rooted in her past, and her future lay in Edinburgh or beyond, not Bristol. But right at that moment there wasn't anyone else and, in releasing her from childhood, perhaps she owed him the chance of a second fling. With Emilio safely discarded, perhaps some fun was what she needed. It couldn't do anyone any harm, certainly not to her. Lorna didn't think for a minute that Austin could feel any differently; that was too ridiculous.

'OK, Austin,' she said, making him grin like a Cheshire cat.

* * *

Lorna was unused to airports, had only once travelled by air by herself, and badly wanted to behave like the assured

159

traveller, knowing which gate to go to, poised and assured. But she was also a little frightened of flying, clutched her bag too tightly at check-in, and needed a stiff drink before embarkation. The security officer who waved her through the scanner looked suspiciously at her STOP THE WAR badge and insisted on searching her hand luggage. She was therefore in a bad mood before she'd even taken off.

The plane was delayed by an hour and Lorna was in a worse mood when she landed. She had expected Austin to meet her in arrivals, but there was no sign of him. She hung around for a few minutes then tried to phone him, but his mobile was switched off and she didn't have a number for his flat.

In desperation, she put a message out over the airport tannoy. The kindly, middle-aged woman behind the information desk smiled at her sadly, obviously concluding that young love had gone badly wrong. 'There's still a flight back to Edinburgh tonight,' she said.

Lorna waited a further fifteen minutes by the information desk, then went outside for a cigarette. Austin, the idiot, was parked outside in his Fiesta. The same car he'd owned in North Berwick, his mother's hand-me-down.

'I thought you meant *outside* the terminal,' was his excuse. Lorna didn't kiss him hello.

'You could at least have come inside,' she protested. 'Honestly, I've been hanging around for ages.'

'Half an hour, actually,' he corrected, pulling out into traffic, 'and don't forget I've had to wait as well. Your plane wasn't exactly on time. In any case, you can't just leave your car outside an airport these days.'

He had a point, although Lorna wasn't going to give in. 'It wasn't my fault the bloody plane was late. Anyway, airports do have carparks, Austin.' She pointed at one as they drove towards the exit, a big sign telling them to turn right for Bristol. Austin turned right.

'... which cost money. Anyway, at least you're here,' he said, 'and it is nice to see you.'

This took the wind out of her sails. She couldn't very well have an argument with someone who was being reasonable, let alone nice. Despite herself, she patted his knee. 'Better late than never, huh?'

On the way into town they chatted about their respective courses and how he was getting on in Bristol. Austin, so he claimed, was in seventh heaven and, as he had described it, living in a *bijou* flat in a bohemian part of town. With a couple of other guys, of course.

They took a short detour to drive under the Clifton Suspension Bridge and Lorna had to concede the brilliance of its engineering, the huge span of the bridge high over their heads.

'Still an inspiration, eh, Austin?'

'The simplest things often are,' he replied. 'Look at it. Pure symmetry, pure brilliance.'

'Pure simplicity?' she suggested.

'Exactly,' said Austin. Then, to her surprise, he said: 'I've always envied you, you know.' He was driving with rigid attention, both hands on the wheel and staring straight ahead. 'I've never been the brightest guy,' he admitted. 'Everything I've done, passing exams, all that shit, I've had to work at. You just seem to sail through things.'

Lorna didn't know what to say. Sure, he'd never been top of the class, but he wasn't stupid either. 'You're at university, Austin,' she eventually said. 'That makes you officially clever. One day you'll get a certificate to prove it.'

'That's not what I meant,' he said, still staring intently ahead. 'It's just that, well, I've always had to try twice as

161

hard as everybody else.' Eventually he smiled. 'I'm trying hard now,' he said.

They stopped for a drink at a swanky pub with polished tables and lots of dull chrome. Hidden lights bounced light off metal walls, floors, and ceiling. Austin thought that it was the height of cool; Lorna thought it pretentious. To thank him for the lift, she insisted on buying the drinks, then wished she hadn't. The plane ticket had been extortionate enough, despite being split down the middle with Austin.

They clinked glasses. To a casual observer, they could have been first lovers, which in a sense they were. Since they'd last met in North Berwick, only weeks before, Austin had affected designer stubble that had scratched her skin when she did get around to kissing him hello. He'd obviously been anticipating her visit and making some personal changes.

Austin's definition of a bijou flat wasn't Lorna's, and nor did it seem to be in a bohemian part of town. It looked like a condemned area just waiting for the bulldozers. Nearby houses were bricked up; graffiti daubed on walls. Only here did Austin's old car really fit in. Lorna sniffed the air, avoiding dog dirt and crisp packets on the pavement.

The flat was reached by a thin and winding staircase, probably a fire hazard, which brought them to a battered door on the third floor. It had probably once been green, but the stair light was too dim to see it properly. A TV was blaring from the flat next door, from which a woman in a sparkly silver dress appeared. The woman had straggly black hair and red lipstick. She looked about forty and much too old to be wearing a silver sparkly dress.

Austin flapped a hand between them. 'Monica, Lorna. Lorna, Monica.'

The older lady was rummaging in her handbag. 'Run out of fucking fags,' she said. 'Going to the shop.' She extracted an inhaler and took a long suck. 'Fucking hay fever,' she announced, before pushing past with a smile and heading for the stairs.

* * *

Inside, somebody had made an effort to tidy the living room. Magazines and DVDs had all been heaped into piles. A computer and games controller sat on a rickety table. Beside it was a wicker basket full of shredded paper. In front of a giant TV sat a leather sofa. Lorna made to cross the room to the window, through which – dimly – she could see the outside world, before realising her feet were glued to the carpet. The flat smelled of stale cigarettes.

'Well, what do you think?' he asked, seemingly proud of his surroundings.

'Very bijou.'

'It's not the Ritz, but it's handy.'

For what? she nearly asked, but swallowed the words before they could escape. Instead, with some difficulty, she prised her feet from the carpet and crossed to the window, her shoes almost sucked off with every step. Through the grime she could dimly see a row of condemned houses and a patch of grass on which sparkled broken glass.

'The others are away for the weekend,' said Austin. 'Leo and Greg. Maybe you'll get to meet them sometime.'

'Lucky me,' said Lorna, now realising why Austin had been so insistent on that particular weekend. A small alarm bell had begun to sound in her head.

Austin chucked his car keys down beside the computer. 'Dump your stuff, have a wash, and let's hit town.' Then he cleared his throat, not looking at her. 'I just thought it might be nice for us to have some privacy.'

That smallest of words. *Us.* Why the hell was she here?

BATH

They went first to a loud pub in the city centre filled with students. Music blared from giant speakers, coloured lights flashed and were reflected off glass orbs hanging from the ceiling. It was virtually impossible to talk unless you leaned very close, which was perhaps why Austin had chosen the place.

Afterwards they went to a quieter pub that did food. The eating area was packed, but they were lucky enough to arrive just as another couple was leaving. Lorna ate fish and boiled potatoes. She was, as she explained, on a meat-free diet. It didn't last.

'But you're skinny as it is,' he told her, digging into steak and ale pie and mopping at it with a bread roll. 'You've always been skinny.'

'I'm not on a *diet* diet. I'm just saving a few animals from being eaten.'

'But not fish,' said Austin, looking at her plate.

They'd moved onto white wine. Austin's treat. He proudly showed her the label, although it meant nothing. Something French and unmemorable. They chatted on about friends and acquaintances, swapping stories. One of Austin's old friends was in hospital having crashed his motorbike. Another had dropped out of medicine to travel round the world. Another had found God and was considering the ministry. One of his flatmates was studying law and hating it. Lorna's friends had also scattered, although they still met up during the holidays. Lorna told him about Suzie's modelling antics.

165

'She's been modelling stuff for years,' he said.

'But now she gets paid *real* money. All she does is put on bikinis … sometimes in places like Ibiza.'

'Maybe you should try it.'

Lorna snorted. 'Do I look like a model? Actually, don't answer that.'

She waited for him to reply anyway, and was disappointed when he didn't. Emilio would have stared into her eyes, said something incomprehensible in Spanish, and told her she was beautiful. Complete claptrap, of course, but words she liked to hear. Instead, Austin speared a chip, dipped it in gravy and transported it to his mouth. 'She's always been your best friend,' he said eventually.

'So?'

'So, haven't you made *new* friends?'

'Of course I have,' said Lorna. 'But that doesn't mean that you have to dump the old ones.'

'Are we old friends, Lorna?' The waitress had placed a lit candle on the table; Austin's breath bent the flame to his question.

'Suppose so. We've known each other long enough.'

'Primary one, to be precise,' he said, spearing another chip and waving it from the end of his fork. 'We'd moved down from Edinburgh. I can still remember crying because I missed my old friends.'

'Poor you,' said Lorna. 'Personally, I don't remember much about anything. You've got a better memory than me, Austin.'

The potato was now immobile on his fork. 'You gave me one of your chocolate biscuits on my first day at school. It meant a lot at the time, being the new boy and everything. Do you remember?'

She shook her head. Her first recollections of Austin were from years later. He looked a little crestfallen;

receiving that biscuit had obviously meant more than the giving of it.

'There's a club just along the road. Fancy it?'

The flight, the delay, and her bad mood earlier had made her tired. 'Do we have to?' she asked.

'Not if you don't want to,' he said, taking one of her hands and squeezing it. 'In fact, why don't we just go home? I've got a bottle of plonk in the fridge. To get us in the mood,' he added, which made her inwardly squirm.

* * *

They took a taxi back to his place – although how he could call it *home* was beyond her – taking the chance that his Fiesta wouldn't be stolen, vandalised, or clamped overnight. She sat in the living room, her feet glued to the floor (under no circumstances was she going to take off her shoes), as he found a corkscrew and lifted down glasses from a cupboard over the fridge. Through the dirty kitchen window, far off, was a glimpse of the suspension bridge.

'I've missed you,' he said, handing her a glass.

'It's been a long time,' replied Lorna, knowing where this was physically leading, but not what was on his mind. The alarm bell was tinkling louder. 'The one and only Austin Bird,' she said, holding up her glass, 'who deflowered me and took my innocence.'

He laughed. 'We were both rather drunk.'

'I lost a perfectly good pair of knickers because of you. I never did find them.'

He put on music, something soft and classical, and lit a candle. No doubt this moment of seduction had been meticulously planned. Lorna sat and waited for it to unfold.

'You don't regret it, do you?' He was fiddling with the

volume control, getting it just right.

'It was fun, Austin,' she said, 'and it had to happen sometime. Actually, I'm glad it was with you. Better you than someone fat and ugly.'

'I'll take that as a compliment,' he replied, although she hadn't meant it to be one, still hearing the alarm bell which was becoming louder.

He finally joined her on the sofa, having arranged everything to his satisfaction. 'I'm just sorry we lost touch. What happened to your Polish friend?' It was said with a smile; but what he really wanted to know was whether he had territorial rights.

'There's nobody else, if that's what you mean. Marcel left me to go back to Prague.'

'I thought your imaginary husband was Polish?'

'Whatever.'

He was quiet for a few moments, frowning. 'Me neither,' he said eventually, although Lorna wasn't one to be judgemental. Either you have someone else or you don't, she thought. She didn't mind either way.

They finished the wine, by which time Austin's symphony had reached a crescendo and switched itself off. He took her by the hand and led her to his bedroom. Lorna noted that the sheets were clean and another candle had been set on the table by the window. They kissed. Austin tasted of beer and beef and ale pie.

They made love but, try as she might, she couldn't raise much enthusiasm. She did her best, making the right noises at the right moment, but her heart wasn't in it and his beard scratched her face. It didn't feel right, although it did last rather longer than the first time. Afterwards, they lay side by side, watching candle-shadows on the wall.

'I meant what I said, Lorna. Back then, on the beach.'

She said nothing.

'I said that I loved you. I meant it. Still do.'

Lorna tried to make light of it. 'It was probably a drugged choccie biscuit, Austin.'

'I don't expect you to love me,' he said. 'I just thought I should tell you what I feel.'

'I appreciate your honesty,' she said. 'I'm just not sure *why* you think you love me. We haven't exactly seen much of each other since ...'

'It must be about seven hundred and thirty days since we last made love,' said Austin. 'I remember those things.'

'You really do have a better memory than me.'

Lorna lay in the dark and listened to his slow breathing. She'd been expecting a light-hearted weekend away, a bit of frivolity with an old friend, and hadn't expected unrequited love.

* * *

In the morning she lay in Austin's bath, wrapped in steam. She'd slept badly, feeling guilty. She hadn't meant to rekindle emotions, to stir something that should have remained extinguished. She shouldn't have come to Bristol.

Austin had left to fetch his car, if it was still where they'd left it.

And then, from the flat next door, came the sound of moaning. With a start of surprise, Lorna realised that the couple next door were making love without inhibition, and noisily. She tried not to listen, not at first, but the sounds were insistent. They seemed to come from the walls, the taps, filling the bathroom, eddying the steam. Then, having no choice, she did listen. From gasped instructions the woman was making, Lorna had a fairly precise idea what they were up to. She closed her eyes, imagining the scene being played out next door. Their pleasure was almost contagious. She'd wanted to feel like that the previous evening, Austin once more coyly slipping on a condom, his back turned. But it hadn't happened; something had felt wrong and out-of-time. What Lorna had to give wasn't what he wanted. The woman next door also had a cough.

Austin, arriving back with his Fiesta in one piece, was hugely apologetic. 'It's Bill and Monica,' he informed her, biting his lip and trying not to smile. 'They're at it all the bloody time,' although he couldn't keep the admiration from his voice.

* * *

After she was dressed, and after he'd apologised again about his neighbours, Austin offered another apology. After a bit of sightseeing, he told her, he had to play rugby for his college. The engineers were playing the chemists. This hadn't been mentioned in any of their pre-weekend planning.

'Look, I'm really sorry,' he said with a hangdog expression. 'But if I do well this year I might get into the university team.'

'You could have said something.'

'I'll cancel if you want me to,' he said. 'Say I'm ill or something.'

'There's no need,' she said quietly.

It wasn't the best of mornings. Austin knew he should have mentioned the rugby, and clearly felt guilty. From Lorna's perspective, she couldn't help but wonder whether he really was in love with her or just thought he was. For different reasons, she also felt guilty. He tried once or twice to hold her hand, but she shied away from him. She'd wanted the kind of pleasure that had come from the neighbouring flat: uncomplicated, with no meaningful words attached. She realised she still had another night to get through, another night of faked noises and listening to words she didn't want to hear.

She watched him play from the touchline, a vile wind whipping in from the Atlantic. Apart from her, there were only three other spectators; all girlfriends of the opposing team. Lorna hadn't expected wind and rain, or to be standing on touchlines, and was consequently underdressed. She stood, cheered to keep warm, and shivered. By half-time, the engineers were so far ahead that the game was effectively over. When Austin had the ball, or when he dived for a tackle, his face still contorted in the way she remembered.

She'd watched him play enough rugby games in the past. But that had been for their school; her school as much as his. She'd wanted the school to win, wanted him to do well. Now, she didn't care about engineers or chemists. She was from a distant place and had no connection with what was going on. In the dying minute of the game, Austin scored a try. Lorna had been thinking about something else, and missed it, then made the mistake of telling him. He didn't look pleased: his moment of glory had passed unnoticed.

Afterwards, in the clubhouse, it seemed as if he was avoiding her. The team were joking and laughing and Lorna was relegated to the periphery, making small talk with the other girlfriends. None of them seemed remotely happy either, and kept looking at their watches. Lorna realised that they were there as drivers, appendages to chauffeur their boyfriends back into town. She felt sorry for them, and then couldn't think of anything else to say to them.

Rounds of beer followed rounds of beer. It was quickly clear to her that an etiquette was in play: first the home team bought the beers, then the opposition reciprocated. Everyone had to contribute a tenner, even Lorna – which she thought was a bit rich – and nobody could leave until all the money was used up.

Somebody started a bawdy song and everyone joined in. Then, another batch of beers appeared. Austin thrust a large glass of white wine into her hand. It was warm and the glass felt sticky, like his carpet, as if it hadn't been washed properly. 'Sorry,' he said, 'but it's the best we could find. Not much call for wine in a rugby club.'

'It doesn't matter,' she replied. 'Anyway, what are we going to do this evening?' Over Austin's shoulder, she saw his team-mates pointing and jabbing each other with their elbows.

'We thought that curry might be a good idea.'

Ah, *we*. 'But I don't like curry, Austin.'

'It's … well, it's traditional. When we win, we have a curry together.'

Lorna remembered that Austin's parents always had a carry-out at the weekend, a tradition that seemed to have passed to their only son. 'I still don't like curry, and I don't much like being leered at.'

'Oh, don't worry about them,' said Austin, turning to look over his shoulder. 'Lighten up, Lorna. They're just having fun.'

'Well, I'm not,' she said, although he didn't hear this. Austin had returned to the bar and had his arm around one of his team-mates. They were both laughing about something and had new pints in their hands.

At that moment, Lorna felt like an intruder without hope of rescue. By not reciprocating his love, she had offended him. By not joining in with his fun, she was making him seem small. The weekend was fast becoming a disaster, and her plane wasn't until the next afternoon.

Instead, she took herself outside, back into the freezing

wind, and phoned the kindly lady at the airport. Then, before she could change her mind, she walked to the main road and flagged down a passing cab. At the airport she made her way quickly through security, just in case Austin had set off in pursuit. Her things were still at his bijou flat, but they didn't amount to much. A change of clothing, nothing more. Everything of importance was in her oversize bag, which was over her shoulder.

Back in Edinburgh, there was a voice message on her mobile.

You bitch, Lorna! How could you do that? Just ... walk out. You didn't even say goodbye! Austin sounded very drunk and very angry.

Lorna stood outside the airport terminal and waited for the city bus. She didn't want to speak to Austin, but knew she had to, even if it ended in a drunken tirade. He would probably have kept drinking and God knows what state he'd be in by now.

Thankfully, his phone was switched off.

'I'm sorry,' said Lorna to his messaging service.

The two words sounded lame and inadequate but she didn't know what else to say. She thought about it for a few moments then ended the call.

T-SHIRT

'Hiya'

'Hi, Lorry.'

Tom was sitting up in bed and already pulling up his T-shirt. On his face was a lopsided grin.

'Wow,' said Lorna. 'Is it sore?'

'It's fine,' said Tom.

She was fascinated by the dressings that were probably covering the little stitches holding her brother together. Someone with a sharp knife would have cut him open. Clever hands would have reached inside to untangle his intestines. A specialist in sewing would have sewn him up. Or would all those things have been done by the same person? She didn't know, and Tom would have been asleep so he wouldn't know either. 'When are you getting out?' she asked.

'Why, are you missing me?' Tom had put on a little-girl voice.

'Not even a teeny-weeny bit.'

'Tomorrow, with any luck,' interjected their mum, who was carrying a plastic bag full of sweets and cans of Coke. 'In the meantime, this should keep you going.' She emptied the bag's contents onto his bed. Tom immediately made a grab for the bar of chocolate, knowing it was Lorna's favourite.

'Maybe Tom isn't allowed to eat yet,' she quickly suggested, her eyes on the pile of goodies on the bed. 'Maybe sweets are bad for him.' Her mother was forever saying that sweets weren't good for them. According to her, they made you fat and rotted your teeth. But if that was true, why did so many people, including grown-ups, eat sweets?

'It's OK,' said her mum. 'I checked with the nurses.'

Her father was at the end of the bed. His lips were pressed together and he seemed to be tunelessly whistling. He had his hands clasped in front of him, locking and unlocking his fingers. 'You look good, son,' he said.

'I'm fine,' repeated Tom.

'Did it hurt?' asked Lorna.

Tom was looking at his sister with his eyes half-closed. 'They gave me an injection,' he said. 'It made me go to sleep.'

'Did you have dreams?' she asked. Lorna often had dreams, usually nice ones, because nothing really bad had ever happened to her.

'Don't be silly,' said Tom, mocking her. 'You only have dreams when you're *really* asleep. Not when you have an injection.'

Lorna nodded; she supposed that made sense.

Her dad had cleared his throat. 'It's called anaesthetic, Lorna. It means you don't feel anything when you have an operation.' He seemed pleased to have added another word to her vocabulary. 'Anyway, we've been here long enough. Come on, we really should be going.'

It seemed to her that they'd only just arrived. She looked at her mother, who smiled; they both knew how much her dad hated hospitals. Her mum kissed Tom and ruffled his hair, which Tom had always hated. 'We'll pick you up tomorrow, lovey.'

Her father was looking happier now they were leaving. 'Be good for the nurses, Tom,' he smiled, twining his fingers behind his back. 'No giving them trouble, do you hear?'

Tom had again lifted his T-shirt for Lorna's benefit. Her mum looked away, not wanting to see the evidence of his illness. 'Of course I'll be good. Don't have much choice, do I?' he said, pointing to his scar. 'Oh, and Lorry ...'

With a smile and a wink, Tom rugby-passed Lorna the bar of chocolate.

* * *

That evening there was a phone call from the hospital. Lorna could hear her father's grumbling voice from the hallway. He seemed to be asking lots of questions and then listening a lot. He was looking worried when he came back to the living room.

Tom had picked up an infection, so he said, although Lorna didn't know what an infection was. Her mother had to explain that germs had got inside Tom, which she could understand. She had always been made to wash her hands before each meal, just in case she swallowed germs that could make her poorly. She knew that germs lived everywhere, particularly in the toilet, and you always had to wash your hands after going there. Lorna also knew that germs were very small and didn't like us very much. Maybe Tom hadn't washed his hands before he ate all those sweets?

They sat for a few minutes in silence, nobody quite sure what to do. Even to Lorna, wide-eyed between her parents, it seemed as if something had changed. She felt momentarily frightened, before realising that doctors and nurses always made people better.

'They said he'll be OK,' offered her father to nobody in particular, and Lorna thought perhaps he was just speaking to himself. 'They said it's not serious.'

'Will Tom still come home tomorrow?' she asked.

'I didn't think to ask,' he admitted, 'but, no, perhaps not. I don't know, Lorna.'

Her mum looked at her watch. 'I can still catch the last train,' she said.

Her father could have offered to drive her into Edinburgh but he'd been under the sink since coming back from the hospital so that would probably have been a bad idea.

The next day, Aunt Meg moved in and, because it was nice and sunny, hung out the washing. A long-sleeved T-shirt belonging to Tom waved damply from the clothes-line.

* * *

A few weeks earlier and they'd been afloat, navigating along narrow rivers and throwing bits of bread to swans and moorhens. On the first day, barely out of the marina, her dad nearly crashed into another boat. They all found it hugely funny, except him, desperately spinning the wheel, their own vessel only slowly changing course as the other boat, sounding its hooter, bore down on them. The two boats missed one another by inches, the other boat's captain shouting rude things. It turned out that her dad hadn't known that you drive a car on one side of the road and a boat on the other side of the river. He hadn't been paying attention during the briefing with the boat's owner. During that holiday, her father often looked preoccupied.

Usually they'd potter aimlessly down waterways until it was time for lunch, or time to moor up for the night. Lorna liked to sit cross-legged at the very prow of the boat. Although her mum had been initially doubtful about this being a good place to sit, she was won over by the fact that Lorna was conspicuously wearing her life-jacket and was always in sight. Lorna liked the feeling of wind on her face. One day, as always, they tied up the boat and went to a local village for lunch. But afterwards, instead of going back to the boat and casting off, her mum and dad decided to look round the shops. This didn't make sense to her: why hire a boat and spend time on dry land?

'I know,' said her father, stopping at a shop window and looking inside. It was a newsagent's, but seemed to sell just about everything else. Lorna peered through the window, trying to see what he had seen. 'Why don't we buy you fishing rods?'

'That's a good idea,' said her mum.

'We could catch our tea,' Lorna said excitedly – she had never been fishing before.

'Well, Tom?' asked her Dad.

Tom nodded. Like her, he was rather entranced by the idea of catching a huge salmon or trout or herring or whatever the Norfolk Broads was teeming with, although neither of them much liked eating fish. Lorna only developed a taste for it much later.

Their boat was moored at the edge of the village, on a wooden jetty that stuck out into the water. They were allowed to take their fishing rods to the riverbank, but had to promise to stay in sight at all times. Her dad showed them how to bait the hooks and cast out the line. Lorna listened to him doubtfully: she had never seen him go fishing before.

She picked a spot, fixed sweetcorn to the hook, and chucked in the line. Tom had walked a short way downstream and was doing the same. Then she sat on the riverbank and stared at the sky, before feeling a tug on her line. She reeled in to find that she'd hooked a plastic bag.

It was a warm afternoon, with a charge of static in the air. Lorna took off her jersey and laid her head on it, then remembered to put her stupid life-jacket back on. She looked round at the boat but neither her mum or dad were in sight. She once more contemplated the horizons of the sky, white clouds churning, and fell asleep.

She woke with a start to find Tom was sitting next to her, his line dipped in the water. Between them was the tin of sweetcorn bait. The man in the shop had said that fish liked sweetcorn, although Lorna hadn't been convinced and, not having caught anything, was less convinced now. She looked at the sky. It was filled with dark and angry clouds. She twisted her head: the sun had shifted in the sky.

Lorna reeled in her line and laid the rod on the riverbank. Tom's rod was clasped between his knees. She then laid her head back down on the jersey and raised her right arm to the darkening sky.

'Zzzzzzzz.'

'Not again,' said Tom.

Lorna waved her imaginary lightsaber in a series of tight circles.

'It's a useless film,' said Tom, as he'd already told her several times.

'Zzzzzzzzzzzzzzzzzz.'

'Please, Lorna!'

'Zzzzzzzzzzzzzzzzzzzzzzz.'

Lorna lowered her arm, smiling to herself. She couldn't explain that it wasn't so much the film, but its ending that she liked. She liked how it was a fairytale in which bad things happened but also came good in the end. She liked how it had a scary baddie and a princess, and that the universe was saved by a nobody like her. She turned her head to look at their riverboat. Two dark shapes were in the middle of the boat and she could hear low voices.

Tom had cleared his throat. 'You said something horrible last night,' he said in a thin voice. Hair had flopped over his eyes, hiding his expression.

Lorna closed her eyes, a gathering wind against her face. She didn't know how to reply. Lorna supposed that she should apologise, but the words were stuck deep down in her throat. She'd wanted to say sorry all day, and now didn't know how.

Then it started to rain, big fat drops of rain, and their father was shouting at them. They hurried back to the boat as the heavens opened. For supper, her mother tipped the remains of the sweetcorn into a bowl of tuna and chopped onion that, now containing fish food, both Lorna and Tom absolutely refused to eat.

* * *

It became a common dream: effortlessly soaring, removed from the world, the wind roaring in her ears. Despite being frightened of flying in aeroplanes, dream-flying held no terrors. In her dreams, she was liberated, free, able to go anywhere. It was as if the bits and bytes of her untangled, that she was simply an essence, part of the wind, part of the sky. She occupied no fixed place, no mass or weight. She was truly free.

Ever since she was old enough, Lorna would take the train into Edinburgh, usually with friends. She'd go shopping or to the cinema or meet up with other friends who had moved into the city. She was jealous of them. They all seemed more assured, more in control. In their company, Lorna felt provincial. They went to the ballet or the theatre and went shopping at Jenners or Harvey Nicks. Lorna could only afford the cinema and had only once browsed in Jenners, marvelling at the prices. Sometimes she went into Edinburgh by herself; she liked the freedom of travelling alone, of being grown up. She liked coming up the ramp from the station and being suddenly

181

confronted by the castle. On the left, the buttresses of the Old Town, on the right, the Georgian splendour of the New Town. Between them, like an umpire, the ancient stones of the castle. In North Berwick, if Lorna walked down the High Street, she knew virtually everyone. If they weren't her friends, they were her mother's friends. In a place where everyone knew everyone, she felt closed in. It was as if she was growing wings: at first, light and insubstantial, beating gently against restraining walls. Lorna was hardly aware of them. But as she grew, their North Berwick home growing smaller, her fledgling wings developed purpose. She no longer belonged in North Berwick. The hidden wings on her back would beat vigorously, trying to lift her away. In Edinburgh, she was anonymous and her wings would fold away to nothingness.

* * *

Only days after Auntie Meg moved in, Lorna was in her bedroom and looking out at neatly pegged washing on the clothes line. Her face was close to the window, breath fogging the glass. It was early morning. The flat was quiet, although she knew that Auntie Meg would be awake. Auntie Meg didn't seem to need sleep. She was always in the kitchen when Lorna woke up, always in front of the TV when she went to bed. If Lorna needed the loo during the night, the portable TV in Aunt Meg's room – actually, Tom's room – would be switched on. Her aunt liked snooker and chocolate biscuits. Padding to the toilet, Lorna would hear the rustle of the biscuit packet. Auntie Meg was a kindly lady, Lorna's mum's sister, and very large. It was a mystery to Lorna how someone so large could move about.

Some of the washing she recognised, some she didn't.

Their small back garden was shared with other flats in the close. The gargantuan string vest clearly belonged to Mr MacDonald on the first floor: he worked on the railways, precise job unknown, and wheezed as he climbed the stairs. Like a steam train, her mum would laugh, although Lorna didn't know what a steam train sounded like. She only knew what Thomas the Tank Engine sounded like and, she supposed, a real one wouldn't sound the same.

There was also a floral dress, red roses on a blue background: that would be Amy McGuire's. She habitually wore floral patterns. Her mum's age, Amy had always longed to live somewhere with a garden. Deprived of that luxury, she'd taken to wearing one instead. Lorna recognised her own nightgown, a stupid purchase from years before, a big hamster face smiling from the material, and made a mental note to get rid of it.

Then she opened the window and, kneeling on the floor, put her chin on the windowsill. The early sun hadn't yet taken the chill from the air and she shivered. From her window she could see the top of the Law and its whale jaw; looking left and right, other small gardens with clothes lines full of other people's lives. A gull wheeled and screeched; Lorna watched it with half-closed eyes.

Her mind was a blank and she felt neither happy nor sad. Instead, she felt nothing at all. She was hungry, but couldn't be bothered to eat. She wanted to play on the beach, but it seemed too much effort. In any case, her friends had stopped calling. The phone had been eerily silent for days. Lorna would sometimes pick it up just to make sure it was still buzzing.

Tom's washing was also on the line: mostly pyjamas and T-shirts, including one long-sleeved shirt that she thought was really cool. It was black and had Chinese lettering on the front. Nobody in their family knew what the T-shirt said, or if it really was Chinese. Maybe it said something rude, or was a call to arms against the Communists who ruled China. Her mum didn't think so because she'd bought it in Debenhams but, all the same, Tom tried to keep it hidden when he saw Chinese people on the High Street. Tom was sensitive like that. He never thought to ask anyone what it said.

Lorna felt a breeze on her face and looked down. A blackbird was picking at the patch of grass below the washing. A tabby cat on the wooden fence was following its every hop, but seemed content just to watch. It was too nice a morning for random carnage. Amy McGuire had tried to plant flowers against the fence, but the close had too many young kids who owned footballs. She'd given up, bought a flower box, and changed her wardrobe.

Tom's long-sleeved T-shirt had caught the small breeze. One sleeve had risen and fallen – almost a wave.

Lorna closed the window and pressed her face to the glass. Then with a forefinger, in the patch of condensed breath, she drew a smiley face.

Tears welled in her eyes, although she didn't know why. It just seemed that Tom's T-shirt was saying goodbye.

It was the morning her brother died.

* * *

Things happen, and you move on, that's what Suzie said. History is what happened yesterday or a minute ago. Good things or bad things: pick yourself up, dust yourself down, babe, and get on with it. Shit happens. That was a favourite expression of Suzie's. But not to our family, Lorna had always thought. We have too perfect a surname.

After Tom's death, she no longer had certainties, and it was then that her wings began to stir. She no longer had faith in her parents. Her mother was just someone who worked part-time in a bakery and her wizard father was permanently under the kitchen sink pretending to look for dishcloths or washing powder.

GREECE

It wasn't every day that Lorna got to drink with an American president, and she was initially rather flattered.

She was outside a beach bar, drinking ouzo, and under her feet was warm sand. Cicadas chirped and a gentle sea ebbed and sucked. It was sunset and gathering shadows were lengthening on the beach. Behind her was the rundown bar; above, the buttress of a cliff. The beach stretched away on both sides, disappearing into darkness. A game of mixed volleyball was noisily taking place in front of the beach bar. Film and rock stars pranced and dived, their feet kicking up sand. Rickety tables had been planted in the sand and surrounded by plastic chairs. Inside the beach bar had been dancing, mostly to mournful Greek music, although Mariah Carey was now pumping out 'We Belong Together'.

Lorna had fallen into conversation with a garrulous man called Bill, who had offered to buy her a drink, then taken her arm and led her to a plastic table perched precariously on the sand. She'd been too surprised to say no, and flattered to have this particular Bill's attention. She couldn't decide whether he was just being friendly or, knowing his reputation, if he was trying to come onto her. Lorna was keeping a close eye on his large hands.

'The simple fact is that eternal life isn't everything it's cracked up to be,' he was saying. Mariah faded away to be replaced once more by bouzouki, plucked strings played in harmony to falling waves. 'I shouldn't really tell you that, particularly since you've only just got here, but

187

it's what you'll hear from everyone else. To be honest, it can be a bit of a bore.' He was, so he'd said, a chief petty officer from Section B, whatever and wherever that was, and had a penchant for cigars. 'Without regular regeneration to shave off a layer of boredom, we'd have gone stark-raving bonkers a long time ago.' Bill puffed happily on his cigar, silver smoke mingling with his silver hair.

'The *concept* of eternity is OK,' he continued, hoisting one leg over the other, 'so I can fully understand why people on Earth lust after it so much. Nobody much wants death to be the end. Most people would prefer to have something to look forward to on the other side. However, the *reality* of eternity comes with contradictions that are more difficult to resolve. Regeneration helps us to come to terms with them. It makes us a little less bored.'

'Is your name really Bill?' asked Lorna. She could have asked any one of a thousand questions. This one, however, seemed of most immediate importance.

If he was offended, he didn't show it, blowing out smoke and examining the end of his cigar. 'It may once have been something else, but I simply don't remember. That's the trouble with Heaven, Lorna … you forget things. It can sometimes be inconvenient but, usually, it doesn't matter. If you've forgotten something, you don't generally remember that you've forgotten it, if you follow me.' He shrugged, then grinned. 'But, to answer your question … ever since I was William the Conqueror, I've stuck with Bill.'

Lorna sipped ouzo while President Bill Clinton ran through a list of names. 'William Shakespeare, Bill Gates, William Holden, Wild Bill Cody, William Shatner, Bill Cosby … you name them, I've been them. The Bill Gates didn't last long. Too nerdy. However, now that this particular Bill is yesterday's man, I suppose I'll have to find someone else.' He once more examined the end of his cigar, then turned his eyes to hers. 'Nice dress, incidentally. Very classy. Anyway, who are you going to be?'

It was the same question Irene had asked. Now it seemed that Bill was making the same assumption. 'For now, I'm happy enough being me,' she told him primly. 'I wouldn't know how to be someone else.'

Bill even had the ex-president's homely drawl and lopsided smile. 'You don't have to actually *be* that other person. Inside, you're still yourself. The same memories, except the ones you've forgotten – the same everything. You just look like them, that's all.' He sipped from his Budweiser then laid the bottle on the plastic table. Underneath their feet was drifting sand. Across the beach the ocean was now dark blue, almost black, the sun's orb sinking deeper. 'It's only a game,' he said. 'Harmless fun.'

Trinity had made exquisite alterations to Lorna's chosen dress, even suggesting what accessories might accentuate its glittering lines. It had to be the Cartier, Trinity had advised firmly, not the Tiffany. *We don't want you looking cheap, do we?* Lorna had never worn anything like it before and was irritated that Bill should assume she'd want to be someone else, as if she wasn't good enough. But earlier, looking in the full-length mirror in her bedroom (another chipped duplicate from the Edinburgh flat, complete with stains on the glass), she'd also felt a contradiction: it wasn't her looking back. It was just someone who looked like her. The real Lorna wouldn't have worn Cartier, Dior, or Tiffany; the real her hadn't wanted those things. She bit her lip. She'd wanted to make a difference with her life, not acquire unnecessary accessories. Her reflection suggested otherwise.

At the next table, a Cameron Diaz was talking quietly to a Beyoncé. Next to them was a Sienna Miller with her arm draped lovingly over a Jude Law. Each in their designer clothes, each looking like a million dollars. 'Maybe I'll think about it,' she said to Bill in a brittle voice.

'Of course, you don't have to,' he replied, then laid both hands on the table, palms down. For a moment it seemed that he was about to push himself upright. Instead he leaned over the table and lowered his voice. 'I didn't mean to offend you, Lorna. I most certainly didn't mean to suggest that you should be someone else. From where I'm sitting,' he said, looking her up and down, 'you are one fine-looking woman.'

Lorna was unused to flattery and blushed, although it did confirm that Bill was chatting her up. It had been a long time since anyone had complimented her. 'So, if changing bodies is a game that everyone likes to play,' she asked, 'why doesn't God join in?'

Bill seemed to find this immensely funny and rocked back in his chair. 'God is God,' he said eventually and struck a match. Cigar relit, he tossed the spent match onto the sand. Lorna watched it dissolve into the beach, a small piece of litter becoming nothing.

'Well, the truth is that religious faith came as a bit of a shock to him. He was warned, of course, but didn't pay any attention. Transferring all that genetic code was always going to cause trouble, but would he listen? No. However, once it became clear that people on Earth had actually started to believe in the old fool, he realised he had to do something about it. He couldn't very well give you faith then ignore you completely. He realised, Lorna, that he had a certain responsibility towards his creation, over and above his other responsibilities to the crew. In other words, he decided to play at *being* God.' Bill grinned and blew out smoke. 'Anyway, in terms of his physical appearance, you invented that for him. A father figure, venerable and unthreatening. Somebody to keep you safe, somebody old and wise. You can't be a god and look like a rock star. People simply wouldn't believe in you. You have to *look* the part. God in his divine vanity decided to go along with the charade you'd created for him. You see, not only does he actually like playing at God, he enjoys looking like God. Ridiculous, of course,' said Bill and shrugged his ample shoulders. 'Why are you here?' he finally asked. 'We don't get many dead people in Heaven.'

Lorna felt momentarily chilled, still unwilling to think of herself in the past tense. 'I don't know,' she conceded, taking a deep breath and exhaling slowly. 'He chose me, so he says.'

'Well, he usually does,' said Bill. 'But always for a reason.'

'He won't say why.' She looked out at the sea where a dying sun was weaving a tapestry of sparkles. 'What's he really like?' she asked.

'You mean, is he a good God?' Bill's eyes twinkled. She looked down then lit a cigarette. Their smoke met over the table. 'Well, I suppose he is, not that we see much of him. Keeps himself to himself, and mostly lets Trinity get on with things. He spends most of his time in his quarters, keeping watch over you and wishing he could be a proper God. Sometimes, of course, he can't help but interfere.' Bill examined the fingernails of one hand. Lorna felt a breath of wind off the sea, struck by another sudden absurdity. She *knew* this place. She'd been here before, or somewhere like it. 'Some of the crew still blame him for getting us stuck here but, well, what's done can't be undone. No use crying over spilled milk, eh? We're here and that's an end to it. He has tried to make up

191

for it, I'll give him that. Radio and television, that kind of thing. Inventions to keep us entertained, Lorna, while we while away the centuries.'

'Will he be here tonight?'

'Good gracious, no. He hates having fun. Oh, hi, Irene.'

Since escorting her to the party, Lorna hadn't seen much of Irene. She'd told Lorna not to be nervous, but she'd been terrified. How could she not be? She was about to meet a bunch of people that she would be sharing the rest of her life with, and that was going to be an infinite amount of time. Lorna had gripped the handrail of the transporter with ferocious strength, and almost had to be physically prised from it.

But she needn't have worried; the ship's crew were welcoming, shaking her hand, asking how she was getting on, and, like Bill, why she was here. Their curiosity was charming; their film star lips all smiled. I'm getting on OK, she said, but it'll take a bit of getting used to. No, I have no idea why I'm here, repeated over and over. The first hour of the party was a blank. She was passed from new face to new face, making small talk with superstars. She'd chatted to two John Lennons, a Tiger Woods, and, despite misgivings, had even danced with a Tony Blair, and had to refrain from slapping him across the face for invading Iraq, before remembering that he wasn't the real Tony Blair. But he was a useless dancer, which made her feel better about being with him. It was Blair who had introduced Lorna to Bill Clinton.

'I brought you a refill,' said Irene, and plonked a new glass of ouzo on the table, then threw the empty glass onto the sand where it turned to liquid and was absorbed. Lorna stared at the damp patch, watching it disappear, once more mesmerised by the small things. 'Well, how do you like the place?' asked Irene.

'It's very Greek,' she replied.

'Excellent!' said Irene. 'Every so often, Trinity asks the crew what kind of a beach they'd like and then goes about the building work. She's terribly clever, absolutely *hates* to get things wrong. Last year, it was Hawaii, the year before Spain. This is supposed to be Crete. Have to take Trinity's word on it, of course, but she does do heaps of research.' Irene gestured over her shoulder to the ramshackle beach bar. 'If you're hungry, there's food inside. However, it mainly comprises of things like stuffed vine leaves and bits of squid in tomato sauce. Things, sweetie, that I don't believe should be categorised as food. Personally, I'd recommend the barbeque.'

Further down the beach, Lorna could see flames. Shadows were mingling around it. A woman was laughing, rich and infectious. It could easily have been Suzie, laughing about nothing.

'Trinity doesn't, however, replicate everything,' said Irene, who had helped herself to one of Lorna's cigarettes, 'just in case you were worried. You don't therefore have to worry about jellyfish or spiky sea urchins. Such unpleasant things serve no function and are, in any case, aesthetically displeasing.'

'So I won't get eaten by sharks?'

Irene didn't smile. 'The sea is artificial, Lorna. It waters our fruit and vegetables, we drink it, and we flush it down the loo. Absolutely clean and containing no organic matter.'

Lorna looked out across the beach, wanting to dip her toes in the water. A full moon was trapped on its surface, silhouetting the barbeque and, she now saw, a solitary chef behind it. He seemed to be turning things over, shying backwards from the flames and smoke, wafting at the heat with one hand. Despite lunch, she was hungry and she'd always liked barbeques. The Pussycat Dolls were blaring from the speakers.

'Would anyone like a hamburger?' she asked.

Neither of them did.

* * *

It turned out that Lorna had met this particular Keanu Reeves earlier, but had still to recognise the nuances of character that allowed you to tell each one of them apart. The Kate Winslet that was Irene was easy. Irene didn't smile much, smoked constantly, and exuded authority. The other Winslets she'd been introduced to seemed more demure and authentic.

Keanu was wearing beige shorts and black singlet; a pair of sunglasses was perched on his forehead. I'm not much into clothes, he said, holding out his hand again. His name was Nico, and he liked cooking. Most evenings he came to the beach with his barbeque. It's a popular place, he said, indicating the bar. In his apartment was a proper cooking stove, he told her, begrudgingly provided by Trinity who saw it as a rebuke to her own cooking. He liked making things, he explained; he avidly watched cookery programmes. He was thinking of opening a proper restaurant, with a real kitchen, serving food that wasn't artificially prepared by Trinity.

He explained that his girlfriend Simone had opened a cocktail bar upstairs, the Broadway. You should come along this Friday, he said. Simone's putting on a medieval night. People think we're a little odd, he confided, lowering his voice. But I enjoy cooking and she enjoys mixing cocktails. Most of the ship's crew, he said, lie in bed all day and watch films. Work isn't compulsory, he added.

Although nobody was eating his burgers, Nico had put on another batch. 'Trinity does everything for us, so

194

there's no need to do anything. Not being nosey, but why are you here?' he asked.

'I don't know,' she replied. 'I wish I did, but I don't.'

'So, nobody's told you anything yet?'

'I mean, I know I must be here for a reason.'

'But nobody's told you what that reason is?' Nico lifted a hamburger off the flames and inserted it into a bun. 'Well, no doubt God will get around to it sometime,' he said, and wrapped the hamburger in a paper napkin.

'Good luck with the restaurant idea,' she said.

Lorna took the hamburger down to the water's edge, kicked off her shoes, and waded in, feeling the thrust and suck of water. Further down the beach, a couple had stripped off and were skinny-dipping, the girl shrieking as the man dived after her. Lorna couldn't see who they were but, like mostly everyone, they looked young and lithe.

The burger was perfection; burnt on one side and almost raw on the other, just as she remembered. Her mother would have been proud of it. She discarded the paper napkin and watched it dissolve in the water's margins.

Then she walked further up the beach, hearing an owl's call. The moon was still reflected in the water, wavelets lapping on the shore. Well away from the beach bar, she sat in the sand and stared towards the horizon. Then she undressed in the shadow of sand dunes, the light breeze touching her skin. The sand was still warm, the water dark and cool. It folded her to its silence; then she broached the surface, tasting the tang of salt on her lips. She swam out then lay on her back, looking at the stars. They were the same stars as on Earth. She recognised The Plough, traced a path to the North Star.

Then Lorna lay on the beach and thought about Tom. Strangely, remembering that he'd died hadn't come as a shock. All she'd done was remember something that was already there, tucked away at the back of a drawer, a fragment of memory waiting to be found. She thought about his Lego creations, his dextrous hands. She also knew it had happened a long time ago. She'd been a child when he died, and she'd come to terms with it, in her own way. Thinking about Tom, it seemed as if other memories were jostling on the edge of her mind, but memories that were still hidden, lurking just underneath the surface like fish motionless in a stream. When she looked, they were gone.

A faint breeze touched her skin, cooling her. She looked down the beach to the broken-down bar, hearing far-off music, laughter, and the sound of a door opening and slamming shut.

Lorna remembered Tom playing rugby, and leaving Austin in the rugby club bar when she stormed off to the airport. She had never really understood why she'd run out like that. OK, she'd felt used, and confused by his protestations of love, but that didn't justify hurting him. But it was then, shivering on the touchline, that she'd remembered Tom darting up and down the field in his over-sized shorts, sliding in mud, and shouting hoarsely for the ball. She'd also remembered how she'd watch Austin play school rugby and how, sometimes, she'd look at him and wish that he was her brother. From the Bristol touchline Lorna had been assailed by that thought. It had distracted her from Austin's try. She had finally realised who he really was, and who he could never be, and what had drawn her to him in the first place.

*　*　*

The door slammed again and Lorna opened her eyes. She stood up and brushed sand from her legs, supposing that she ought to be sociable and rejoin the party. For a moment she felt guilty about leaving – but, as always, the lure of the sea had been too much. Lorna had grown up beside it. It was part of her. She and Tom used to jump from the harbour wall, much to their mother's dismay. It was stupid of them: they shouldn't have told her. But Lorna had always floated easily. She couldn't remember a time when she couldn't swim. Jumping from the harbour wall was an adrenaline rush, not dangerous. But her mum had been insistent. She'd promised faithfully not to go harbour-jumping again, with or without Tom.

Except for her, the beach was deserted. The volleyball game had long since ended, although the party in the beach bar still seemed to be in full swing. A woman's voice was raised in laughter. It sounded again like Suzie's laugh, brazen and uninhibited, living for the moment. Suzie who, despite their different backgrounds, had always been her best friend, always looking out for her, always spilling of Lorna's secrets to the world, including – worst of all – the episode with Austin in the sand dunes. At the time, she'd been livid with Suzie for blabbing it around town, then livid with herself for telling Suzie in the first place. But it wasn't Suzie's fault she couldn't keep secrets and Lorna should have known that.

Secrets, she thought, feeling suddenly nauseous. Her left cheek had begun to hurt and she put a hand to it, feeling fearful. A shard of memory had twisted free and for a moment Lorna had seen Suzie's face contorted with rage, felt Suzie's hand against her face. Lorna took a deep breath, forcing herself to calm down. She'd never hurt Suzie in her life. Suzie therefore had never had cause to be angry with her. They were best friends and always had been. The pain in her cheek immediately faded, the fragment of false memory dissolving. But still she felt fretful and unsettled, an inner equilibrium disturbed. Lorna took another deep breath and, looking over the beach to the dark water beyond, vowed never to drink ouzo again.

On her wrist was a Cartier bracelet; around her neck, a flawless diamond on a golden chain. She searched fruitlessly for her underwear in the sand dunes and smoothed out creases in her Dior dress.

'Trinity, can I go home, please?'

Of course, Lorna. Floor-level lighting will guide you to the nearest exit which may be behind you. I trust that you had an enjoyable time?

'Thank you, Trinity,' said Lorna following small fairy lights that seemed to lie just under the sand. The trail ended at a transporter stop, seemingly set into the cliff face. She looked for a moment at the revelry on the beach then stepped inside. Moments later she was back in her apartment.

On the bed was the pair of knickers she'd just lost on the beach.

I didn't think that you had discarded them intentionally, so I retrieved and washed them for you. You can, of course, trust to my utter discretion, even if it's just lost underwear. To be frank, you'd be surprised by some of the things I get asked for. Mostly by the Hugh Grant lookalikes, although that may just be coincidence. My advice to you is simple: enjoy yourself and, above all, don't feel guilty about being here. Many are taken, few are chosen. The countdown to transition has now begun. Shit! said Trinity, with just a hint of exasperation. *I didn't mean to say that. It is, I regret, yet another electrical fluctuation.*

All the lights in Lorna's apartment had gone out again.

* * *

A few close friends and family had been invited back to the golf club. Her mum thought the idea was preposterous, accusing her father of horrible things. Her dad said that some of them had come a long way; it was the least we could do. He'd have a word with the Secretary, he said. Lorna supposed that the golf club was usually a happy place for him. He went there often enough, as her mother was forever grumbling. Lorna saw him take out a small plastic bottle from his jacket pocket and swallow a couple of pills. Her mother was missing. This was a gathering she simply couldn't face; Aunt Meg had taken her home and was staying with her.

Lorna would much have preferred to have gone with her mum. She didn't know why they were having a party at her father's golf club. It didn't seem proper that they were having a party and Tom hadn't been invited. She would have liked instead to have gone to her bedroom and turned the TV up loud.

Although Suzie's parents weren't close friends with her parents, they'd come along because of Suzie. Like everyone else, Suzie also looked uncomfortable and didn't know what to say. Neither of them had been to a funeral before; neither knew what to say to the other. They'd have preferred to be outside, but it was still raining. Worse, Lorna had heard someone laugh. She didn't recognise who it belonged to, but it didn't seem right.

At first, Lorna wandered the room eating crisps. Then she gravitated to the only person in the room who was her age, who was sitting in a chair and swinging her legs.

'I'm really sorry, Lorna,' said Suzie's mother.

There was an awkward silence. Suzie's parents were smiling thinly. Lorna didn't know if she was supposed to say anything.

'Thank you for coming,' she said eventually.

'It was the least we could do,' said Suzie's mother, and

pulled her daughter from the chair. Like Lorna, Suzie had been eating crisps. 'Why don't the two of you go off and play?' As she said this, Suzie's mother frowned. She didn't know what to say either.

The grown-ups were crowded round a long table, on which had been placed trays of sandwiches. The other end of the room was empty. Lorna and Suzie sat in plush armchairs and watched golfers proceed up the first fairway. She saw that they weren't holding up umbrellas, then realised it had stopped raining. There was a patch of blue in the sky. A rainbow was arched over the town. Maybe they could go outside after all.

Lorna was wearing her best dress. It was dark red and knee-length. The last time she had worn it was to a birthday party, a happy occasion with cake and pass-the-parcel and lots of running about. Her mum had deemed it dark enough for the funeral; she didn't want to dress her daughter in black.

Outside was a paved porch with wooden bench seats, each donated in loving memory of a dead golfer. Lorna wondered if her dad would donate a wooden seat for Tom, even though they couldn't afford it and Tom had never played golf. The porch was sheltered by the overhanging roof of the clubhouse. Suzie and Lorna sat side by side on one of the wooden benches.

'What did Tom die of?' asked Suzie, swinging her legs. Lorna saw that the cut on her knee still hadn't healed. They'd been playing on the beach and Suzie had fallen and cut her knee on a piece of broken glass. It seemed like a carefree eternity ago.

'Germs,' she told Suzie.

It started to rain again, the sky darkening over. There was a rumble of thunder out to sea. Big raindrops dripped from the overhanging roof and fell into a bed of blue flowers bordering the putting green.

'Hello, you two.'

It was her dad, glass of whisky in one hand and a wicker basket full of sausage rolls in the other. He handed the basket to Suzie.

'Thank you, Mr Love,' said Suzie, and popped a sausage roll in her mouth. Then another, before she'd swallowed the first.

'You should try and eat something, Lorna,' he said, although Lorna hadn't seen him eat anything – except pills from his plastic bottle, and that didn't count. He looked out across the putting green to the first hole, where a group of golfers were sheltering by the professional's shop. 'My father used to say it never rained on a golf course,' he said. 'When I was your age, I believed him.'

Lorna guessed that he had no idea what to say either, like everybody else, and had said the first thing that came into his head. Now that he'd said it, it seemed to be the only thing in his head. The golfers by the pro shop were packing up and heading back to the car park. If anything, the sky had darkened still further, rain falling vertically, and thunder edging in from the Firth of Forth.

'I'm sorry about Tom,' said Suzie.

His glass needed refilling and he had half-turned to go back to the clubhouse. Now he stopped, his bottom lip trembling. 'Thank you, Suzie,' he said before escaping to the bar.

Lorna watched him, his slow ponderous progress. Until recently, he'd seemed like a rock, upright and strong. Now his shoulders were full of sand and sagged.

* * *

Inside, adult hands patted her and said soothing things. Lorna knew they were trying to be nice, but she wished that they'd say nothing. She didn't need any more sympathy, and she didn't need to know that Tom was with God or, worst of all, that only good boys and girls go to Heaven.

That was said by a maiden aunt who Lorna rarely saw and whose breath smelled sickly-sweet. Her mum sometimes smelled the same when she'd had a glass of sherry. Not only didn't she know whether Tom had been good — he'd only weeks before pushed her off their canal boat — but she didn't want the same thing to happen to her. She didn't want to go to hospital and catch germs.

'Only the good die young,' said the maiden aunt, thinking this was a nice thing to say. She was smiling sadly, one plump hand resting on Lorna's shoulder.

She was large and had smudged lipstick. Lorna couldn't remember her name or why she was related to them. All she knew was that she was a maiden aunt and lived a long way away. Lorna looked at her and felt tears prickle. Her aunt shouldn't have come all that way, just to say something like that.

By now, most people had left. Her father was still at the bar, his glass full. Suzie had her coat on, her parents hovering at the door.

'We could give you a lift home, Lorna,' suggested Suzie's mother. 'Your mum's at home, isn't she?'

Lorna nodded and fetched her coat. She didn't want to be there, and hadn't wanted to come in the first place. Suzie's mother had a quiet word with her father and Lorna saw him look over and wave.

It was the first time she had been driven in a Porsche. The back seat was cramped but the engine sounded like a wild animal. She liked it when Suzie's father revved the engine like a racing driver.

They were only able to park some distance from the

202

flat. The small High Street was packed with day trippers who were sheltering inside the town's many coffee shops.

Suzie walked with Lorna to her front door.

'My dad says your dad should sue the bastards,' said Suzie suddenly. 'That's what I heard him telling Mum. He said that Tom shouldn't have died.' A raindrop clung to the end of her nose then fell. 'My dad's a lawyer. He knows about things like that.'

'Stop it!' Lorna hadn't meant to shout; it had erupted from nowhere. She didn't want to know that her brother needn't have died, that the germs could have been defeated.

'Anyway, that's what he told Mum,' said Suzie.

'Please stop, Suzie.'

'I just thought ...'

'Please, Suzie!'

Lorna put both hands over her ears, turned on her heel, and marched off. Back home, her mother had gone to bed. Aunt Meg was in the kitchen, but not really doing anything. Lorna didn't know what lawyers did, except that they drove nice cars and got people money, if you could afford them. She heard the Porsche accelerate down the High Street.

'Your mother's asleep,' said Aunt Meg, whose bulk filled most of their small kitchen. 'It's been a tiring day, poor dear. Do you want something to eat? I could fix you a sandwich or something.'

'There was stuff at the golf club,' said Lorna, although she'd only eaten crisps. 'Dad's still there,' she added, just in case Aunt Meg was worried about him.

He came back much later and slept on the sofa in the living room. Lorna could hear his snores through her bedroom wall. He also seemed to be muttering in his sleep, although the words were just a low grumble.

By then, she had taken kitchen scissors to the drying

area at the back of their house and cut Tom's T-shirt into little pieces. Then she'd put the pieces into the bin and replaced the scissors in their drawer. She didn't want to be good. She didn't want to die young.

Then she walked to the beach. She wanted to be alone, to gather her thoughts. It had stopped raining and the sky had cleared. Under a full moon, Lorna could see stars.

CURTAINS

On her birthday before Tom died, Lorna's parents bought her a bicycle. She chose it from a shop in the Grassmarket in Edinburgh. High above Mike's Emporium, the gaudy shop which her dad had been recommended, was the looming mass of Edinburgh Castle. On the way, he spouted history in a loud voice.

'See that pub there?' he asked, waving airily. 'That used to be the city prison. Long time ago, of course. Before I was born, in fact.' He paused theatrically to laugh, then gestured further down the street. 'Now, see *that* pub? It's called The Last Drop. Know why that is?'

Lorna shook her head, trying to keep pace with him. When he strode purposefully, which was rarely, it was hard to keep up. 'They used to take the criminals to be hanged on the Royal Mile,' he informed her. 'But, being nice people, the jailors would first take the condemned man for a last drink.'

Lorna looked at him blankly.

'For a last drop before the last drop,' he finished. 'There, we're here.'

She had wanted a new bike for a long while now. Her old bike, a dilapidated Raleigh, had gears that slipped and a chain that kept falling off. Her father, bemused by anything mechanical, couldn't mend it, and nor could Tom, not that he had even bothered looking at it.

The shop was dimly lit and it took her eyes some moments to adjust. She then saw that the Emporium was lit from above with small lights, each angled theatrically to illuminate particular machines. Lorna walked around the shop reverentially, touching and gazing, pausing at a particular bicycle, then moving on to the next, only to pause again and look back to the one before. Most of the bikes were for big boys. She was joined in her search by a tall man with grey teeth.

'They're all lovely bikes,' he confided, bending towards her and lowering his voice. 'See anything you fancy?'

Lorna shrugged. 'Just looking.'

The shop assistant – Mike? – cleared his throat but didn't speak for some moments. He had large ears like radar discs that stuck out squint. Her dad was standing by the door and surveying the street. He said, 'You choose, Lorna. It's your birthday.'

'In that case,' said the shop assistant, 'we'll have to find you something really special.'

Her father brushed a hand through his hair, stroking it flat against his scalp. 'What kind of bike were you thinking of?' the shop assistant asked, clasping her shoulder and steering her towards the girls' section of the shop. 'A racing bike, perhaps? All the kids are after them, you know.' His challenge to her conformity hung like a question mark. 'It's the telly that does it,' he confided to her dad, who had his hands in his pockets, jangling change. 'The Tour de France, all that stuff. Yes indeed,' he added, motioning Lorna towards a particular machine. 'What about this beauty? Take my word on it; ask anything you like.'

'She's maybe a bit young for a racing bike,' said her father.

'Then how about this one?' asked the shop assistant.

It was perfect. It smelled of oil and gleamed like silver. Lorna didn't need to ask any questions. She already owned the bike and was far away, bent tightly on a sweeping bend, a roaring breeze in her ears. It was like the feeling of flight, of being free.

'French-made, reliable, and very reasonably priced. Go on,' he urged, anxious to please, indicating that she could try it out. Lorna felt the contours of the bike like a blind person, running her fingers down the handle bars, sensing its speed and oily newness.

'Sit on it,' whispered the shop assistant, his breath against her cheek. Once again she was hurtling on a down-slope, gears cranked forward for maximum speed, feet churning in slow sweeps.

'It's very nice,' she said.

The shop assistant clapped his hands together, setting up an echo. 'I told you, didn't I?' although Lorna had no idea what he'd told her.

Her dad had brought old blankets which they spread across the back seat of his car. The bicycle lay on top of the blankets and jerked and twitched as they drove home to East Lothian. They took the coast road, her dad, as always, driving too fast.

Coming into North Berwick, she saw Suzie sitting at a table outside a café, flanked by her parents. They seemed to be eating fish and chips. Suzie recognised the car and waved. Lorna waved back.

'Who's that?' asked her dad, who did try occasionally to take an interest in her friends.

'Just somebody from school,' she replied, still not sure if someone as posh as Suzie could be friends with her.

They parked her bike at the bottom of the communal stairwell and her mum came down to admire it, wiping her hands on a dishcloth. Upstairs was the smell of baking, and birthday candles laid out on the kitchen table.

* * *

Suzie became her best friend the Christmas before Tom's death. Lorna was looking through curtains, watching her parents' progress to the front row. The curtains were heavy and black and she wasn't really supposed to be peering through them. She was wearing a green dressing gown and a towel was wrapped round her head and she thought, with some reason, that she looked ridiculous. Completely bastard shit fucking ridiculous. Despite her feeble protests, Lorna was the mother of God.

She saw her dad make his way through the auditorium and was again reminded by how tall he was and how he stooped when he was around people, as if embarrassed by his size. He was wearing a grey suit, white shirt, and purple tie. Her mum was wearing a blue dress and her hair was newly cut and set. She was smiling at anyone she recognised. Her father, who didn't know many people, was looking nervous.

'Places, children!' Mrs McPhail clapped her hands and Mrs Thomson sat down behind the piano. Lorna let the curtain fall back, obscuring the sight of her mother finally taking her seat. Her father, hands twined on his lap, had been in his seat for some minutes. As the curtain flopped closed, she knew that he'd seen her. He'd winked towards the stage in the same way he did when pulling money from her ear.

Writing the Nativity play had been a collaborative activity. Everyone was asked their views on the birth of Jesus and many of those ideas had been incorporated into the script and storyline. Mrs McPhail, so she told everyone, was very keen on amateur dramatics and attended night-classes in creative writing for the theatre. This year's Nativity play was therefore an experiment. By allowing free rein to collective imaginations, she had rewritten the story to make it more relevant to our own lives, or so she told the school. Mary and Joseph were therefore a pair of tourists in Edinburgh who couldn't find a bed for the night. That being the case, Lorna really didn't see why she should be wearing a green dressing gown and a towel on her head. Mrs McPhail told her we must mix the new with the old. That made absolutely no sense because Lorna had never seen anyone in Edinburgh wearing a green dressing gown with a towel on their head.

The curtains were hauled back by Mrs Crabtree, who had to pull on a rope. She was a large woman and not very fit and the curtain opened erratically to uncertain applause. Nobody seemed quite sure whether they should applaud at the beginning or the end or both. This underlined in Lorna's mind that they weren't really theatre people. Everyone knew that you only applaud at the end, and only if the actors deserve it.

Although they had been through a full costume rehearsal, Lorna was uncertain in the bright lights. She looked out at the audience but could only see shadows. A chair creaked. Someone coughed. She stared out at where she knew her parents were sitting. Her mum would be rigid in her seat with a handkerchief knotted through her fingers. Her mouth would be fixed in a set smile. Her dad would be thinking about something else. He often was.

The first scene involved Lorna walking slowly round the stage holding Joseph's hand. Suzie was Joseph. Mrs McPhail had convinced herself that this gender reversal was a good experiment. However, the fact was, only Suzie had wanted the part. None of the other kids had wanted the leading roles. Having talked her way into Joseph, it was Suzie who had talked Lorna into Mary. But under the bright lights, hearing coughs and someone swearing, she was terrified. The dress rehearsal hadn't been too bad; the hall had been empty. Now it was full, and hundreds of pairs of eyes were following her around the stage.

To make things worse, there was a cushion shoved up

her dressing gown. Her hand was trembling in Suzie's. Suzie squeezed hers, but it was no good. Lorna's mind was fast becoming a blank. The rest of the cast, all dressed casually in jeans and T-shirts, marched around the stage singing a Christmas song about Santa Claus. Mrs Thomson, on piano, was vainly trying to get them to march and sing in tempo.

Lorna and Suzie were deposited at the end of the song beside a door. Above the door hung a sign saying HOTEL. Lorna knocked loudly on the door, which was opened by a small boy in a suit. He said that all the rooms in the hotel were fully booked, and had they not thought to phone and make a reservation. The audience laughed. Lorna could hear her mother joining in.

'No,' said Suzie loudly, declaiming to the gods as Mrs McPhail had taught her, 'because the telephone hasn't been invented yet.' More laughter from the audience, who now understood that this year's Nativity play wasn't the traditional fare they'd been expecting.

At this point Lorna was supposed to burst into tears and say, '*Whatever are we to do?*' On cue, she burst into tears, but couldn't say anything. Words had become glued together. Her mouth had dried up. Suzie, also dressed in a shapeless gown with a towel on her head, glanced at her and realised that the tears were genuine. She too was also momentarily without words. However, unlike Lorna, she had wanted to be in Mrs McPhail's stupid play. To compound Lorna's misery, her cushion had slipped. Now, she thought, I don't just look pregnant, but stupid and obese.

'Whatever are we to do,' hissed Mrs Peacock from the wings. She was holding one hand to her brow. Most of the audience heard and someone laughed. Suzie heard the laugh and gave Lorna's hand another squeeze.

'Whatever are we to do?' exclaimed Suzie boldly, and

led Lorna across the stage to another door. This also had a sign above it. This sign said STABLE. 'I know,' she said, although this was also Lorna's line, 'we can sleep here for the night. The animals will keep us warm.' Lorna was looking at Suzie open-mouthed. Her cushion was in danger of falling out completely. 'Let's go inside,' Suzie said loudly and pointed to Lorna's cushion. She was ad-libbing for all her worth. 'It looks as if little Jesus might be born soon.'

The audience roared with laughter. Mrs McPhail had both hands to her brow and was shaking her head. But it seemed as if Suzie was in her element. A fish that had found water. Speaking Lorna's lines and hers, she was invincible and Lorna couldn't help but feel that she had been saved. It was then that she made up her mind. Suzie was her best friend ever in the whole world.

* * *

Trinity hadn't yet fixed the short-circuit, and Lorna's apartment was still in darkness. She was lying on her back, her head against the rattan headboard. She could have been back in Edinburgh, except for the absolute silence. In Edinburgh, there was always the distant throb and pulse of the city, something Lorna found comforting; a reminder that she was surrounded by people. Then Lorna felt a stab of pain. It started in her shoulder and worked its way down her arm. She winced with the pain, took a sharp intake of breath. She'd seen Suzie's face for a fleeting instant. It had been contorted with anger, eyes blazing. Although the image of Suzie only lasted a moment, Lorna was able to feel her anger as sharply as she could feel the pain in her arm. Its was a jagged pain, like a stabbing knife. Both Suzie's anger and Lorna's pain were equally real, except her mind wouldn't

211

tell her why. The pain was frightening. It came and went without warning, and could presage a lifetime of enduring pain. But if I'm dead, she thought, I have no lifetime. And if I'm dead, I shouldn't feel pain. Thinking about this made her want to cry or scream. *None of this is real!* she wanted to shout. Instead, unbidden and unwanted, her mind threw out a snapshot of the day after the Nativity Play.

* * *

It was the first time she'd visited Suzie's house, and its size marked their families as coming from different planets. Lorna's home was a small flat where you could hear the neighbours squabbling, or cars roaring down the High Street just underneath the front window, or drunks trying to find their way home on Friday nights, which shouldn't have been difficult as it was such a small town. It was a flat where you could listen in on other peoples' lives whether you wanted to or not, or admire their washing hanging out to dry. Suzie's house was a world apart: set back from a quiet road, with a red gravel drive that scrunched under her feet, and a downstairs and an upstairs – and, looking up, another upstairs above that. There was a garage for the cars, grown over with climbing roses (garage not cars), and a summerhouse under trees at the bottom of their garden. The silver Porsche was parked on the driveway. The house itself was painted white and had bay windows that looked onto manicured grass, on which was set a round wooden table and chairs. The lawn overlooked the town and the sea. What struck Lorna first, once she'd negotiated the loud drive, was the silence. Their house was always filled with sound: shoppers and cars, revellers, and the crash of waves. Here, simply the distant grumble of an aeroplane on its descent to

Edinburgh airport. Lorna swallowed nervously, despite Suzie now being her official best friend in the whole world.

'Why, hello you!'

The front door, painted lustrous red and framed between dwarf conifers in bronze ceramic pots, had been opened by a tall women in blue jeans. She was wearing a pink cashmere jersey, her hair cut short. She had pearls round her neck. 'I'm Susan's mother. And you must be Lorna.' She was smiling and seemed to be an exact replica of Suzie, only very old.

Lorna had pushed her bike up the driveway and didn't know what to do with it, thinking there might be a special shed for bicycles, perhaps with a servant to park it. After some indecision, she propped it against the wall of the house.

The hallway was cavernous and hung with paintings that Lorna knew were called Modern Art, because they seemed like random blobs and streaks of colour. They didn't look like anything. If she'd done something like that at school, Mr Downie would have told her to go back to her desk and do it again *properly*. Lorna's home was filled with pastel watercolours of sea and beaches, some painted by her mother, rather badly. Her mother was given to random enthusiasms. The previous year she had taken up painting, bought a smock, churned out several masterpieces (her word, not anybody else's), and given up – all in the space of a few months. The year before, it had been yoga. The year before that, modern dance when she'd come back from her weekly class all hot and sweaty and wearing a sparkly jumpsuit, which was utterly gross. Suzie's hall was dominated by a giant (real) Christmas tree and around its base was already stacked an acreage of parcels in festive wrapping. Lorna looked jealously at the parcels. Lorna's tree was small and plastic and didn't have presents underneath it. Any smaller and it would have had AIR FRESHENER written on it.

Then there was an eruption of noise and from the shadows at the end of the hall bounded Suzie, grabbing her arm, and pulling Lorna towards the stairs.

'Whoa there, you two!' said Suzie's mother. 'I haven't been introduced yet.'

'This is Lorna,' said Suzie. 'Right, we're out of here.'

'Susan, manners, please!' Her mum turned to smile at Lorna. 'Your mother works in the bakery, doesn't she?'

Lorna nodded.

'I thought so. Next time I'm in I'll introduce myself properly. Bet you're looking forward to Christmas.'

Lorna didn't know if this was a question, so just nodded again.

'Is there anything special you're hoping to get?'

She furrowed her eyebrows. 'A hamster,' Lorna said eventually.

'A hamster? Well, if it's what you want.' Suzie's mum wrinkled her nose, making Lorna wonder what she had against rodents. 'Anyway, I thought the Nativity play was simply wonderful!' Suzie's mother seemed to mean this. 'Very enjoyable and so … different! Not what we were expecting at all. And it had a tiger in it.'

'It was a lion,' said Lorna, acutely aware that the lion had said more than she had.

Suzie's room was at the very top of the house. It was surprisingly small, smaller than Lorna had imagined, but it was her very own kingdom. She even had her own bathroom, with a fancy shower and a bidet, which Lorna looked at blankly and had to ask Suzie what it was for. Even when Suzie told her, it didn't make any sense. Her bedroom was painted in vivid reds and pinks. On a polished oak desk sat a large stereo system. CDs were scattered over the carpet, competing for floorspace with discarded clothes. A poster of Guns'N'Roses was pinned above her bed, unmade, which had cream cotton sheets. Lorna had always suffered nylon. In the morning her hair stood on end and crackled. She would give herself electric shocks eating toast.

Suzie put on a Red Hot Chilli Peppers CD and jumped around on the bed. Lorna wandered to the window and looked down into the town, then called out excitedly to Suzie.

'Look! That's my bedroom window!' She had recognised her blue striped curtains. It felt strange looking at her bedroom from a new angle, and to be connected with Suzie like this; it also reinforced Suzie's otherworldliness, like she was a princess in a castle.

Suzie had rushed to a cupboard and was rummaging through clothes and toys. She bounded back, waving a torch. 'We could talk to each other,' she announced, eyes wide and shining, golden curls framing her face, 'when we're in bed.' Suzie switched the torch on and off, on and off, shining it into Lorna's eyes.

Lorna thought for a moment. 'We'll need a code.'

Suzie didn't know what a code was. Lorna explained that it was how secret agents talked to each other. 'Like, one flash means *Yes*.'

'And two flashes means *No*.'

'And three flashes means *How's things*?'

After that, they sat on the floor and tried to puzzle out what else they could say in torch language. They agreed that four flashes would be *Hi* and five flashes *Goodnight*, but after that they ran out of ideas. It was all very well saying *yes* and *no*, but how could they ask questions? Lorna suggested that they could use short and long flashes to mean different things. She'd seen a programme about ships at sea and that's what they did. Suzie suggested

215

moving their torches sideways or up and down, or in circles. It was clear that inventing torch language was going to be very hard.

* * *

It was during that afternoon of new friendship that Suzie, now Lorna's best friend in the world (ever), told her about the birds and the bees, which came as a surprise because there were no birds or bees involved, if Suzie could be believed, which wasn't always the case. Such was the shock that Lorna couldn't later remember how the conversation had come up: perhaps from the Nativity play and how the son of God had come to be born.

It was after Suzie's mother had fed them tea, cake, several kinds of biscuits, and various sandwiches. They'd walked to the beach and for a while they threw stones into the water, watching them being devoured by waves.

'I'm going to be an actress,' said Suzie. After the previous night's triumph Lorna had asked her what she was going to do when she grew up. 'I'm going to be in magazines and on the telly,' she added, sounding utterly convinced.

Lorna didn't know how to be famous, or whether she really wanted to be. All she knew was that she couldn't compete with Suzie. Even then, Suzie was the school beauty. Pre-pubescent boys would bring her little bunches of flowers stolen from local gardens or the cemetery. 'What does your dad do?' Lorna asked instead, thinking about the shiny Porsche outside their utterly mammoth house.

'He's a lawyer.'

Lorna thought for a few moments. 'What do lawyers do?'

Suzie explained that her father went into Edinburgh in the morning and came back in the evening. He had an office in the New Town, with his own parking space. Lorna supposed that this was a nice thing to have. Her father, when he was working, which wasn't often, took the train, and didn't need a parking space. Sometimes, said Suzie, he looks through big jotters full of important letters. Sometimes he writes things down with a pen. Sometimes he types things on the computer. Suzie, imparting banal information, eventually conceded that she had no idea what her father did.

They were walking along the east beach and past the grand houses that front the sea. The east beach was Lorna's favourite bit of North Berwick. It was rocky, not pristine sand like the west beach, but it always felt more real to her; the west beach looked constructed, the east beach – with its jumbled rocks and crab-infested pools – seemed authentic.

The tide was in. Grey clouds were chasing across the sky, uniform and formless. Lorna pointed to a grassy bank between the shoreline and the cliffs.

'I was born there.' Although her mum could never be sure of the exact spot, Jack and Alice Brotherstone were, and while Jack jogged very slowly into town (being American he was somewhat large), Alice had stayed with her mother. The Brotherstones were therefore able to accurately identify the spot to the local paper.

'Jesus! Really?'

'Really.'

'You were born next to a rusty beer can?'

Lorna looked along Suzie's extended finger. 'I don't suppose the beer can was there then.'

'But maybe it was,' said Suzie. 'Maybe your mum drank it, and that's why you were born there.'

'Mum says it was a dodgy prawn sandwich.'

'So she didn't plan to give birth by the seaside?'

'God, Suze! Why would anyone want to do that?'

Suzie kicked up sand and shrugged. 'Why does anyone do anything?' she said, which sounded wise, but wasn't, because it was Suzie saying it. 'Like sex. Why would anyone do that?' Her eyes had gone big and round, like a kitten's.

Lorna understood the concept of sex, but not the nitty-gritty. She knew about kissing and how *things* could get out of hand. She'd seen enough TV programmes to know that people got sweaty and took their clothes off, and then sometimes gazed at the ceiling and smoked cigarettes.

'First the boy's thing gets big and hard,' said Suzie, not waiting for Lorna to answer, which she positively hadn't intended to do. Lorna had an inkling she didn't want to know what happened between getting sweaty and smoking cigarettes.

Lorna didn't know what Suzie was talking about.

'You know, his *thing*,' said Suzie. She had golden ringlets and big blue eyes and looked like a Barbie doll, according to Lorna's mother, who had suggested giving her one for Christmas and who evidently didn't much like the idea of a fluffy rat in their home.

'What thing?' was all Lorna could manage.

'The thing between his legs.'

This Lorna could understand, having seen her dad's thing before. He seemed unable to lock bathroom doors, or maybe didn't know it had a lock. Feeling a little sick, Lorna had never realised that boys' *things* could be multi-functional.

'What!'

'Then he puts it between your legs.' Suzie pointed graphically with one finger.

'What!'

'Then he squirts stuff into you which makes babies.'

'*What!*'

'It's what married people do when there's nothing on

TV,' concluded Suzie, looking triumphant.

Lorna thought this was both disgusting and very unlikely, and queasily said so. Her mother would never let something as gross take place under her roof. She couldn't see why anyone would want an erect *thing* being stuck inside them and then being squirted with stuff. It would be like the man going to the loo inside you, which was an utterly horrible thought. Lorna's life was framed in certainties, and although the adult world to which she aspired had a nuanced vocabulary from which she was often excluded, she also assumed that she knew the ground rules: that grown-ups didn't have much fun, had to work to earn money, got married, and had children. Against those certainties, she had never thought to ask why or how. She knew where babies came *from*, but had never wondered how they got there in the first place.

Dark, scuddy clouds were now crowding in, making the horizon cold and indistinct, and a couple of seagulls were quarrelling over a scrap of something at the water's edge. It somehow seemed possible that Suzie's truth could have some basis in fact. That between cute puppies and dog poo was a middle way: that the truth was malleable, without precise definition. Looking east, the far horizon was uniformly grey, sea and sky melded together. Suzie had seemed very sure of herself. Nevertheless, even if any of it was true, which Lorna doubted, she absolutely vowed that such unpleasantness wasn't *ever* going to happen to her. It was a promise she didn't keep, but sometimes wished she had.

That evening, Lorna sat in the kitchen and read a book. Her mum was pottering and she could hear the rustle of homemade Christmas decorations being hung in the hall. Her dad had a glass of whisky in one hand and was standing silently by the kitchen window, immobile. She had no idea what he was thinking or, worse, what his *thing* was thinking, because he'd said earlier that there was absolutely nothing worth watching on TV.

FLATULENCE

Lorna had only once eaten in a posh restaurant, and that was on Suzie's birthday. Suzie wanted to be grown up and for the two of them to be the only people at the table. Of course, her dad was paying. The evening started out badly. Lorna was wearing a frilly blue dress (from the Red Cross), which she hated. Suzie was wearing a red cotton dress, which she also hated, although it had a proper label from a proper shop. They were also about a millionth the age of anyone else in the restaurant. To make things worse, most of the menu was in French, and the things on the menu that were in English didn't seem edible.

'Pumpkin soup?'

'Ugh!'

'Squid cooked in its own ink?'

A shudder, Suzie biting her lip.

'Veal?'

'Cruel.'

They were in Suzie's dad's favourite restaurant with Marcel, the head waiter, fussing around them, treating them like royalty, bowing as he approached the table and bestowing warm smiles at Suzie, who had been to the restaurant with her parents many times before. Lorna was more used to the occasional Pizza Hut. The room's walls were lined with gilded mirrors, and it seemed that several Marcels were advancing on them from different directions.

'Your usual, mademoiselle?' enquired Marcel, his pen poised.

'Yes, please.'

Lorna looked at Suzie for help. At the doorway to the restaurant, where an unctuous young man with slicked-back hair had taken their coats, had been a small fountain with naked cherubs holding up a large potted plant. The waiters were dressed in white. Marcel's gold pen hovered over his pristine notepad.

'The steak is excellent, mademoiselle,' he whispered, 'as I'm sure young Miss Bryce will attest to.'

'Is that what you're having?' Lorna asked.

Suzie nodded.

'Does it come with chips?' Lorna asked Marcel, blushing. In the places where she was usually taken for special treats, everything came with chips, and you didn't need to ask for them.

'But of course, mademoiselle. It can come with whatever you want it to come with.'

'I'm also having deep-fried camembert to start with,' said Suzie.

'Deep-fried *cheese*!'

'It tastes better than it sounds,' confided Marcel.

Lorna nodded uncertainly.

She could see other diners watching them. How, they were thinking, can such young girls be *allowed* to eat in here? How could they *afford* to eat in here? 'I've never been to a place like this,' Lorna whispered over the table, and picked up a fork. Around her place setting was a profusion of other knives, forks, and spoons, and she was entirely mystified as to which ones to use.

'My dad can afford it,' said Suzie.

'Are all lawyers rich?'

'I expect so,' she replied. 'All the ones I've met have been rich.'

'With big cars?'

She nodded.

Lorna reached into her pocket and handed over an oblong box. 'That's from me,' she said.

Suzie peeled off wrapping paper and extracted a Kylie Minogue tape. It was one that Lorna knew she'd been wanting.

They finished with ice cream and raspberries and then, unexpectedly, all the lights went out. In the sudden darkness, all Lorna could see were pinpricks of light from the candles on each table. Then she realised that one of the candles seemed very bright and was moving towards them.

Marcel was holding a small cake, into which has been stuck a sparkler. Two other waiters were beside him. Marcel led everyone in singing Happy Birthday and, bit by bit, the other diners joined in. At the end, everybody clapped and the lights came on again.

At that moment, Lorna wished she knew what lawyers did, because the steak and the deep-fried cheese had been delicious, and Marcel had made her feel like someone really important, not just the daughter of a bakery worker, and had ignored her ill-fitting dress. She wanted to eat in places like that again and again.

* * *

Her dad used to say *better out than in*, which usually preceded him farting loudly. Fathers weren't supposed to fart, Lorna would think, let alone draw attention to it. She found this utterly gross. But on their Broads holiday she had realised that her dad's intestinal workings were plumbed differently, and she would have to put up with it. Or that his mental faculties were plumbed differently and didn't see that breaking wind in public was something that most people didn't do. (Some boys at school did it, to guffaws from classmates, but they didn't count.)

She would have been happier if out-rather-than-in extended beyond flatulence, because Lorna had never really had a good conversation with her dad. She always hoped he would pass on nuggets of wisdom acquired through his great age and huge experience. But, on reflection, he wasn't experienced at very much: only at living in North Berwick, travelling to work in Edinburgh, and venturing to the Auld Hoose or the golf course. Her mum was much the same, working in the bakery, indulging in her transient passions. So Lorna never had the benefit of parental advice, nor much in the way of encouragement. To them, in their different ways, life wasn't what you made of it, but about accepting what it made of you.

Maybe that's why she wanted to be best friends with Suzie. She was different. She had dreams and ambitions that extended beyond bakery aprons with STAFF written on the back. She had parents who wanted her dreams to come true. On her birthday, the year they went to the posh restaurant, Suzie had a portfolio of photographs taken by a professional photographer in Edinburgh. She'd had to shout and pout and stamp her feet to get the second part of her present. But Suzie was nothing if not tenacious, and could be *loudly* tenacious, and her parents had no option but to concede defeat. Copies of her portfolio were sent to a number of modelling agencies in London.

To Lorna's surprise, but not Suzie's, one of the agencies responded and said that they might have a job for her, for a children's clothing catalogue. It involved Suzie travelling to London with her mum for more photos, at which point she was taken on, which was OK because it was the start of the Easter holiday and, apart from eating chocolate, Suzie didn't have much else to do. She disappeared off to London, her mum driving to the airport and Suzie in the passenger seat wearing dark glasses, which she'd never done before. It seemed to Lorna, standing on Suzie's gravel driveway and waving goodbye, like a rehearsal for a future she could never aspire to.

It was that which Lorna envied; how Suzie had charted a life for herself, not long after leaving primary school. She envied her certainties, and it threw her own uncertainties into sharp focus. It made Lorna wonder about the meaning of life, and try on her mum's bakery apron. It was still too big, but it wouldn't be long before it fitted perfectly.

* * *

After leaving school, Lorna and Suzie both moved to Edinburgh: Lorna to study law, Suzie to go to drama college. Ever since the ghastly Nativity play, Suzie's heart had been set on films or modelling or both. For a while, Lorna lived in halls of residence, returning home to North Berwick most weekends, then only on occasional weekends, much to her mum's disappointment. She was appalled by 9/11, but also about its aftermath: the invasion of Afghanistan, the tide of blood. Not to mention the whales, which she'd always liked.

Her father had by then almost stopped speaking. He much preferred to sit in front of the TV, watching game shows he'd once disdained. He'd even taken to shouting out the answers on *University Challenge* or *Who Wants to be a Millionaire?* though invariably his were wrong: the capital of Australia wasn't Sydney; an isotope wasn't a breed of dog; and Tolkien didn't write *Harry Potter*. Lorna used to wonder why he bothered reading newspapers and watching the news: his knowledge of current affairs was dismal. Mum may have had difficulty naming the prime minister, but her dad's utterly *crap* views on almost everything were ridiculous, even to her.

We were quite right to invade Afghanistan, he said. We were quite right to invade Iraq, he said. War might be a failure of politics, Lorna had decided, but that didn't make it right.

Suzie was living in a small flat in Leith and hating it. They decided to rent a flat together. This wasn't a big deal for Suzie, whose parents were rich and who was also modelling for clothing catalogues, disappearing for days at a time and returning with ridiculously large cheques. Not so for Lorna, who realised she'd have to work part-time to pay her share of the rent. She weighed up her options, then said yes to Suzie, who immediately took it upon herself to find the perfect flat. Lorna wasn't convinced by this strategy, and said so. Most things, in Suzie's world, came marked *expensive*. Suzie merely touched the side of her nose with one elegant finger and winked theatrically.

Lorna's mobile rang a few days later when she was shopping in town.

'The flat's in Arthuria Road, sweetie. Know where it is?'

She did, vaguely. Suzie's voice was almost drowned in traffic noise. 'Polwarth?'

'Close. Merchiston. Go past the King's Theatre and it's third on the right. I'll see you there, OK?'

'When?'

'Now, babe.'

It was on the top floor and, being an old tenement, didn't have a lift. Suzie was already there when Lorna arrived, wrapped tightly in an Afghan coat, ridiculously large earphones clamped around her head. There was snow on the ground and a howling wind. The communal stair needed painting. Bikes were parked in the bottom hallway, reminding Lorna of her own bike which was stolen a few months after she'd been given it. What with everything else, it hadn't been replaced.

'Find it OK?'

Lorna nodded. She had walked miles from the bus stop and was frozen. She had a woollen hat pulled over her ears and her breath hung like cigarette smoke in the stairwell. 'Are you sure this guy wants to rent it to us?'

'I've told you, petal. He's a friend of Dad's. That means he's not going to rip us off.'

'I suppose,' said Lorna.

'Never suppose!' commanded Suzie. 'Just *do*, babe. Well, shall we visit our new abode?' She produced a set of keys, rattled them in front of Lorna's face, and smiled her dazzling smile.

Lorna often wondered why they were best friends because, in many ways, they were opposites. Lorna's ambitions were rooted firmly in the possible; she remembered those old sepia photographs of North Berwick and the threat that they posed. When she dreamed, she dreamed sensibly. Her nightmares were about failure. Not so Suzie, with her long blonde hair and model figure, with her huge blue eyes and pouting lips, and her crazy dreams that might just come true. Suzie had never been studious. She was loud and crass and didn't care what people thought. She attracted superlatives and didn't read books. Whereas Lorna's feet had always been on the ground, Suzie's head was stuck firmly in the clouds. Opposites attract, Lorna supposed.

The flat had seen better days. The woodwork was chipped and the hall carpet was stained with muddy footprints. The kitchen, all wood and Formica, was a throwback to the 1960s. But it was warm, the rooms were decently proportioned, and the bathroom was mercifully clean. But it was the view that sold the place to Lorna. The climb up to it had been tiring, but the vista from the living room was restorative. She was able to look all the way across roofs and chimneys to the buttress of the castle.

'Well, what do you think?'

'It's OK, I suppose,' replied Lorna, still mesmerised by the view.

'It's better than OK,' said Suzie. 'Two decent bedrooms, newish bathroom, and a kitchen with a cooker that actually works.'

Lorna was convinced, but it wasn't anything to do with the flat or its fixtures. It was everything to do with what lay beyond the glass; a thousand years of stones and battlements, seemingly adrift in the night air. 'The fridge light doesn't work,' Lorna complained with a smile.

* * *

Shortly after moving in, Suzie disappeared off to Italy for a week, returning tanned. Lorna felt jealous, reminded again of the glamorous world to which Suzie was gravitating. By then, Lorna had found a part-time job in a local mini supermarket. The shop manager who interviewed her didn't ask many questions and didn't bother to write down any of her answers. He introduced himself as Mr Sturridge, although his lapel badge said KEVIN – HERE TO HELP. He offered her the job on the spot, then told her she'd been the only applicant. The rest of the staff were friendly enough, even the ones who worked there full-time. In the staffroom at the back, with its plastic chairs, kettle, and chipped mugs, Lorna would sit and read her law books, depositing cigarette ends into an ashtray that nobody ever seemed to empty. KEVIN was transferred to another branch shortly afterwards, replaced by Mike, who kept asking her to go for a drink with him, or to the cinema, or for a meal, and who didn't seem able to take no for an answer. Mike was fat and smelled so it wasn't a difficult decision for LORNA to make, although he was kind in a fatherly sort of way. She had also been down to North Berwick. Her mother's face seemed more wrinkled, her father slumped in an armchair and shouting *Sydney* or *dog* at the TV. His eyes were bloodshot and his hands trembled so much that he tried to keep them in his pockets out of sight at all times.

HEAT

A year after visiting Austin in Bristol, Lorna was once more in an aeroplane, although this one was bigger and the passengers were more boisterous. In the seat beside her, reading a magazine, was Suzie. Lorna still had an aversion to flying and listened intently to the safety briefing, making sure she knew precisely where the nearest exit was, even if it was behind her.

They'd travelled from Edinburgh to Newcastle by train for the flight, having been unable to find a cheap deal from a Scottish airport. From the proceeds of a modelling job, Suzie bought breakfast on the train, an extravagance that Lorna hadn't before experienced, and marvelled at how the waiters and waitresses could balance salvers of bacon and tomato while being buffeted around corners. From Newcastle they caught the metro to the airport, where Lorna went straight to the bar.

They were early and, inevitably, their flight was delayed by an hour. Having been able to drink additional anaesthetic, Lorna was comparatively relaxed when they finally did board the plane. Suzie, of course, was dressed to kill. Or thrill, Lorna couldn't decide which. A diamanté stud gleamed from her belly button and the shortest of short skirts accentuated the length of her legs. A pair of sunglasses, perched on the top of her head, was almost lost in blonde foliage. Lorna was wearing a cream pair of jeans and a blue cotton shirt. Suzie sat by the window, Lorna by the aisle, as far from the window as possible.

After take-off, Lorna bought two vodkas and tonic and

a small bottle of white wine from the trolley. It was going to be a long flight and she didn't want to experience it completely sober. She jumped when the wheels retracted after take-off, jumped again when the flaps wound into the wings, and gripped her seat when they'd achieved cruising altitude and the engine pitch changed.

'Relax, babe,' Suzie advised, flicking the pages of her glossy magazine. 'Statistically, the train journey to the airport was the dangerous bit. Planes don't crash anymore. It's a known fact.' Suzie had said much the same in the bar at Newcastle airport.

'I prefer my feet on the ground,' replied Lorna, fizzing open a can of tonic and adding it to vodka, 'or, perhaps it's just that I have too much imagination.' She stirred the contents of her plastic glass with a swizzle stick, looking suspiciously at the wing for signs of structural failure.

'Bloody hell!' said Suzie, who had temporarily discarded her fashion glossy for the airline's in-flight magazine. 'What in God's name is going on?' She tapped a page with a manicured finger and handed over the magazine.

Lorna smiled. The flight wasn't going to be so bad after all.

'Thought you'd be pleased,' said Suzie. 'Well, I think it's all crap. If they're going to show a film, why can't they show a *decent* film?'

'I suppose they have to cater for all ages,' said Lorna and looked up the aisle. Mostly families, many with young children. A large and solid man with a Newcastle United shirt waddled to the rear of the plane. Lorna shrank into her seat to let him pass, as far from the outside world as she could get. 'That's what *Star Wars* does, Suze. It's for the young and the old and everyone in between. Anyway, you never know … you might enjoy it.'

'It got crap reviews and I absolutely won't like it.' Suzie was adamant, and slipped the in-flight magazine back into its pocket on the seat in front. 'I don't like stupid films about space and I don't like things I can't believe.' She had picked up another magazine and was randomly turning pages. 'But you're quite right about one thing, sweetie ... Unlike me, you're able to believe in complete bollocks.'

'How true,' said Lorna and bought headphones from the stewardess.

Shortly after the film finished, the plane began its descent. The nose tilted downward and the engine noise changed again. By then, dreaming about far, far away, Lorna was fast asleep.

The plane landed and she woke with a startled yelp. Hitting the runway hadn't woken her, but the noise of everyone clapping had.

* * *

They embarked from the rear of the plane into a wall of heat. Lorna felt she had to force her way through it to get down the steps. This was a new kind of heat, relentless and clinical. Grey mountains were carved against the sky. The colours were different, the landscape alien. Suzie took a deep breath and said 'Bloody hell' in a low voice. Inside the terminal, the air was cooler and they sat on plastic seats and waited for their cases to come through. Lorna lit a cigarette, ignoring the No Smoking signs. Well, everyone else seemed to be ignoring them, including a couple of Greek policemen who were lounging against a wall.

Suzie had made her promise not to smoke in their hotel bedroom, laying down rules that also applied in their flat in Edinburgh. Their bedroom had a balcony, according to the brochure, so it wouldn't be a problem. At the baggage reclaim, the metal carousel rattled to life and bags clattered onto it. Lorna's suitcase wasn't large and she could pull it behind her on its extension handle. Suzie's was gargantuan and could only be moved by an elephant or trolley. By the time Suzie realised this, all the trolleys were in use.

'You shouldn't have brought so much stuff,' Lorna grumbled, struggling to help Suzie move the case through customs.

'I haven't brought a lot of stuff,' said Suzie huffily. 'I've only brought what I think I'll need.'

'Such as what? Lead bars?'

'Very funny. Not. I like. Looking. Good. OK?' It was clear that, right or wrong, more criticism would be unwise.

Outside, they had to manhandle Suzie's bag across a car park to their bus. The bus driver, doubling up as baggage loader, could barely lift her case off the ground. In Newcastle, it had seemed lighter. But there again, they'd had trolleys at Edinburgh station, Newcastle station, and the airport. In the baking heat, the short journey across the car park had coated them both with sweat. Lorna saw that divine justice had been achieved: Suzie's exquisitely applied make-up was smudged. Smiling inwardly, Lorna didn't tell her.

Suzie had taken out a guidebook to compose herself and was reading it. They were sitting towards the back of the coach, cocooned in air-conditioning. 'This is one Greek island where time really does stretch back for an eternity. Crete straddles the junctions of Europe, Africa, and the Middle East, and has been a place of trade since the Neolithic era as well as a target for invasion for the Myceneans, Romans, Venetians, and Turks.' Suzie snapped the booklet shut. 'And now us, babe,' she said.

They drove through landscapes that were mostly barren. The hills in the distance could have been on the moon; baked and lifeless. In places, jets of water irrigated small farms. In the lee of farm buildings were tomatoes and watermelons; trellised vines offered protection from the heat. Suzie pointed to an old woman in black riding side-saddle on a donkey. Lorna pointed to an old man with a luxurious moustache sitting on a wall by the roadside.

'At least we know we're in Greece,' said Lorna.

'Probably paid by the tourist board,' commented Suzie.

The road wound down to Agios Nikolaos on the north coast and then upwards across a precipitous headland. Ag Nik, they'd been told, was the place to be. Filled with nightclubs, you can't help but have fun. Suzie, of course, wanted to stay there; Lorna had thought otherwise. It's a bit pricey, she'd been told. Suzie had eventually capitulated, muttering about the price of taxis.

Their small hotel, in the next town, was up a side street from the beachfront. Their room was white and spotlessly clean and the balcony overlooked a small drying area at the back. Sheets and towels were hanging out to dry. A gecko was clinging to a shaded corner of the bedroom; Suzie flapped at it with a towel until it disappeared. In their small loo was a modern toilet, much to their relief. It can sometimes be a bit primitive, they'd been warned, and you shouldn't flush toilet paper.

In the late afternoon sun, they headed for the beach, bags partly unpacked, both of them wilting from the effort of carrying Suzie's case upstairs. The woman who had met them in reception had looked at it and eloquently shaken her head. No porter today, she'd said, discovering a few words of English. Son not here.

Lorna was feeling both fulfilment and relief. Here she

was in a foreign land – and, against all odds, she had survived the flight.

They had to wade far out to sea before the gently-shelving beach dipped into deeper water. Here, Lorna dived, listening to sand being dragged across the ocean floor and, turning over, watched light sparkle on the sea's surface.

Afterwards, wrapped in towels, they sat in a beach taverna. Greek music played softly in the background. Suzie ordered bottles of lager. At their feet, in the shade of a bamboo awning, the sand was scattered with cigarette ends. Then Suzie ordered ouzo, because they were in Greece and you have to try it at least once, petal.

Lorna was fascinated how the colourless liquid became milky when you added water. She liked how things could transform into other things. It had always been the little things that most interested her. She was so fascinated that she ordered two more, just for the simple pleasure of watching the liquid change colour. After downing the second, she felt that she was growing to like ouzo. The aniseed tasted sweet and sharp; the alcohol innocuous.

'What's wrong, babe?'

'Jesus Christ, I don't believe it!' Tired and slightly tipsy, Lorna could have sworn she'd just heard a familiar voice. Looking round, and with mounting horror, she realised it belonged to Austin Bird.

236

REALITY

'I *fucking* can't believe you said yes!' Lorna was angrily stuffing a T-shirt into a drawer, one of the few Suzie hadn't already filled.

'Oh, come on, Lorna! What the hell was I supposed to say?'

She pushed the drawer shut and put her hands on hips. 'Well, *fucking NO* springs to mind.'

'Look, sweetie, they're going home tomorrow. It's only for one bloody night.'

Suzie had a towel wrapped around her head but was otherwise naked. Water dripped from her shoulders and ran in rivulets between her breasts. 'Anyway,' she continued, rubbing her hair, 'it's not as if you have to sleep with him.'

'Suzie!'

'Well, that's what this is about, isn't it? Christ, Lorna, you haven't seen him for ages and, well, he's no doubt forgiven you.'

Lorna removed her hands from her hips and slipped a sundress onto a hanger. She hung it in a wardrobe which was also bulging with Suzie's clothes. 'There was nothing to forgive.'

'You did walk out on him,' Suzie reminded her.

Lorna snapped shut her empty suitcase and placed it on top of the wardrobe, then went onto the balcony and lit a cigarette. Below, sheets and towels still waved in the drying area. They'd specified a sea view, but the old woman had simply shrugged. It didn't much matter; the hillside above the town was spectacular enough: olive groves rising to high mountains etched against a darkening sky.

'You could have asked me first, Suze.'

'You were in the loo. I had to say something, so I said yes. Look, it's only for one night,' she repeated. That was the galling part; Austin and his friend Leo had waited until Lorna had gone to the toilet before springing the question. The loo had been revolting, a ceramic hole in the ground, festooned with flies. When she got back, she was confronted by the prospect of an evening with an ex-boyfriend, who may or may not have forgiven her for abandonment.

'I'll feel awkward,' said Lorna. 'Maybe he loves me, maybe he hates me. I don't *know*, Suzie, and I don't want to find out.'

'Maybe he neither hates you nor loves you,' Suzie suggested, trying to cram another pair of knickers into an overfilled drawer. Lorna had the distinct impression that the whole chest of drawers might explode, showering them in Dolce & Gabbana.

'He probably knows to the precise second when he last saw me.'

'Don't be silly, sweetie.'

'He did last time, Suze – down to the exact number of days. It was creepy.'

'I think it's rather cute. Heartfelt, you could say. '

'He doesn't have a heart,' said Lorna, realising this sounded a bit stupid.

'I still think "cute" sums it up.'

Lorna stared angrily at her friend, feeling that she should be showing a little more support. 'Anyway,' said Suzie, 'his pal is quite nice.'

'Don't get any ideas,' warned Lorna. 'If you go off with Leo, where the hell will Austin sleep?'

Suzie indicated their narrow beds with a tilt of her head, which finally made Lorna laugh. 'Well, OK, like you say – it's only for one night.'

'That's better!' said Suzie, finally pulling on underwear and joining her on the balcony which housed a small table, two plastic chairs, and a drying frame on which their swimwear was already folded. On the table was an ouzo bottle, glasses, a bottle of water, and a plate of peanuts, which they'd bought on the way back from the beach. 'To old friends,' said Suzie and handed Lorna a glass.

But unlike the ouzo, I'm not going to transform, she thought. The somebody that I am is not about to become a somebody else, however many glasses of ouzo that I drink. Austin is history, end of story. I am also in a beautiful place and am free to do as I choose. 'To old friends best forgotten,' she said, tasting aniseed.

* * *

'Well, this is a coincidence,' said Austin Bird. Having spent two weeks in the sun, he was lithe and tanned. His hair was shorter, although he still had designer stubble. His friend Leo had fair hair and wore strings of beads around his neck. His hair was much longer and bleached into blonde highlights by the sun and sea. He was taller than Austin and moved with languid purpose, like a wild animal, hair blowing across his face. He had high cheekbones and was tightly muscled; his teeth were very white and rather pointed, as if used to chasing down prey. Lorna thought he was cute.

They'd arranged to meet back in the same beach bar. Remembering the flies and the hole in the ground, Lorna was determined not to use the loo again. She'd replaced ouzo with white wine and soda. She didn't want to be told anything that she didn't want to believe.

She wanted to keep her wits about her. Austin had gone from friend to lover back to friend again, maybe. He had already transformed from one thing to another, and she didn't want any more confusion.

'So what made you choose here?' asked Lorna. 'I mean, out of all the bars in all the places in the whole world, why this place?'

'Connie McGregor mentioned it,' said Austin. 'She came here last year. Raved about it.' Connie had been in their year at school, now finishing a course in art and design in Leeds.

'In which case, coincidence solved,' said Suzie who, being arty, had kept up with Connie. 'It was her who recommended it to me.'

Austin raised his glass. 'It's a small world,' he said.

'It certainly is,' said Lorna, not meeting his eye.

Leo and Austin were at that stage of their holiday when, given half a chance, they could easily have decamped to Greece permanently. Austin said he wouldn't mind working in a bar; Leo's idea of heaven was to start a jet-ski business, then laze about in the winter. Perhaps go travelling, he said, maybe do nothing. It's what the Greeks do, he said. They make all their money in the summer and spend all winter in bed watching films.

Under a setting Greek sun, dreary British skies didn't hold much appeal, nor did the thought of another year of studying. Austin, who had always liked bridges, wasn't so sure about them now.

'It's all about lifestyle, isn't it?' he said, suddenly serious and knotting his fingers. 'It's about deciding on careers we might have to do for the rest of our lives. And then, twenty years from now, realising that we've made a bollocks decision.'

'You've always wanted to be an engineer,' said Lorna.

'You were born with a spanner in your mouth. Don't tell me you've got cold feet?'

'No, of course not,' he conceded. 'It's what I've trained for and it's what I'll be. But just look around you, Lorna. Now, tell me honestly. Where would you rather be?'

In front of them was a sheltered bay, around which lights had begun to appear and become captured just below the surface of the still water. Behind, the towering buttress of a mountain range. In between, white sand and the shimmer of falling waves. 'Here isn't home,' said Lorna. 'You wouldn't really belong here.'

'I would if I learned Greek.'

'Not so easy' she countered. 'For a start, they've got a different alphabet.'

Austin held up a hand and, counting off fingers, offered a few Greek phrases. '*Kalimera,* I am reliably informed, means good morning. The same reliable source, who happens to be the old crone who cleans our room, tells me *kalispera* means good evening and that *kalinichta* is good night. *Efharisto* is thank you. See, I'm almost a native.'

'A very polite native,' said Suzie. 'But, there again, the old crone who cleans your room is probably a very polite Greek lady.'

'*A ghamesou,*' said Leo.

Austin laughed. 'He's just told me to fuck off,' he explained. 'Well, OK. I may not belong here, but I would like to stay a bit longer. The sun's hot, the beer's cold, and the sea's warm. Right at the moment, reality seems like a bit of a bore. That's the trouble with holidays,' he said, picking up his beer bottle and realising it was empty. 'Just when you start to chill out, it's time to go home. Anyone fancy another?'

Leo and Austin knew all the bars to go to and the

tavernas to avoid. They knew the affordable places and the pricey clubs that catered for the rich set. Nick the Greek's in Ag Nik was *the* place to go to, although it got crowded. Right on the beach, said Leo, and most of the action takes place on the beach, if you follow me.

Leo pointed to the headland. 'There's a taverna over there. Just follow the path, you can't miss it. A bit ramshackle, but nice and quiet. It's also on the beach,' he added, looking at Lorna with a question mark in his eye. She wondered just how much Austin had told him, perhaps explaining bitterly how she hadn't even had the decency to properly break up with him. Dumped by a two-word phone message, the cold-hearted bitch. 'But the very best place to eat in the whole of Crete is, by strange coincidence, right here. Well, me and Austin like it, so we thought we'd treat you.' He pointed backwards to the small town. 'In any case, after all the beer I've had, it's probably not a good idea to get caught short in this dive.'

A bit later, walking into town, Leo said: 'Sorry, but I couldn't help but notice your face. Much earlier, I mean, when you came back from the loo. It wasn't a pretty sight.'

'My face or the loo?' asked Lorna.

Leo grinned and tossed his mane of hair. He had blue eyes that sparkled. He was smiling. 'The appropriate phrase, Lorna, is *pou eena ee twaleta, parakalo*. Remember that and you'll always be able to find a toilet. However, any country that invents democracy and taramasalata can't be that bad.'

* * *

For starters they had stuffed vine leaves, bread, squid in tomato sauce, and – Leo's choice – taramasalata. Lorna

242

took only a small bite of the squid because she'd never tasted it before, and didn't like it very much. Once bitten, she wouldn't be tasting it again. It had also been Leo's choice; he liked the taste of the sea. Their seats were on a low rooftop, a bar and kitchen immediately below; it overlooked a scrubby patch of grass through which thin cats stalked. The taverna was set towards the back of the town and, from their rooftop table, they had a view across white roofs to the beach and dark sea. Cicadas chattered from olive trees set in the burnt grass. Austin and Leo drank bottles of beer, Lorna and Suze drank ice-cold white wine that came in a metal jug. The waiter said it came from Sitia, an area on Crete. Lorna thought back to their coach trip from the airport and the moonscapes in the hills. She'd never much thought of Greece as a wine-producing country.

With this night being their last, both boys were determined to enjoy themselves. Although they were leaving the next day, neither had packed. That final act could be put off until the very last moment. In any case, said Leo, I travel light. Just a rucksack. I can carry it onto the plane as hand luggage.

Lorna raised her eyebrows at Suzie, whose wardrobe now encompassed every square inch of their room, dresses hanging on doors and the curtain rail. Leo was also looking at Suzie – trying, and mostly failing, Lorna thought, to look at her face and not down her cleavage.

'So what is it you do?' he asked.

'Drama school,' said Suzie. 'Actually, just finished.'

'So you're an actress?'

'Technically, I'm unemployed.'

Leo persisted. 'But it's what you want to do, right?' With amusement, Lorna saw that Leo had instinctively leaned closer to Suzie; the moth attracted to her light. 'I mean, does that mean you're going to be a film star?'

'I certainly hope so,' said Suzie and, for effect, swept back luxuriant hair with one hand. It was a gesture she was forever doing; it drew attention to her face, made people look at her. 'Actually, I've just had my first audition.'

'Wow!'

'I doubt anything will come of it,' said Suzie, 'so I'm not getting my hopes up.' Lorna knew precisely how much it meant to her. Suzie had been to London twice to see producers and casting directors. 'It's a film called *School's Out!* Basically it's a load of crap, but it does have Hugh Grant.' Suzie shrugged theatrically. 'I also do a bit of modelling. If you look in the right mail-order catalogues you'll find me showing off this year's beachwear specials. Apparently,' said Suzie, 'my bum is the perfect size.'

At this, Leo looked down, but the tablecloth was in the way. 'For what?' he asked rather stupidly, not knowing what else to say. Lorna had to stifle a grin.

'There are models,' said Suzie, 'who only use their hands. You see them on telly advertising hand cream or washing-up liquid. The ad people only use them because they have long fingers, perfect nails, and, importantly, they don't get the shakes when they're nervous. On the other hand, my bum is perfect for swimwear. But no, Leo, I haven't a clue why.'

Lorna expected Leo to lean closer, drawn still further towards Suzie's glamorous light. Instead he leaned back and looked out over the rooftops. 'Austin tells me you're going to be a lawyer,' he said to Lorna, signalling the waiter for more wine and beers. They were now onto their second metal jug, and the main courses hadn't yet arrived. Lorna's resolution not to drink too much had gone out the window.

'Hopefully,' she said. 'Unlike Suze, I have no

244

ambition to be the next Julia Roberts and my bum is only perfect for sitting on.'

Leo and Austin laughed; Suzie merely pouted.

'It's also what I'm doing,' said Leo and, to her surprise, leaned towards her. 'So, tell me, what made you want to do law?'

* * *

Afterwards, they sat on the beachfront drinking more beers and white wine. A trip to Ag Nik had been suggested, to show them the best places, but even Suzie was beginning to flag. It had been a long day for them, what with lugging Suzie's suitcase across Europe. Sitting in the late evening warmth and watching the world go by seemed a better ending. Woozy and sleepy, Lorna kicked off her shoes and kneaded her toes in the sand. They were sitting on plastic seats around a rickety table. Lorna lit a cigarette and blew smoke at the stars.

Suzie and Leo were on the dance floor, being shown how to do a Greek dance. They were in a long line of other tourists and bar staff, their arms around one another. In time to the music, they shuffled left and right and kicked out with their legs. Suzie was shrieking with laughter and flicking back her hair. Lorna watched the slope of the bar staff's eyes. As always, Suzie was the centre of attention.

Lorna had been too tired to take to the dance floor; she hadn't wanted to make a fool of herself – and Austin's moves were all confined to the rugby field. He could feign and dummy, he could side-step, but he couldn't dance. He was now playing for the university and scouts from the local professional side had been to watch him.

'So you might yet play for Scotland?' She was pleased for him. It's what he had always dreamed about; now he was making it happen.

'I doubt it, but who knows.'

She had noticed how he had filled out since the last time she'd seen him. His shoulders were broader, his arms more muscled.

Lorna smiled. 'You really didn't mean that crap about chucking it all in and moving here, did you?'

He shook his head. 'End of holiday angst, that's all.' He sighed, at a loss for words. Suzie was still shrieking from the dance floor. 'But I'd much rather not be going home,' he said.

He looked up, met her eye. Lorna didn't know what to say. Instead she looked out to sea; a cruise liner was passing on the horizon. She couldn't see it, only its lights.

'I'm sorry about that rugby match,' said Austin. 'I'm sorry I was so incredibly stupid.'

He had every right to be angry. Instead he was being apologetic. 'I'm sorry too, Austin. I shouldn't have gone off like that. Time of the month, or something.' Out to sea, the liner was disappearing behind the headland.

'Meeting you here was just ridiculous,' he said. On his face was a crooked grin. He was handsome and hunky and she'd always liked that about him. He was solid, dependable. But there was still that something else about him, that hint of someone else. She looked away; a twinkle of fairy lights was caught in her wine glass. 'It's just that, well … I still feel the same', he said.

Now he too looked away. Back in the bar, a new bouzouki tune had started; plucked strings over which a man was softly crooning. Lorna turned to look; Suzie was still dancing, although with less enthusiasm. Leo still had one arm around her shoulders and was kicking out of time.

'That's silly.'

'I know.' He made no attempt to justify how he felt. 'I

246

also know it's not what you want to hear.'

'I'm flattered, Austin, really I am.' Distracted, she lit a cigarette, then realised that an unfinished one was still burning in the ashtray, 'and you don't have to apologise about the rugby. Anyway,' she said more brightly, 'that was then and here is now.'

'And yet I still feel the same way, Lorna. Silly, I know, but there it is. I'd prefer it if I didn't, but I do. Don't get me wrong,' said Austin quickly, holding up a hand, 'because it's not as if I haven't been with other girls. I haven't exactly been pining away.' Lorna drew smoke into her lungs. She didn't want to be listening to this; she wanted Leo and Suzie to come back and an unwanted spell to be broken. 'It's just that I keep comparing them with you and they never quite match up.'

'We were kids when we went out, Austin. What you're saying doesn't make sense.'

He too had kicked off his flip-flops and was sitting legs extended, feet dug into the sand. 'Because something is nonsensical doesn't make it untrue. Anyway, why does *anything* have to make sense?' he asked.

* * *

Soon afterwards, to her intense relief, Suzie and Leo flopped into chairs. Applause followed from the dance floor. Leo ran a hand over his perspiring brow. Suzie demurely dabbed at hers with a handkerchief. Austin smiled ruefully, knowing a moment of truth had come and gone.

'If that's dancing,' said Suzie, 'then it's all Greek to me. Christ, I'm knackered.' She was clutching a bottle of chilled beer and tilted it to her lips. Lorna watched it glug down her throat. She set the bottle on the table, where it frothed. 'Oh, and thanks, guys, for supper. Much appreciated, wasn't it, Lorna?'

'Except for the squid,' agreed Lorna.

'Well, thanks for coming,' said Austin, not quite looking at her. 'I suppose we've got an early start,' he added, not wanting to leave but knowing his evening had come to a close.

'Yeah, me too,' said Suzie and also rose. 'Unlike you lot, I need my beauty sleep. It pays the bills,' she added, smoothing down her dress. 'You coming, babe?'

Lorna still had a glass of wine to finish, and she also wanted a few minutes to herself, to luxuriate in the warmth of a Greek evening. 'In a minute, Suze. Just leave the door open, will you?'

There were kisses goodbye and then Lorna walked to the water's edge, carrying her shoes in one hand. She trailed her feet in the water, trying not to feel guilty about Austin. She'd never meant to hurt him, and hadn't liked being compared to his other conquests. The passage of time should have changed things for both of them.

Without meaning to, she had picked her way along the beach, away from the town. Now, stopping and looking up, she saw how far she'd walked. She noticed a path that rose over rocks and round a small headland. The sea breeze had revived her, cleared her head. Carefully in the light of a full moon, she walked up the path and round the headland.

She stopped to look up. The sky was a patchwork of huge stars, so large she could almost reach up and touch them. Lorna had never been so far from home before, and neither of her parents had been to Greece. It made her feel liberated, free; she was able to do as she wanted. She inhaled deeply, smelling warm air tinged with salt.

After a ten-minute walk she arrived at the next beach. This one was much smaller, and sat in the lee of a steep escarpment that rose high above her head. Hundreds of feet up, she saw car lights on the mountain road down which they'd travelled that afternoon. Set back from the beach was the ramshackle beach bar.

It looked as if it had been put together from driftwood. A wooden sign hung from a chain over the taverna door. *Nico's*. It was closed although a solitary light burned inside. Her footsteps echoed on the bar's wooden decking and she looked around, fearful that she may have disturbed someone. A large barbeque was set against the shack's wall, cooking utensils scattered on a table beside it. The beach was deserted; waves lapped on the shore and were sucked away.

She sat at one of the taverna's tables and lit a cigarette. It was warm and, after her walk, felt supremely peaceful. Austin wasn't her problem, she had decided, he was his own.

'Hi,' said a voice beside her. 'Christ, sorry! Didn't mean to startle you.'

'Startle me? You nearly gave me a fucking heart attack!'

'Sorry.'

Lorna's heart slowed to a canter.

She looked at him. 'It looks like you've been following me, Leo.'

'Not in a creepy way, if that's what you think. I just didn't fancy going to bed. I also didn't fancy wasting my last night here. Tomorrow I can sleep, tonight I don't have to. I saw you disappear over the headland.'

'So you decided to follow me?'

'Actually,' he said, grinning inanely, 'I still want to know why you want to be a lawyer.'

'Is that some crappy way of trying to chat me up?'

He shrugged. 'I'd just like to know, that's all.'

She was looking at him suspiciously, drawn in by his impossibly good looks but doubting that anyone followed anyone in the middle of the night to ask inane questions. He had one eyebrow raised, his mouth puckered. He seemed on the verge of smiling, but not quite, perhaps unsure how well his entrance had gone down.

'What on earth for?' was all Lorna could think to say, busily prevaricating. She didn't know who this person was, except that he was a friend of Austin's; she didn't know what his real motives were.

'Because I don't want to be a lawyer.'

A bird rose unseen from the olive trees, its wings softly beating. Lorna looked at him evenly. He'd followed her, but seemed unthreatening. His expression was guileless, now smiling; small creases at the sides of his mouth. His mouth was a little too wide, she noticed, his eyes a little too close together, his long nose bent. Lorna realised that she was trying to focus on his negatives to avoid being overwhelmed by the positives. 'Then if you're serious about being bored to death, you'd better pull up a chair.'

'That's the spirit!' said Leo.

LION

'Jesus, you're an idealist!'

'Not sure about that, but I do have ideals.'

Leo had nicked one of her cigarettes, although he said he didn't usually smoke. 'It's the same thing,' he said. 'An idealist is a person who has ideals. That sounds suspiciously like you.'

She'd been stupid enough to tell him that, in her opinion, without law there was nothingness, an entirely imprecise word that she immediately regretted saying and, having drunk a bucketful of Greek wine, found difficult to pronounce. She didn't really know whether she really believed it anyway, this idea of law bringing order from chaos. It seemed far removed from dusty books and the trivia of legal precedent, but it's what she'd kept telling herself. They sat in silence, listening to the flop and retreat of waves.

'An idealist also harbours unrealistic expectations,' said Lorna eventually, not entirely sure if this made sense either. 'I may be idealistic in some respects, but I am not unrealistic.'

'Austin says you're a Trotskyite leftie.' In the darkness, she couldn't be sure whether he was just making fun of her.

'So, what's wrong with that?' she demanded.

'Nothing at all,' said Leo quickly. 'I'm sorry, I didn't mean to sound condescending.'

Lorna took a deep breath. A car passed on the road above, its headlights momentarily turned out to sea.

'Actually, I'm not a Trotskyite leftie, whatever Austin thinks.' Lorna wondered how much Leo did know about her, Austin pouring out love/hate diatribes. 'OK, so why are you doing law?' she asked, to move the conversation away from Austin.

She saw his shoulders rise and fall. 'I have no idea, none whatsoever. I thought you might be able to give me a clue. That's why I wanted to talk to you.'

'That's ridiculous,' she said.

He was looking up the stars, his eyes half-closed. Then he leaned forward and planted his elbows on the table, cupping his head in his hands. 'I don't want to be poor but, unlike you, I have no idea how *not* to be poor. In other words, Lorna, I have never had the slightest inclination to do anything in particular.'

'So, being congenitally undecided, you chose the world's second-oldest profession.'

Something stirred in the undergrowth beyond the olive trees, momentarily silencing the cicadas. She looked round fearfully, realising how dark it had become. On the walk across the headland, she'd been slightly drunk and the full moon had guided her. Now she was relatively sober, except for difficult words, and the moon had passed overhead.

'My father's a lawyer,' said Leo, 'and he was forever badgering me about it. He owns a practice in our part of Devon. Mostly conveyancing and divorce, that kind of thing. Not doing a lot for ordinary people because they can't afford his fees. There's no money in legal aid, so he says. Our family doesn't therefore specialise in righting wrongs. Anyway, he kept telling me to think about law because, one day, his business could be my business.'

'That's the trouble with rich people like you, Leo. You make poor people like me work all the harder.'

He laughed. The cicadas had started up again.

'Actually, I kind of meant that, Leo. I grew up hating people like you. Posh accents, rich parents, a good job at the end of it. People like you think that the world owes you a living.' She realised she had probably said too much. 'Then you get married to someone called Samantha, have two adorable children, and drive them to primary school in some ghastly 4x4.'

'But I don't know anybody called Samantha.'

'But you will, Leo. Racing certainty. It's how the circle of privilege turns. You probably went to public school and own a cravat.'

'Marlborough. So, yes, I did go to a public school. But, no, I don't own a cravat. Or a cardigan, or whatever else you're going to accuse me of.'

'Cardigans aren't posh, Leo,' said Lorna. It was what her father habitually wore, with the buttons done up all wrong so it hung squint, and with gravy stains down the front that wouldn't wash out.

'My father believes in family,' said Leo, who didn't seem to have been offended. Austin must have warned him about her dodgy views on social justice. 'He also thinks that happy families have lots of money. He wants the best for me, I guess.'

'So, the richer you are, the happier you are, is that it?' She had never had his advantages and for a moment was angry with him again, for following her, scaring the shit out of her, and then telling her how well-off his family was. She didn't want to listen to a rich boy's sob story.

'No, Lorna, I don't believe in all that crap.' There was a pause and Lorna looked closely at him. He was almost beautiful, she decided, like a Greek god: tall and strong, with his mane of untamed hair. 'But to be honest,' he said, clearing his throat and looking upwards at the stars again, 'I don't have the courage to stand up to him.'

'Courage? Sorry, where does courage come into it?'

'I don't want to disappoint him,' he admitted, his face in shadow, 'and if I say *no* that's what I'll be doing.' He ran a hand through his hair, brushing it from his eyes and turning them to hers. 'Maybe I just don't want to spend the rest of my life in a boring office.'

'I hope you don't want me to feel sorry for you,' said Lorna.

'I wasn't looking for sympathy.'

'In which case, I can't help you.'

He smiled. 'Actually, I didn't think you could.'

Her anger had become a knotted pulse in her abdomen. 'But that's not really why you're here, is it?'

'It isn't?'

'Austin.' She said it evenly and watched him closely. His head was cocked to one side and shadows, like camouflage, moved over his face.

'You think that ...'

'Yes, Leo, I do. He sent you.'

Leo merely seemed amused, leaning back in his chair and stretching out long legs. 'He didn't.' Leo smile was now displaying sharp white teeth. 'Although he still feels guilty, stupid sod, about inviting you to Bristol and then rushing off to play rugby.'

Lorna's head was tilted back. 'He's just an old friend,' she said.

'He says he's in love with you.'

'He only *thinks* that, Leo. He can't possibly be in love with me because we haven't seen each other for years. It was a childhood thing, that's all.'

'Then what happened?'

'We grew up. That's what happened. End of story.'

'But you did come down to Bristol, didn't you? No, don't answer that ... none of my business. I'm simply telling you what he's told me. It's what he says, Lorna, so who am I to disagree? He hopes that one day it might all

254

magically come together for you guys. In some respects, of course, he is a rather dull dog with very few tricks. Once he decides on something, you can't easily persuade him otherwise.' He laughed gently. 'He says that the only bridge he wants to build is between the two of you. Not a very imaginative cliché, if that's what it is, but that's Austin for you. So, what do you think?'

'About what?

'About you and him.'

Lorna abruptly stubbed out her cigarette, then pushed the butt out of sight between the slats of the wooden floor. 'You weren't following me because you saw me on the headland, were you? You're here on a spying mission.'

'Lorna ...'

'Austin did put you up to it, didn't he?'

'Lorna ...'

'You *bastard*!' she said loudly, frightening the cicadas, and swept up her cigarettes.

'Austin doesn't know I'm here.'

But Lorna was in full flow and wasn't listening. 'Christ, how gullible do you think I am? All that *shit* about doing law ...'

'He doesn't know I'm here,' he repeated. He was holding up his hands, palms upward. 'I told him I wasn't tired and was going out for a drink. That's not why I followed you.' His voice was soft but insistent and something in its shaken tone made her pause. Now he was standing with his hands palms-down on the table. Somehow, in standing, his chair had toppled backwards.

'Then, why?'

'Because you're a sexy lady, that's why.'

'For fuck's sake, Leo! You spent half the bloody night dancing with Suzie.' Having failed to coax her into bed, he was obviously pursuing the second-best option. Suzie was the sexy one; those beachwear catalogues couldn't all be wrong.

'She's not my type,' said Leo. 'But that's why I needed to know about you and Austin. I didn't want to say something stupid.'

'Stupid?'

'I didn't want to say anything stupid to you.'

'I'm not sure I follow.'

'I wanted to ask,' he said, peeling off his shirt, 'if you wanted to go for a swim.'

* * *

Her first reaction was *Oh My God!* He was a stranger, for Christ's sake! Well, not quite a stranger, but close enough. She again felt a pulse of anger, at the ambiguity of his suggestion and what his definition of a *swim* might actually mean. Say no and it would seem prudish, say yes and, well, what would he assume she had agreed to? And did he mean *skinny* dipping? She watched him warily as he stood by the water's edge, his shirt discarded to the sand, hands deep in the pockets of his khaki shorts and his lion's mane ruffling in the breeze from the water.

'It's the best time to swim,' he said over his shoulder. 'It's when the temperatures of the air and water are closest together.'

'I've never swum at night before,' she said, prevaricating. The North Sea was deathly cold even on the hottest day. Nobody, but nobody, ever went swimming in North Berwick at night, no matter how much they'd had to drink.

Leo seemed lost in thought, his feet being sloshed by incoming waves, face fixed on the horizon. She followed his gaze to a far point where featureless sea was met by stars. They seemed to be closer here; larger, more luminous, and more of them. In Scotland, the stars seemed cold and distant; here they felt warm, each one a small sun warming her skin. It was then that she really did feel herself to be in a place far away; a distant country, a place where normal rules need not apply. Her eyes returned to Leo.

Partly, of course, it was the alcohol. She no longer knew whether Leo had been sent on Austin's fool's errand, but it now seemed of little importance. She didn't really believe that Austin still loved her but, whatever his feelings, they were his to sort out. She hadn't led him on, so was innocent of hurting him. Immediately, she felt both alive and peaceful. The evening with Austin had passed off without incident; emotional fireworks had failed to detonate. She was safe from his professed love.

There was only the sound of cicadas and the lap of water. The water seemed to beckon her, recognising a child who used to jump off harbour walls and, without further thought, she slipped off her clothes and joined Leo at the water's edge. This was a place of contradictions, a ramshackle taverna that could only be supplied by boat, but which was only a few minutes' walk from a bustling town. The evening before, she'd been packing in an Edinburgh drizzle and now here she was by a warm sea. Above was a road, above that the stars. In front of her was also Leo.

'Sorry, didn't think to bring a bikini.'

'Me neither.'

'Believe me, Leo, a bikini wouldn't suit you.'

'Even a nice pink one?' He seemed rather startled by her nakedness, not sure whether to look at her.

'Well, maybe a lacy pink one. Samantha could choose it for you.'

'If I ever meet her.'

'*When*, rich boy. You are *destined* to meet her.'

She ran into the sea and dived. She had always felt

safe under the water. Once she had been pulled from North Berwick's swimming pool by a lifeguard. She'd been under the water for so long he'd thought she might be in trouble. But she hadn't been; she'd only been lying on the bottom, listening to silence.

Lorna broached the surface, tasting salt on her lips, and laughing for no reason. She felt free, filled with sudden energy. The cocktail of sea and stars had released her, making her innocent of anything she might now do.

Lorna frowned at this thought, and sat by the water facing out to sea. She didn't know Leo, and he was Austin's best friend and here they were, naked, Lorna sitting languidly in shallow water by the beach to watch Leo slide down his trousers. This was the strangest contradiction of them all and it sent a frisson down her spine; he was a stranger, but a friendly stranger who had followed her. She drew up her legs and laid her chin on her knees. A larger wave, the wake of an unseen ship, toppled her and she lay, laughing in the surf, trying to sit up again. Then Leo was at her side, his strong arms pulling her to her feet. Intentionally or by accident, his hands found her breasts. She hesitated for a moment, then turned to him, absolved of everything, and pulled him down to the sand. He tasted of salt and his lion's mane was plastered to his scalp. A cocktail of time and place had removed all inhibition, leaving only this moment under the Greek sky and strong arms holding her tight. In the moonlight, the beach was the colour of yellow brick-dust. Lorna put a finger to Leo's lips and shook her head; she didn't want to hear words he might not mean.

* * *

Afterwards, they lay on the warm sand, Leo on his back looking at the stars, Lorna on her side with her head on his chest. She listened to his heart, her eyes closing, and they lay silently for a long while, half asleep, waves touching their feet. Lorna felt immensely peaceful. It was a new feeling for her. She was unused to freedom, from being away from books. Her nerves were energised: like the princess and the pea, she could feel every grain of sand under her body.

Lorna nuzzled into his chest hair, tasting salt, and gently stroked his face. Her eyes were closed and she was remembering another holiday, much further back when she was part of a proper family, and when she'd first fallen under Darth Vader's spell. She knew that bad things were starting to gather, but on that riverboat they were insulated from them. She knew that Tom was ill, but it didn't seem serious. He'd just be a little bit sick, then he'd feel better. She also knew that her dad had lost his job, but who cared about that? The world was full of people who worked and her father was just another person. It was the first time she'd tasted lamb cutlets. The best day of all was when they returned the boat. They had time to kill before heading north. Best let the kids run riot, her mum had said. That way they'll sleep in the car. I know, I'll make us a picnic.

Her dad turned off the engine and then removed the key from the boat's ignition. 'Finished with engines,' he said, like a real ship's captain. Lorna thought he looked sad.

They ate the picnic by a riverbank, with river boats puttering up and down. Lorna remembered the long grass on the riverbank and how it rustled in the breeze. Her mum, perennially unsure what her family liked in sandwiches, had made every combination possible. The result was the best picnic ever, on the sunniest day of the year. On the river was a white barge, water bubbling from its stern as it put its engine into reverse and negotiated its way to a small wooden jetty. The boat moored against it. There was also a pub, she remembered, and another man came out of the pub to help. He helped the elderly man on the boat to thread the heavy mooring lines into large rings on the jetty. He was wearing a sailor's cap and at his feet, darting everywhere, was a small terrier.

Lorna snapped her eyes open. She knew that Leo was also awake, his pulse had quickened, and his eyelids fluttered. She kissed his chest and felt seawater slosh against her ankles.

'These kids of mine,' he asked. 'Do they have names?'

'Gemima and Alexander.' She smiled. 'Perfect names for the offspring of a Leonard.'

'And will I really own a 4x4?'

'Compulsory, I'm afraid … Goes with the territory.'

He raised himself on one arm to look at her, and kissed her on the nose. 'Do you hate everybody you have sex with?'

'Not everybody, no.'

'Just me, then.' She couldn't tell if he was being serious; his lion's mane had blown across his eyes.

'Not even you, Leo.' She smiled, kissing him back, her hands framing his face, memorising it with her touch.

His strong arms had pulled her close, and she hoisted one leg over his. 'Lorna, you're a teeny-weeny bit mad.'

'Probably. Didn't Austin tell you?'

They kissed for a while, listening to the cicadas, as a faint glow on the horizon signalled a new day. He kissed her forehead and her eyes. 'You could always just fuck me again,' she suggested.

'Might as well live dangerously,' he replied.

MUNCHKINS

'Lorna, you slut!

'Suzie!'

'Well, what else am I supposed to think? First you warn me off him then you shag him yourself!'

'For heaven's sake, Suze, shut it!' Lorna leaned across the table, trying to indicate that other hotel guests were within earshot. 'It wasn't like that,' she protested in a hissing whisper.

Suzie grimaced, then waved her hands. Lorna had lit a cigarette.

They were having a late breakfast on the pavement outside the hotel, shielded from the morning sun by a stripy red awning. Suzie was wearing a fat grin.

'And did the earth move?' she asked, theatrically lowering her sunglasses. Across the street, an elderly Greek man sat in a café drinking a miniscule cup of coffee. Most of his teeth were missing; those that remained were stained dark brown.

'It did sort of tremble a bit,' conceded Lorna in a low voice, casting an eye around the other tables. Most seemed occupied by young couples interested only in each other. However, close by, were a middle-aged man and woman who seemed to be spreading margarine onto their rolls with excessive care. 'But, *please* ... not so bloody loud.'

Suzie, as Lorna well knew, wasn't equipped with volume control. 'Little Miss Love on a one-night stand! Whatever would her mummy say?'

Across the street, the old Greek had unfolded a newspaper. In one hand was a rosary; small beads dripped between fingers.

'Shut it, Suze! People are listening!'

'Then *let* them listen, sweetie!' She looked around, spotted the middle-aged couple, and smiled sweetly. Both returned her smile and went back to their rolls. 'So, how much trembling did the earth actually do?'

Suzie had been asleep when Lorna eventually got back, creeping up the stairs to their room like a guilty schoolgirl. But at least Suze had left the door unlocked. Lorna had brushed her teeth and dropped into a deep sleep. She hadn't needed to tell Suzie anything but, since they were best friends, reticence wasn't an option.

'It trembled quite a bit actually,' she said.

'In which case,' Suzie commanded, once more lowering her dark glasses and winking across the table, 'I demand that you tell me everything. Every single, little detail, babe. Leave nothing out. Auntie Susan wants to know precisely what you've been up to.'

It was usually Suzie who got to tell these tales. Suzie, with her blonde hair and curves. Not usually Lorna, with her head in a law book. In hindsight, she detected a hint of jealousy.

'I hardly dare mention it,' said Suzie, 'but what about Austin?'

Lorna looked across the street where the old man was talking loudly to an old women dressed in black, and who had even fewer teeth than him. Didn't they have dentists in Greece? 'Leo promised not to say anything.'

'But can he be trusted?'

Lorna stubbed out her cigarette. Austin and Leo would be at the airport. 'Que sera, sera,' she said, realising that she hadn't eaten anything, that Suzie had scoffed all the rolls, and that her coffee had gone cold.

* * *

She supposed that Leo could be trusted because he had no reason to tell Austin anything. They shared a bijou flat together, listening to Bill and Monica going hell for leather next door – so sharing a confidence that might, no, *would*, cause trouble was utterly pointless. At least that had been Lorna's conclusion as they'd walked back to the town hand in hand in the early morning.

'We could always just elope,' said Leo. 'Run away somewhere. Live happily ever after.'

'Ah, somewhere. Where exactly is *somewhere*?'

'Anywhere,' he said, squeezing her hand. 'Somewhere romantic. A cave perhaps, but with hot and cold running water. A *nice* cave, somewhere hot, near the sea.'

She leaned against his shoulder, bumping him. 'And have to share it with Osama bin Laden? Nice idea, Leo, but no. The HappyMart needs me.'

'The ... *what*?'

'Suzie gets to be a model. I work on the checkout at HappyMart. It's a sort of downmarket Tesco, mainly selling sausages. It's in Edinburgh,' she added, to make it sound more glamorous.

He gave a low laugh. 'Sounds lovely! That's probably what I'll be eating tonight. Sausages.'

'Back to reality, eh?' She thought for a few moments. 'What will you tell Austin?'

He took a few moments to reply. 'Don't know. Does he need to know anything? Probably not, so probably nothing. Might just say I slept on the beach. I've done it a couple of times this holiday.'

Lorna jabbed him in the ribs. 'What, picking up other desperate girls and forcing them to have sex? You've done that to *other* innocent victims? God, Leo, you're not just posh, you're a posh *monster*.'

He squeezed her hand again. Now they had reached the far side of the headland, the town laid out ahead of them, and their pace had slowed to a crawl. 'I didn't force you to do anything. I was going to swim with my clothes *on*. It's the way I usually go swimming. It's the way *most* people go swimming. Except you, of course. Or is it a Scottish characteristic?' He stopped, faced her. 'I do want to see you again.'

She put her arms around his neck and they kissed. Then she broke free. 'I'm not called Samantha.'

'You could change your name,' he suggested. 'Little Gem and baby Alexander. What about them? They'll need a mother.'

She smiled and looked across the sand to the town. Early risers could be spotted in the water, all wearing swimwear as far as she could tell. 'It did mean something, didn't it, Leo?' She threaded her arm through his. 'You'll call me, right?'

He extracted a mobile phone from a pocket and dutifully tapped her number into it. Lorna double-checked that he'd entered it correctly, the lawyer inside her making sure of the detail. But she couldn't reciprocate because her phone was in her hotel room. 'You could come to Bristol,' he suggested; then after a pause, 'although that might not be a good idea.'

'Not good.' she agreed, 'especially since you live in a complete dump. Has anyone ever thought to clean that carpet? It's a health hazard!'

'The thought has crossed our minds. Several times, actually. But we haven't quite got around to doing anything about it. Beer gets spilled on it, that's the trouble. So there's no real point in cleaning it because more beer will get spilled on it.'

Now moving at a snail's pace, they arrived at a fork

in the road. Up one street was Lorna's hotel; his was up the other. 'I could always come and see you,' he said, not quite looking at her. 'I've never been to Scotland. I'd like to see those strange-looking cattle. I could come to your shop and buy some *delicious* sausages.'

'They're not delicious. Leo. They're crap. But you've got my number, right?' said Lorna, suddenly tearful, wondering what the last few hours had been about and who Leo really was. Christ, she didn't even know his surname and now, on the point of goodbye, it seemed an irrelevant piece of information to extract. 'But if I don't see you again, good luck with your life. Remember, Leo, in twenty years from now you'll have a fat wife, two adorable children, and a planet-destroying car. Maybe you'll be happy.'

'With a *fat* wife? You never said anything about Samantha being *fat!* How did that happen?'

'Too many chocolates, I expect. What with you being such a successful lawyer, she doesn't need to get off the sofa.'

'Lazy cow.' He looked genuinely upset, as if Lorna had accidentally mapped out a life for him that he had secretly been dreading. 'You know, if I ever do meet a real Samantha, I'll run a mile. No matter how attractive she is, I now *know* she'll turn into a large sloth.'

'Well, you've been warned.'

He shuffled his feet, kicking up dust. 'It was fun though, wasn't it? A bit unexpected, but fun. I'll miss you,' he added.

Lorna wasn't sure if he was saying so long or goodbye, and didn't want to think about it. 'Call me, posh boy,' she said and kissed him hard on the mouth, her arms entwining his neck and then, with tears in her eyes she broke free, turned and hurried up the hill, forcing herself

265

not to look back. She thought he might run after her, calling her name, and listened for his footsteps but when she reached her hotel, cleaners already mopping at the tiled reception floor, and did look back, he was lost to sight.

* * *

After breakfast Lorna and Suzie went to the beach. Lorna lay on her towel and read a book from behind dark glasses. Suzie, topless and with only a thong for company, had brought a stack of magazines. Soon, however, she was playing beach volleyball with a bunch of Greek boys. The boys had first circled, like sharks, then sent an emissary who could speak English. It was Suzie they wanted although, since they were Greek and polite, Lorna was also invited. They wouldn't take no from Suzie, but were happy enough to accept it from Lorna.

It wasn't a game of skill, but an art in showing off. It wasn't about playing a winning shot, but about who could jump the highest or smash the ball the hardest. Winning wasn't important, bravado was everything. After every point there were high fives and macho posturing. In the middle was Suzie, the only girl. Lorna saw that the Greek boys didn't offer to pick up the ball when it came Suzie's way; it was much more interesting watching Suzie bend down to pick it up. If Lorna had seen this, she knew Suzie would have noticed. But unlike her, Suzie didn't mind. Effervescent and without nerves, Suzie loved attention. She enjoyed the way men's eyes followed her, surreptitiously drinking her in. It was the same with cameras. She flirted with them without fear. The stud in her navel caught the sun as she jumped and turned.

Lorna positioned herself under their beach umbrella and closed her eyes. She dozed, thinking about Leo, about water lapping at their legs, the first smear of a new day lighting his face. Thinking about Leo brought her abruptly to Austin, and she opened her eyes just as Suzie lay down beside her, perspiring.

'Suze, you're a tease,' said Lorna. Her mouth was dry and she sat up and drank some water from a plastic bottle. It had been in the sun and was tepid.

'If you've got it, flaunt it, babe.'

The Greek boys had lost interest in beach volleyball now their star had left the field. They were in a huddle, chatting, casting around for a new mascot to take Suzie's place. Like a pride of lions, they had snared their prey only for Suzie to escape.

'Fancy a swim?' asked Suzie.

* * *

Afterwards, Suzie made Lorna take her the headland to the next beach. A caïque was in the shallows by the beach, a rope from its prow tethered under a large stone. Crates of beer and vegetables were being unloaded by a posse of young Greeks wearing beige shorts and white T-shirts. In the darkness, the cove had seemed magical; a hidden place that was theirs alone. In daylight, Lorna saw litter below the olive trees, an empty Coke can floating by the water's edge. The beach now teemed with people, some brown, others alarmingly pink. She spotted a grossly fat couple who had been on their plane. Yesterday, the man had been wearing a football shirt and she'd shrunk into her seat to let him pass by. His solidly large wife, unwisely wearing only bikini bottoms, was eating cake.

'Bloody hell!' said Suzie, eyeing up the woman. 'Blancmange eating blancmange. Fucking munchkins.'

The ramshackle taverna had come to life. Mournful Greek music played from speakers tied under a plastic awning. A grapevine trailed up the wooden supports and dripped from wooden beams. Underneath, where Leo had peeled off his shirt and dared her to follow, red tablecloths had been spread out. The bar had regained purpose; the barbeque lit and smoking. A waitress with red hair was circling the tables with trays of beer and soft drinks. Further up the beach, Lorna saw several couples who were completely naked, including another couple she recognised from the plane and who were, judging from their colour, already in danger of inconvenient sunburn. This beach, Leo had told her, is called Paradise Beach. The next beach down, which you can only get to by boat, is called Super Paradise. You don't want to know what goes on there, he'd said. When pressed, it turned out that Leo didn't really know. He hadn't been to it, he'd just heard stuff.

They found a table out of the sun and ordered kebabs, salad, and beer. The salad came with plump tomatoes and goat's cheese. Suzie had finished most of it, and the bread, before Lorna had even finished her cigarette.

'So where exactly did the deed take place?' asked Suzie. 'I have a curious desire to know *all* the details.'

Lorna pointed to the seashore. The caïque was being pushed from the beach, its motor puttering to life in a plume of dense smoke. The boat turned and headed towards the headland.

'Maybe they'll erect a plaque,' said Suzie. '*Lorna Love got laid here.*' She seemed to find this hilarious and cackled. 'Will you see him again?' she asked, demolishing a bowl of black olives.

'I don't know, Suze. It was a silly, silly thing that shouldn't really have happened.' She ground out the cigarette, not really knowing what she did feel, and pushed the remains between the floor's wooden slats. She could still feel his arms around her, his mouth against hers. Her memories were raw yet they felt unreal. Had she really taken all her clothes off? Had *it* really taken place? She hardly knew him, but remembered the stars and a welling sense of liberation. 'If I saw him again, it wouldn't be the same.' Lorna shrugged and made a grab for one of the last remaining olives. 'Everything might be a let-down. I think he probably feels the same way.'

'You only *think* he feels the same way?'

'I didn't ask him, Suze. Maybe I should have asked, but I didn't. There again, I didn't really want to know.'

'It's just that fuck 'em and leave 'em has never been your motto, Lorna.'

'For God's sake! Shush!' Suzie, as always, was oblivious to other people, simply not caring what secrets she shared. Lorna sighed. 'I don't even know his surname,' she admitted feeling, despite herself, a little sluttish.

'Dove. Austin told me.'

'Dove, like the bird?'

'What other kind of *dove* is there, sweetie?'

Lorna thought for a few moments, looking over the sea. 'Then if we ever do see each other again, we'll be the Loveydoveys. God, that's worse than the Lovebirds!' But at least she would have progressed from a generic form of wildlife to a specific species, and smiled to herself. When she looked back to the table, all the bread and olives had been eaten by Suzie, who now looked at her watch. 'All being well, they'll be landing soon. But it does seem a pity,' she said, 'to have had the earth tremble and not want to repeat the experience. Earth-trembling is so very rare. Suppose he does tell Austin,' she suggested, lowering her sunglasses and looking at Lorna over the top rim. 'What then?'

'He won't.'

'But he might,' persisted Suzie.

'So what's there to tell? We talked, we went for a swim, we made love. End of story, Suze. It happened, now it's over.'

'Not for Austin it isn't.'

'I refuse to feel guilty about Austin,' said Lorna with some venom. It was her life and she had a right to get on with it.

'D'you know, it's a pity he still fancies you,' said Suzie, unexpectedly wistful. 'Know what, sweetie? I've always, *always* fancied him to bits.'

The waitress with the red hair brought them plates of kebabs and another bowl of salad. She spoke with an Australian accent and was forever casting loving glances towards the barbeque and the dangerously good-looking chef in beige shorts and white T-shirt who was behind it, who slightly resembled Keanu Reeves. Lorna stared open-mouthed at her friend. Suzie had never *ever* mentioned that she fancied Austin.

* * *

After lunch, Lorna lay in the shade and read her book. She didn't want to get burned on the first day. Suzie had gone to the other end of the beach to join the naturists, determined to achieve the perfect tan. Once again she dozed, her book folded against her chest, and thought about Leo. Had he arrived back safely? Had his plane disintegrate in mid-air?

Suzie rejoined her later in the afternoon and they went back to the beach bar for large slabs of watermelon. The Australian waitress brought over their plates, then lingered.

'Just arrived, huh?'

'Yesterday,' said Lorna.

The waitress said that her name was Simone and that,

like them, she'd come here on holiday. She was originally from Sydney and had been working in London, mostly in bars around Earl's Court, which is more Aussie than English. Then she'd come here and met Nico, whose family owned the taverna, and stayed. Nico was the chef, she explained. They were married now, and had a place in town. 'He is rather gorgeous, don't you think, and how did you like his kebabs? Now I feel as if I've been here forever. That's the trouble with Greece,' said Simone. 'You lose track of time. I don't know what it is about the place, but I just love Crete. When we got married,' said Simone, 'my mum came over from Oz. Had to, really. Nico's family couldn't all afford to go to Australia. Where are you guys from?' she asked.

'Scotland,' said Lorna.

'Edinburgh,' added Suzie.

'Well, have fun,' said Simone, finally realising that she had other customers and rushing off to serve them.

Lorna switched on her mobile. She had only one voice message, from Austin.

You utter bitch, Lorna! How could you do that to me! I know you don't feel like I feel but, for God's sake, my best friend? My ex-best friend, as it happens. I was on the balcony this morning. Saw you hand in hand on the beach. Christ, Lorna! Anyway, I hope you're both really enjoying your holiday.

'Trouble, babe?'

Lorna handed over the phone and Suzie listened to the message. 'It would appear, sweetie, that Leo did tell him.'

'I don't suppose he had much option.' Lorna stared across the beach, her stomach in a tight knot. But what exactly had she done wrong? She wasn't Austin's property. The fat couple from the plane were now the colour of beetroot. Two children at the water's edge were throwing a frisbee to one another.

'I refuse to feel guilty,' she said. 'Jesus, Suze, what gives Austin the right to slag me off?

She couldn't face speaking to him, but knew she should say something. She pondered what to do, the knot in her stomach growing tighter, then decided that she didn't want to spoil the sunshine by having an argument, or listening to another tirade. She certainly didn't need to justify what she'd done. Why the hell should she? She might have hurt him, but she was innocent of doing it intentionally.

Instead, she sent him a text.

I'm sorry.

It wasn't until later that she remembered sending him the same two words from Edinburgh airport. Then, at least, she'd had the courage to speak them.

* * *

Leo didn't text or phone. She had expected some form of communication, if only to explain what had happened between him and Austin, and didn't know what to think when there was nothing. Had they fought like knights over her? Each declaring their eternal love for the weirdo leftie? Or talked it over in the pub and decided that Lorna Love was a slag not worth bothering about? That seemed the more likely outcome. She had, after all, flown to Bristol on a whim for a casual weekend with an *ex*-boyfriend and then, on another whim, had enjoyed casual sex (twice) on a beach with someone whose full name she didn't know.

Maybe, she decided, he'd phone when she got back, and held tight to this thought until, slightly panicked, she thought, no, he's lost his phone *and* her number. Or maybe he didn't like telephones, or the million-pound expense of phoning Greece. Suzie's agent didn't call with either good or bad news about her audition and so at regular intervals each day both girls could be found frowning at their mobiles and mouthing obscenities, Suzie audibly. Most nights they went into Ag Nik. Gemini was good and had a mosaic of small lights over the dancefloor; it was like dancing across stars. The Adelphi was good too, and had cargo nets hanging from the roof. It was in the Adelphi that Suzie met Asim, a computer programmer with a thin moustache from Birmingham. He was on holiday by himself and Suzie spent a few nights at his hotel. Suzie didn't hugely like him, she explained, but he was exceptionally good … if Lorna knew what she meant. The computer programmer flew home the day before they did.

They decided to spend their last night quietly. They still had to pack – Suzie especially. So they crossed the headland and ate in the beach bar. As always, Nico was at his barbeque. He waved and smiled, recognising them from previous visits. Simone brought over a jug of chilled wine, not having to be asked, then grilled fish and salad and fussed around them. At the end of the meal she brought sweet liqueurs, on the house, and hoped they'd had a good holiday. Will you come back? she asked.

Of course, they said automatically.

Oh, and would you mind if my brother contacted you? He's coming to Edinburgh. He's finished with college. Fancies a year out. You don't have to put him up or anything. He's already got himself sorted. Just show him about, that sort of thing. He wants to work in radio, said Simone.

Of course, they said again, not expecting ever to see Simone's brother.

His name's Joe. Joe Crowe, she said.

STARS

Mercifully, Trinity had mended the chewed wires and the lights had come back on. Lorna opened her eyes to bright light. For a while she lay and looked at the ceiling, fruitlessly willing herself to sleep, then dressed in shorts and a T-shirt, and, opening her front door, padded soundlessly along the corridor. At the end of the corridor was an open space in which leather chairs had been placed around a glass table. On the table were well-thumbed magazines and, in a crystal vase, a bunch of wilting daffodils. She'd always liked daffodils; they reminded her of spring and new beginnings. There was often a large bowl of them in their sitting room window in North Berwick.

She pressed her face to the outer observation window and looked across space to Heaven's other hull.

Trouble sleeping, petal?

Lorna didn't answer, just stared outwards.

It's all been a bit of shock, hasn't it? Not at all what you expected.

'I didn't know what to expect,' said Lorna. The glass was cold against her forehead and again she felt a stab of pain in her arm. Involuntarily, she winced.

It'll pass, sweetie. In time.

'But how much, Trinity?' Other memories had been nudging in. 'And why is my friend angry with me?'

I cannot say.

Lorna suddenly felt close to tears. 'For God's sake, Trinity, why am I here?' Lorna was almost shouting, voice cracking. There was a short silence.

He has a plan for you, Lorna. That's all I know.

Lorna, still looking outwards, noticed that only the centre portion of the other hull was illuminated. Most of the huge structure was in darkness. It looked desolate and empty and, again she realised, much too large.

Now that Leo had come into sharp focus, Lorna realised that she hadn't quite told Suzie the truth in Greece. Yes, the interlude with Leo had been otherworldly, an encounter in a place far away, and yes, it had been an experience that could never be repeated. But she had wanted to taste the reality of him again, to see how it would compare. He hadn't called and so she had had to think of their brief relationship as a holiday fling – a bit of harmless fun before the plane left for Bristol. He hadn't got to shag the drop-dead gorgeous one and had had to make do with her plainer, slightly weird friend. Is that what Leo thought about her, she had wondered? Was that why he hadn't called? Or was he simply being practical, feeling that the distance between them, from Bristol to Edinburgh, was too great? Lorna hadn't blamed him, whatever his reasons, and maybe it had been best that they'd left it at that. While Leo's silence had signified a rejection, perhaps, she'd thought, it was also a kindness.

Slowly, the dull ache in her arm subsided and she walked back to her apartment. It wasn't home, and could never be home, however many IKEA furnishings Trinity installed. Home contained hope, and here there was none; just random memories recreated in chipped mirrors and cigarette-burnt sofas. She lay down on her bed and no sooner had she closed her eyes than she found herself walking in a place she did not recognise. She could feel a breeze on her cheek and smell summer. Although she had never been there, it seemed so real. There was a river, swollen by a recent storm. The ground was wet and her feet sloshed through mud. It seemed a dream of utter loneliness, almost of despair, and Lorna woke up feeling tired and wretched, her head throbbing and her arm sore once more.

Good morning, sweetie.

'Good morning, Trinity.'

Sleep well?

'No.'

Trinity seemed to sigh. *Regeneration, young Lorna, is a process of change, and change takes time. It doesn't happen overnight. But before I forget, Irene wants to see you on the High Street.*

'The High Street?'

North Berwick High Street. She thought you might like to have a bit of home in Heaven.

'North Berwick High Street?'

It's the main street in North Berwick, I believe.

'I know that, Trinity. But what's it doing here.'

It's just a street, petal, so it doesn't really do *anything. Can you be more specific?*

'For starters, how could a bit of North Berwick have found itself here?'

I had a rummage in the local planning department and compared the original plans with Google Earth.

'OK, then maybe somebody should have asked me first, Trinity. I don't want to be reminded.'

Reminded of what, petal? Of being dead?

'There's enough weird stuff going on my head. I don't need any more weird stuff.'

In which case I shall discuss it with Irene. Or perhaps you'd like to do that? She's waiting for you now.

* * *

The flat in Arthuria Road had brought with it a sense of liberation. She had grown up and spread her wings, escaping the claustrophobia of her North Berwick home and the petty rules that her mother laid down. At home, shoes had to be taken off at the front door; the table had to be properly set for supper, which always had to be on the table at seven o'clock, after which Lorna would wash up the saucepans and plates while her father dried. It wouldn't have been so bad if she could have sometimes done the drying-up, and she did occasionally suggest it, but after years of practice their household had its unspoken rules. Lorna rather doubted whether her father could be flexible and wash a saucepan. The first weeks in her new flat were a blissful release from banality, which her brief stint in halls of residence had done nothing to assuage.

In Arthuria Road she could lie in late without someone having a shower and waking her up. She could work late without her mother turning on every light in the room in case she damaged her eyesight. And she didn't have to listen to her father's titanic flatulence when he thought nobody was listening. Sure, Suzie wasn't exactly quiet, but Lorna usually found them comfortable sounds – even the bass notes booming from her bedroom – because they each sounded like freedom. She was an adult, with her own flat and front door, through which Lorna would generally appear at about ten thirty at night, Monday through Thursdays. Not to mention the occasional dayshift, eight to four, at weekends.

Her job at the HappyMart had not yet instilled any burning desire for a career in the retail sector. Far from it. But it was a world she knew. Her mother worked in a bakery, and most of her mother's friends – and most of her relatives, come to think of it, except Aunt Meg who was on invalidity benefit on account of being *a little heavy*, as her mother diplomatically put it. Before Tom's death, Lorna could remember Aunt Meg standing on the landing outside their front door, hands on hips, face putrid, having only had to negotiate a couple of flights of stairs.

Lorna had experienced a small moment of panic when she first handed her job application to KEVIN – a brief stab of fear that the HappyMart might be the pinnacle of her career, and that the next forty years would be spent selling packets of bacon and crisps, which seemed to make up most of the HappyMart's sales. When someone bought a lettuce, Lorna had to refrain from congratulating them, although the gaudy badge on her livid pink tunic did make it seem a little better. LAURA – HERE TO HELP. She'd lost her correct name badge after her first week, and that was the closest that Mike's small tools and personnel drawer could come up with. She didn't complain; working under an assumed name was better than doing it under her real identity, because if the HappyMart was to trap anybody, it would be Laura's fate, not hers.

Her first day was taken up with training: mainly being shown how to scan through items and take card payments, and then having to do it for real while one of her new colleagues stood at her shoulder. She had to memorise what was on special offer and how to tempt customers to purchase from the *Buy It Today Otherwise Its Gone!!* shelf beside her checkout. She was told how to ask for ID for alcohol sales, what to do if someone took ill in the shop (dial 999), or if they detected shoplifters (dial 999), or discovered a fire (dial 999). She was also instructed to always ask if customers wanted help with their packing. This she quickly decided to ignore. There were old people who were clearly incapable of packing, and who were probably unsure why they'd just purchased eight packets of Jaffa cakes, but who insisted on packing everything themselves and holding up the queue; equally, there were adolescent boys who thought it was a good laugh having someone package up their baked beans and jumbo chocolate bars for them – until she defiantly stared one youth into submission and gave up asking if customers needed help. From then on she acted independently, packing for those who looked as if they needed it, and handing an empty plastic bag to those who didn't.

At knocking-off time, tired from a day at college and an evening at the shop and with a dissertation still to write which had to be handed in the next morning, Lorna would sometimes, and against her better judgement, take home a Pot Noodle for supper. At her interview, KEVIN had breathlessly advised her that staff earned discounts on all purchases, making the HappyMart sound generous and benevolent, and explained that the level of discount rose in line with length of service. Lorna supposed that if she did work there for the next forty years, she could probably live for free, although the food it sold would no doubt have killed her long before then. Across the road was an Indian mini-market which sold real vegetables with earth still on them and real meat that didn't come in shrink-wrap plastic with cartoons of smiling cows. Lorna usually did her weekday food shopping there, much to Mike's palpable astonishment.

Within days, she had started playing the checkout game, which she was told everybody played. It wasn't really a game – there were no winners or losers. It was an exercise in imagining what customers' lives were like or, if that was too hard, what they were planning to cook for their supper. In many cases, it was too easy: the pregnant women who came in for cigarettes, young mothers who came in for pureed baby food and cigarettes, tired-looking professionals who would rummage in the chilled foods section and emerge with one TV dinner (and come in every night and buy the same thing), an older man who would buy a bottle of whisky every evening then hide it in his briefcase, or the very old scruffy man who would regularly buy four tins of dog food and who Lorna would sometimes see in the street but never with a dog.

Everyone complimented her on her tan when she came back from Greece, even Mike, who said she was looking *bronzed and gorgeous* and then, staring at her chest, added: *Isn't Laura looking gorgeous?*, making her wonder if in the HappyMart's mirror-world you were obliged to become whoever your name badge said you were.

On Saturdays she was usually early and forced to wait on the pavement, pacing up and down until one of the managers arrived with the keys to open up. For a shop that sold so little of any value, including nutritional value, there was an inordinate number of locks and keys. Then there was the rigmarole of switching off alarms, switching on lights, making sure the chilled items hadn't been lost to an overnight power cut, checking the float in each till, stacking shelves, checking inventories, and cleaning floors; tasks that were all meticulously itemised on a weekly rota pinned to a corkboard in the staffroom. For some reason, the staffroom, the only part of the shop that was a genuine health hazard, was maintenance-free. Discarded newspapers that had once told yesterday's news now told last month's; the ashtray never spilled over but was never empty, remaining permanently full of butts. It stank of neglect, disillusionment, and stale smoke, which could only be partially alleviated by opening the small window that looked onto the customer car park, and wedging it open with a plank of wood handily placed there by management. Even with the window open it was a depressing and dank place. On cold days, they could have used it as a chill cabinet; on hot days it became a sauna, except for the litter and health and safety notices pinned to the corkboard. Stained and chipped coffee mugs belonging to the HappyMart family were stuck to the room's small table, glued there by a potent mixture of tomato ketchup and salad cream, or so it looked to LAURA, who only dared venture into the staff hell-hole if the weather outside was utterly awful, or if she had a piece of law she absolutely had to learn. Usually she would take her breaks huddled on a bench around the corner, obeying Mike's edict that staff were not allowed to smoke on the pavement directly outside the shop.

It was therefore with waning enthusiasm that Lorna now walked, term over, from her flat to her place of employment, books still under her arm and her laptop in a bag over her shoulder, the sense of freedom that moving into Arthuria Road had kindled being doused daily by the monotonous *beep-beep-beep*, hour after hour, evening after evening, and occasional Saturdays. She had to keep reminding herself that this wouldn't be forever, that it was a means to an end, then feel guilty and traitorous for thinking this: she was the only part-time student in the HappyMart, and shouldn't be thinking bad thoughts about the realities of ordinary peoples' working lives. For most people, this kind of job wasn't a stepping stone or a brief interlude before something better. This was it, year after year, until their shopping bills were entirely paid for by management's generosity.

Yet for the most part, despite the normal grumbles, the rest of the HappyMart family seemed quite content to be there. Maggie, for example, a little overweight and who didn't like to stack the lower shelves in case she did her back in, said that it was the best job she'd ever had. As Maggie was in her mid-forties, Lorna couldn't imagine how bad her other jobs must have been; but Maggie hummed as she worked, and was always smiling. Then there was Vlad, a good-looking boy from Poland, who was lucky to possess a healthy sense of humour since he had to listen cheerfully to Impaler jokes every day. His girlfriend, also Polish, had an utterly improbable first name, with lots of 'z's and 'w's, but had a badge which read GOSIA. Lorna noted how easy it had been to procure VLAD and GOSIA badges from the small tools and personnel drawer, and how difficult a replacement LORNA badge seemed to be. She wondered if this was Mike's revenge for turning his advances down. There was also a nervous young single mother called Steph who the others said was secretly mad, although Lorna saw no evidence of it, and nobody could say why they'd reached this conclusion.

On Saturday morning, just before eight o'clock, Lorna stood impatiently on the pavement as a series of locks were unlocked and, with metallic protest, a thick steel grille, the size and strength of a blast door, thought Lorna, ratcheted upwards. Then there was the inner glass door to open and a complex alarm system to deactivate. The code for this was Top Secret and known only to a select handful of employees, of whom Lorna wasn't one. Once inside, Lorna braved the staffroom to change her fleece for the company's smock, then busied herself with inventories, delivery schedules, and floats for the tills. Other members of staff had now arrived; mostly part-timers like her, but ones who only worked at weekends.

Would Lorna please report to the manager's office. Thank you.

Mike's voice, seeming to come from every surface of the shop. Lorna swallowed her irritation. His office was next door to the staffroom and all he'd had to do was open his door and ask her himself.

She knocked and went into the holy sanctum – little more than a large cupboard – to find Mike behind the rickety desk that took up most of one side of the office and was surrounded by boxes, mostly cartons of cigarettes. A battered steel filing cabinet and plastic chair were the only other items of furniture. There was a laptop open on his desk, switched off, and beside it, a tannoy system with a microphone on a flexible steel tube. Hung from the ceiling were two TV sets, which relayed CCTV pictures from inside the shop. Lorna could see Maggie filling the top shelves of the bakery section, Vlad stacking bread rolls into the lower shelves.

Like the staffroom, Mike's office had a small window overlooking the car park but, unlike the proletariat's, his didn't need a plank of wood to keep it open. A warm breeze sighed through the open window as Mike motioned her to sit down. He appeared to be reading a manila file which on closer inspection had her name on it. Being management, he was allowed the luxury of a crisp white shirt, with HappyMart stencilled on the right breast, and a green tie. However, being of Auntie Meg proportions, his shirt buttons were straining alarmingly and his collar was too small to fasten. It wasn't a good advertisement for the company.

'Thank you, Lorna, for coming to see me.'

'That's all right, I was here anyway.'

Mike looked at her sharply, then put down the closed manila file on his desk. 'Thing is, I've got some rather exciting news to impart to you.' He sat back as he said this, nearly toppling into a large box of Sterling Superkings and looked pleased with himself.

Lorna's heart sank. She just wanted to pay her rent; exciting news from HappyMart was superfluous to requirements. 'I'm all ears,' she replied brightly.

Mike again looked at her sharply and leaned over the table, giving his shirt buttons some respite. 'You've been here a while now, haven't you?'

Lorna nodded warily, wondering what was coming next.

'And you've been ... how shall I put this? ... an exemplary employee. Always punctual, always reliable. A credit to our family.' Christ! thought Lorna, at the mention of *family*, her heart sinking further still. I'm about to be baptised with baked beans. 'Which is why,' Mike continued, 'I would like to be the first to offer my congratulations.'

Lorna had been wondering how Mike managed to circumnavigate his desk to sit behind it, or whether he had to climb over it to reach his switched-off laptop. 'Thank you,' she said after a few moments. 'Um, for what exactly?'

'On your second star.'

'My ... *what?*'

'You have been a checkout operator long enough, Lorna,' said Mike, and with a flourish, handed an envelope over the desk. She opened it to find a single plastic gold star nestling inside. 'From now on, you are a checkout *supervisor*!'

Below LAURA's badge was stuck one gold star. On Mike's badge were four gold stars, denoting his great rank.

'Does it come with a company car?' she asked, trying to decide if her heart could sink any lower and concluding that it had reached rock bottom.

'A modest hourly pay rise,' Mike replied, looking pained, thinking perhaps that Lorna should be turning cartwheels round his cupboard or, better still, kissing him on both cheeks, 'and the satisfaction of knowing you've earned it.'

'Well, put like that ... thank you,' she said. 'May I?' She indicated her badge.

Mike leaned back in his chair, again stretching his

buttons to breaking point, and looking at her like a kindly father on Christmas morning, his young offspring about to open the best present ever. Lorna stuck on her second star, wondering how generals felt when they stuck on theirs.

Mike stood up and reached one arm over the table. Lorna took his hand, muttering *thank you* several times as tears prickled her eyes. She should be happy; other people would be happy. Her mother's bakery apron didn't have any stars on it. His handshake was limp and moist and Lorna had to resist the temptation to wipe her hand down the side of her trousers.

'Perhaps we could celebrate later?' suggested Mike, ever-hopeful, and raised an eyebrow.

Back in the shop, Maggie asked what the pow-wow had been about. 'Not been fired, have you? Shit, that wouldn't be good.'

Lorna indicated her badge.

'Fuck me!' said Maggie. 'You've been promoted! Here, Vlad, look at this! Little Miss Clever's been made a fucking *supervisor*!'

Lorna sat bleakly behind her checkout, wondering what her supervisory duties entailed, if they were any – Mike hadn't mentioned anything – now fully aware what the other members of the HappyMart family called her behind her back. For a few minutes, it was all she could do to stop herself crying. The others would have thought they were tears of joy, and she couldn't have faced that humiliation. A second star! And only working part-time! Well done, girl! No need to cry! Wish I could get a second star! She was also aware of the CCTV camera at the front of the shop, relaying black-and-white pictures back to Mike's office. Perhaps he was looking at them now, the kindly father looking after his flock, and abruptly she pushed back her little swivel chair and marched outside for a cigarette. She badly needed to regain some composure and fill her lungs with something more wholesome than Mike's body odour.

* * *

For the rest of the day, she glumly *beep-beeped* through her customers' groceries, not playing the game, not bothering to deconstruct peoples' lives from chocolate biscuits, tea bags, and buy-one-get-one-free washing powder. She only had to stare down one youth who, playing with his MP3 player, expected his cigarettes, vodka, and cans of lager to be bagged for him. Seeing the look on her face, he'd hurriedly packed them himself, making Lorna feel marginally better. None of her regulars commented on her second gold star. It probably wasn't something anybody noticed. As the day wore on, it seemed as time itself had slowed down; she would look at the wall clock over Mike's door and, when she looked again what seemed hours later, only a minute would have passed.

During her induction to HappyMart, KEVIN had explained the corporate ethos behind the franchise and its slogan *Where The Price Is Always Happy*! It was a brand, he explained, that represented good value, a brand in touch with the aspirations of ordinary people. More than anything, he explained, it was a brand that reached out to today's shoppers, whoever they were. Our corporate colours, he explained, represent the colours of the rainbow, from dawn to sunset, of different people within the HappyMart family working together within one integrated whole – a new concept of retail modernity, he continued, now reading word for word from a company leaflet, and obviously not convinced by the seemingly random splodges of colour that represented their corporate identity. Lorna looked at the small smattering of customers in the shop. There was an old man in a grey mackintosh whose only purchase, nestling at the bottom of his wire basket, was a jumbo packet of sausages. In aisle three, a rather large young mother had bought ice-cream and chocolate cake. Her baby daughter slept serenely in a pushchair. In aisle four, an elderly lady in a tweed coat was humming loudly to herself, and had been staring at a freezer cabinet of frozen vegetables for several minutes. The HappyMart family, staff and customers alike, often seemed to Lorna to be equally dysfunctional.

'Babe!'

Lorna looked up from her reverie to find Suzie standing beside her checkout, the first time her friend had ever braved the shop. 'Lorna, I've got news!'

Lorna pointed to her badge.

'Oh right,' said Suzie. 'Laura, I'm sorry.'

'Don't worry, people are always confusing us. Peas in a pod, we are. If you like, I could pass on a message?' she suggested.

'Thank you, Laura. Anyway, I'd be *so* grateful if you could tell Lorna that I got the part.' Suzie started to jump up and down and clap her hands, something that Mike had obviously spotted on his TV monitor because he was now outside his cupboard door and looking over. 'They want me, babe! I got the part!'

By then, Lorna was on Suzie's side of the checkout, both girls jumping up and down and squealing. The elderly customer in the mackintosh, now clutching a packet of digestive biscuits to accompany his sausages, stood forlorn and unnoticed, a banknote in his hand. 'Oh God, Suzie. Great! Fantastic! Well done!'

Suzie stopped jumping and held Lorna's shoulders in both hands. 'We must drink wine and celebrate!' she intoned loudly in a French accent, now holding up one hand and placing the other across her chest – Suzie's utterly unconvincing Napoleon impression.

'But it's not four o'clock, Suze …'

Suzie didn't bother looking at her watch. 'It is now, sweetie.'

CLICK

Lorna was barely able to change out of her smock and into her fleece before Suzie had swept her out of the HappyMart and marched her into central Edinburgh and into The Broadway, a basement cocktail bar much favoured by Suzie, dimly lit by candles that had melted over bottles. Drinking cocktails was one of Suzie's affectations, one she had adopted before even leaving school and, although Lorna didn't much care for them, it was Suzie who was paying and had the right therefore to choose where they would start the process of getting 'utterly shit-faced, babe'. First impressions of The Broadway weren't good. It smelled unpleasantly like Mike's office.

'Death by Cointreau?'

'Yuck!' Lorna pulled a face.

'Vampire's Bite?'

'What?'

'Hm. Mostly vodka and tomato juice. A bit Bloody Maryish, with a splash of Jamaican rum, Tia Maria ...'

Lorna's mouth puckered to a sour oval. 'God, no! Isn't there anything remotely drinkable?'

'There's Arthur's Quest.' In the bad light, Suzie had to squint at the menu. 'A subtle blend of whisky and green ginger ...'

'No!' Lorna shuddered.

'Or a Passionate Knight, perhaps? Something to *really* get you going. Apparently.'

'Is that with a "k" or an "n"?'

'K'

'Ah well, just as long as he takes his armour off first. What *is* it?'

'Lots of gin and Bacardi.' Suzie looked doubtful, then brightened. 'Shall we?'

'I suppose,' conceded Lorna.

'Suppose nothing!' commanded Suzie.

She returned to their table with two brimming bowls of opaque liquid topped with spreading foliage and, inserted through a slice of lemon, a red umbrella. 'Bottoms up,' said Lorna, and tentatively sipped from her oversize glass. 'God, it tastes as awful as it sounds.'

Suzie patted her on the knee and sipped from her bowl. 'Actually, it's not that bad. It just takes a bit of getting used to.'

'It's ghastly, Suze!'

'Well, it's Saturday night and cocktails are perfect for getting pissed.' Her long fingers wrapped round the glass and she winked across the table.

'It's still afternoon by my watch,' said Lorna, and was momentarily distracted by laughter from the next table as a tray of exotic cocktails was brought across by a tall man in leather trousers. Some were in the same goldfish bowls that Lorna and Suzie were drinking from, others in impossibly long flutes. One of their glasses had a lit sparkler that fizzed brightly in the dim bar. Lorna saw that several of the other men in the group were wearing leather trousers.

Lorna leaned across the table. '*And* you've taken me to a gay bar!'

Suzie shrugged, having obviously never given it much thought, and finished her glass. 'Drink up, petal. We've got Arthur's Quest to try next.'

'Well, it can't be any worse than this,' said Lorna, looking cagily about and hoping there was nobody she knew there.

'I suspect it could be quite a *lot* worse,' replied Suzie. 'You really don't like cocktails, do you?'

'Suzie, you *know* I don't like cocktails,' she said, tasting a strange mixture of alcohol on her tongue and reaching for a cigarette. 'What exactly *is* Demon's Revenge?'

Much later, they ended up at a champagne bar in Leith, which looked out over a disused wharf on which floated crisp packets and plastic bottles. It was a part of Edinburgh's gentrification: redundant warehouses finding new leases of life as up-market homes; old streets being reinvented with gastro-pubs and themed restaurants. How or why they came to be there Lorna couldn't remember the next morning. It was probably somewhere that Suzie had been recommended. On first inspection, it was much like The Broadway; the same candles melting over bottles, lots of exposed brickwork, and bare wooden flooring. The candles did little to lift its reverential gloom, and Lorna almost had to feel her way to the bar, her feet sliding in sawdust.

Suzie was already there and drumming her fingers impatiently on the counter. 'Who do I have to sleep with to get a drink around here?' she demanded.

Suzie was more than a little drunk and alarmingly loud, even by her standards, and immediately there was frozen silence. A dozen heads turned in their direction. It did, however, attract the attention of the barman, a spotty youth with lank hair who had been leaning on the counter and chatting to a couple of customers. He rushed down from the other end of the bar, his face flushed.

'That would be me,' he offered hopefully with an encouraging smile. His encrusted face looked like the surface of the moon.

'In which case,' said Suzie, enunciating clearly and

brushing back hair, 'we'll have a bottle of house champagne and two glasses. Oh, and peanuts. Might as well push the boat out,' she said over her shoulder. Lorna was wishing she was invisible.

They found a corner seat, looking out onto dark water. Across the disused dock was a building site, with long shadows and a tall crane. Through the shadows she could discern an advertising hoarding, announcing the imminent arrival of two and three bedroom executive apartments. Lorna wondered when an apartment could be considered *executive*. Were factory workers *allowed* to live in an executive apartment?

'Just in case I haven't said it already, congratulations,' said Lorna, for about the hundredth time.

It wasn't exactly a starring role but Suzie would have her name in the credits. Much further up the pecking order were Kate Winslet and Hugh Grant. She'd been on tenterhooks throughout their Greek holiday, but had heard nothing and assumed the worst. Then, that morning, out of the blue, an assistant producer had phoned to give her the good news. Filming was due to start and Suzie was required immediately.

'Just don't do anything stupid,' said Lorna.

'Like what?'

'Like sleeping with him.'

'Who?'

'Who do you think? Hugh Grant.'

Suzie thought for a minute. 'Is that the best advice you can come up with?'

'It's the only advice I can come up with.' Lorna was aware that this had emerged as one long blurred word. 'He does have a reputation,' she added slowly, enunciating each word, as if she regularly read *Hello!* magazine.

Suzie had spilled most of her glass on the table but

seemed oblivious, planting one elbow in the pool of liquid and holding her almost-empty glass at a precarious angle.

Squinting through befuddled eyes, Lorna saw a younger Suzie: the Suzie who liked horse riding and ballet. Her parents had bought her a part share in a dappled mare that Suzie would gallop through waves on Gullane beach. Lorna remembered her singing along to Mariah Carey with a hairbrush, the volume turned to seismic, gyrating her hips and jumping around her bedroom until her mother came upstairs and told her to shut up, a not uncommon occurrence. She was big into Vanilla Ice, and Bryan Adams' 'Everything I Do' would make her cry. Where had the years gone? In between, Lorna had read books, learned maths and English, then precedent and jurisprudence, hunched over their Arthuria Road kitchen table while, from Suzie's bedroom, the bass notes of her latest rock group, and the familiar sound of Suzie jumping about, this time without a mother to tell her to shut up, sometimes alone, sometimes with Pete, or Dan, or Rob, or Carlo, or once a wiry Chinese boy called Dennis. And those were the ones she could remember, which was hard, now that the bar had begun to spin like a fairground roundabout.

Overcome with sudden affection, Lorna placed a hand over Suzie's. 'You're my best friend,' she said, realising that all drunks said that, and then removed her hand, just in case Suzie had taken her to another gay bar.

Suzie placed her glass with some difficulty on the table and beamed at it, as if not falling over was a clever trick deserving of praise. 'What's wrong, babe?'

Lorna had been thinking about Mike's watch, a huge lump of metal that not only told the time in Edinburgh but in most of the world's other capital cities, and which incorporated a stopwatch for lap times and a time-lapsed facility, particularly handy for warning you when your scuba air supply might be running low, an activity that Lorna didn't think Mike was capable of pursuing. He was inordinately proud of his ostentatious watch and constantly telling his staff – and presumably family and friends, if he had any – about its endless features. It was, he admitted, a fake. *Made in China, or somewhere*, he said. *Why buy a real one when a fake is just as good?*

'I'm OK,' said Lorna.

'No, you're not, sweetie,' and then when Lorna didn't reply, added: 'Anyway, I've got news that might cheer you up. Dad's given me his old car!' To add to the effect, Suzie dangled car keys under Lorna's nose, grinning like a Cheshire cat.

'He's *given* you his old car? Just like that?'

'Well, he can afford to, sweetie. It's a kind of twenty-first birthday present rolled into a well-done present. Actually, I think it was Mum's suggestion. But the good news is that I made him promise to put you on the insurance.'

'Christ, Suze, I can't drive a Porsche.'

'Oh yes, I forgot,' said Suzie, not smiling. 'You don't like rich people, do you?'

Lorna wondered what Suzie saw looking over the table. The young Virgin Mary, perhaps, with a precarious cushion stuffed up her dressing gown? Or the young adolescent trailing in Suzie's wake, awed by the price of jewellery or clothes, and never being able to buy anything? Or the older adolescent on a visit to the zoo, shouting *You're not an endangered species!* at a squirrel in the pygmy hippo enclosure? (Suzie had immediately bettered the joke by running away from the lions' enclosure screaming *They've escaped*!) Or the young woman, hunched over books in the kitchen, while Suzie entertained Pete/Dan/Rob/Carlo/Dennis in her bedroom?

Once she'd emerged drunk in her underwear to announce that one of them (Lorna couldn't now remember) had dumped her. *But only after I'd given him a blow job!* she'd complained bitterly. *Why couldn't he have dumped me before I gave him a blow job?* Lorna had made soothing noises, and introduced her to her two Uni friends who were also at the kitchen table, now hurriedly putting on coats and scarves.

'I don't like *privilege,* Suze,' Lorna said, her mind clouded by Passionate Knight and Arthur's Quest and, for some reason, Mike's watch. 'There's a difference, you know.' She forced herself to smile. 'Are you being serious? About me being able to drive it?'

'Absolutely, sweetie.'

Lorna frowned into her almost-empty glass. She had always coveted Suzie's father's cars, each one more silver and shinier than the last. 'Wow! I get to be rich by association.'

Suzie pocketed her car keys and looked at her evenly over the table. 'Lorna, what the *hell* is wrong?'

'Don't know, Suze. Too much to drink, I expect.' She thought back to Mike nearly toppling into a cardboard box of cigarettes, an inane smile on his face; the kindly father bestowing a treasured gift. 'Anyway, I'm also going to be fabulously rich. As an esteemed and highly valued member of the HappyMart family, I have been awarded a second star.'

'A second *what*?'

'A second star. I've been promoted.' She blinked several times, forcing back tears. 'This morning I was a humble checkout operator. This evening, I'm a checkout *supervisor.*'

Suzie coughed and smiled uncertainly. 'Look, you're only doing the crappy job until you graduate. What the hell's wrong in that?' She paused to fill up their glasses.

'And isn't getting promoted a good thing? For a start, it's more money.'

'I did ask about a company car,' she said, watching the bubbles in her glass, 'but I think you need to have about a zillion stars to get one. And even then it would probably be a clapped-out Skoda with splodges of colour all over it. Christ, Suze, I'm pleased for you ... really I am ... but I just feel so fucking miserable.'

Suzie patted her hand absently. 'I'm still going to pay the rent, if that makes any difference. I don't intend to actually *move* to London.'

'Bollocks, Suze. Famous people live in London. Famous people don't live in Edinburgh.'

'J.K. Rowling?' prompted Suzie. Lorna remembered that Suzie had read at least one Harry Potter book, or at least bought it, or maybe just been given it or simply stolen it.

'Except her.'

Lorna found her hand gripped suddenly by Suzie's. 'But I like it here,' said Suzie in her little girl voice, the one she would adopt if she was in trouble with her mother. 'I don't know anybody in London.'

Lorna lit a cigarette and looked outwards at the shifting water. It was slick with oil and sparkled green and blue. 'You know *tons* of people in London. You're always down there. Anyway, in six months you'll have forgotten about us,' she said. 'You'll have celebrities drooling over you. You'll have your photo in the *Daily Star*.'

Suzie was looking serious. 'I still don't want to go.'

'Of course you do! You're a tart, Suzie! Now you've got the chance to be a *real* tart.'

'Moi? A tart? Pot, kettle, black, babe.'

'Oh, admit it, Suze ...'

'I still remember Crete,' said Suzie more loudly, as if their holiday had been years before. She had one eyebrow

298

raised and was waving her glass at Lorna, spilling wine. 'You and what's-his-name.'

'Leo.'

'Sparrow? Eagle?'

'Dove, actually.'

'That's a film, babe. Also with Hugh Grant in it.'

'Whatever, Suze.' Lorna was also going to say *Don't be ridiculous* but, in framing the words in her head, she knew that the word ridiculous would be hard to say. Her glass was also somehow empty. Lorna couldn't remember having drunk it, or if Suzie had drunk it for her. Suzie's elbows, now on the table, were soaking up slops. 'You're forever doing stuff down there,' Lorna managed, changing the subject.

'But I don't *know* anybody,' Suzie repeated. 'Proper people. People I can talk to. Like you, babe. Will you miss me?'

Lorna clicked her lighter twice, two small bursts of flame.

'Lying toad,' said Suzie, then looked thoughtful, or as thoughtful as Suzie could ever look. 'You liked him, didn't you?'

'Who?'

'Leo ... *him*.'

After a pause Lorna flicked her lighter once.

'Then call him.'

Click. Click. In any case, she didn't know his number, or if he was still in Austin's flat, or if Austin had stabbed him to death and hidden the body.

'Because of Austin?'

Click.

'Stupid bloody cow!' said Suzie. 'And are we reduced to talking in torch language?'

'It's a lighter. Too drunk to speak.'

'Fuck's sake!' Suzie's arms were held out over the

299

table, dripping champagne. 'How the bloody hell did *this* happen?'

Something strange happened to Lorna on their Greek holiday, and not just the interlude with Leo. She'd brought it back with her from Crete, but couldn't put her thoughts into words. She'd put it down to post-holiday angst, or time of the month, and tried to ignore it. Something had been altered, an inner chemistry displaced, making her question herself and the certainties she had always held firm to. Becoming a lawyer had been everything. Working for Amnesty, perhaps, or Greenpeace, or some-such charitable endeavour – she wasn't naïve enough to believe that she could change the world, but simply wanted to make a difference: to do something worthwhile. Was it something Leo had said? The rich boy who wanted to throw away that opportunity, but who hadn't the courage to say no to his dad? Well, perhaps, she conceded, and felt another trickle of tears at the back of her eyes.

Then she said it. 'I don't want to be poor,' putting into words an alien thought that she shouldn't have allowed inside her head, but said so softly that Suzie couldn't have heard, and maybe Lorna hadn't wanted her to hear. In any case, Suzie's goldfish attention had wandered again; she had ripped open the packet of peanuts and was demolishing them in small fistfuls, some of which were making it to her mouth. The rest, like shrapnel, were bouncing off the table behind her which, thankfully, was unoccupied. Then Suzie leaned conspiratorially towards Lorna, her forearms once more mopping up the last of the spilled wine, 'I'm also doing an advert for bathroom hygiene.' Suzie had dropped her voice, as if imparting a State secret, although Suzie's stage whisper would have been audible to enemy spies on the other side of the bar.

'Bathroom *what*?'

'Hygiene, sweetie,' said Suzie. 'I'm going to be the new face of toilet paper.' She tried to look serious, then gave up. 'Lorna, for God's sake, it's not that funny!'

REGENERATION

It was North Berwick, but it wasn't. Superficially it looked the same – the same granite, the narrow one-way street, the same cars parked down one side. The air also smelled the same: the tang of the sea and, above, the whirl of seabirds against grey cloud. But it was wrong. The cars were spotlessly clean: everything was scrubbed, immaculate. Lorna touched the bonnet of a car. It seemed like it was made from plastic. She crossed the road and looked up at her house. In the window was a bowl of wilting daffodils but when she tried to push open the door it wouldn't yield.

It was as if she was home, but couldn't quite get home: somewhere in limbo, unable to take the final step, to open her own front door. It too felt plastic. She felt tears well up.

'We thought you might like it,' said Irene.

'I don't like it,' she said flatly, trying to swallow emotions. 'It's not real.'

'Well, of course it's not real. That would just be ridiculous.'

'I've no idea what ridiculous is any more.'

'Oh?'

She gestured around her. 'I appear to be in the street where I grew up. It's far beyond ridiculous, Irene! This isn't Heaven, is it?'

Usually there would be moving cars on the High Street, sometimes long lines of them. Cars parking, cars pulling out; the slam of car doors. But she was now able to stand in the middle of the street, listen to birds calling, hear the distant slap of waves. Irene paused to light a cigarette and nod politely at a Bono who was standing in a shop doorway talking to a Sting. Across the road was someone who was in Franz Ferdinand. All three were wearing blue tracksuits and smiled at Lorna as they walked past. Looking about, she saw that familiar shops had changed their identity and now bore the same labels as in Heaven's other shopping complex. Where the butcher should have been was Prada; in place of the greengrocer, Dior; a craft shop called Presence was now Valentino.

'Your memories are nearly complete, young Lorna. Then you will be at peace. Memory integration takes time, you know that.'

'But I keep getting pains in my arm. I keep having nightmares.' She was breathing heavily. 'Irene, I'm frightened. I don't know what to think any more.'

'About what, sweetie?'

Lorna gestured to the fake shops and shiny cars. 'This place. Heaven. It's not real.'

Irene smiled briefly. 'What's real and what isn't real is of no importance,' she said. 'Reality is subjective. You're in a place where we can artificially recreate anything. The boundaries of reality can therefore be misleading. What is important, petal, is that you learn to decide which is which.'

'I don't understand.'

'Then think of it like this,' said Irene, once more extracting a cigarette and momentarily looking upwards. 'Do you know what a toaster looks like?' Her lighter flashed; she sucked down smoke and plumed it at the circling seagulls. 'Of course you do. But what would happen if someone secretly altered your toaster to make it look like a giant mushroom? The next morning, you'd go into the kitchen and find that your toaster had disappeared.'

'I don't see what you're getting at.'

Irene smiled again, this time seeming to mean it. 'But that's the point, don't you see! Your toaster *is* still in the kitchen. It just doesn't look like a toaster anymore.' She waved her cigarette at the shops. 'That's what happens in Heaven, Lorna. You're seeing things that may or may not be real. It's for you to decide.'

'That still doesn't make any sense,' she said.

'Probably not,' conceded Irene. 'Anyway, God wants to see you.'

They walked on, past the familiar and the unfamiliar, and down to the beach. Here, Lorna suddenly felt both hot and cold. If she turned her face towards the dunes, a chill Scottish breeze touched her cheek. But when she faced the sea, she felt a wall of heat, then a stab of pain in her arm, like a needle. She flinched, thinking she'd been bitten.

At the top of the sand dunes they stopped and looked over the golf course, and Lorna half expected to see her father, bent under his golf bag. Instead, a young Jack Nicklaus was playing up the fairway with a Tiger Woods. Tiger selected a club, addressed his ball, and sent it a few yards into a bunker.

Irene beamed. 'He may not be very good, Lorna, but last week he could hardly hit the thing.'

On the way, Lorna's eye was caught by something glinting in the sand dunes. She went closer. It was an empty vodka bottle and, as she watched, it melted back to nothing.

At the other end of the beach, Nico was pushing his barbeque along the sand. Here and there, couples lay on beach towels. Some were bronzed, others lily-white. A fat couple eating cake were burned red. Once again, she felt chilled on one side, a burning sun on the other side. The pain in her arm had subsided.

She was in a jumble of places she recognised, some real and some not so real, and all contained within a spaceship of unimaginable size. It was that which unsettled her. It was what she'd thought when she'd first watched *Star Wars*, moorhens cackling and Tom puking his guts up over the side of the boat. Why did the evil Empire need such impossibly huge spaceships?

God was waiting for them in the Greek beach bar which had seen Lorna's welcome party. In front of him was a glass of beer. Music was playing softly from loudspeakers tied to the plastic awning. As always, he was wearing a cream tracksuit. With a start of recognition, Lorna realised that without his beard, he would be the double of Sean Connery. Not James Bond, but Sean Connery as an old man. Now seeing this, she wondered how she hadn't noticed the similarity before.

He rose chivalrously from his seat and motioned her to a vacant chair. 'I trust that all your memories are coming back?'

Lorna nodded. Irene placed a white wine and soda in front of her. Lorna looked at it, wondering – not for the first time – what time of day it was or whether it mattered.

'Memory integration is a bit of a bore,' he continued, 'but it's a process that can't be speeded up. The human mind is terribly complicated, Lorna. Even Trinity has a hard job understanding it. By the way, how are you settling in?'

'I don't know.' The pain in her arm had returned; she felt momentarily sick. She blinked; again feeling hot and cold.

'Excellent!' said God and beamed happily. 'If there's anything you want, you just have to ask. Nothing is too much trouble, is it, Irene?'

'She'd much rather not be here,' said Irene, who had lit

a cigarette and was blowing smoke up to the torn awning. Vines had broken through the plastic; a corner flapped in a gentle breeze from the sea.

'Understandable, of course,' said God. 'Moving home is always traumatic.'

The pain in her arm had blossomed, and shards of memory were spinning, giving her a headache. She wanted to cry.

'It's just that I don't know why I'm here,' she said. 'Until I understand *that*, I can't believe in anything, particularly you. What I *don't* know is why you didn't bother to invent a cure for poverty or cancer. Or stop illegal wars ... often conducted in *your* name! A proper God would have done that.' Lorna looked at him accusingly. 'I also want to know what's happened to everybody. Despite TV and blockbuster films, most of the crew have left, haven't they?'

There was a silence. Lorna looked between them. Irene was staring out to sea, God seemed to be examining his glass and frowning.

'It's just that Heaven is too big,' she said more calmly. The pain in her arm had eased. Under an artificial Greek sun, Lorna again looked from God to Irene. 'Much too large for the number of people who live here.' All those empty corridors, a shopping complex that nobody visited 'Where did everyone go?' she asked.

'I told you she was perceptive, God,' said Irene, blowing smoke towards the hanging loudspeakers. Soft music was still playing. 'Now there's no point in *not* telling her.'

Across the beach, Nico had set alight to his barbeque. Alone on the white sand, he had no customers.

God pointed at Nico with a bony finger. 'The first sign of trouble, Lorna, is when people start to work. It signifies that they have regained a sense of purpose; that mere leisure and pleasure are no longer enough.' God paused, took a sip of his drink, and looked at Nico with pursed lips. 'You see, Lorna, the regenerative technologies aboard this facility were only supposed to work for a year or so. The expectation was that, even if we were stranded in deep space, rescue would arrive relatively quickly. Nobody had ever considered how regeneration might work over many centuries. It isn't, I regret, the eternal panacea we thought it would be.'

God drank more beer and placed the glass back on the table. Lorna watched bubbles rise. 'The process does keep us young and healthy so, in theory, we could all remain here until the end of time. In Heaven, eternity should mean eternity. But regeneration is about much more than physical renewal. It stops us becoming bored,' said God with a wistful smile. 'It allows us to enjoy ourselves for century after century, doing the same things over and over again. But, as we now know, its effects do wear off. As I said, Lorna, the system was never designed to work indefinitely. Trinity has tried to modify the process, but the human mind is just too complicated. The first indication that the process wasn't perfect was when some of the crew started to work again. At first, Lorna, it was only a small handful, and I didn't worry much about it. Over the centuries, more handfuls ...'

He placed a hand on his beer glass. Over his head the torn plastic awning was flapping. 'When people regain purpose, Lorna, it means that, sooner or later, they put in for a transfer.'

'To where?' She was mystified.

'Where do you think, sweetie?' said Irene. 'To Earth.'

* * *

Then Suzie was gone and the flat felt empty and cheerless. Lorna had kissed her off at Waverley Station, heaving great suitcases from the taxi to the train. The Porsche could only have accommodated Suzie's make-up bag, and only with difficulty, and there wasn't an aeroplane large enough to take all Suzie's luggage. She'd therefore decided to leave the Porsche in Edinburgh, at least for the time being. It felt strange having the flat to herself, no longer competing for the bathroom with Suzie's never ending string of boyfriends, or working against the background of loud rock music from her bedroom. Instead, there was silence, which Lorna initially found discomfiting. In the long summer break, without lectures, tutorials, or dissertations, Lorna opted to work additional shifts in the shop, building up a campaign fund, so she called it, for her last year at university. She didn't know what she'd spend it on. So most mornings now found Lorna outside the Arthuria Road flat, pausing on the pavement, her eyes always drawn to the silver Porsche in their resident's space. Lorna loved it, but rationed her outings in it. It drank too much, and working at the HappyMart wasn't enough to quench its thirst. But she did drive past the shop one afternoon and by coincidence Mike and Vlad were outside having a cigarette. Lorna waved airily to them as she drove past, the roof down, and Suzie's Versace sunglasses on her nose, then speculated if this might affect her nickname. Nor could she resist driving down to North Berwick and showing it off to her parents. Her mother had insisted that Lorna drive her down the High Street, again with the car's roof down, while she grandly waved to friends and acquaintances with a big grin on her face.

In a break from filming, Suzie came north for a long weekend. She now shared a flat with three other aspiring actors in Battersea. The lump of the old power station, now an art gallery, was almost next door. Lorna asked her about Hugh Grant. 'Is he absolutely gorgeous?'

'He's very charming and raffish.'

Lorna leaned over their kitchen table. A bottle of wine had been opened and mostly consumed. 'That's not what I meant, Suze.'

'I don't fancy him, if *that's* what you meant. Christ, Lorna, he's old enough to be my father! Actually, he's quite sexy,' she conceded, 'but in a sleazy way, if you get my drift.'

'So you haven't slept with him?'

'Not yet, but I'm working on it. And if we get married, I insist on you being maid of honour.'

'Will I get to wear a pink dress?'

'The pinkest of pink, sweetie, like a flamingo, although you don't have to stand on one leg.' Suzie wrinkled her nose; in Suzie's absence, Lorna had been known to have the occasional cigarette inside. That morning had been spent with every window open and Lorna spraying the place with several cans of air freshener. 'I'll even make sure you catch the bouquet.'

'Don't think I'm ready for marital bliss just yet, Suze. Mister Right seems inexplicably to have got lost. Best if I wait til your third or fourth wedding.'

Suzie kicked off her shoes and swung her long legs onto a kitchen chair. 'And how have you been? All alone in this place.'

'Oh, you know. OK, I suppose.'

But she wasn't OK, not really. There was still that sense of dislocation that she'd unwittingly brought back from Greece. A small but unspecified gathering of doubts, nothing she could pin down, and so ephemeral she was usually able to ignore them, forcing herself to be cheerful, making smiley small talk with her customers, and insisting that she did at least an hour of revision each evening, even if it was still the long university holiday. Maybe it was that which had made her drive past the HappyMart in Suzie's car, driving round the block several times, knowing it would be Mike's break, and that he usually went outside for a smoke with The Impaler. Why had she done *that*? To show off? To somehow say that she was *better* than them? She'd felt ashamed afterwards, because she wasn't better than anybody, and it wasn't even her car.

In her new solitude, Lorna did sometimes still think about Leo, but he was slipping from sight; a holiday romance that hadn't properly ignited, although she sometimes wondered if he'd found the courage to disappoint his father. Either way, it didn't much matter.

The next morning, Mike emerged from his office He was holding open a copy of *The Sun* and laid it down on Lorna's checkout. 'Isn't that the loud person who was in here a few weeks ago?' he said, stabbing a large finger at a showbiz picture. Suzie appeared to be emerging from a nightclub. She was wearing a sparkly silver dress and was smiling over her shoulder at someone just out of camera shot. The caption described her as 'Suzie Bryce, model and actress, taking a break from filming *School's Out!*' Lorna looked through all the grubbier tabloids without finding other pictures, then texted her.

U r in The Sun!

Suzie texted back later. *And nt on pg 3*

That evening, Lorna watched a programme on Iraq, the generals and politicians seeming confident that, apart from some insignificant difficulties, life was improving for ordinary Iraqis, despite an unreliable electricity supply and water shortages and the daily risk of being shot or blown up or dying from dysentery. Then, tired and depressed, she made herself a cup of hot chocolate and stood at the window and looked out at her castle, which was usually enough to lift her spirits.

The phone was ringing.

'Hello.'

'Is that Lorna or Suzie?' He had an unfamiliar voice and sounded hesitant.

'It's one of us,' agreed Lorna.

'I mean … sorry … It's just that Simone said I should call. To say hello.'

Lorna had no idea what he was talking about.

He persevered. 'Simone. My sister. She runs a taverna in Crete?' The rising inflection of his voice suggested he was Australian, and Lorna did remember.

'Oh yeah. Simone. Married to Nico.'

'Well, Simone said that you two were cool and that I should look you up when I got to Edinburgh.' There was a small silence. 'I'm Joe, by the way. Joe Crowe.'

* * *

It was clearly a subject that God found painful. His eyebrows furrowed, he continued in a low voice: 'The ones who want to transfer have grown tired of eternity. Maybe they feel they've lived long enough. But the isotope that protects my crew in Heaven offers no such protection on Earth. They know that, but still they ask for their transfer. Like everyone else, they become prey to illness and disease. If they're lucky, they grow old before they die. They also know that it's a one-way ticket. If they choose to leave, they can't come back. That was one of my rules when the first crew members asked to leave, a decision that even Irene agreed with. I thought it would be a deterrent. Why go on a suicide mission when you can live forever?' He shrugged, then looked at his glass.

'Your crew is defecting to Earth?' asked Lorna.

'Not defecting. Merely choosing a different kind of

life.' He sat up straight as he said this, looking her in the eye. 'But don't think I just let them transfer to Earth willy-nilly! My purpose, Lorna, is to give *them* purpose. Only if they agree will I authorise their transfer.'

Irene had been tapping her foot in time to the music, seemingly lost in a private reverie. 'God's primary responsibility has always been to his crew, Lorna. He is God of this facility, and his first concern is for our well-being. This beach, for example,' said Irene and gestured round with a manicured hand. 'He authorised its construction for a purpose. To entertain us, yes, but also to recreate a bit of Earth in Heaven. He thought it might stop people wanting to go there.'

'I was wrong, of course,' said God. 'I simply wanted to provide my crew with a new form of entertainment. That's the trouble, Lorna. You can only really enjoy yourself in a limited number of ways, even on a beach.' Here, mischievously, he winked, making her blush. 'However, once you've tried everything a million times, it does become repetitive. Regeneration was supposed to stop that. For a time, it did.' Lorna opened her mouth but God motioned her to be quiet. He seemed agitated, pulling at his beard then fiddling with his strings of beads. 'But I do care, Lorna, and I do what I can. In terms of medical and other advances, my crew have helped your people to develop all manner of things. Lister, Pasteur, Archimedes, Socrates, Alexander Bell, James Watt, Bill Gates, Galileo ... I could go on, Lorna, but I won't. All were friends and colleagues and I miss all of them.'

God took a deep breath. 'As for world poverty, well, it's your world. I may have created you, but how you choose to run things is your affair. Mine not to reason why, young Lorna.' He looked again to the beach where Nico was turning hamburgers and wafting away smoke with a small towel. 'As you well know, there's more than enough food on Earth to feed everybody, so half your world needn't starve. So it's really just a question of organisation and resolve, and your people seem to possess neither.

'I have given Earth electricity and the steam engine, vaccines and the internet. The Wright brothers were both crewmen and, from their humble beginnings, you are now reaching into space. But I can only work within the context of what you know. I couldn't very well send the Wright brothers back to invent the jet engine, could I? To cure cancer, you have to truly understand the workings of DNA, which you don't. But you will, Lorna! I have helped you map out the human genome and clone Dolly the sheep, and you are inching ever closer to a final cure. So you see, where I can, I have helped you achieve great things. Many of the miracles of your science have come directly from this space facility. I'm not a bad God,' said God and stroked his beard. 'But I am a realist. For every great scientific advance on Earth, I lose a member of crew. However,' said God more brightly, 'most of them do achieve the tasks that I set them. In return for mortality, they generally keep their end of the bargain.'

'Not all,' said Irene.

'No, not all.'

'Not, for example, David Beckham.' Irene shook her head.

Lorna had been listening in silent awe. 'David Beckham's an alien!'

God once more furrowed his eyebrows and looked at her sternly. 'We are both genetically similar, young lady. Please don't think of us in those terms, as I certainly don't think it about you.'

'I'm sorry,' she stammered. 'I didn't mean it to sound like it did.' Now that God had said it, it made a perfect kind of absurd sense. She'd always thought there was

314

something odd about the Beckhams.

'He was supposed to go to Earth and advance your thinking on free-electron lasers. They have, or will have, both a medical purpose and a central role in faster-than-light space travel. I felt it was about time I gave Earth's space programme a bit of a jolt. David, I regret, hasn't yet achieved the purpose I gave him.'

Irene had fetched two more glasses of white wine and soda from the bar and now handed one to Lorna. 'He was football daft, even here. Captain of Heaven's soccer team, always practising, always watching matches on the telly. We have a small stadium on the other side of the golf course,' she said with a wave of one hand. 'It was always likely that Earth's temptations would prove too much.'

'But largely,' said God, 'my crew have proved successful. For that, at least, I am profoundly grateful.'

A few couples were wandering in from the beach, towels over their shoulders. Two girls in bikinis were chatting to Nico, although not eating his burgers. The sun had slipped lower, a cool breeze had sprung up off the water. 'Why am I here?' she asked.

God finished his beer and stood up. 'So I can offer you a choice, young Lorna.'

'A choice?'

He was stroking his beard with one hand, running beads through his fingers with the other. 'When all your memories have returned, your regeneration will be complete. At that point, and not before then, I will reveal that choice to you. It explains why you're here, Lorna. It explains why I chose you.'

STAR WARS

She couldn't rid herself of the small but bewildering sense that her trajectory was wrong, and at first (having ruled out post-holiday angst) she put it down to the long summer break from college, having the flat to herself, and the mind-numbing drudgery of the HappyMart. But eventually she started to admit that some of Leo's doubts had been passed to her, and it kept her awake at night, staring at the ceiling, feeling confused and lonely. She continued to work additional shifts at the shop, but didn't socialise with the rest of the HappyMart family, despite being asked to a couple of staff outings, which always involved grotty pubs or a curry, and generally both. Little Miss Clever supposed that the others probably thought her stuck-up. She didn't really know why she turned down their invitations, and was saddened one Friday evening when it became apparent that they were all off for a few drinks before heading home, and nobody – including Mike – had bothered to mention it to her. She didn't want to fritter away money on socialising. She liked Vlad and Maggie and the others, and absolutely *wasn't* better than them, but she couldn't risk their fate. Becoming a lawyer had been her only fixed star; and beside that one bright star in her sky, nothing mattered. Those grim back-and-white pictures from the North Berwick museum were still etched into her memory, so too the cupboard under the sink and her mother sinking, exhausted, onto the sofa each evening.

One night, after a particularly dull evening at the

HappyMart, Lorna dreamed she could fly but had forgotten how. She was in the countryside in warm sunshine, in a meadow filled with yellow flowers, with a sparkle of water at the meadow's margins. She knew she could fly and she *had* to fly, because she was miles from a railway station or bus stop and had to get back to Edinburgh. It was how she'd got to the meadow in the first place, lifting herself off the ground with the merest flick of a wrist, and floating upwards from the city, turning to the coast by pointing her face towards it, and riding the thermals. Now she was stranded, her feet rooted to the ground. Lorna tried running and flapping her arms, then realised she had a canvas bag over one shoulder and decided it might be too heavy for take-off. She placed it on the ground and ran round it, arms outstretched. Gradually, Lorna realised that the gift of flight had been taken from her and now she was no different from anyone else. She wasn't horrified by this. In her dream, she merely accepted it.

Not long after Tom died, Lorna had started to talk to a man with a big grey beard and twinkly eyes. He wore a long black cloak, like she wanted her father to wear, and had a large red nose, like a beacon on a lighthouse. He was very tall, almost as tall as the sky, she used to think. When he smiled, his whole face would light up, and he would bend down and ruffle her hair, and tell Lorna stories about long ago. Sometimes she would ask his advice or just tell him what she'd been doing at school. He had very large ears, so was a good listener. Her mum said that Lorna shouldn't talk to him, not only because he was a stranger, but because he didn't exist.

But he existed to her and together, sometimes, they would rise up from the ground, Mr Tomkins holding tight to her hand and float off into the night sky. She loved Mr Tomkins and was sad when, after she'd grown up a bit, she no longer thought about him.

The Chinese believe that a person's soul lives for as long as they are remembered on Earth. When Lorna found this out, she worried about Mr Tomkins. Had she inadvertently killed him, even though he was a figment of her imagination?

The next morning after her dream, as she showered, she thought about Mr Tomkins because the dream seemed to signify something, but as the day passed it became smaller until she forgot all about it.

She decided that some exercise might do her some good and dutifully bought a pair of running shoes. For two days she drove the Porsche to the foot of Arthur's Seat, a large hill on the fringes of central Edinburgh, and ran around it. The first half of the run was excruciating as it involved a stiff climb; the second half less so as it was downhill all the way. On the second day she was caught in a freezing downpour and lay shivering in the bath for half an hour, her limbs aching and her lungs burning. For a while she vowed to give up smoking, then decided that jogging wasn't for her. Then she tried swimming and, after her shift in the shop, would walk briskly to the Commonwealth pool and force herself to do thirty lengths. But after two days, despite her love of swimming, realised that she had fallen out of love with swimming pools. Greece had spoiled her, the warmth and silence of an empty sea compared with the shrill mayhem of small children, and the equally shrill whistle of lifeguards trying vainly to keep order.

She occasionally met up with friends, for a drink or outings to the cinema, but most had moved back home for the summer, and *home* meant anywhere from Shetland to Washington DC. Lorna found herself looking forward to the start of the new term, her last year, and to the point where her planned trajectory would became reality. She made resolutions to do more with the time available to her at university, to adopt new pastimes, join clubs and societies – and then felt that disquieting sense of dislocation: she had never joined societies or clubs because she always shunned distractions, except the occasional demo. Now, lying awake and staring at the ceiling, she didn't know what to think, and whether meeting Joe for coffee would be a good or bad idea.

Although Simone had said he'd got himself fixed up, suppose he hadn't? Suppose his cheerily friendly phone call was a prelude to asking her for a place to stay? Suppose he was broke, or mad, or a rapist? After the initial loneliness, she'd become accustomed to having the flat to herself. Sure, she missed Suzie, but she was able to walk around the place in her underwear and not lock the bathroom door; able to sit at the kitchen table and work without the inconvenience of earplugs. So she approached her meeting with Joe with a steely resolve: she wasn't going to offer hospitality, merely the civility that any stranger deserved.

The rendezvous they'd planned was like something from a bad spy film. He was medium height, medium build, with dark, straight hair, and would be wearing a red shirt. They'd arranged to meet at a Starbucks in the city centre. Lorna walked down from the HappyMart, glad of the exercise, and saw him immediately through the glass window, sitting at a corner table and reading a book.

'Hi!' she said brightly and stuck out a hand. He looked up, seemingly flustered, and shook it. First impressions of Joe weren't promising. His hair was unkempt and badly needed cutting, he was not of medium build, although not quite of Auntie Meg proportions. She waved airily in the direction of the coffee machines. 'Back in a tick.'

She returned to their table to find he was again reading his book, which Lorna thought a little rude. He looked at her warily as she sat opposite him, a smile painted on her face. 'How long have you been here?'

'About five minutes,' he offered, biting his lip.

'I meant in Edinburgh?'

He was now looking a little alarmed. 'I've always lived here,' he said. 'Look, do I know you, or something?'

It was then that Lorna spotted another man in a red shirt at the other end of the coffee shop. This one, Lorna saw with relief, did seem to be of medium build. 'I'm really sorry,' said Lorna. 'It was the red shirt. Stupid of me ... Sorry.'

Lorna picked up her cup, apologising again, and hurried across the room.

'Joe?'

He stood up immediately, rather chivalrously. 'Yeah, you must be Lorna. Good to meet you'

'Let's get this straight,' she replied. 'Joe Crowe, right?'

He nodded.

'From Australia?'

He nodded again.

'Well, thank God for that! I've just been chatting to someone else in a red shirt.' She pointed across the room. 'He wasn't you, incidentally.'

She looked at him more closely, and was immediately reminded of James Dean. Her mother had fancied James Dean, once forcing Lorna to watch *Rebel Without A Cause*, which she'd hated because it was in black and white. Now Lorna had the strange feeling of looking at someone though her mother's eyes. He was tall and slim (not exactly the medium she'd been expecting), but looked strong. His forearms, sleeves rolled up, were muscular. He had a chiselled chin and a lock of dark hair flopping over one eye. She soon found that he had an infectious smile, and a more infectious laugh.

He was in Edinburgh because his grandfather had emigrated from Scotland and he'd always wanted to see the place. Through a distant relative of Nico, husband to Simone, who seemed to have extended family in all corners of the world, a bar job had been secured for him. It wasn't much of a job, as he readily admitted, pulling pints and cleaning ashtrays, but he wasn't in Edinburgh to work. Not *proper* work, if she knew what he meant. He'd already visited Inverness, where his grandfather had been born, and had hitchhiked round the north of Scotland. He'd seen mountains and wilderness but, despite a good look, hadn't seen the Loch Ness monster. Joe had also been to his sister's wedding and eaten in the Greek beach bar: it gave them a point of connection, and reminded her again of Leo.

At first she was wary, having programmed herself to be merely friendly, whatever he was like. Instead, she was unwillingly captivated. He had an easy charm, and had already found himself somewhere to stay. He wasn't therefore looking for favours and, over that first coffee, apologised for phoning her. 'But I promised big sis that I would,' he said with a small shrug.

'And how is Simone?'

'Getting to grips with learning Greek, that's the hard part.' Joe had one hand on his cup and pushing back his lock of falling hair with the other. 'It's not just the language, it's the bloody alphabet. It's completely different.'

'It's all Greek to me,' said Lorna, which made Joe laugh, even though it wasn't very funny. She remembered saying much the same thing in Greece, with Austin and Leo. But she also felt curiously flattered, looking at him more closely: green eyes flecked with blue, and that infuriating lock of hair. It made her want to lean over the table and push it back, and she had to resist the temptation.

'Strangely enough, that's *exactly* what she says.'

Outside, a group of serious-looking Japanese tourists with camcorders were filming each other. A busker with a guitar was playing 'She Loves You' by The Beatles. His guitar case was open by his feet. 'I didn't really get to know her,' admitted Lorna. 'We just ate there a few times, that's all.'

'Well, she remembers you,' said Joe, hand still clasped to coffee cup. 'You and your actress friend. Simone reckons you two were cool.'

Lorna sipped her latte, remembering. 'Suzie. Stick around long enough and you'll get to meet her. We kind of still share a flat, except that she's never here. She's in *School's Out!* if you're interested. The new Spielberg film? It's a romantic comedy, apparently.' Lorna lifted her cup. 'It's got Hugh Grant in it.'

'I'm not sure I like romantic films,' said Joe. 'Being blunt, I thought that *Notting Hill* and *Love Actually* were crap.'

'In that case, you're not going to like *School's Out!*'

Joe smiled. 'And what's your favourite film?' he asked.

'You'd laugh, so I'm not going to tell you.'

'I won't laugh.'

'Everybody laughs, Joe.' Then, after a pause for dramatic effect. '*Star Wars* … Sorry.'

He was smiling, but not laughing. 'Sorry? For what?'

'For liking a film that's complete bollocks.'

'It's not!' He was pushing back his lock of hair again. 'But can I ask why?'

Lorna still didn't really know why she liked *Star Wars* so much. She'd never been into science fiction and didn't like *Star Trek*. She thought the other *Star Wars* films were garbage in comparison. It was just the first film that she loved. It was a fairy story, love story, and adventure story all wrapped together. At the time, her parents bickering on the deck of the riverboat, Lorna would sit at the prow of their boat, like Kate Winslet in *Titanic*, and try not to listen. On the gently rocking boat, in front of the TV, she had found another world. And in that mirror-world, with everything going wrong, things could also be put right.

'Don't really know,' she said.

Curiously, it was also a favourite of Joe's, or so he said. Lorna didn't know him well enough to believe him.

'Joe, you're just saying that.'

He held up his hands, palms outwards. 'Why would I lie? Listen, it's a great film. It paved the way for the sci-fi stuff that's come since. Actually, not just the sci-fi stuff. The special effects, for Christ's sake!' He returned his hands to his side and grinned. 'In any case, I also fancied the pants off Princess Leia.'

'I rather liked Han Solo,' conceded Lorna.

He was a year older than her and had completed a degree in media studies. He had offers of work lined up, he said, but didn't quite know what to do. Taking time away from Australia might help him decide. That was the real reason he'd come to Scotland. He'd always wanted to work in radio drama, he said, maybe as a producer, maybe in front of the microphone. Like Suzie, Joe seemed to be a bit of a show-off. Even at first glance, Lorna knew it.

'But why radio?' she asked.

'It's more intimate than TV,' he explained. 'People listen to the radio because they want to. People generally watch TV because they can't think of anything else to do. I like the spoken word,' he added, 'and I like to listen to it without the inconvenience of pictures. Good radio drama allows you to invent your own pictures. Does that make any sense?'

Lorna thought about it. She too liked the written word,

and liked the easy pleasure of inventing pictures to go with them. 'Actually, I suppose it does,' she said.

'In any case,' said Joe with another laugh. 'I have the perfect face for radio.'

He was wrong, of course, and probably knew it, but Lorna rather admired him for his lack of conceit. Suzie would have hated to work in radio; Lorna rather doubted that she'd ever listened to a radio drama in her life.

'So, you're going to be a lawyer,' he said. 'If you don't mind me asking, what kind of lawyer?'

It was a question she had yet to resolve and she found Joe's question unsettling: in that moment, she couldn't immediately remember what had attracted her to law in the first place. 'A good lawyer,' she said.

'That's not a very good answer,' said Joe.

Outside, the busker was playing a Rolling Stones number, presumably thinking that his passing audience all remembered the 1970s. 'I just want to do something useful.'

'Oh God!' said Joe with the lock of hair back over one eye. 'You're an idealist.'

'Socialist, yes. Idealist, no.'

'Well, a socialist with principles.'

Lorna smiled; he was teasing, but not mocking – in much the same way that Leo had done. She smiled at Joe, drawn to him, her ramparts crumbling.

Then her mobile rang. It was her mother and she was crying.

'Something wrong?' asked Joe.

'Family trouble,' said Lorna. 'Look, Joe, I'm sorry. I've got to go.'

GUILT

The wooden bench overlooking North Berwick harbour was exactly as she remembered it, although she couldn't recall the last time she had sat on it. In the harbour were small boats, their rigging clicking and clacking in the faint breeze. The tide was out and the boats sat stranded. The sun shone wetly from a grey and overhanging sky. She'd driven down at high speed and she was seething. 'Mum, he could have been hurt!'

'Aye, but he wasn't. He's in bed with a sore head, stupid bugger. Ashamed of himself, so he is.'

Lorna shoved her hands deeper into her coat pockets and sighed while, beside her, also wrapped warmly, her mother shook her head in exasperation. 'I didn't know what to do,' she said, a tug in her voice.

Her dad, almost home after a visit to the Auld Hoose, had fallen down the communal stairs. Working only sporadically from home as an insurance advisor, it was a journey he knew well, drunk and sober. 'He could have been hurt,' Lorna repeated, looking towards the Bass Rock, as always, swathed in circling birds. 'You should have got someone to help you.'

'By the time I found him, he was snoring his head off. He didn't *need* anybody's help, Lorna.' Finally alerted by his absence – the pub would have long since closed – her mum had found him in the stairwell. He was too heavy to lift by herself, and she didn't want to involve neighbours. She didn't want to broadcast her domestic problems. So she'd pushed a pillow under his head and hoped to God he'd wake up before neighbours used the stairs in the morning.

'Of course he needs help,' said Lorna. 'He's needed help for years.'

'He needs a well-aimed kick up the arse, that's what he needs,' said her mother, who had given up not swearing. Now that Lorna was grown up, she often used words that had always been forbidden. 'But he's finally, *finally* promised to see the doctor,' she added.

'Well, it's a start.'

Her mother sighed. 'He's feeling awfully stupid about it, as well he might. But I think it's frightened him a wee bit. Made him realise things, if you know what I mean. That's why he's agreed to the see the doc. Not before time,' she added.

Lorna placed a hand on her shoulder. 'Well, let's go and see the stupid bugger, shall we?' If her mum could now use forbidden words, Lorna didn't see why she shouldn't.

'I'm sorry for dragging you down.'

'It's not a problem, really it's not. I'm glad you did.' Lorna squeezed her shoulder, noticing how thin her mother had become.

Her dad was propped up in bed and wouldn't meet her eye. He kept saying he was fine, but didn't look fine. His face was ashen and there was a small bruise on his forehead. His hands were trembling.

'I should really get up,' he said, looking at the window. 'I've got things to do.'

'What things?' asked Lorna.

'Just *things*. I'm not completely useless, you know.' He said this with a smile, except it wasn't a real smile. 'Despite what others might think,' he added in a louder voice for the benefit of his wife who was pottering in the kitchen.

'Mum says you're going to see the doc.'

'I suppose –' Still not meeting her eye.

'Please, Dad.'

He nodded, hands bunched together, not looking at her.

Afterwards, her mother suggested they went to the bakery to pick up a sandwich. Lorna noted that no money changed hands at the bakery.

They ate their sandwiches on the same familiar bench, looking out across a familiar sea. The tide was beginning to turn, the boats starting to float, to regain purpose. Midstream in the estuary, a grey battleship was heading upstream, bound for the naval dockyard in Fife.

'He seems OK,' offered Lorna, 'although he's not.'

'Apart from everything else, Lorna, he worries about you.'

'Me?' Lorna turned to face her mother who was staring straight ahead. 'Whatever has he got to worry about?' Between them on the bench was carved a faded inscription: *Austin Loves Lorna*, circled with a heart. Bloody Suzie, all those years ago, cackling, a penknife in one hand, forehead knotted in concentration. Lorna had completely forgotten, and inched closer to her mother to obscure the offending words.

'He worries whether you're doing the right thing.'

Lorna was hungry, but no longer wanted to eat. Through an alcoholic haze, her father was accusing *her* of stupidity. 'That's ridiculous,' she said, throwing the remnants of her baguette into the metal-lattice bin beside the bench. She could have fed it to the seagulls, but wasn't feeling charitable.

'He also feels guilty.'

So, thought Lorna, I now have a father who is both worried and guilty, but who can't walk up stairs. Once again, she felt enclosed by the small town and her parents' inadequacies. 'I don't understand, Mum. Guilty about what?'

The wind had blown hair across her mother's face. Lorna saw how grey it had become; she'd not noticed this before, or the etched lines around her eyes.

'Because Tom's death was somebody's fault, wasn't it? In clever words, the hospital admitted as much.'

'This isn't making any sense.'

'Your father thinks that you've always been looking for someone to blame. He feels guilty about not doing something about it when Tom died. Suzie's dad said that we should have taken action against the hospital. He told us it was the right thing to do. Your dad thinks that's why you want to be lawyer.'

Lorna couldn't think of a sensible reply. 'Is being a lawyer such a bad thing?'

'Of course not, darling. We're both hugely proud of you. Enormously proud, Lorna. Please don't think we're not. He worries about whether you're following your heart or your head.'

'Lawyers could have got us some money,' said Lorna, realising, the moment the words left her mouth, how utterly stupid this sounded. She closed her eyes, remembering how she had cut up Tom's T-shirt and guiltily hidden its remnants in the bin. But it wasn't clear whether her mother had heard her because, when she opened her eyes, her mum had silently risen from the bench and left. Lorna watched the battleship head further upstream, then drove back to Edinburgh.

* * *

When she got back to Edinburgh, depressed, she phoned Joe. Talking to her parents had unnerved her.

'I'm not really phoning for a reason,' she said. He was

330

living in a flat in the Old Town, sharing the rent with a couple of medical students. Lorna could hear voices in the background. 'Probably just to apologise for running out.'

'I enjoyed meeting you,' said Joe.

'It's not every day I phone people I've only just met. Sorry,' she added, twining the telephone cord between her fingers.

'That's two apologies. You OK, Lorna?'

She forced out a small laugh. 'I just feel a little down, that's all. My dad had a bit of an accident.'

'Geez, not serious, I hope.'

'No, no, nothing like that.' Seeing her father's ashen face and shaking hands had brought conflicting emotions into sharp focus. 'I was also wondering what you were doing tomorrow evening?' She pressed her eyes together. She had never been this forward before.

'Tomorrow? Yeah, nothing, I guess.'

Lorna then shakily poured herself a large glass of wine, hoping her father wasn't doing the same. *Brazen bitch*, she said aloud.

* * *

Lorna had read somewhere that during the Falklands War penguins were so entranced by the novelty of low-flying jet fighters that they'd lean backwards to watch the planes cross the sky – and lean further back, and back, then fall over. She thought this was hilarious and recounted the anecdote over and over before finding out, years later, that it was a myth. But it nearly happened to her the evening after her visit to North Berwick, as she turned to watch Joe walk to the bar, unintentionally tilting her chair backwards so it was balanced on two legs, then realising with a pang of alarm that she was about to end up on the floor.

Was she in love with him even then? After only one cup of coffee – actually, not even that: she'd only drunk half of hers – and a white wine and soda? Lust, certainly, she wouldn't deny that. She'd never believed in love at first sight; unlike Suzie who had fallen in love several times, so she claimed, often on the merest whim, and then straight out of love the next morning once the alcohol had worn off. But can you love someone if you don't *know* them? Lorna's relationships had always been measured – except Leo. She wasn't built to cast her soul to the sea, and relationships also spelled distraction. She didn't need love; she didn't need its complications. So why behave like a mythological Falklands penguin?

They clinked glasses.

'Next time, let's go out properly,' he suggested, that infuriating lock of hair across one eye. Did she know him well enough to push it back? She decided against; she might be a brazen bitch, but not that brazen, not yet. 'To the cinema, get something to eat. Or both,' he smiled.

Lorna readily agreed, trying not to grin like a Cheshire cat.

Later, walking home, she had an unaccustomed spring in her step. Such a stupid cliché, but how true; her feet did seem to be attached to springs. Lorna hardly minded that it was raining, the air heavy with the first taste of autumn. Above, the sky was grey and molten; muddy clouds churning like waves. She unfurled her umbrella, turned up her coat collar, and hurried on, oblivious to everything.

* * *

She felt safe with Joe and trusted him, and for some reason felt able to accommodate distraction. She stopped being single-minded. They went to the cinema then, the next week, to the theatre and, late one Sunday morning, walked to the top of Arthur's Seat. Below were rooftops stretching to the sea and, against the horizon, the hills of Fife. Joe held tight to her hand.

On the way down, scampering and giggling on the muddy path, Joe said that he knew a pub near his flat that did huge portions of Sunday lunch. So they ate roast beef and shared a bottle of red wine, listening to a fiddler playing Hebridean tunes. Joe seemed nervous; inwardly smiling, Lorna guessed why. On the way out, he pointed to a chalk board advertising a cocktail night.

'God, no!' said Lorna.

The living room of his small flat on the Royal Mile looked out over a disused bus station, which disappointed her. Living on Scotland's most historic street, he deserved a better view. On the mantelpiece was a skull.

'You're supposed to kiss it,' ventured Joe. 'Bob and Sarah-Ann insist that every new visitor give Eric a quick snog. It's a sort of initiation, I suppose.'

'But they're not here,' she replied. 'In any case, it's revolting.'

'They're medical students,' he reminded her. 'Medics have a peculiar sense of humour.'

'Why Eric?' she asked, looking more closely at the skull.

'Named after a lecturer neither of them likes very much. Actually,' he said, taking it from the mantelpiece, 'it's plastic.' Stamped on the skull's base was *Made in China*. 'It's not real. Utterly artificial.'

He poured her a glass of wine then sat in an overstuffed chair and watched her drink it slowly. She was by the window, looking over the old bus station and thinking about nothing. Soft music was playing and shafts of light played on the flat's worn carpet. She put down her glass and sat by him, on the chair's soft arm. Joe was still looking nervous. Lorna touched his face with the fingers of one hand, running over its contours.

'I've run out of things to say,' she said.

'Likewise.'

'Then it's probably time you seduced me,' she suggested.

His small bedroom, with one single bed, had clearly been tidied in anticipation of visitors. The sheets were clean and the room smelled faintly of furniture polish. He drew the curtains then helped her to undress, kissing her gently. She closed her eyes, still thinking about nothing, but feeling warm and safe and wanted.

Afterwards, he said something surprising. 'You're very beautiful,' he told her.

Lorna was at the window and about to light a cigarette. Although Joe didn't mind her smoking, standing by open windows had become a habit.

She paused, the cigarette not yet lit. 'I don't think so, Joe,' she replied, suddenly aware of his eyes on her naked back. 'But it's nice of you to say so.'

He was propped up on pillows, his hands behind his head, his face in shadow. 'Well, for what it's worth, I think you're beautiful.'

Lorna replaced the cigarette in its packet then lay down beside him. After a moment, she rested her head on his chest. 'You don't have to say anything you don't mean, Joe.'

'I never do,' he said. 'I do actually believe in honesty. In relationships, I mean.'

'Is that what we have, Joe? A relationship?' Lorna was smiling.

'Well, I suppose so,' he said, holding her tight. 'After all, we've just had sex.'

'I prefer the term making love,' she corrected, 'as in making love to Love.' Lorna squinted up to see if he was smiling.

He shrugged. 'Anyway, I only ever say things I mean. If I don't mean something, I don't say it. So, believe me, Lorna, if I tell you you're absolutely lovely.'

'The term you used was beautiful,' she reminded him. 'Apart from which, you're not so bad yourself. My mother would fancy the pants off you.'

'Would I want to have sex with your mother?'

'Doubt it, but you never know.'

Lorna laid her head back on his chest and closed her eyes. Inside, she felt an unbidden emotion, something she hadn't felt for a long time, and realised she was happy.

She could only suppose that she was falling in love with him. There seemed no other explanation. She had never been in love before, not properly. Austin had been a rite of passage, a friend; Leo a strange interlude on a Greek island. The other men in her life hadn't made it onto the Richter Scale. This totally new emotion could only be love. There was nothing else that it could be.

* * *

She had come to believe that it was easier to see life's injustices when you had to look up; she'd never had the luxury of being able to look down. After her father lost his job, money had been tight, and most of her clothes had come from charity shops. Holidays were a distant memory. They'd struggled for years, watching her father spend what they did have, and his red eyes and shaking hands. After that first afternoon in bed with Joe, feeling buoyed and exuberant, she felt guilty about her dad and phoned him when she got back to her flat.

She hadn't spoken to him for days, although her mother had kept her updated on progress. He seems to be better, her mother said, making it sound like a twisted ankle or bout of flu. Her father answered, sounding tired

335

and distant, as if he was speaking from outer space.

'I just phoned to see how you were.'

'In other words, whether I'm sober.'

'Something like that.'

'I'm still taking pills,' said her dad, sounding resigned and unhappy. 'I'm going to see a therapist, whatever they do. As of now, I've no idea. Have you any idea what a therapist does? You're the clever one, Lorna, not me. After that, there's a group I can go to.'

'I've no idea, Dad. But it's a start.'

'As you say, it's a start.' There was a small silence. 'For what it's worth, I'm sorry.'

She was confused. 'For what?'

'For not being strong.' His voice was soft and Lorna could hear him breathing.

'You don't have to apologise for anything.'

'You've always been the strong one, Lorna.'

She didn't know what to say to this, or how to tell him she wasn't strong. The patina of her resolve was made of soft metal. She wasn't strong, but had become good at pretending – so good that only she knew it. She had developed a chameleon's skin; she could change colour and hide behind a false façade. She wasn't made of steel. She still sometimes slept with a light on, and still sometimes heard a small child crying.

'We're both so very proud of you,' he said.

'I'll see you soon,' said Lorna.

SECRETS

Suzie's next visit back to Edinburgh was at Christmas. Now that filming had finished for *School's Out!* she was in demand for modelling assignments, and auditioning for other parts. She regaled Lorna with stories of people she'd met, things she'd seen, the parties, the nightclubs. Now back at college but still working shifts at the HappyMart, Lorna's life seemed inconsequential by comparison.

'I mean, *Jordan*!' Suzie was saying. 'You only have to shake hands with her to be in the newspapers.'

Lorna had only a vague idea of who Jordan was so didn't reply.

They were in the flat, Suzie settling herself more comfortably on the sofa, in her favourite spot, legs tucked up behind her swimwear-catalogue behind. 'But the exciting news, sweetie, is that I may be into a relationship.'

'Only *may*?' Lorna also saw that she was frowning. 'With Hugh Grant?' she asked. 'That's a bit quick, Suze.'

'For God's sake, no!'

'So why the long face?'

Suzie had now stretched out on the sofa and was looking at the ceiling. 'I'd rather not talk about it, not *quite* yet.'

There had rarely secrets between them, and even fewer that Suzie had successfully kept. This was uncharted territory. 'But why not?' asked Lorna. 'Is he someone to be ashamed of? A Latvian dwarf? Someone old enough to be your grandfather. Christ's sake, Suze! You can't just announce exciting news then clam up!'

Suzie made a zipping motion across her mouth. 'Best if I explain everything soon,' she promised.

'God, it's someone famous, isn't it.' Lorna thought for a moment. 'Christ, it *is* Hugh Grant!'

'Not Hugh Grant.' Behind Suzie's head, the castle as always was floating, beating unseen wings.

'An actor?'

'Lorna, let's not play guessing games. I'll tell you soon.'

'When?'

'Soon. Anyway, what about you, babe?'

Faced with Suzie's evasiveness, Lorna didn't know what to say. 'I dunno,' she said, then dried up. 'Do you remember last summer?'

'Crete?'

'The beach bar. A redhead from Oz called Simone?'

Suzie did remember, with a sudden cackle. 'The place, as I recall, where you had carnal knowledge with what's-his-name.'

'Well, her brother phoned a while ago. He's working in a bar in the New Town.' Lorna was looking at her castle and smiling. 'Anyway, he phoned to say that Simone was OK and still happily pandering to Nico. He was also asking about places to go, that kind of thing, so I met up with him.'

'And? Lorna, stop beating about the bloody bush.'

'Well, it turned out he is gorgeous.'

'More gorgeous than Hugh Grant?'

'I haven't met Hugh Grant,' Lorna reminded her. 'But that's all I'm telling you, Suze, because you're telling me fuck-all.'

They went down to North Berwick for a few days over Christmas, Suzie driving the Porsche for the first time in weeks, and giving Lorna palpitations. Suzie's concept of driving involved maximum velocity then remembering, with some surprise, that roads also have corners and other cars. Lorna's overnight visits to the town had become fleeting. It felt strange sleeping in a familiar bed that had become unfamiliar. Her bedroom felt smaller, the sea louder. Their ornate Victorian bath seemed more chipped. On Christmas Day, they ate turkey and all the trimmings. Her parents asked lots of questions about her studies, most of which they'd asked a hundred times before. Her father drank mineral water; the cupboard under the sink now only contained cleaning fluids. Lorna checked. Later, they watched *Star Wars* on the TV. It was the first film, the one that she remembered so well and in one of the commercial breaks Suzie suddenly appeared holding up toilet roll. She was in some kind of spaceship, and was wearing a skin-tight silver jumpsuit. This, presumably, was the reason that Suzie had been picked for the role – the jumpsuit could simply have been silver paint, sprayed on. At the end of the advert, Suzie intoned to camera: *It's toilet paper, but not as we know it.*

Immediately afterwards, Lorna's mobile phone rang.

'Did you see it?'

'Of course, Suze.'

'I *knew* you'd be watching that stupid film. So, was I wonderful or just marvellous?' Later, as Lorna was going to bed, she saw a torch flashing from up the hill, just as it had years before. She fetched a torch from the hallway cupboard and, laughing, flashed back.

* * *

Every year, ever since Suzie had become her best friend in the world, Lorna was invited to the Bryces' for leftover lunch. Every year, there were exactly the same leftovers, the same red-chip driveway, so too the obligatory Porsche

339

that adorned it. This year, with Suzie at home, there were two Porsches, making her house look like a dealership for posh people. The year before, there had been a houseful of leftover relatives, the afternoon descending into inebriation and spontaneous games of hide-and-seek and charades. Lorna had been given the film *Anchorman: The Legend of Ron Burgundy*, which didn't seem easy, but all she did was point at an empty bottle of red wine and Adele, Suzie's mother, had guessed immediately. This year it was just the four of them. There was champagne in the drawing room, as Suzie's mum preferred to call it, while Suzie recounted tales from London, Adele rolling her eyes when Suzie wasn't watching. Then they ate in their cavernous kitchen, surrounded by marble, stone floors, and gleaming chrome. Lavender, their purebred Siamese, sat quietly and disdainfully by the French windows, too refined to miaow or beg for food. She'd never once brought a dead mouse into the house, so Suzie said. In place of napkins were folded up sheets of toilet paper.

'It's a bit creepy having a loo roll that's not as we know it,' said Graeme, Suzie's dad. His steely hair was cut short and he had piercing blue eyes. He unfolded his toilet paper napkin theatrically and placed it on his lap.

Suzie tossed her head, making her hair cascade. 'I don't make up the words,' she grumbled. 'We have scriptwriters who do that.'

'Gosh!' said Adele, placing dishes of ham and turkey on the table. 'Scriptwriters. Plural! Just to write one sentence!'

'They wrote several sentences,' Suzie muttered, feeling got at. 'Then those sentences were sent to groups of people who decided which one they liked the best.'

'A focus group for toilet roll slogans,' said Graeme, trying, and failing, to sound sincere. 'I wonder how they choose these people. Can anyone apply for jobs like that?'

Suzie grimly chewed a mouthful of ham, saying nothing.

'Imagine!' added Adele. 'All that effort just to wipe your bum.'

Lorna was wearing an off-the-shoulder chunky jumper, a Suzie cast-off from a modelling assignment. It was oversized and knitted, grey with silver threads, and she was wearing it with jeans (Oxfam, ho-hum) and a silver belt. Adele was wearing much the same, although with less make-up and with more designer labels.

After lunch, Lorna was quizzed by Graeme. He was perplexed that she had still to make up her mind about which branch of law to pursue.

'Dad, she's a pinko leftie,' Suzie advised him, demolishing a bread roll. Everyone else had finished eating. 'She wants to change the world, don't you, sweetie?'

'Suze, that's not true.' Lorna said, realising that she was expected to say something on the subject of her future. 'I haven't decided yet,' was all she could think to say.

'Lorna likes little people,' said Suzie, buttering another roll and filling it with ham and salad. 'She also wants to save big fish like whales.'

'Fish aren't little people,' said Graeme.

'Actually, whales aren't really fish,' said Lorna.

Everyone was looking at her. 'I just want to feel good about what I do, that's all. It doesn't have to be about little people, or *fish*, or anything stupid like that. Despite what Suzie thinks,' she said to Graeme, 'I'm not a completely hopeless idealist.'

'There's nothing the matter with ideals,' said Graeme. 'Idealism is only to be expected in the young. It's what distinguishes the young from the old, I suppose. Keep to your ideals, Lorna. Unlike my daughter, you might end up doing something worthwhile.' He winked at Suzie, who pretended to be angry.

'It's toilet paper, but not as we know it,' said Suzie's mum through giggles. Lorna was stuck again by how similar mother and daughter were, like Russian dolls that fit inside each other. On the few occasions that Lorna had been to their home for parties, she had always seen how Adele Bryce was surrounded by men, the centre of attraction, the focus of the room, with other wives keeping a close eye on their husbands. That was certainly the case with her parents, her father drawn like a moth into her light, her mum – wearing beige – smiling grimly from the other side of the room. Suzie's mother's genetic code seemed to have been passed in its entirety to her daughter who now said through gritted teeth: 'OK, OK. Very funny. Not.'

Suzie's parents had only once been invited to Lorna's home, and it hadn't been a success. It couldn't have been long after Tom died, and the unmentionable subject hung on everybody's lips. To avoid it, Adele talked about a recent long weekend in Venice, seeing the Grand Canal, Saint Mark's Cathedral, the Palazzo Ducale – the list went on and on, including a visit to a glass factory on Murano where she'd bought an ornate green vase which she presented to Lorna's mother as a thank you for their meal. Lorna's mum placed it on the mantelpiece alongside Tom's picture, her father pouring another glass of whisky and not looking at it.

'I used to have ideals,' said Graeme, ignoring his wife and daughter. 'Still do, I suppose. Like you, I wanted to be a lawyer. Like you, I thought that it would be a secure career. Like you, I wanted to do something worthwhile.'

'He became a lawyer anyway,' said Suzie and cackled.

Her father continued to ignore her. 'The choice I had

to make was the same choice that you have to make. Inevitably, Lorna, it all comes down to choice.'

'And what choice did you make?' she asked.

'I chose corporate law.' He sipped from his wine glass. 'Not, perhaps, the best choice for a young man with his heart set on making the world a better place. But at the time I couldn't think of anything better.' He put down his wine glass then smiled round the table. 'I still don't think it was a bad choice.'

Nobody was going to doubt him. He was a *somebody* in the Edinburgh legal world, with flattering profiles in the broadsheet newspapers, and had driven fancy cars since Lorna was old enough to tell the difference between a Vauxhall and a Ferrari. He exuded authority – was someone to be respected, to be trusted. 'It's also the reason we sent Susan to school here in North Berwick and not to some expensive school in Edinburgh. To give her a sense of what everybody's life is like.'

Lorna thought about this. 'I always thought you were a fascist.'

'Forthright, as ever.'

'Well, maybe not a fascist, but you know what I mean.'

He inclined his head. 'No, I don't think I do.'

Lorna opened and closed her mouth several times. 'OK, I want to do something useful with my life. What that something is, I don't know. I just don't want to end up doing something that I'll regret. But, maybe, yes, I am a pinko leftie, whatever that means. Sorry,' she added, 'you're probably not a real fascist.'

'You could do worse than choose what I chose.'

'I wouldn't fit in.'

He laughed. 'The world, Lorna, isn't full of little people and big people. The world is just full of people … in my experience, mostly good people. You could, of course, specialise in defence. But, and I say this honestly, few of the clients truly require the services of a lawyer. Most require other things, like drug rehabilitation, which they rarely get. On the other hand, most good people work for companies who provide them with salaries and pensions. Corporate law is about making those companies succeed, so it is also about helping people.'

There was a small silence. 'Jesus Christ, Dad!' said Suzie. 'Do you actually believe that bullshit?'

Even her father laughed. He again lifted his glass, watched red wine swirl in the subdued light. 'OK, you want to do something useful with your law degree ... charitable stuff, right?'

'I just don't want work for fat businessmen and tell them how to get fatter.'

'If it helps, we also represent some of Scotland's largest charities. Mostly for peanuts, sometimes for free. I've always believed in that side of things. Social responsibility, Lorna. Giving something back to those less fortunate. We're also involved in the administration of aid to Rwanda, among other places.' He raised an eyebrow. 'If you wanted, I could have a word with Toby Redmarsh. Do you know him?' Lorna shook her head. 'Nice fellow. I'm playing golf with him at the weekend. You may not have heard, but he's taking over from me at Wilsons. I've decided to call it a day. Time to retire.'

'Retire?' said Lorna, prevaricating. 'You're barely out of short trousers.'

Although Lorna had never heard of Toby Redmarsh, the gilded name of Wilson, MacGraw & Hamilton needed no such introduction. Discreet to the point of invisibility, its clients owned Scotland and large chunks elsewhere. This was a firm that had no need to chase business; clients aspired to be represented by Wilson, MacGraw & Hamilton. It was everything she'd always stood against; a

344

caste of privilege stretching back centuries. And yet she'd always liked Graeme and his easy charm, and the silver sports car she could glimpse through the kitchen window.

'Anyway, they wouldn't want me,' said Lorna. 'Not posh enough.'

'Don't be silly. They want talent.'

'Didn't go to the right school.'

'Neither did Suzie … Really, Lorna, it doesn't matter, not these days.' Graeme Bryce was smiling. 'But you do, in your free-thinking sort of way, kind of believe in capitalism?'

'Not unbridled, greedy capitalism, no.'

'But in bridled, *un*-greedy capitalism?'

'Look, Graeme, a firm like Wilson's wants posh *and* talent,' she persisted. 'Listen to me! My accent! I can't even speak proper English.'

'Sorry,' interrupted Suzie, 'but did anyone understand what this bumpkin actually said? Anyway,' she now added, turning to her father, 'unlike you, she has *real* principles.'

* * *

Lunch extended into late afternoon, but without charades, and Lorna escaped uneasily back to Edinburgh. Usually the Bryces' Boxing Day lunches were all about frivolity and exchanging stupid – and by unmentioned agreement – very cheap Christmas presents in bad taste. Lorna had given the Bryces a HappyMart box of seasonal chocolates with a smiling reindeer on the box; in return she'd been given a multi-pack of toilet tissue in a plastic container the size of a car engine that Suzie promised to bring with her to Edinburgh the next day. But this year had been different. Her conversation with Graeme had been an unnerving reminder that she had to start making decisions.

It had all been very well studying to be a lawyer, and deciding to be a good lawyer, whatever that meant, and wanting to make a difference, even a *small* difference, but what did that actually mean? Joe came round and they finished a bottle of wine and watched an old black and white film on TV. She didn't talk about her uneasiness; it was still Christmas, the season of goodwill. Reminded again how comfortable she felt in his company, they had no need to talk. They lay, curled together on the cigarette-burned sofa then went to bed. After making love, they slept: Lorna on her side, Joe behind her, one hand softly on her breast. In only a few weeks her life seemed to have turned on its axis. She hadn't meant to find love, and maybe she hadn't, but Joe seemed too perfect to throw back. Suzie was forever throwing back frogs; Joe was still a prince, much to her surprise. The wings on her back were tightly folded against his chest; she couldn't have flown, even if she'd wanted to. He was breathing softly; the touch of it on her shoulder like a sea breeze. She hadn't yet mentioned him to her parents; she didn't want to frighten him. At times strong and wild, he didn't look as if he wanted to be tamed. Joe had spent Christmas in Edinburgh with one of his flatmates, and Lorna had nearly invited him down to North Berwick. Tom's room still had a bed in it, rarely used.

Towards dawn she felt Joe's breath against her ear; felt his lips on her neck. She rose from dreamless sleep and turned over; felt his arms around her, pulling her close. She held to him dreamily; kissing him back.

Then she pushed him on his back and knelt over him, guiding him into her.

'I've got a suggestion,' he said.

'Can't it wait for a bit?' she replied, eyes closed. At that moment, at the end of the night, she simply wanted to be wanted.

'Simone called yesterday. She's having a baby.'

'Good for her.'

'The thing is, Nico wants a big family get-together. You know what the Greeks are like about family.'

'Joe, why not just make love to me?'

'Fuck you, Lorna!'

'That's the spirit,' she said.

Afterwards she opened the curtains and they lay and watched the dawn touch the city. 'I'd quite like to go and visit her,' said Joe. 'You know, wet the baby's head.'

'You do that when they're born.' Her head was on his chest and she could feel his heart thumping, then slowing. 'Anyway, when would this *get-together* actually happen?'

'In a few weeks.'

'But it's the middle of winter!'

'It'll be warm. Well, warm*ish*. It's Greece, remember.'

'It's also term-time, Joe.'

'It'll only be for a few days, Lorna. Anyway, you could take books and stuff with you. It's why computers and email were invented.'

'Then think of the expense, the plane tickets …'

'At this time of year, they'll cost peanuts.'

'Quite a few peanuts.'

He scratched his head then laid one arm across her back, tracing the contours of her spine with a finger. 'Come on, Lorna, it'll be a blast.'

She lay in his arms feeling safe, light thickening in the sky and, despite herself, made some mental calculations. Now she was a two-star supervisor, and had worked through the summer break, she'd got a bit of money saved and, strangely, the thought of taking time off no longer bothered her. She'd worked and worried all her life and, although her ambitions hadn't changed, she now seemed able to accept other things into her life, even if she couldn't yet discern principle from ambition. She wanted to tell Joe this, to try and explain it, but it was too early in the morning and his eyelids were closing. Maybe a holiday would do her good. The HappyMart and the University of Edinburgh could manage without her for a few days.

'Why the hell not,' she said.

TOWERS

It couldn't be Heaven because, after her meeting with God, her headache had gone from bad to worse and all she could do was sit in the beach bar and stare out over a warm sea. On her face, a Greek sun; at her back, the place of her birth. Then in a moment the sea and sand disappeared and her body felt heavy. Weights seemed attached to every part of her, even to her eyelids. She tried to open them, but couldn't. She was back in blackness, but not quite black. The darkness was shifting in interwoven columns, climbing upwards, becoming dispersed. Lorna looked up and, through darkness, could see the sky: flickers of blue amid mud grey. There seemed to be a noise like distant thunder and it echoed as if in an enclosed space. Then the smoke shifted again and she saw the same shattered houses that she'd seen before. There was smoke rising, figures hurrying, looking upwards. The same woman was at the centre of her screen, soundlessly wheeling, the small child in her arms. She was still unable to get anyone's attention. Lorna had assumed it was some kind of suicide bombing in a place far, far away but suddenly she knew it wasn't a suicide bombing. She'd remembered, because she'd seen it on the television news and in the newspapers. It was a stray bomb from a US jet that had hit an Iraqi village. Military commanders said it had been a mistake. Bad intelligence, said a general to a bank of microphones. He didn't look contrite, preferring instead to talk about the fog of war and collateral damage. He had grey, cropped hair and an air of righteousness. He had a voice born of giving orders and on his tunic were rows of medals, suggesting that he sometimes got things right. Only at the end of his short statement did he remember to apologise for the loss of innocent life. Then the news report switched to the scene of the bombing, to smoke and dust and broken-open houses. A US soldier was cradling a rifle, pointing it at the camera, motioning the camera crew to back off. In the background were women dressed in black and a child in a bloodied T-shirt. At the time, Lorna had thought that *mistake* didn't really cover it.

She thought back to the night she'd lost her virginity, the boys in the kitchen talking football and discussing David Beckham's riches and, much later, of her voice raised in protest at a war in which she wanted no part, but which had happened anyway. Collateral damage. It was the first time she'd heard the expression, her blood boiling with its banality, and the truth lying in bloodied people, not the fog of war.

Her headache eased and she walked back to the High Street. There was blue sky above and she could hear water lapping onto the shore. The shops and cafés were deserted. Lorna helped herself to a copy of *The Times* from a rack and settled down in a pavement café, flipping pages. As with everything from Earth, it was all out of date. Before the beach party she'd turned on her TV, tuning into a soap opera she liked, only to be disappointed; signals from Earth took several months to reach Heaven and she'd seen the episode before, on another television in another kind of life. She supposed it was the same with newspapers. On the front page were the same faces from Iraq: another suicide attack, or maybe the same attack. Faces with blood, anguished faces telling of loss. Children had died; a mother was cradling a dead daughter. Lorna frowned, feeling nauseous, once more sensing that a fragment of torn memory was flapping, signalling for her attention.

She walked further up the High Street and paused beside a small shop selling exquisite watches, and on a whim she pushed open the door and went inside. Her attention was caught by a display case in which sat Mike's watch and she reached inside and extracted it. It was heavy, like Mike, and had the same impressive range of dials to give you the time in Sydney or New York and the phases of the moon. But when she looked closely, the hour and minute hands were stuck solid to the watch's casing. Like everything else, it was real, but it wasn't. For a brief moment she felt a pang of affection for Mike. Despite his faults, he had made the HappyMart his universe and seemed content with it, and she was overcome by a sudden urge to phone him and apologise for not having been at work.

It was the same with the dress she'd chosen with Irene. Overnight it had gone from chic and exquisite to tatty, with poor stitching, a hem that was coming loose and a red stain down one side, barely noticeable, that could have been blood or tomato sauce. So too her diamond and emerald bracelet; it now appeared to be nothing more than moulded plastic, glittery and gaudy but capable of convincing the very young or terminally gullible.

She'd been told that she was a temporal anomaly: dead in one place, alive in another. But Lorna didn't feel dead. She didn't feel devastated by her death, because she could no longer believe she had died. Equally, she didn't feel elated by continued life either. It was as if she had become two people, with different consciousnesses in different places; the real and nonsensical place in which she existed couldn't be death, and she now sometimes heard intruding, familiar voices, as if there was talking in another room. Reality is subjective, Irene had said, lecturing her about toasters and giant mushrooms.

When she came out of the shop, Nico and another man were sitting at another pavement café, and they beckoned her over. Lorna saw that the other man was a young Omar Sharif double. Nico introduced him as a research supervisor.

'I'm Asim,' he said in an exotic accent.

They sat and drank coffee, until Nico announced that he had to get down to the beach and start cooking. Asim asked if she'd like to see where he worked and, as he seemed nice enough, she said yes. He led her off the High Street and into a maze of identical corridors, each one white and antiseptic. Then they turned a spotlessly white corner and were suddenly in countryside. They were in a huge and open place, with lush grass and woodland through which a small stream meandered and birds darted. Lorna watched a butterfly flit from flower to flower. It was a summer day, and Lorna felt a faint breeze touch her cheek.

'God thought this place would be a good idea,' said Asim. 'Somewhere for the crew to go jogging, read books, or lie in the shade of an oak tree.' He waved an arm at the trees and the rolling hills in the distance. 'Turned out to be one of his less inspired ideas.'

They entered the woodland and had to cross a small stream on the way, Lorna slipping off a rock and getting her foot wet. She stopped and listened to birds' calling, to the hiss of wind through branches. Asim was standing beside a blank wall, tapping one foot impatiently, and then pressed a blue button on the wall, a hidden door sliding open to reveal a large room with workstations neatly arrayed in long rows. At first glance it seemed no different from a call centre that Lorna had once visited, except that this one was empty.

'This,' he said, gesturing around the room, 'is a

research department devoted to collating material on Earth's biodiversity.' He sat her down behind a computer screen and showed her how to tap into the datastream that Trinity was downloading from Earth's own research computers. Each research report, he explained, had to be searched for key findings, and those findings cross-referenced with other reports. That way, said Asim, we build up a comprehensive picture of things like carbon emissions and climate change. By tapping into everything, he said, we can see the bigger picture.

'But why do you work?' asked Lorna.

He stroked his pencil moustache. 'Originally, I was a hyperspace engineer. Back then, of course, our main engines hadn't fallen off. After they did, I retrained as an astrophysicist. It might have helped us find out where we were. Then, once we'd given up on any hope of rescue, I retrained as a botanist. My speciality was orchids, if I remember, and I made several trips to Earth to identify each species and their habitats. There are still samples lying about somewhere, if you'd like to see them. Then, when God decided we'd done enough research, I retired.'

'But you're working now,' she reminded him. On one cream-coloured wall were fixed a line of clocks, each giving the time in New York, Madrid, Bali, and London. All the clocks seemed to have stopped.

'Well, some of us do, Lorna, although I did stay retired for a very long time. Then, quite recently, I decided that I needed some purpose to my life. I decided to come out of retirement and do something useful. If nothing else,' he said, looking mournful, 'it passes the time.'

'Will you transfer to Earth?' she asked.

'Maybe.' He shrugged. 'But I don't want to die.'

'Neither did I,' Lorna agreed.

For a few minutes she watched the datastream from Earth: one from the University of Bogota on the disappearing Amazon rainforest; another from Cologne University on the genome of the fruit-fly; and a third from a Japanese think-tank on the growing menace posed by the whale population. She frowned at this.

'Well, that's about it, I'm afraid. Not much to see.'

'Thanks, anyway.'

'If you like,' he suggested, 'we could go back to my place. Watch a film, smoke some dope ...'

She shook her head and Lorna now saw that, in his disappointment, he didn't really look like Omar Sharif. His good looks were superficial, like make-up: a chameleon skin stretched over a false frame. He was just somebody pretending to be Omar Sharif: an impostor, and a bad one at that. His dark eyes weren't mysterious, they were blank. He pressed a button on the outer wall and ushered her back into the woodland.

She didn't go home at first, and for a while she just walked. It was good to smell flowers again, to touch bark, to feel the brush of grass. She walked further into the woodland, no longer believing where she was and no longer caring. Trees stretched out in all directions, oaks and willows, small streams bubbling between them. In small clearings were daffodils and the drone of bees. She may have walked for hours or minutes, clambering on stepping-stones over streams, following grassy pathways up hillsides, feeling the wind on her face. She was in a familiar place, but somewhere she had never been to before. She kept looking, trying to find the clue that would tell her where she was. Then she found herself on the top of a hill, clear of the woodland, with a steep grass slope facing towards the sea. In the distance were two tall towers, and smoke was billowing from one of them.

* * *

She woke with Joe's arms around her and lay, warm and safe, listening to his slow and measured breathing, instinctively pushing herself back into him so they fitted together like spoons. Then her mobile phone alarm went off. Just before Christmas, she'd set it to make a quacking sound, like a duck, thinking it would wake her up with a smile, the closest thing to a dawn chorus that her phone offered. This was the first morning she'd experienced it and realised it was intensely irritating. Being woken up was bad enough; being woken up by an electronic duck was worse. She reached up to switch the bloody thing off, knocked her phone onto the carpet, and swore.

'Nice wake-up,' said Joe.

'Sorry ... thought it would be funny. But it's not.'

His arms were still around her and she folded herself back into him. 'Definitely not,' he agreed, sounding half-asleep.

She ran her tongue around her teeth. 'Promise I'll change it. No more animals.' They lay there a little longer, while Lorna thought about what she felt. It was still the passionate start of their relationship, the fiery beginning where they made love every time they saw one another, but not yet confident enough to put how they felt into words; the part where they wanted each other all the time, and always had to touch one another and hold hands. But emotions were still being skimmed over, particularly by Joe, although he would always hold her tight after they'd made love (a term he never used) and tell her she was beautiful – which she didn't believe, but what the hell. But she'd not known what he felt, and whether they were on a similar wavelength. It was the not knowing that troubled her. She'd never pushed him, never asked what he felt, not wanting to scare him away, but aware that he was an itinerant Australian and would one day travel home. And then what? She didn't dare think about it.

Instead, she forced herself to break free from his embrace and sit on the side of the bed. 'The HappyMart awaits, Joe. Duty beckons.'

He groaned. 'Want some coffee?' she asked.

'Hmmm …'

'Which means what exactly?'

'Yes,' he said into the pillow.

'Then, go make some, Joe. I'm going to have a shower.'

By the time she'd showered and dressed, Joe had made coffee and, unusually for him, had also made toast and they sat like a newly-married couple at the kitchen table smiling at one another. His hair was dishevelled but now she knew him well enough, she stroked it flat with one hand. 'You really are a mess in the morning, Joe.' She picked up her mug and cradled it in both hands. 'Did you mean what you said last night?'

'About Greece? Yeah, of course.'

'In which case, I'll need to buy thermal underwear.'

'It won't be that bad. It's Greece, and Crete is quite far south.'

'All the same …'

Lorna had been thinking about the HappyMart which stocked a small selection of clothing, mostly nylon socks and shoddy underwear but not, as far as she could remember, anything warm. In the intervening hours, another thought had also come to her. They were about to go to a place where the main men in her life had both made a cameo appearance; Austin professing love, Leo never phoning – and now Joe. Would they also make love outside Nico's taverna? Would that help expunge Leo's ghost? 'You won't forget about tonight?' she asked, moving onto another nagging worry.

'Dinner here, right? I finally get to meet your glamorous friend.'

'She's a flirt, Joe. *Don't* flirt back. That's an order, not a request.' She bit her lip, having long experience of Suzie's charms, particularly now she was an actress with a real film about to be released, while Lorna was a check-out operator … no, *supervisor*, which didn't make her feel any better. 'If you even so much as look at her, I will kill you..'

He was smiling. 'But suppose she says something to me. I'll have to look at her.'

She smiled back. 'You know what I mean.'

He kissed her goodbye and she listened to his footsteps on the stairs, then went to the window and watched him on the pavement, turning up the collar of his coat and looking up the window where she was standing. He waved, and she waved back, wanting to run down the stairs after him and … what exactly? Drag him back upstairs and into bed? Tell him she loved him? He'd been gone for only a minute, and already she was missing him.

She went back to the kitchen to finish her coffee, and was surprised by the front door being opened, and Suzie appearing in the doorway. She'd stayed the night in North Berwick and Lorna hadn't expected to see her until that evening. Suzie heaved a jumbo-sized bag of toilet rolls on the kitchen table. 'Your Christmas present, remember?' she said.

'What on earth are you doing here? This, for you, is officially dawn.'

'To speak to you, that's what.' Suzie made herself a cup of coffee and sat opposite Lorna, occupying the space that Joe had just vacated. She could still smell his aftershave, still see his fallen lock of hair.

'OK …'

'Christ, Lorna, your brains have turned into mush! Has that fucking shop made you deranged?'

'Only partially.'

'It's just that I can't believe you said yes!' Suzie seemed genuinely angry.

Lorna had seen the way that Suzie had scowled at her on Christmas Day, knowing a rebuke would follow at some point. That point seemed to have been reached. Lorna took a deep breath and ran a hand through her hair. 'For God's sake, he's only going to have a chat about me on a golf course! Where's the harm in that?' As Lorna said this, she had a mental picture of her own father hopelessly lost in the Auld Hoose, not making it to the first tee.

'I'm only looking out for your best interests, babe,' said Suzie, scowling as Lorna lit a cigarette.

'But where's the harm in it?' she repeated and, sighing, opened a window. A weak sun was still low over the rooftops but the wind was blowing the wrong way and most of her smoke was ending up inside the flat.

'Chats on golf courses are often fatal,' said Suzie. 'They *lead* to things.'

'Don't be ridiculous.'

'I'm. Not. Being. Ridiculous.'

'What, like an interview?'

'Exactly, Lorna. Before you know it, you'll be on a slippery slope to nowhere. What's happened to you, babe?'

'I don't know what you mean.'

'You know *precisely* what I mean. OK, you've never aspired to be Mother Teresa. At the same time, sweetie, I've never had you down as a fucking corporate lawyer.'

Lorna said nothing. It was too early in the morning to have to justify anything, let alone something she couldn't yet justify to herself.

'I'm your bestest friend, remember?' said Suzie. 'I just want to know what's happened to you.'

'Nothing, Suze. Just life.' Lorna looked at her watch,

realising what the time was. 'I have to go,' she said, then paused. 'Joe's also asked me to go back to Crete with him, visit Nico and Simone. She's pregnant, apparently.'

'How nice,' said Suzie. 'When?'

'In a few weeks.'

'In a few *weeks*! What's the point in going to Greece in the middle of winter?'

'They're having a party,' said Lorna. 'Joe thought it would be nice if we went.'

Suzie raised an eyebrow. 'You *must* be mad.'

'It's a family gathering, Suze.'

'Then maybe you are making the right choice, Lorna. Now that you're about to sell your soul, you'll soon be able to afford to do whatever you like.'

Lorna felt her blood rising. 'And what exactly is your point?' she demanded. 'You're the actress, not me. You're the one with the Porsche, not me! You're the one whose earning Christ knows how much! Not me, Suze! I work in a shop, remember, with mush for brains.'

'Well, that's what it seems like, Lorna.'

'Don't you dare lecture *me* about being able to afford stuff.'

'I'm not lecturing you!'

'It's what it sounds like, Suze.'

Suzie plonked her empty cup in the sink and turned, arms crossed over her chest. 'At least I'm doing what I've always wanted to do. Not exactly making the world a better place, but that's your thing. I'm more interested in my world. But the Lorna I *used* to know always wanted to do something useful with her life. Maybe, past tense, babe.'

'I haven't changed,' she mumbled.

'But something has … something has.'

The two girls stared grimly at one another. Suzie eventually broke the spell. 'Anyway, I've got an announcement to make.'

'An announcement?'

'A boyfriend announcement.'

Lorna, still angry, was late, and she hated being late, even for Mike. 'Then it'll have to wait, Suze,' she said, turning on her heel and leaving Suzie looking unusually crestfallen.

MINKE

There was nothing that Mike liked better than staff meetings, judging by his beatific smile and gleaming eyes, as he ran through that week's not-to-be-missed special offers. It was one regular occasion that Lorna found particularly depressing. 'Christmas is over, boys and girls,' he was announcing, beads of sweat on his forehead, the HappyMart heating having accidentally been turned up to tropical overnight, 'and that means it's going to be New Year in a few days.' Mike paused to let this not unexpected information sink in. Lorna was perched on one corner of her checkout, while Maggie, Gosia, Vlad, and Mad Steph had formed a rough semi-circle around Mike. Lorna was always struck by Mike's enthusiasm, which seemed to be shared by the other managers she'd met and even some of the staff; he genuinely seemed to consider his small empire both challenging and rewarding, and would regularly emerge from his cupboard to march proudly around his domain, offering inspirational encouragement to his staff, before returning to his office ... to what? Climb over his desk and check actual sales figures against forecasts? Chase up delayed deliveries? Go to sleep? It was hard to know what Mike did in his cupboard, but Lorna couldn't help but admire his enthusiasm for the tedium of his existence. Her bored indifference to her job made her feel like an imposter – someone who shouldn't have any stars, let alone two. She forced herself to concentrate. 'That means that mince pies go on special offer. Likewise,

Christmas pudding, lager, and own-brand whisky. Everyone likes a party at New Year, don't they, boys and girls,' he said, smiling, embracing them within the HappyMart family, as Lorna's attention drifted back to Suzie and her stinging denunciation. Had she changed? Lorna didn't think so, but did know that she was now aiming in a slightly different direction; her ambitions were no longer about nonsensical ideals, but about practicalities. The HappyMart was a constant reminder of her need to escape, to never again have to listen to Mike's encouraging speeches: to aspire to better – and to not feel guilty.

Suzie was going back to London for New Year, having been invited to several parties that would be attended by people she *utterly* had to meet, sweetie. Producers and casting directors; the glittery people that Suzie now mixed with. Joe would be working on New Year's Eve, the busiest night of his pub's year, and Lorna had invited a few friends over for the evening. They would probably drink far too much, then at midnight watch the firework display over the castle, counting down the hours and minutes until Joe came round after his shift, sober and exhausted. At the thought of him, she smiled, and Mike smiled back, delighted to see his checkout supervisor sharing his enthusiasm for food retailing.

* * *

Later that day, in the early afternoon, she found a frog sitting in the middle of aisle four. How it got there was anybody's guess. It was green and slimy, its throat pulsating and its neck craned backwards. It seemed to be looking at a box of cereals. The front of the box was dominated by a cartoon frog holding a large spoon and wearing a large smile. The frog on the floor wasn't smiling, although it was hard to tell. Steph put it in a cardboard box and said she'd release him after work. (How did she know the frog was a *him*? Lorna wondered). Steph lived near a pond, so she told everyone. The HappyMart family agreed that would be best, glad of be relieved of any responsibility. Only Mike disagreed and suggested killing it and making frog's legs, which Lorna assumed to be a joke although with Mike, being obese and much given to constant snacking, largely from the Snacks'n'Nibbles range, she couldn't be sure. The frog didn't seem to mind being incarcerated in a box but, deprived of its cartoon counterpart, did look a little lonely, or so it seemed to her. It bore a distinct resemblance to Mike.

* * *

The only living thing that Lorna had ever seen that was bigger than Mike or Aunt Meg was a whale, and it wasn't properly alive. It wasn't a very big whale. It was a minke whale to be exact, and it washed up on North Berwick's east beach one morning. This was good, because the town's famous golf course fronts onto the west beach, and all those American tourists presumably didn't want to be distracted by police and coastguards and the stench of a decomposing whale.

Lorna had always liked whales, although she'd never seen one before. On TV, they seemed placid and kind, their size making them magisterial and wise. She liked the way they weren't proper fish, and had to breathe air, and lived in families and looked after one another. She liked the mystery of them; how scientists didn't really know how they navigated the oceans, or understand the clicks and squeaks of their language. One day, she used to think, she would study whale language and translate it. Would they be spouting wise philosophy? Describing the conjunction of stars in the night sky? Or just complaining, *Bloody hell! Not fish again for tea. I wish we had some sweetcorn.*

It was Dora Prentice who heard about the whale and texted Suzie, who texted Lorna. She had no idea how Dora got to hear about it, since you couldn't see the beach from the bike sheds. Even Lorna's mum had heard about Dora's burgeoning reputation although, being Catholic, she was more forgiving. *It's her jeans*, she told Lorna, which didn't make any sense.

The whale was surrounded by yellow tape, presumably to stop small boys prodding it, and by men in uniforms wearing walkie-talkies. Occasionally the walkie-talkies would make a squawking sound and then voices came through. The words were indecipherable; like whale language that only whales could understand, it seemed that walkie-talkie language only made sense to large men in uniforms. There was also a Land Rover parked beside the whale, with COASTGUARD written on its side. Lorna looked out to sea, half expecting to see the rest of the whale's family, but there was only a large tanker heading upriver towards Edinburgh.

Suzie joined her beside the yellow tape. She was wearing tailored blue jeans and a cream blouse, neither of which would have come from a charity shop, unlike Lorna's jeans and T-shirt. Several charity shops had taken to calling their clothing pre-loved, which made them sound nice rather than secondhand, which made them sound shoddy. Pre-what? Lorna wanted to ask. Pre death? Pre realising that shapeless, baggy jeans just aren't fashionable? Her mother, whose taste in fashion should have been a criminal offence, had tried to persuade Lorna that her friends would be really jealous, depositing a few meagre coins on the shop's counter and handing her the plastic bag containing Lorna's new pre-loved jeans and pre-loved T-shirt.

'It's a big brute,' said Suzie, looking at the whale. Was that mascara around her eyes? A hint of blusher on her cheeks? She brushed blonde hair from her eyes and pouted at the whale, half closing her eyes against a gust of wind. 'Do you think it's really dead?'

Lorna was flattered that Suzie had asked her, as if she could possibly be an expert on whales. 'I expect so,' Lorna replied. 'Anyway, it's not moving.'

This wasn't quite true, as the whale's tail was still in the water so that, with each incoming wave, its tail would move up and down, like it was trying to flap its way further up the beach.

'So what are they going to do with it?' Suzie asked, brushing a grain of sand off her lipstick. Lipstick? Lorna's mother had made clear that make-up was for grown-ups. Girls are made of sugar and spice, she would say, and don't need make-up.

'Maybe just dig a big hole,' Lorna suggested.

'It would have to be the biggest hole in the whole world,' said Suzie.

'A really *fucking* gigantic hole,' agreed Lorna, which made Suzie cackle. Lorna liked it when Suzie laughed. It was uninhibited; it seemed to spring from every part of her body. Her laugh was contagious; when Suzie laughed, everyone laughed.

But it wasn't really funny. The dead whale's eye seemed alive, its blank gaze fixed on Lorna's face, following her as she moved around its great carcass. She wanted to touch the whale, to stroke its flank, to tell it not to worry, and that she, Lorna, would look after other whales from now on.

Later that afternoon they lifted the whale with a big crane onto a large lorry, then covered it with a tarpaulin, and took it away. The next week, the local newspaper put a picture of the whale on its front page. In the background, almost invisible among the crowd, were Lorna and Suzie: Suzie looking pert and demure, and Lorna in her baggy jeans looking like a refugee.

* * *

Her dad had an old record player and he'd sometimes dig it out from the living room cupboard, plug it in, and play some of the classics, as he termed them. The Beatles. The Stones. It's not just the music, he would say, eyes dimly remembering a past where a younger dad might be gyrating on a dancefloor, can of beer in one hand and a girl on the other. Her mother? Or an even younger dad with who-knows-what girl. He was a crap dancer. Dads shouldn't be allowed to dance, she would think, but he wasn't playing records: he was replaying memories from a time when she didn't exist. Lorna couldn't imagine him as a young man, and he didn't have any photographs of himself from long ago, or he said he didn't. Lorna therefore had to imagine him as he might have been: tall and chunky, not yet a wizard, and with everything in front of him, including her. But she soon gave up trying to reconstruct him as he might have been.

During her painting phase, her mum painted a picture of Lorna, a watercolour on a sheet of A4 paper. Her idea was to paint it from a photograph taken on their Norfolk holiday. Lorna was standing with her back to a river and her mother made her stand on a riverbank for ages, her chin tilted to an afternoon sun, before she clicked the camera. Then, back at home, she changed her mind about wanting to paint her from the photograph and made Lorna stand for ages and ages in the living room, in the same pose, peering intently over her easel, sometimes with a paintbrush in her mouth, trying hard to appear like a real artist like Rembrandt (whom she once compared herself to, eliciting quizzical looks between Lorna and her dad). She didn't understand why, if her mum had taken a photo with a camera, she now needed to pose for *hours* in the living room. Her mum finally put down her paintbrush with a satisfied flourish and turned the easel around.

The finished picture horrified Lorna. She'd always thought of herself as pretty in a tall and gangly way, but the picture she was presented with depicted some sort of Rosewell alien, with a large forehead, big eyes, and colourless lips. At first, Lorna tried to laugh it off, knowing her mum was utterly *shit* at painting. Then another thought dawned: maybe she wasn't that bad at painting, and this was how she saw her daughter. Maybe, God forbid, this was how she actually looked. Lorna stood in front of the bathroom mirror and held up the painting next to her face, willing the two to be different. To Lorna's horror they weren't that dissimilar: not only was she an alien, but her mum thought so too. She could have painted me differently, she thought, glossed over my faults, but she hadn't. Did that mean she didn't love me, and didn't care what I would feel? Or that she *did* love me, and was simply telling the truth? Her mum often said she always should tell the truth and that God didn't like fibbers. (This didn't make a huge amount of sense because earlier that week she'd told Mrs McIntyre, who they'd met in the street, how much she liked her new dress, and later told Lorna how horrid it was. It therefore seemed that telling fibs was also a nice thing to do. To have told Mrs McIntyre that her dress was disgusting wouldn't have been nice, even though it was the truth.)

Lorna didn't keep her mother's picture but, just in

case, still didn't like having her photograph taken. She had come to see people as they were, and no longer tried to imagine what they might once have looked like.

* * *

Her anger with Suzie dissipated during the day to be replaced by a nagging worry about that evening, with Joe meeting Suzie for the first time and the dangers that entailed, and the larger worry about Joe himself. Would he stay or would he go? No, he would go; like her, he had lofty ambitions. And if – when – he went back to Australia, would she go with him? What then for all her well-laid plans? Could she put Joe above all of them, whatever *they* now were?

During the day she told Mike that she'd soon be going to Greece for a few days and would tell him the dates as soon as she knew, a piece of information that immediately became common currency among the rest of the staff, and it seemed by their demeanour and comments that Little Miss Clever was now not only too good for the likes of them, but suddenly rich as well. Her drive past in the Porsche had not gone unnoticed.

'Never been to Greece,' was Maggie's comment, as if it was a strange planet. 'Costa del Sol's where I go. In the summer, like when you're supposed to,' she added pointedly, as Lorna fruitlessly searched the HappyMart's limited clothing range for anything that might be useful, to an endless soundtrack of Christmas songs, from the religious to the secular, from the St Paul's Choir singing 'Silent Night' to Slade belting out 'Merry Christmas Everybody'. Again Lorna was struck by how this seemed to lift the others' moods. Maggie whistled along to Bing Crosby's 'White Christmas', and Gosia hummed to Aled Jones' 'Walking In The Air', hour after bloody hour, while Lorna tried to blot out the racket with a stream of half-formed doubts and worries.

She was bad tempered and weary when she arrived back at the flat to find Suzie sprawled on their sofa wearing the shortest of low-cut red dresses. 'Nice day at the office, dear?' she enquired solicitously.

'Don't ask,' said Lorna, who had decided not to repeat that morning's argument. Right then, there were more pressing things to discuss. 'Joe's going to be here in a minute,' she said.

'Yes, I know that, sweetie. And to mark the occasion, I'm going to cook Greek. To get you in the mood, as it were, for your *holiday*.'

She made it sound as crazy as Maggie had earlier. Lorna advanced towards her friend. 'So absolutely no making eyes at him, Suze, okay? No giving him ideas, all right?'

'Have I ever …?'

'Yes, Suze, you have. Maybe not intentionally, but yes.'

'As if,' said Suzie and wiggled her bottom. Lorna saw that the shortest-of-shortest red dresses also had a slit up one side, accentuating the length of her legs and the apparent fact that she wasn't wearing underwear. 'Moi?'

Lorna sighed and shook her head. '*Please*, Suzie.'

'Don't worry, babe, I'll behave.' Suzie grinned like a Cheshire cat, then stopped smiling. 'But are you sure everything's OK?'

'You asked me that this morning.'

'And I didn't get an answer.'

'No secrets, Suze. Scout's honour.' Lorna tried to mimic a Baden-Powell salute, feeling slightly queasy at Joe's imminent arrival and Suzie's lack of clothing. She caught sight of herself in the mirror: a slightly-stained yellow polo shirt with the HappyMart logo on one breast, and black trousers, also stained. She also looked tired, her hair lank and needing washed – and Joe would be here any minute. Did she have time for a shower? Could Suzie, dressed like *that*, be trusted alone with him? Could Joe be trusted with her?

Suzie looked at her thoughtfully then, twirling round to sit properly on the sofa, planted both feet on the carpet and smoothed down her dress. 'Anyway, to change the subject, it's maybe time for me to share my little secret with you.'

Lorna raised her eyebrows.

'A rather big, *delicious* secret,' said Suzie more loudly, biting her lip and looking worried. 'I should *perhaps* have told you earlier.' Lorna saw that Suzie seemed to be blushing. 'It's just that, well … I didn't know how you'd react, sweetie.'

'React? Told me what earlier?' asked Lorna. 'Secrecy, Suze, doesn't suit you. You aren't programmed for secrecy. Don't worry, I'll get it.'

It was the doorbell and Joe was standing on the doorstep, a bottle of wine in one hand. Beside him, looking sheepish, was Austin Bird. Alarmingly, he had a large suitcase in his hand.

'What the hell are you doing here?' asked Lorna.

'You invited me,' said Joe, raising a smile.

'Not you, *him*.'

'Actually, sweetie,' said Suzie from behind. 'He's my little secret.'

NIGHTMARE

'I know I should have told you …'

'What?'

'We didn't know what you'd say …'

'What!'

They were in the kitchen, door firmly closed and Lorna, feathers ruffled, was screeching like a demented crow. Her only coherent thought was that this couldn't be happening. She had somehow entered a parallel universe where the utterly improbable was somehow reasonable.

'He wasn't supposed to get here until tomorrow. I was going to tell you this evening …'

'What!'

'I swear I didn't know he was going to be here tonight …'

Lorna took several deep breaths. 'Suzie, what the *fuck* is going on?'

'Listen, I only found out this afternoon that he was going to be early.'

'Then you could have *bloody* told me!'

'I *was* going to tell you, sweetie.'

The initial shock of seeing Austin Bird, large as life in her flat had passed. Lorna was now thinking instead about his luggage.

'You know I've always fancied him,' said Suzie, looking as apologetic as she could ever look.

'You still should have told me! Christ, Suzie! You're supposed to be my friend.'

'We didn't know how you'd react.'

Lorna snorted. '*We*!' She took several more deep breaths. 'Probably a bit like this.'

'Exactly. Look, I was just *on* the point of telling you. How the hell was I supposed to know he was going to turn up early?' Suzie flicked her hair, making it clear that none of the nightmare was her fault.

'You could have phoned me at the shop.'

'I thought I'd have time to tell you face to face.'

'He's got a suitcase,' said Lorna, with her lank hair and stained HappyMart polo shirt, and stared angrily at Suzie with her perfect hair, immaculate make-up, and not-quite dress.

'Well, aren't you the perceptive one?'

'Suzie, what the fuck is going on?' she said, then realised she'd asked exactly the same question only moments before.

'I've asked him to stay for a couple of days,' said Suzie. 'Oh, come on, petal! In the privacy of my own bedroom, I can do whatever I like. With whoever I like, OK?'

Lorna said nothing, her mouth in a thin line.

'Look, Austin was working in London and we hitched up during a break in filming. We've been pretty much together ever since. Does that answer your question?'

'No. Someone should have told me. Actually, not someone. You.'

'You'd only have thought that he was using me to get at you.'

'Really?'

'I didn't know *what* to think! OK, at first I *was* worried that he might still harbour brutish thoughts about you. However, after shagging his brains out for a few weeks, I realised he did seem to actually like me. Not you, sweetie. The Lovebirds era is finally at an end, believe me.'

'Is that so?'

'Yes, Lorna.'

'God, this is a *bloody* nightmare!'

'Then wake up from it, sweetie. And please don't start screaming again.'

Lorna had lit a cigarette without bothering to open a window, then angrily stubbed it out. 'I'm going for a shower,' she announced.

* * *

Suzie had cooked lots of olives and salad and feta cheese and lamb but, thankfully, no squid. But, with Austin there, it simply reminded Lorna of Leo and the upset he had caused. She sensed that Austin was thinking much the same thing, although he did repeatedly apologise for his unexpected appearance. He also explained that he was going to be on secondment to an engineering firm, translating theory into practice. Books and lectures can only teach you so much, he said. The London firm he was temporarily attached to had given him the chance to work on different projects. That way, he said, you get experience of different things and see what you're best suited for. He would be in Edinburgh for a few weeks in the spring on a land reclamation project; a derelict site was being cleared to make way for high-rise flats for the upwardly mobile. A deprived part of Edinburgh was being revived. After that, it was back to Bristol for his final exams. He was still in the same flat, although he didn't describe it as bijou anymore.

Lorna said virtually nothing to his monologue. Suzie mostly studied her plate. Joe simply looked bewildered.

By accident or design, the washing up was left to Lorna and Austin. Suzie had dragged Joe off to the living room to be interrogated. Lorna stacked dishes beside the sink, not knowing what to say, feeling a pulse of anger and struggling to control it.

'Suzie was supposed to have told you about us,' said Austin apologetically.

Lorna turned the tap off. She could hear voices from the living room. 'Your actress friend,' she replied, 'sometimes forgets to tell people anything.'

'It'll only be for a couple of days,' said Austin. 'You don't mind, do you?'

'You've got a rather large suitcase for a couple of days.'

'I'm going back to Bristol for New Year.'

Lorna had been out-manoeuvred, and knew it, but refused to meet his eye. She pushed her hands into warm water and extracted a serving spoon, which she elaborately washed. Having Austin in her flat made no sense. For a moment she felt herself transported back to a time when she was the centre of his life. Then, despite herself, she felt guilty, remembering terse messages on his phone. 'Somebody should have *bloody* told me.' She scrubbed at a pan and set it on the draining board.

Austin was busy drying another saucepan; frowning, just like she remembered when they were in class and he had a maths question to solve. 'Leo says hi,' he said, also not meeting her eye. 'He sends regards or love, whichever is appropriate.'

'Well, that's nice to know.' Lorna kept her eyes fixed on the sink, her hands deep underwater.

He was hard at work on the pan, burnishing it to a shine, still not looking at her. 'It's because of me,' he finally said, 'that he never got in contact with you.'

'I'd sort of guessed.' Lorna kept all inflection from her voice.

'He knew I was furious and didn't want to make things

worse. At the time we were sharing a flat. Well, you know we were. Also,' said Austin, finally looking at her, 'he didn't know if you'd be pleased to hear from him. He thought it might just have been a holiday fling.' He was almost babbling, getting everything out in the open.

Lorna dried her hands, framing an answer. 'I have nothing to apologise for,' she said slowly and deliberately, the pulse of anger forming a rhythmic beat in her temples.

'But I do,' said Austin. 'I'm sorry.'

Lorna said nothing, her anger turning to a burning headache.

'He's in Spain, in case you're interested. He finally said no to his father. Dropped out to set up a jet-ski business. His dad's livid.' She thought back to Greece and how neither Austin nor Leo had wanted to go home, and then Austin answered a question she hadn't asked. 'He still talks about you, now we're on speaking terms again. I think he regrets not picking up the phone.'

'It doesn't really matter now, does it?' She dried her hands on a dishtowel which she then threw onto the table, then turned to face him, hands on hips. 'Austin, you behaved like a complete bastard.'

'Lorna …'

'An utter *shit*!'

He was looking at the floor. 'I really like her, Lorna, although I haven't a clue why she likes me.' He frowned again, the little boy trying to solve a maths riddle. 'I can't go on apologising forever.'

'So you finally gave up the Lorna habit?'

He looked up, eyes bright. 'That's exactly what it was, a habit. Like those,' he said, nodding at the kitchen table on which was a packet of Lorna's cigarettes. 'I kicked the Lorna habit.'

'Do you know what, Austin? I don't really want to continue this conversation. I've got a headache and I'm going to bed.'

She went to her bedroom and, opening a window, smoked a cigarette, her elbows on the windowsill, her thoughts miles away. Why the *hell* hadn't Suzie told her about Austin? Christ, she'd nearly had a heart attack when she'd opened the front door. And Joe was *still* in the living room *and* she could hear his laughter through the wall. What the *bloody* hell was so funny? She threw her cigarette butt out the window and watched its parabola to the pavement below, then brushed her teeth and went to bed. From the living room, Joe was still laughing. She now had the uncomfortable thought that they might be laughing at her, regaling Joe with stories of their youth, and of the stupid things she'd said and done. *I was the person she first had sex with*, she imagined Austin telling Joe. *And that beach bar of Nico's? Well, she's had sex on the beach there as well. No, not with me, but with a friend of mine she'd only just met.* She had to prevent herself from creeping along the corridor and listening at the door. In any case, their flat had creaking floorboards that would have betrayed her. Instead, she lay in bed seething, her headache blossoming to a sharp peak before gradually subsiding. Joe eventually slid in beside her after what may have been minutes but seemed like hours and put his arms around her. 'Well, that went well,' he said.

CHOICE

The offices of Wilson, MacGraw & Hamilton occupied a corner site in Charlotte Square, Edinburgh's most prestigious business address, although it merely whispered its splendour with a small brass plate, polished to a burnished gleam. Lorna walked slowly round the square, smoking a last cigarette, composing herself. Then, squaring her shoulders and smoothing down her blue trouser suit, a special purchase for the occasion, she pushed open the door.

On the reception desk was a large bowl of exotic white flowers. The receptionist, accentless and beautiful, welcomed her with icy civility. A grandfather clock ticked in an alcove and on the wall behind her were other clocks in burnished aluminium telling her the time in Edinburgh, Mumbai, New York, and Sydney. At her feet was a briefcase, another special purchase, containing a writing pad, pen, several copies of her CV, paper tissues, and a jumbo bar of chocolate, half eaten. She looked around at the leather sofas, the intricate silk curtains at the windows; the understated power and privilege that pervaded every surface, piece of furniture and ornament, and which extended to the glacially exquisite receptionist who saw Lorna looking over and smiled professionally. Lorna closed her eyes and wondered if she was selling her soul to the devil. But she had to qualify, she reminded herself: obtaining a law degree wasn't the end of the process. She had two years as a trainee ahead, and only then could she call herself a solicitor. And where better, she'd told herself over and over, than *here* – Scotland's premier legal practice, which would sit well on her CV and open other doors. Perhaps then she could reclaim her soul from Satan supposing, of course, that the public-school toffs who ran the place gave her that chance.

'Lorna?'

She opened her eyes to find a fleshy man with wispy brown hair standing in front of her. He extended a hand. 'I'm Toby Redmarsh.'

He led her up a grand staircase, where the portraits of long-dead legal grandees hung in gilt frames. Their footsteps were soundless on thick carpet. His office was palatial and overlooked the square. Coffee and biscuits had already been arranged on a low walnut table. Lorna took the proffered cup – real porcelain – while Toby Redmarsh brushed imaginary crumbs from his immaculate suit.

'Graeme Bryce tells me you might be interested in joining us,' he said. Like the receptionist, his voice was clipped and accentless. Unlike Suzie's dad who went jogging and loved sailing, Toby Redmarsh was softer and more rounded. He was wearing half-moon spectacles that winked in the overhead light. Lorna supposed that his hobbies extended no further than the golf course.

She said yes, her eyes travelling round his huge office. Like the main staircase, the walls were hung with bewigged men in legal robes wearing stern expressions. Lorna felt oppressed by their history, still not convinced that she really did mean yes.

'Think of Wilson's as a kind of family, Lorna. We look after our people, our family, because we choose only the very best. Among the many, only a few are chosen to work here. That could be you, Lorna.'

'I'd like that,' she said, inclining her head.

'Graeme, of course, speaks highly of you. Of your

fortitude,' he said, although Lorna could only guess at what he meant. 'I've also taken the liberty of speaking to your faculty. I hope you don't mind,' he added, looking over his glasses. 'They too speak highly of you. Excellent grades and several distinctions. To fortitude, that also suggests application.'

'I've always worked hard,' she offered.

'Wilson's isn't just a legal practice,' continued Toby. 'Oh, no, that it most certainly is not. The firm dates back to the reign of Charles II and over the centuries we have advised governments and kings. Nowadays, we have offices and associates across the globe. Our clients have colonised the world and brought great wealth to Britain's shores. We are therefore not merely part of Scotland's legal history; we have played a part in the history of the nation.' Toby smiled. 'I am led to understand that you are a closet socialist. Is that true, Lorna?'

The chat on the golf course seemed to have touched on quite a few subjects. Lorna shifted uncomfortably in her seat, again feeling oppressed and out of place. 'Socialist, maybe. Pragmatist, certainly.'

Toby laughed. 'An excellent answer, if I might say so! Here at Wilson's we need all kinds of people because our task, Lorna, is to understand the political and economic landscape from all possible angles. Only then can we best advise our clients.' He paused, his glasses down his nose, appraising her. 'So why do you want to join us?' he asked.

She had all sorts of answers prepared. To earn enough to buy my own Porsche; to buy a house with Joe and raise dozens of children; to help her parents financially; to escape *their* life; to do something useful, something that might change the world just a little bit, because marching through Edinburgh had achieved nothing. Little Miss Clever took a deep breath.

* * *

The plane pushed back from the stand, and she instinctively grabbed Joe's hand, then gripped tighter as the engines started. Joe was looking out the window, seemingly lost in thought. He didn't look worried; he obviously didn't think they were going to die in a fireball. Lorna looked at him and wondered: do you love me? Finally he looked round. They were approaching the runway. Lorna had begun to sweat.

'You don't like flying very much, do you?'

'Planes crash, Joe.'

'Never one I've been on.'

'Well, this might just be the first.'

She had insisted that they got to the airport ridiculously early. Joe, who seemed convinced that their aeroplane would stay glued to the clouds, had sighed and scratched his head and ordered a taxi. 'Anyway, thanks for coming,' he now said, smiling stupidly, his lock of hair over one eye.

The engine note changed, becoming a screech. They jolted down the runway, picking up speed.

'Jesus Christ!' said Lorna.

The in-flight film was an action thriller, with lots of running about and gunfire. It seemed to involve good guys becoming bad guys and bad guys becoming good guys, until she couldn't make out which was which, and instead flipped through the airline's magazine and was amused to see that a forthcoming film would be *School's Out!*

The summer before, she had emerged into raw heat. Now it was barely warm, with a scent of rain. Before, the sky had towered over them; mountains precisely etched. Now, the sky was ochre, the mountains indistinct. Simone and Nico were in Arrivals to meet them. Simone was jumping up and down with excitement to see her brother; Nico, in white T-shirt, black jersey, and jeans, shook her hand rather formally. Simone kissed her on both cheeks like an old friend.

Nico drove with Lorna and Joe in the back seat. He drove rather like the boys on the Greek beach had played volleyball. It wasn't simply an exercise in getting from A to B, it involved bravado. On a precipitous road, Nico would drive with one hand on the steering wheel, look studiously at Simone, and light a cigarette at the same time. To Lorna's surprise they came to a stop outside the same hotel that she and Suzie had stayed in.

Nico only spoke limited English, but was learning. Simone spoke limited Greek, but was also learning. 'We speak only love,' said Simone, slamming the car door shut. She was only just pregnant; no bump yet. 'It means he doesn't have to listen to my crap opinions and I can't understand his. Maybe once we understand each other a bit better, we'll get divorced.'

In the hotel's reception was the same dowdy Greek woman who Lorna remembered from her last visit. Now, she was introduced as one of Nico's aunts, and actually smiled. Before, she'd shrugged at the idea of a sea view; now, their balcony looked over the Mediterranean.

Lorna slept alone for the rest of the afternoon. Joe and Simone had a lot of catching up to do. Later, he came back to the room and made love to her. He tasted of warm salt; he'd been swimming.

She stretched, sleepily happy, then went down to the empty beach. Joe wanted a nap, and Lorna fancied a swim, despite the lowering sun and tugging breeze. She lay on her back in the sea, her ears under the water, listening to the tug and pull of sand, a winter sun on her face and the mountains dimly silhouetted against the sky.

***

The party was at the beach bar, which had closed for the winter. Several antique relatives had been transported by boat from town, then carried onto the beach by other relatives. Joe explained that some of them had flown in from Athens, a cousin had come from New York. The Greeks, he explained, value family more than we do.

The taverna's wooden tables had been pushed into a U-shape and covered with white paper tablecloths. Huge mushroom-shaped gas heaters were sprinkled around the table, and a bonfire was blazing on the beach. The litter that Lorna remembered from the year before, gathered under the olive trees, had been cleared away. Music was playing from speakers strapped to the awning and a torn plastic corner still flapped in the breeze.

There was a scent of distant rain, clouds crowding onto the mountain peaks. Despite the gas heaters and bonfire, everyone was wearing warm clothing.

Plates of food had been laid out on the tables. One of Nico's brothers was in charge of the barbeque; Nico had his arm around Simone. They were whispering in one another's ears. How much they understood was anybody's guess.

After the food there were toasts and, after the toasts, dancing. The antiques looked on, clapping. Old ladies in black smiled and catcalled. Old men with stained teeth and rosaries between their fingers leaned on sticks. The youngsters on the dancefloor, arms around one another, swayed left and right.

'Hi, how's it going?' Simone flopped into a chair beside Lorna. Joe was in another corner of the bar talking to one of Nico's sisters. Joe could talk to anyone, even if they couldn't speak English.

'Good, thanks.'

'Nico says I shouldn't be dancing in my condition,' said Simone, extracting a paper napkin from a silver dispenser on the table. She mopped her brow then discarded the napkin on the wooden floor. She was drinking orange juice and held out the glass. 'The bastard's banned me from drinking alcohol,' she said, casting a not-unfriendly glance in her husband's direction. Nico was at the centre of the dance, a handkerchief in one hand, one end of which was held by the next dancer, one of his brothers.

Lorna was watching Joe, who seemed to be communicating with the young Greek girl in sign language. She was laughing. Lorna had also noted how beautiful the Greek girl was. Simone saw the direction of Lorna's gaze.

'He's a good boy, usually,' said Simone. 'But keep a close eye on him, Lorna. He's a bit of a rogue.' Simone was smiling. 'He's got his life mapped out. Right now, it's all about having a good time. Then, it's back home and into radio. He's very single-minded. OK, maybe that doesn't make him a rogue, but he always gets what he wants.'

'That just makes him ambitious,' said Lorna. 'Nothing wrong with that.' She knew that Scotland wasn't going to be Joe's permanent anchorage, despite reminding him repeatedly that Scotland also had radio stations. 'We're just enjoying being together,' she said, lying through her teeth.

Simone saw that Nico's back was turned and quickly gulped back some of Lorna's wine. 'I don't know why I listen to the bloody man,' said Simone, wiping one hand across her mouth. 'A few drinks never harmed anyone.' Simone took another surreptitious swig from Lorna's glass. 'I just don't want to see you hurt when he

383

eventually ups sticks. Even if he is my brother,' she added.

'I won't be,' promised Lorna, refusing to think about it.

They were interrupted by Nico asking Simone to dance, having temporarily forgotten what condition she was in. Lorna watched them for a while, distracted. She had come back to a place she didn't think she'd ever visit again. Time and space seemed to have fused together; she now had a blue trouser-suit hanging in her wardrobe and had worn it several times in the intervening weeks, meeting Toby and other colleagues. Joe was still waving his hands around; the Greek girl was still laughing.

Lorna walked down to the sea. Behind her, she heard a door close, a voice raised in laughter. The sea hissed and foamed at her feet. She was wearing a cream cardigan and she wrapped it more tightly round her shoulders. A cool breeze was coming off the sea. By accident or design, she realised she was standing on the exact spot where she'd made love with Leo. The same waves were flopping onto the shore; the same sky framed against the mountains. The conversation with Simone had saddened her; made everything seem temporary.

She heard footsteps behind her and knew who they must belong to.

'Lorna, I saw you wandering off. What's wrong?'

She shook her head, not speaking.

'You're crying.'

'I'm not crying,' she replied, trying to make light of it. 'It's just that my eyes are leaking.'

Joe put a hand on her shoulder then gathered her to his arms, and she stared over dark water. 'I used to have a teacher called Mr Sullivan,' she said softly, not caring if she was making sense. 'He had just got divorced and he had problems. Up here,' she said, releasing a hand to tap her head. 'I've realised that, in me, he saw a kindred spirit.'

Joe had one arm around her middle and she leaned into him, grateful for his strength. 'Toby Redmarsh phoned this afternoon,' she said. 'He was phoning to offer me a job. Actually, a provisional job, until I pass my finals.'

Joe stroked her hair.

'I said yes,' she told Joe, wondering how Suzie would react.

Lorna waited for Joe to say something, to tell her she'd made the right decision, but he said nothing. Instead, he continued to stroke her hair. She remembered him saying that he only told people the truth, and if he couldn't be truthful he didn't say anything. Through his silence, Lorna didn't know what he was thinking or what he really felt about her. Behind them, she could hear baleful Greek music. Ahead, the dark sea had trapped reflected lights from the taverna and drowned them.

LOVE

They were only in Greece for four days, but long enough for Lorna to be added to Nico's family. His brothers took her to the ruins at Knossos; his sisters, including the sultry beauty who had captivated Joe at the beach party, took her on a shopping spree to Heraklion. Lorna bought a revealing cream dress she doubted she'd ever wear and Nico's sisters bought her an enamel pendant on a leather thong. It wasn't something she would have chosen. It had an eye motif. For good luck, she was told. An elderly aunt drove them to their family farm in the hills above the town. Under a trellis festooned with vines, Lorna drank homemade wine and dipped warm bread in olive oil. On the coast, with its tourist developments, was one Crete; a few miles inland, away from the sea and beaches, another. The older Greeks didn't much like what was happening to their island. It was being transformed into a place devoted to other people's pleasure. People even make baby on the beach, said the elderly aunt, making Lorna blush. At the same time, they told her, other people's pleasure gives jobs for our sons and daughters. It means they can stay here, with us.

They swam every afternoon, even though it had grown even colder, and even on the two days when it rained. After swimming, they would go back to their hotel and make love. That for Lorna was the best time of day; lying in Joe's arms, feeling complete, watching the sun sink to the sea, listening to the rhythm of his breath.

One afternoon, Lorna cut her big toe on a shard of

glass on the beach. Simone was with them and she took her to see the old woman in their hotel. She washed the cut and pressed on a bandage seeped in blue-grey liquid.

'It's a herbal thing,' said Simone. 'It's something that only grows here in Crete. The old folks use it instead of disinfectant.'

Lorna stood up tentatively; the old woman now washing her hands and saying something to Simone.

'She says that the plant is called *eronda*,' said Simone.

On their last night, bags packed, Lorna woke from a bad dream and, wrapping herself in a towel, soundlessly padded out to the balcony. It was almost dawn and first light was rising from the horizon. It was cold. An aeroplane that inexplicably hadn't crashed, carved a vapour trail across the morning sky. She'd been dreaming about Joe, but he hadn't been in her dream. She'd been looking for him, searching through her flat, but he wasn't there. Yet she could smell him, feel that he was around, if only she could remember where. But it wasn't that which had made her suddenly wake up. Something was wrong, something she couldn't put a finger on.

Without thinking, she lit a cigarette, brow furrowed. Then she peered back into the bedroom to make sure that Joe was still there. He was lying on his side, facing away from her, a sheet wound round his legs. His back was slightly arched and in the morning light Lorna could see every knot in his spine.

She ground out the cigarette. She supposed it was just pre-flight nerves and the emotion of departure. This time tomorrow, she thought, I will be back in Scotland. At this, she felt a lump in her throat, remembering her dream and how she'd frantically searched through endless rooms for a person who was no longer there.

Lorna slipped back into bed and put her arms around Joe. He stirred against her, still sleeping, and they lay still for a while; then she kissed the nape of his neck until he woke up.

They made love, without words, as the sun rose. She studied his face as she kissed him, running a hand down the contours of his forehead, eyes, cheeks, and chin. When he smiled, which was often, a small dimple would appear on his chin. Lorna held him tight, feeling languid and warm in his arms. But her brow was still furrowed; she had a sense of something. Perhaps it was the aftermath of making love, or the end of their holiday, but it felt like something else was ending. She didn't know and absently ran a finger down his spine, feeling its sinuous contours. He was feigning sleep; Lorna could sense tension in the muscles on his back. His eyelids were closed and for some moments she examined his face, shadowed in the early light, like a Greek god, strong yet vulnerable: his sculpted chin, the curl of his eyelashes, the pale pink of his lips.

'Say something, Joe.'

There was a short silence. 'Like what?' he asked, his words slurred into the pillow. She knew she had chosen precisely a wrong moment to start a conversation.

Instead, she bumbled on, trying not to sound needy or pushy. 'I don't know. Something. Anything.'

He reached to his chin and scratched. It made a sound like sandpaper and his eyes momentarily opened. She was watching him but couldn't see what he was thinking. 'It's the middle of the night,' he told her, extracting himself from her arms and turning over, excluding her, making her feel stupid, like a limpet that has been chiselled away.

Then her phone trilled. A text message from Suzie. *Expext u want me to pik u op*, obviously written in haste at crack of dawn in Edinburgh. Lorna texted back, then lay back on the dishevelled bed, not touching Joe. He'd shifted in irritation when her phone had beeped, and she had the distinct impression that he also blamed her for Suzie's text. He was lying at the furthest extremity of the bed, the sheet wound tightly around him. Her bad dream lay between them and she didn't know how to explain it to herself. He often told her that she was lovely, but had never mentioned the word *relationship* again. Nor had she, because it would have seemed presumptuous. She didn't want to frighten him away or bind him too tight with silky words. When will you leave me? she wanted to ask, but didn't dare, needing the reassurance that he cared, or felt *something*. They lay, without more words, each now pretending to be asleep.

* * *

Love: such a small word, encompassing so much. All emotions, good and bad, hopes and fears, squeezed into four letters. Lorna sensed in Joe a missing part of her. Is that what love is? Discovering a missing jigsaw piece and finding that it fits? Are we all born incomplete, compelled to search for the lost bit of us? Lorna only knew that she was both exultant and terrified. What will happen when he leaves? she kept thinking – an uncomfortable mantra in her head. Joe was easy-going, always smiling, always reaching out to her; but he didn't do meaningful conversation, or talk much about his past. Lorna knew that he had been born near Sydney. His parents, both doctors, owned some land and kept horses. He had two sisters, Simone in Greece, and one in the USA – a biologist researching new treatments for malaria. She wanted him to map out his childhood, to describe the heat and dust, the names of the horses. Lorna tried to describe her own childhood, without embellishment, in an effort to encourage him, but he would shy away, change the subject. Joe was good at that, effortlessly skating back to trivia and platitude. He wasn't being evasive; he just didn't see the point of talking about the past. To him, it was unimportant. What had been, was gone.

Lorna told him that she'd been born in the open air right beside the sea. I now have an affinity with the sea, she laughed. It must have been the first thing I saw and heard. He raised an eyebrow but didn't reply. After making love one night, Lorna asked him about other girlfriends. Have you ever been in love, she asked? She'd rehearsed the question, making it sound insubstantial, without hidden meaning. Only you, she'd hoped he'd say. But he didn't. He talked briefly about a girl called Myrtle, a cheery soul with buck teeth, but didn't say much about her. Was Myrtle the person you first had sex with? she asked. Again, it was asked lightly. Lorna didn't want to know about Myrtle or her poor dentistry; she wanted to know about herself, where she stood. No, he replied; that happened earlier. In the darkness Lorna couldn't tell if he was smiling, then he kissed the top of her head, almost fatherly, like her dad used to do. But his kiss was also a full stop. He wasn't going to talk about Myrtle, or anybody else, including her, and Lorna soon realised from his breathing that he was asleep, one arm flung wide across the duvet, the other around her shoulders, holding her close, keeping her safe.

Was Joe missing a bit of jigsaw, she wondered? If so, was it Lorna-shaped? Or was he already complete, his own country, with impermeable borders? It was hard to tell, although it seemed likely. To him, the past was irrelevant; it may have shaped him, but it wasn't worth the bother of describing it. It was only the present that mattered. Instead, Lorna bought jumbo boxes of condoms, in every permutation and flavour, constantly gratified by how many they were using, and hoped that the act of love could become the fact of it. That was her strategy, pure and simple, and it would have to do. It was enough.

* * *

To Lorna's surprise, Nico's whole family came to their hotel to see them off. Frowning, Lorna watched Joe kiss the beautiful Greek girl on both cheeks, his hand hesitating on the small of her back for just a moment longer than necessary. To her relief, Simone drove them to the airport. Nico was on a shopping expedition to buy a new awning for the taverna. The holiday season would be starting again soon.

At the airport, Lorna drank a glass of retsina and took a second glass to the plate glass window overlooking the tarmac. Their plane was close to the window, the two pilots visible on the flight deck, running through a checklist. The co-pilot, with three stripes on his shoulder and a clipboard in one hand, had just said something to the other pilot, with four stripes. They were both laughing. Joe was at a table in the airport bar, nursing a beer, his mobile pressed to one ear.

Lorna sat down and lit a cigarette. 'Who were you phoning?'

He shrugged his ample shoulders. 'Just telling the guys when we're getting back.' He reached into his backpack and pulled out a bottle of Greek brandy. 'We're going to give this a try tonight.'

Lorna had only briefly met his flatmates. Her flat was much nicer, her bed much bigger – so they usually ended up at her place. It was clear that, after several days in his company, Lorna was being excluded.

'Can I ask you something, Joe?'

'Sure, go ahead.' He was sitting with one leg draped

over the other. Behind dark glasses, Lorna couldn't see his eyes.

'It's just that my parents would like to meet you.' She watched him carefully, but he didn't flinch. 'Joe, they know I'm in Greece with a boyfriend. They know we've been seeing each other for a while now. They'd just like to meet you, that's all.'

'Understandable, I suppose.'

Lorna ploughed on. 'I told them that, if you weren't busy, we could go down this Sunday. It's no big deal,' she finished, feeling breathless.

His hands had settled quietly on his lap. Lorna still didn't know what he was thinking. 'Sure, Sunday's fine.'

'It really isn't a big deal,' she repeated, feeling foolish and defensive, 'so please don't think I'm being ... well, you know.'

He smiled but didn't offer any words to make her feel better. Only hours beforehand they'd made love, morning sunlight patterning the bedroom ceiling. Even then, his thoughts had been locked away.

'Don't worry about it,' he said, planting both feet on the ground and standing up. He indicated the bookshop at the end of the concourse. 'I'd better get something to read on the plane.'

Lorna took a deep breath, pleased that the visit had been agreed, then irritated that she should feel so awkward about it. He was her boyfriend; she had every right to parade him in front of them. She was also their daughter and they had every right to meet Joe. When he was out of sight, Lorna unzipped his backpack, took out his mobile phone, and checked the last number dialled. He hadn't lied: he had been phoning his flatmates, she'd been wrong to doubt him.

Lorna swigged back her retsina, then a disembodied voice said that their flight was ready for departure.

393

Lorna slept on the plane, having consumed two further small bottles of wine. Joe, in the window seat, read his book. When she dozed off, he was reading page six and when she woke up, two hours later, he was only on page ten. Although the book was open on his lap, he seemed content only to look out the window. Lorna placed her head on his shoulder and a hand on his knee. He placed one of his hands over hers then kissed the top of her head.

Suzie met them at the airport, having spent the last week in Edinburgh between modelling assignments. Although it was freezing cold, Suzie had lowered the Porsche's roof. Being the smallest, Lorna was squeezed into the back seat with the luggage. Suzie dropped Joe off at his flat. He gave Lorna a hug and kissed her on the lips.

'Are you sure you won't come back?' asked Lorna.

He shook his head. He had things to do, he said, clothes to wash. Already, still in his presence, she was missing him. It was late afternoon and they hadn't made love since the morning, and she missed *that* as well; the scent of him, the press of his body against hers, the way they fitted together perfectly.

'Thanks for the lift,' he said to Suzie, hoisting his bag to his shoulder, a lopsided grin on his face and a lock of hair across one eye. Suzie had parked by the side of the Royal Mile and a tourist coach was impatiently waiting for them to move.

'Think nothing of it,' Suzie replied, with a sideways look at Lorna. 'I was going to the airport anyway to pick up my rapacious capitalist friend.' Lorna had sent Suzie a text from Crete, telling her about the job offer.

The tour bus blared its horn, the driver gesticulating through the windscreen. Suzie smiled sweetly then raised one finger.

Lorna sighed. 'We'd better go.'

They accelerated away, Suzie giving another raised

finger to the coach driver, Lorna turning in her seat for a last glimpse of Joe. She barely had time to fasten her seatbelt before Suzie started in. 'Do you know, Lorna, I didn't realise you're actually just like the rest of us.'

'That's a little unfair,' said Lorna.

'Well, what am I supposed to think? The soft-centred Lorna I thought I knew turns out to be someone else. I was right, wasn't I?'

'About what?'

'About people having chats on golf courses. I did warn you.'

Despite having slept on the flight, Lorna was still tired. She'd survived another journey by aeroplane. The open-top car, wind rushing in, magnified the chill. Involuntarily, she shivered. 'That's just stupid,' she said, gripping the edge of her seat as Suzie swung round a corner, tyres squealing on the cobblestones. 'It'll be valuable experience,' she offered, 'and I need to qualify. *Then* I'll do something else.'

Suzie stayed silent for a while, itself something of a rarity. 'You've changed, babe,' she said, again stopping at a red light and revving the engine. A group of young men, crossing in front of the car, turned to stare, perhaps recognising someone who wore silver jumpsuits on TV. Suzie drummed her fingers on the steering wheel and pretended not to notice. 'The Lorna I used to know would have said no to my father.'

* * *

The next few days were warm and cloudless. Suzie said it had rained non-stop for days and that Lorna must have brought back some Greek weather with her. The visit to North Berwick loomed large in her mind. Joe was on night duty for the rest of the week, so she wasn't able to see him or gauge how he felt. At the same time, her parents had a right to meet the person who, they probably assumed, was sharing her bed. On the morning after coming back from Crete, she woke to find he wasn't there, then realised he'd spent the night at his own place. Nothing wrong with that, she thought, but felt his absence keenly, then remembered her troubled dream of search and loss.

Lorna tried to explain something of this to Suzie, each on either side of the kitchen table. Lorna was drinking strong coffee she'd brought back from Crete. Suzie was drinking a herbal tea that someone had told her was good for her complexion. Suzie, who didn't need to diet or take exercise, was prone to taking bad beauty advice.

'It was just a dream, sweetie.'

'But it seemed to *signify* something, Suze.'

'Don't be so bloody silly.'

'Suzie, I don't think that I am being silly.'

'Lorna, he's crazy about you.'

Lorna sniffed. 'How the hell do *you* know?'

'He told me, for God's sake! You were in the kitchen with Austin doing the washing up.' Lorna narrowed her eyes. 'He told me he'd never met anyone like you before. He actually did say he was crazy about you.'

'I suppose,' she conceded.

'I keep telling you ... don't ever suppose!' commanded Suzie.

Lorna checked her emails and to her surprise, found one from Leo.

Lorna

Austin finally gave me your email address. Hope you don't mind my writing. I gather that Austin was staying with you for a few days over Xmas. Him

396

and Suzie, who'd have thought it! One word of advice: don't ever let him cook spag bol. It's revolting!

He's probably told you that I'm now in Spain. God, you'll hate me, but an aunt died and left me some money. But the English legal establishment is probably better off without me.

By chance, a pal of mine in Bristol is Spanish and, to cut a long story short, we're starting a water sports business just up the coast from Marbella. Have to see how it goes, I suppose. It's not going to be much of a business this year, but we've got plans! There's good scuba diving here, so we'll maybe do that as well next year. That is, if we can buy a proper diving boat. Carlo, my pal, speaks good Spanish (well, he's Spanish!) so that helps. I just prance about the beach and look pretty (ha ha!)

I'm sorry about not contacting you. Well, you know why. For what it's worth, I'm sorry.

It would be great to hear from you.

Love to Love

Leo (and Samantha, who's heavily pregnant)

Lorna, smiling, reread his email, remembering his mane of hair, the predator who had followed her across a headland, and made love to her at the water's edge. She looked out across rooftops to the castle. In daylight, it was attached to its rock, grey and solid and rooted in the past. Lorna looked again at Leo's email, feeling momentarily connected to him, then printed it out. But he too was in the past, and she tore the page into pieces then drizzled them into the waste bin.

TELEPHONE

On the Sunday, as planned, Lorna picked up Joe in the Porsche. She was unnaturally nervous, checking to make sure he'd shaved and had brushed his hair. Although she was only introducing him to her parents, it felt momentous, and she knew that it would also feel momentous to them. She'd never introduced any of her boyfriends to her parents. Austin didn't count; they known him from school.

'My dad's an alcoholic, Joe.'

'You've told me.'

'So, if he takes you to the pub, which he might well do, you mustn't allow him to drink anything.'

'I can hardly stop him, can I?'

Suzie's Porsche was growling, eating up miles. 'Then, Joe, please *try*. Oh, and don't tell them I still smoke. They think I've given up.'

'Maybe you should.'

Lorna was still running through a check-list of do's and don'ts. 'My mother's also quite religious, Joe. So don't tell her any nun jokes.'

He looked pained. 'I don't know any.'

'She might also want to say grace before we eat. So *please* don't do anything stupid like snigger.' Her mum had always said grace before meals, her father winking across the table.

Joe was looking at her sideways, noticing her grim concentration. 'Anything else?'

But, working through worst case scenarios, Lorna

wasn't really listening. 'Not for now,' she told him. 'Just behave, OK?'

* * *

The door to her parents' flat was already open by the time they reached the landing. One of them, probably her mum, would have been watching the street and seen the Porsche throb to a standstill. Her father was brushed and groomed, and had put on a grey suit and tie. Her mum had laid the dining table with the best cutlery. Three wine glasses had been set out. In the centre of the table was a lit candle. Lorna couldn't remember the last time she'd seen a lit candle in the house. Candles were for church or power-cuts. Her parents obviously saw significance in the visit.

'It's nice to meet you at last,' said her mum to Joe. Inwardly cringing, Lorna recognised her mother's best telephone voice: the voice she cultivated when posh people came into the bakery, the voice that was the perfect accompaniment to lit candles and their best cutlery. 'Lorna's told us so much about you.'

Joe kissed her mother chivalrously on the cheek, then shook hands with her dad. 'Nothing scurrilous, I hope,' said Joe, which made her mum laugh rather too loudly and her father look uncomfortable.

'And what is it that you do, Joe?' asked her dad once they were seated in the living room. Her father, of course, knew *exactly* what Joe was doing, so didn't have to ask. It seemed to her a question designed to winkle out Joe's long-term prospects, and Lorna's toes curled inside her shoes.

'At the moment, working in a bar. The Rose and Thistle, on Rose Street, if you know it,' said Joe. Bracketing her father with a bar was not a good idea and her toes curled further.

'But I'm trying to get into radio,' continued Joe. 'That's what I really want to do. I've got a couple of interviews lined up. Next week,' he added, looking at Lorna.

She hadn't known this. He'd not mentioned anything about interviews. He hadn't even told her he was looking for a proper job. As far as she knew, he'd been planning to return to the other side of the world, but not telling her when. Now she didn't know what to think. Did this mean that he might stay? With her?

'That's nice,' said her Mum. 'I like listening to the radio.'

'What kind of radio?' asked her father, who listened only to the TV.

'On the production side, ideally. But I did a bit of DJ-ing back in Oz, so I can do that as well. Anything, really,' he concluded, smiling engagingly, 'that gets me experience.'

'It does count,' said her father with some vehemence. 'Experience, I mean.'

Lorna was sipping at a glass of white wine and soda. Mostly soda: she was driving. Joe was drinking a glass of beer. He usually drank straight from the bottle but had poured his beer into the cut-glass tumbler that Lorna's mother had given him. Every time he picked up his glass, Lorna willed him to replace it on the plastic coaster on the side table.

'I hope you like lamb,' said her mother.

'My absolute favourite!' said Joe, laying it on a bit thick for Lorna's liking. 'Your daughter's been telling me what a good cook you are.'

This made her mother flush. 'My daughter talks rubbish, Joe. Although you probably know that by now, don't you?' She chuckled. Joe smiled back. As far as Lorna could remember, she hadn't told Joe anything about

401

her mother's cooking. Like a ham actor, he was making it up as he went along. She shot him a warning glance that he chose to ignore.

'I understand you play golf,' said Joe to her father.

'Badly, I regret. What about you?'

'Love it.'

Lorna nearly spluttered into her glass then, in mounting surprise, listened to Joe explaining that he had been a schoolboy golf champion, then the captain of his university team. 'I'm a bit rusty now, of course,' he added with a winning smile.

'You should have mentioned that Joe plays golf,' said her dad in mild rebuke, now clearly approving fully of his daughter's boyfriend. Lorna smiled back thinly, wondering what else she didn't know.

Then dinner was ready and they sat in the window alcove looking down into the street. The Porsche was parked under a streetlight opposite. 'Now,' said her mum, once they were all seated, 'let's say grace and then we can eat.'

'Please,' said Joe, 'let me say grace.'

'Lorna!' said her mother. 'It's no laughing matter.'

* * *

Joe was witty and said the right things. He didn't offer her dad any wine, but didn't make it obvious. He listened intently to her father's opinions about the government's economic policies, told solemnly by the failed accounts clerk, and laughed along with her mum when she recounted baking disasters. He was so successful that after supper her father abducted Joe to the pub to show him off to his friends.

'Suzie sends love, by the way,' Lorna said to her mum once the men had departed for the Auld Hoose.

'Sexy Sue? That's nice, dear.'

Her mother didn't seem to be listening, nervously twirling her wedding ring. She heard Joe laughing in the street below. 'He seems a nice boy,' her mum said. Suzie Bryce wasn't uppermost in her mind. 'Is it serious?'

Lorna shook her head, then nodded. 'I don't know, Mum. I haven't asked him.'

'But do you like him?' she persisted.

Again, she nodded.

'He's a bit like that boy you went out with. Austin somebody-or-other. Bird, that's it. They're quite similar, you know.'

Lorna was looking at a framed photograph on the mantelpiece. In the background was a riverboat. In the foreground were her parents, their hands on their children's shoulders. Everyone was smiling. She couldn't remember who her dad had roped in to take the photograph. Beside the photograph was the vase that the Bryces had brought with them. 'I suppose they are a bit,' said Lorna. 'Yes, Mum, I like him lots and lots.'

The men came back from the pub. Joe smelled of beer. Her father didn't smell of anything and, according to Joe, had only drunk two soft drinks.

It was time to go.

Her dad kissed her on both cheeks and shook Joe's hand with genuine enthusiasm. 'Next time, bring some clubs,' he said. 'We'll play a round together.' He was rubbing his hands together, already relishing the challenge.

'Wait, I've got you something,' said her mother.

There was a small box on the hallway table on which sat their telephone. Inside the box was a golden butterfly brooch. 'I saw it in Henry's. You know, the jewellers. It made me think of you.'

Her mum fixed the brooch to her blouse and gave it a

rub with her sleeve. 'All grown up, and flown the nest,' she said. 'This is to remind you to fly back sometimes.'

* * *

On the way to North Berwick, the Porsche had growled. Lorna had wanted to get there quickly, or as quickly as she dared, and get the evening over with. On the way back to Edinburgh, the engine purred. She wasn't in a hurry. One hand fingered her mother's brooch. 'Do you really play golf, Joe?'

'Of course. Wouldn't lie about something like that. Seems a nice guy, your dad. Maybe I'll take him up on his offer.'

'Well, they both seemed to like you,' she conceded, accelerating past the town petrol station and onto the open road, 'although I don't remember ever having told you about my mother's cooking. She's not that good, Joe.' She couldn't see whether or not his eyes were closed.

'All women like to think they're good cooks,' he said. 'I read somewhere that it's something to do with their nurturing spirit. Anyway, I thought a bit of flattery wouldn't be a bad thing,' he added, turning towards her and giving Lorna a smile.

'Nor,' she went on, warming to her subject, 'did you tell me anything about job interviews.' She knew she was sounding unreasonable. She didn't want to be angry with him. 'I just don't know what to think, Joe.'

'About what, for Christ's sake?'

'About you! About us, for God's sake! First I find myself going out with an Aussie bloke. Then I introduce him to my parents, knowing that *sometime* he's going to go back home. Then I find out he might not be going home after all. And, worst of all, I find out he plays golf! All that, Joe, I had to find out this evening.' He was looking ahead, his eyes on the road. Lorna let out a deep breath, then fished in her handbag for cigarettes. 'We just never talk, that's the problem.'

'We talk all the time.'

'Not about things that matter.'

'OK,' said Joe eventually. 'I should have told you about the interviews. But I haven't seen you all week, have I? Honest, I was going to tell you this evening. It was going to be a kind of surprise.' He opened his window to let out cigarette smoke. 'Anyway, you've not exactly been totally open with me.'

Lorna didn't know what he was talking about.

'You didn't tell me your father was a wizard,' said Joe.

* * *

Back in Edinburgh, the car safely parked, Lorna poured a large glass of white wine. She still didn't know what to feel. Suzie was out somewhere and was due back in London the following morning. Joe had gone to the toilet and she wanted to go to bed. She wanted to be held tight, to feel his passion, to feel wanted. She had planned to wake early, to savour the early morning, to feel Joe solidly beside her, before going to college and then to the HappyMart. The pulse of her existence had returned to normal, but with a real degree and a real job on the horizon. His mobile phone was beeping. He'd left it on the living room table and, remembering Heraklion airport, she picked it up and pressed the green button.

Joe came back from the toilet and looked at her quizzically.

'Joe, can I ask you a question?'

He shrugged. 'Of course.'

'Who the *fuck* is Sarah-Ann?' Lorna waved his mobile phone at him, taunting him to tell the truth.

'She's my flatmate.' His words were without inflection, but his eyes were more eloquent. Lorna could see confidence drain through his shoes.

'I know that. But she's more than that, Joe.'

'Don't be ridiculous!' He didn't know whether to be angry or to laugh, but colour had left his cheeks.

Lorna hurled the mobile phone at his face. With a blurred movement of one hand, he irritatingly caught it. 'I swear, Lorna … there's nothing's going on.'

'She called you *darling*, Joe. She asked if you were coming home tonight.'

'She shouldn't have said that.'

'But she did.'

'That doesn't prove anything,' he persisted. Except she wasn't listening to his words; she was watching his face, and the way he couldn't look at her.

'I don't *have* to prove anything,' said Lorna, determined not to cry. 'Why, Joe?'

He sat down heavily, looking down. 'It doesn't mean anything,' he finally admitted.

Joe, her great redeemer, had built her up only to knock her into pieces. In that eviscerating moment, her blood had turned to ice. Her wings, long folded to her back, wanted to beat at his face. Joe, immobile on his chair, could only mumble.

'Just get out,' she told him.

'Lorna, please let me explain.'

'No!'

'Please, I can explain…'

'There's nothing to explain.'

'Please!'

'I don't want your bloody explanations, Joe! I just want you to get the *fuck* out of here!'

He left, recognising a volcano about to explode, leaving her feeling stupid and abused, and then she did cry, wet tears for what might have been. Suzie came back later but, by then, Lorna had gone to bed, lying in the dark, not wanting to talk about it. Joe had betrayed her and it now all seemed such a waste. All those emotions invested ... and for what? For nothing. She thought about all the nights she'd lain awake, worrying about Joe, what he felt about her, about when she'd have to wave him off at the airport – or, just maybe, walking hand-in-hand through an airport departures gate. Instead, she had been taken in by him, won over by his smile and the lock of hair that fell over one eye, and now she felt worthless and foolish, and couldn't stop crying.

GANNETS

Everyone was sympathetic, saying how sorry they were, how she'd get over it soon, not to worry, babe, because you're strong. Suzie was all for finding some of their more dubious friends from North Berwick to go round to Joe's place and kick the shit out of him. It was a tempting thought, but Lorna said no. She went down to North Berwick to tell her parents that Joe wouldn't be coming down to play golf, and they too fussed around her, telling her everything would be for the best, just you see. Her father looked better than he had done in years and her mother had dyed her hair to cover the grey and looked a decade younger.

'You could stay over for the night,' her mother said. 'Your bed's still made up.'

'Sorry, but I've got a Christmas party to go to.'

'Christmas party, dear? But it's not Christmas.'

'It is where I work,' said Lorna.

Rather than go straight back to Edinburgh, she took a detour to the beach and sat on rocks on the east sands staring out to sea. Waves broke at her feet and sucked at the sand. Looking out at the Bass Rock made her think of her mother; memories of paddling in the sea, sloshing through water, watching waves roll in and fold on the beach. Her mother never went near the sea. She'd watch Lorna from further up the beach, her fingers knotted together. Except once, because she once took Lorna on a boat trip to the Bass Rock.

The water had been effervescent, coursing in bubbles

from the bow of the boat, which rose and fell in small thuds, sending up shards of water that splashed back. The water was mud-brown and Lorna could hear its hiss over the putt-putt of the boat's small engine. The boatman stood in the stern, his hand on the wooden tiller, staring out to sea, his face creased. He had an unshaven face, his stubble grey, and wore a thick grey jumper. The sky was blue with sharp white clouds. Her mother sat in the centre of the boat, her hands gripped to the wooden slatted bench. Above their heads was a canvas awning that intermittently blocked out the sun as the boat rocked forward.

Lorna trailed her fingers in the water, feeling its weight, feeling her hand being tugged backwards and numbed by the cold push of the sea. She took her hand out of the water and licked one finger, tasting salt. A larger set of waves, perhaps the wake of a passing oil tanker, slapped loudly on the hull, making the small boat buck and jerk. The boatman shifted the tiller, turning the boat into the waves; more threads of water plunging over the stern, pricking Lorna's face.

She'd never been to the Bass Rock before and this was a special treat. They were the only passengers in the boat, although it was evident that her mother wasn't enjoying the experience. She'd said nothing since leaving North Berwick, sitting rock-still in the centre of the boat, hands gripped on the wooden seat beneath her, her face set in an expression of stoic resignation. She was wearing a headscarf and dark glasses hid her eyes.

They moored at a jetty, the boatman threading heavy ropes into big metal rings. The jetty was white with bird droppings, and slippery. He helped Lorna (wearing a stupid life jacket) from the boat onto the island. Her mother shook her head and smiled bravely. Above Lorna was the vast whiteness of the Bass Rock, and a cacophony

410

of gannets; they filled the sky, screeching and wheeling and diving to the water. She climbed a little way from the landing-place; there were the remains of a castle and a more modern lighthouse. Below was the surge and splash of water.

She climbed higher from the small jetty, further into noise. There were shadows everywhere; the swoop and whirl of gannets. Out to sea, the birds were falling to the water, wings folded, like missiles. There was an iron railing to which she held fast; the ground was wet, and the drop alarming. From up there, the water looked blue-grey, a shifting patina of dark colours: tensile and strong. North Berwick seemed far away. She looked down, amazed at how small their boat had become. The boatman was standing on the jetty. Little puffs of smoke dribbled from his lips. Her mother hadn't moved; but Lorna knew she was watching her.

She had overcome her fear because she had to: Lorna couldn't have gone alone on the trip. So her mother sat at the very centre of the boat, saying nothing, every sinew taut, for the simple reason that Lorna had always wanted to set foot on the Bass Rock and she hadn't wanted to disappoint her daughter. That's what love is, thought Lorna: unconditional, selfless.

Now, on the beach, she remembered the screech and smell of the place, the dizzying height of the sheer white cliffs and, far below, the ebb and surge of dark water.

* * *

Her colleagues at the HappyMart had also seemed genuinely distressed for her. Maggie, having guessed that something was wrong, cajoled Joe's treachery from Lorna, and for a few moments Lorna wondered if this was where she really belonged, surrounded by a surrogate family of Poles and misfits, rather than in some stuffy law firm with its bulldog spirit and stiff upper lips. Even Mike looked concerned for her, although she did also detect a renewed optimism, as he placed a hand on her shoulder, telling her how sorry he was, and leaving a damp patch on her polo shirt. But their concern made her realise how unsocial she'd been with them, turning down their regular invitations to the pub after work, and not wanting to spend precious money socialising with co-workers who would soon be ex-family. This was why Lorna was now on her way to the HappyMart Christmas party and, despite everything, quite looking forward to it. Their sales figures for the quarter had exceeded forecasts (which had prompted an excruciating email from HQ in Bradford, telling them how *simply wonderful* all the staff were at HappyMart, Edinburgh (Central & South) and *how proud management was to have such a loyal and hard-working family*). It did, however, mean that they were entitled to a less-than-generous bonus. By happy coincidence, during a period of freezing weather, pipes above the false ceiling had burst, cascading water into the shop, ruining some stock, and forcing them to close for a couple of days while repairs were made and new roof tiles installed. It was, therefore, the perfect time to spend their Christmas bonuses on a party.

Lorna joined them in a pub beside the King's Theatre, having driven back from North Berwick, parked the car, and walked down. She was wearing a baggy sweater that had seen better days, and her jeans were stained with seawater. There was sand in her hair and, as she kissed everyone hello, she was painfully aware of grains of it falling into people's drinks. To her embarrassment everyone else had made an effort to dress up for the occasion. Mike had replaced his HappyMart shirt with a blue shirt (correct size) and silver tie (correctly knotted), while Maggie and Gosia were almost identical in black dresses, although Maggie's was several dozen sizes larger. Mad Steph was wearing black jeans and a cream polo shirt, the two tied together with a silver belt, and Lorna had to look twice at her. In the shop, Steph always appeared nervous and plain, happy to potter in the background; now she had emerged from a chrysalis and, Lorna saw, was really rather beautiful. She noticed how Mike kept looking at her, presumably having reached the same conclusion and perhaps planning how to engineer Steph a second star. Nobody had yet managed to tell Lorna why they thought Steph was mad. Vlad, dressed in a grey suit with an open-neck white shirt, was holding Gosia's hand.

Mike thrust a bottle into her hand. 'Here, get this down you.'

Lorna looked at the label, which didn't immediately make any sense.

'It is Polish beer,' said Vlad gravely, extracting his free hand from Gosia to point at the few words of English on the label. 'It is very good beer. It is coming from Warsaw, where I is also coming from.'

Lorna was used to having semi-English conversations with Vlad. 'Well, happy Christmas, everyone!' she said, raising her bottle. Maggie, Gosia and Steph had gone to the trouble of blusher, eyeshadow and lipstick and Lorna was again aware that grains of sand, like bad dandruff, had gathered on her shoulders.

* * *

After a few more Polish beers (Lorna, Gosia and Vlad), several pints Mike) and more than a few gins and tonic (Mad Steph and Maggie) they walked a little erratically across the road to an Indian restaurant. It wasn't the kind of food that Lorna would have chosen, but the evening had all been planned out by Maggie, seconded by Mike, and agreed by the others, who all seemed pleased that for the first time Lorna had condescended to go out with them. Once again she felt slightly remorseful for having declined their other invitations.

'Here,' Mike was saying to her. 'I've got a great name for a curry house.' He held out one large hand to point at the sign above the restaurant. 'I'd call it CRAP. Stands for curry, rice and popadums.' Lorna did her best to laugh politely.

To her relief, she was placed at the girlie end of the table with Steph and Maggie, with Gosia providing a protective barrier against Mike who had launched into a lengthy dissertation on the tribulations of Scottish football, while Vlad did his best to look interested. Down the other end of the small table, Steph had announced, out of the blue, that she probably wouldn't be staying on for too much longer at the HappyMart. She said this softly, with one hand to her mouth, trying to shield her words from Mike, who was still in full flow about striking centre-forwards, whatever they were, and 4-4-2 formations. Maggie, for whom the HappyMart was the pinnacle of her career, looked shocked. Gosia merely nodded in a mid-European, fatalistic way.

'Whatever for?' asked Maggie, also in a stage whisper. 'Think of the discounts, girl.'

'I've got the rest of my life to think of.'

'So do we all, dear,' said Maggie.

Mike pushed his chair back and announced that he was off for a pee. With Mike gone, Maggie leaned in. 'So what's up? What's brought this on, eh?'

For a moment, Steph looked at the table, once again the shy girl that Lorna had always known. 'I'm hoping for a place at university,' she now said, looking up. 'I went to a useless school, fucked everything up … but I've been studying nights … get to sit my Highers soon.' She might have been a couple of years older than Lorna, who now saw that Steph's eyes were gleaming with sudden ambition.

'To get a degree in shopkeeping?' asked Maggie. 'Bugger all good that's going to do.'

'Politics,' said Steph.

'Excuse me,' asked Vlad, 'but you want to be MP? You go from shop, to college, to parliament?'

Steph was again looking at the table, her cheeks red. 'No, nothing stupid like that. Get a job as a researcher, or something.' She looked up, meeting Lorna's eye. 'You know what I mean, don't you?'

Maggie laughed uproariously. 'I told you she was mad, didn't I? Fucking bonkers! Always knew there was something weird about you, girl!'

Lorna now looked at the table, embarrassed by the gleam in Steph's eyes, the same gleam that had once been in hers, and again Lorna wondered what had become of her, all that anger and energy and idealism. Mike then came back from the loo and, being senior management, tried to be authoritative, ordering for everybody as if he instinctively knew what they each liked, although the effect was rather ruined by the fact that he'd forgotten to zip up his flies. Meal ordered, and with bottles of beer and wine on the table, Mike leaned back. 'Listen,' he said, 'I've got a great name for a curry house…'

* * *

Lorna did her best to eat some of the curry, although Mike appeared to have ordered only the very hottest things on the menu and even Maggie, who was something of a curry fan, so she told everyone, had to order water and fan her

415

face with her napkin, while black mascara tears rolled down her cheeks, making her seem like a sad clown.

'How long you going to be staying?' asked Maggie, eating a potato pakora, her mouth full and small bits scattering the table between them. It took Lorna a few moments to realise that the question had been aimed at her. On Lorna's plate was mostly rice.

'July, probably.'

'Then what?'

'Then I start work.'

'What, you've got yourself a job already? You never said nothing.' Maggie's clown face registered disappointment, and again Lorna felt a pang of remorse at not having shared more of herself with them.

'Sorry,' said Lorna, 'only just found out.'

'Where?' persisted Maggie.

'You won't have heard of it. Wilson, MacGraw & Hamilton.'

'Fuck me! It's the only law firm I have heard of! Everybody's heard of that lot! How the hell did you manage that? Well, I suppose that joining them is a good enough reason to abandon the HappyMart, eh, Mike.'

Mike did his best to look pleased for her. He was also sweating as profusely as Maggie and Lorna could smell him from two chairs away, and felt momentarily sorry for Gosia.

'They'll pay better than the pittance we get,' said Maggie, looking sideways at Mike. 'It'll help you afford the petrol for that Ferrari of yours.'

Lorna didn't bother to correct her.

* * *

'Myself and Vlad are going to the cinema at the weekend,' Gosia later said to Lorna, as more beers and

416

bottles of wine mysteriously appeared on their table, not seemingly having been ordered. 'We enjoy cinema very much.'

Lorna had asked Gosia what they liked doing on their days off, realising how little she knew about any of them. Despite seeing them almost every day, they were also strangers, particularly Mad Steph who had proved a revelation.

'We are planning to see *School's Out!*' said Vlad.

'I'm going to see it tomorrow,' said Lorna. 'I'll report back.'

'But it is receiving bad comment in the newspaper,' said Vlad, who was always reading a newspaper in his breaks, temporarily stolen from the newspaper rack, to improve his English. 'They say it is not very funny. Not good jokes.'

'I know someone who's in it,' admitted Lorna. This shut everyone up. 'She's a friend of mine.' She looked at Mike. 'You saw her, remember?' she told him and, for no reason, felt her face flush. 'Then you found a photo of her in the newspaper ... You showed it to me...'

'The tarty blonde who dragged you away...'

'Well, dipsy, maybe...'

'...and it wasn't even four o'clock!' Mike was looking disappointed. 'Look, I'm no thespian but I did think she had a bit of a strange accent.'

'She was pretending to be Napoleon.'

'Napoleon?'

'Bonaparte,' said Lorna.

'Well, and you can tell her this from me, I could do a better Spanish accent than that,' said Mike.

'She's also on the TV,' said Lorna, feeling the need to stick up for her friend, dipsy or otherwise. 'The toilet roll advert ... set on a spaceship?'

Mad Steph picked up her beer glass and held it up as if

to camera. *'It's toilet paper but not as we know it*. I love that advert … makes bog paper sound all romantic. I remember her now. I was stacking shelves on aisle three. Was that really her?' Steph looked wistful. 'Wait till I tell my Derek! I almost got to meet someone famous.'

'She's not exactly famous yet,' said Lorna.

'Here, Mike,' Steph said, 'couldn't we get one of those blue plaque things stuck on the wall outside.' She held up a hand and moved it slowly in a small arc. *'Someone nearly famous was once in this shop.'*

'It's an idea,' he conceded, not looking happy. Mike didn't like fun being poked at his empire, 'but we don't actually stock that brand of toilet paper.' That Lorna did know: the HappyMart only stocked toilet rolls recycled from used toilet paper and other industrial effluent, and then labelled as ecologically responsible.

Without warning, Maggie erupted into a dirty laugh, made louder by gin and tonic and several glasses of wine, and dabbed her eyes with her napkin, smudging her mascara still further and turning her from a sad clown into an enormous giant panda. 'Christ, Little Miss Clever's joining the only bloody law firm that I've ever heard of, drives a Ferrari, and mixes with the jet set. Fuck's sake, girl, the HappyMart's no place for the likes of you.'

DECISIONS

'Bollocks to critics,' said Suzie and speared a radish. 'Critics are paid to criticise. It's their damnable job! What's actually important is what the paying public think. That's you, babe, despite the film being entirely set on Planet Earth. So, what did *you* think, sweetie? In a word, was I wonderful or just marvellous?'

As always, Suzie's volume control was set at loud, although it didn't matter. They were in a favourite Italian restaurant, close to their flat, and equally loud opera was playing from the speakers.

'It wasn't exactly a big part, Suze.'

'That's not the point,' said Suzie, wolfing salad. 'The point is whether or not you enjoyed it.'

In the film, Kate Winslet was a harassed young mother. Hugh Grant, improbably, was the widowed father of a young daughter. Suzie was the daughter's primary school teacher. She appeared in two scenes and said four lines. Clever make-up had toned down Suzie's natural beauty and added years to her. Mostly, her task was to hand Hugh Grant's daughter back to him, until he realised that he was in love with Kate Winslet and emigrated to New Zealand. The film had been almost completed and in post-production before Suzie was called upon. Things hadn't gone well during filming, scriptwriters had been fired and new producers brought in. At the last minute, the new team felt that some additional London footage was called for to better ground the narrative angle, before Hugh Grant chased across the world in search of love.

Suzie's primary school was therefore a last-minute idea, to suggest how much of his old life Hugh Grant would be leaving behind, and the sacrifices that true love entailed. The film had been mostly filmed in New Zealand, to a backdrop of mountains, and involved a series of misunderstandings about Maori culture. Privately Lorna agreed with the critics; it wasn't very funny, despite the lead actors hamming it up in a vain attempt to rise to the poor script.

'Of course I enjoyed it, Suze,' said Lorna, 'or what little I saw of it.'

Suzie had barely stopped talking through the whole film. If it wasn't a commentary on what a particular actor was like, it was about how a particular scene had been shot, what the weather was like, and how the bloody children never-fucking-*ever* kept quiet. On screen, Suzie's primary teacher had been saccharine and honey, ruffling small heads with a pat of a hand. Off screen, the real Suzie could have murdered the lot of them several times over. On two occasions, other cinema-goers had turned round and asked her to shut up.

Suzie was looking worried. 'Actually, that's not really an answer, Lorna.'

'I thought you were great,' said Lorna with more enthusiasm.

'Better than Kate Winslet?'

'She did have rather a bigger part, Suze.'

'That's not the point,' grumbled Suzie, loudly.

On the way out of the cinema, two teenagers had noticed Suzie and nudged one another. Suzie was oblivious; only Lorna had seen them. She was used to men nudging and pointing at her friend. Lorna didn't begrudge Suzie her good looks, and Suzie didn't pay much attention. Being beautiful was a passport, nothing more. Lorna was unsure whether the two teenagers had recognised Suzie the film actress or toilet-roll model. Perhaps both or neither. Maybe they were just gawping.

'I *know* it's had crap reviews but the public do seem to like it,' Suzie was saying. 'Not adults, obviously, not *real* people. Kids mostly.' She chewed thoughtfully for a few moments. 'You're not eating.'

'Yeah, sorry ... Christmas party last night.'

Suzie stopped chewing for a moment. 'But it's not Christmas.'

'Does it have to be Christmas to have a Christmas party?'

'Well, usually ... Otherwise it's just a *party*.'

'Not at the HappyMart, Suze. Our Christmas bonuses came through late. My co-workers and I celebrated with a traditional Indian curry.'

'Ah, so *that's* why you're not eating. May I...?' and without waiting for a reply, Suzie helped herself to a slice of Lorna's pizza. 'Anyway, that's enough about moi ... How about you, babe?'

'I'm okay.'

'Have you heard from the bastard?'

Lorna shook her head.

'Maybe he'll turn up with flowers and apologise.'

'Doubt it, Suze.'

'All men are bastards, sweetie. Take my word on it.' She chewed on another slice of Lorna's pizza. 'Well, most of them. Not Austin, obviously.' She looked dreamy for a moment, the way she'd looked at Hugh Grant at the start of *School's Out!* before he decided to emigrate. 'Anyway, what would you do if he did bring flowers and say sorry?'

'Austin?'

Suzie kicked her under the table. 'Joe, you imbecile!'

Lorna took a deep breath. 'He's a young guy on a gap year. He's single, unattached and over here to sow his wild oats ... or whatever it is that men are supposed to sow.'

'Men don't think with their brains, that's the trouble.'

Lorna put down her knife and fork, having realised that what remained of her pizza was now on Suzie's plate. 'I'm not sure that we do either,' she said.

* * *

But Joe didn't try to contact her and, slowly, the question of her forgiveness became immaterial. Without Joe actually standing there, in person, apologising from his heart, there could be no forgiveness. Instead, she hardened her heart and threw herself at her studies, and even consented to further after-work drinks with Mike and the rest of the HappyMart family, which she again enjoyed, wondering if she shouldn't tell Wilson's to shove their job and instead aim for a third star. She got to know them all a little better – including Mad Steph, who wasn't mad at all; they were on the same wavelength and shared the same political ideals, although Lorna seemed to be losing touch were hers. The whales seemed less important, Iraq a distant place not worth bothering about. Lorna was a little jealous of Steph. The bright light that had once shone from both of them, now burned brighter from Steph.

Over the weeks that followed, Joe did not phone or text, and didn't now seem likely to. Lorna was forever fearful of bumping into him in the street. Edinburgh wasn't a big place, so it wasn't easy *not* to meet someone accidentally. Making love, they'd fitted together like spoons in a drawer; she still couldn't bear to think of him being with someone else.

Suzie continued to flit between Edinburgh and London. Austin was mostly in Bristol, studying for his finals. After that first ghastly night at Christmas, Lorna had decided to bury the hatchet; Austin seemed happy with Suzie and he no longer had the capacity to make her feel guilty. When she next saw him, she would treat him with civility; as an old friend who had once meant more. Mostly, Lorna had the flat to herself and, lonely and a little broke after Greece, took on extra weekend shifts at the till, beeping through more sausages and chips.

But then her doorbell rang. Suzie was in Edinburgh but out for dinner with some advertising people. There was talk of Suzie graduating from bathroom hygiene to Burberry. There was talk of other films, including a sequel to *School's Out!* Provisional titles included *School's Back!* and *School Break!* Lorna was in front of the TV, but was only half watching it. She had a law book open on her knee and was reading through paperwork.

On the doorstep was Joe, remorse on his chiselled features. 'Lorna, we have to talk.' He was carrying flowers and a half-empty bottle of Greek brandy.

She was astonished to see him and could barely speak. 'Why?' she managed after a few false starts.

'Because I made a mistake, that's why.'

'That's not an apology, Joe.'

'Look, I just wasn't thinking straight. Sometimes I wonder if I have a brain.'

He was looking down, a lock of hair over one eye. 'We all make mistakes, Lorna. I'm truly sorry for the one that I made.'

She opened the door to him, which she shouldn't have done. Having watched him walk backwards in her mind's eye, becoming smaller and smaller, he was now back in her flat and, by simply turning up on her doorstep, hadn't given her enough time to secure her defences. A phone call or text would have allowed her space to think; to rationalise what she felt, to rehearse things, to consider carefully what she would and wouldn't do. Perhaps that's how he planned it, a surprise assault because, when she opened the door, she didn't know what to think or what not to do. He looked much the same, and even seemed apologetic. Lorna ushered him back in, remembering the good times, particularly Greece, before that last night and her dream of loss. Too late, as she allowed herself to be undressed and to lie on the floor beside the TV, did she remember why they were no longer together. On the screen was Clint Eastwood and, between her legs, a man who she could once have loved.

But this time it was goodbye, tearing up her last photograph of Joe and chucking the pieces from the window, watching them turn and tumble across the night sky. He'd not come round to grovel or to beg. He'd come to see if, somehow, normal service could be resumed, as before, but without regard for her feelings. That's what galled Lorna the most: he was happy enough to have sex with her, not happy to make love to her, and uncaring as to the effect it might have. Now that she knew that, she could move on; she might once have loved him, or thought that she did, but he wasn't worth it. The incident on the floor had given her strength to put Joe into a box marked *Mistakes* and place him firmly on a shelf in her mind that she hoped would soon become a distant shelf, and then dusty and eventually forgotten.

* * *

Some weeks later, she started to feel sick; sometimes in the morning, sometimes in the evening. Once, during a tutorial, she had to excuse herself and rush to the toilet. This time, she was actually sick. Lorna sat in the loo wondering if anyone had heard her. Then she realised that she'd missed her period. Normally, her body ran like clockwork, and with trepidation she bought a pregnancy testing kit, then sat with shaken incredulity as it changed colour. It seemed as if more of her foundations were being bulldozed away, walls crashing down; certainties churned to sand. It had been the same with her father; she'd always believed him to be a magician, a kindly wizard able to do great things, if only he could properly reveal himself, or so he'd tell her, as she listened spellbound and believing every word. She'd felt the same answering Joe's mobile, and realising that he didn't love her; or, in Greece, saying yes to Toby Redmarsh, and realising that, perhaps, she wasn't going to be a good lawyer after all. Her battlements no longer seemed impregnable; she no longer knew what certainties she still had left; she no longer quite knew who she was.

'What the hell am I going to do?' she asked Suzie.

Lorna was in Edinburgh, Suzie in London. There were auditions to attend, a modelling job for a new face-cream. 'That, sweetie, is a big question.'

Lorna closed her eyes, not wanting to think about what might happen next. Sometimes, she thought, she could be either child or adult; the child not worrying about consequences, or if there were any, or not caring; the adult unwilling to face up to them, or what they might be, or caring too much. She'd always wanted children, but on her terms, with the right person. That could have been Joe, but now wasn't. He'd had his chance, and blown it. She'd never thought too much about the distant future, or the entrapment of nappies. Lorna didn't begrudge new mothers proudly pushing buggies; nor was she gooey over new babies: she simply saw motherhood as something that would happen, when the time was right. Now, it was neither right nor the right time.

'Okay, but if you were in my shoes, what would you do?' It was the child's voice, querulous and hesitant; asking the right question, but not wanting an answer.

Suzie didn't hesitate, not even for a second. 'Get rid of it, petal. It's the only thing you can do.'

Lorna knew that was what Suzie was going to say. Suzie, utterly practical, saw everything in black and white. In front of Lorna's eyes were shades of grey. 'I'm not sure, Suze.'

'But what's the alternative?' said Suzie, then paused theatrically to let the idea of single motherhood sink in. 'Exactly!' Suzie continued, although Lorna hadn't said anything. 'There isn't an alternative.'

* * *

In another quadrant of the galaxy, outside a beach bar that was neither Greece nor Scotland, Lorna had nibbled on a croissant and crumbs were drifting across the wooden table. Inside, she felt rising panic; a tightness across her chest. She was in an absurd place that no longer seemed like a real place. She was remembering things, faster and faster, random memories plucked from nowhere scattering across her mind; some blissful, others painful, and joined by loss and separation. The beach was still empty and Lorna was alone. But then her arm became suddenly sore. She felt sick. Lorna blinked away tears and found voice. 'Trinity, where am I?'

You're in Heaven, sweetie.

'That's not an answer.'

In which case, what answer would you like me to give?

Across the beach was the suck and pull of small waves. 'The truth,' she suggested.

A short pause. *The truth is what you choose to make it, young Lorna. The truth is what you choose to believe. Would you like a glass of wine?*

'I'd like an answer.'

To what, sweetie?

'Okay, let me put it like this. Is Heaven a toaster or a giant mushroom?'

Another pause. *Heaven is neither a vegetable nor a bread-cooking device. Would you like another packet of cigarettes? I see you don't have many left.*

'No thank you, Trinity. But if reality is just a question of choice, perhaps I'm just imagining being here. Perhaps none of this is real. Perhaps Heaven doesn't exist.'

It's a thought, Lorna. Perhaps I don't exist.

'That's just *crap*, Trinity. Okay, why does God choose people to come here?'

For a reason, Lorna.

'For the same reason or a different reason? For *fuck's* sake, tell me!'

Trinity took a few moments to reply, and for Lorna to calm down.

Usually for a good reason, petal. For example, Einstein. He could get the E and MC part of the equation, but didn't think to square it. God brought him here to explain things. Florence Nightingale was another recent visitor. God hates germs and wanted you to know how important it is to wash your hands. I'm sorry about your brother, by the way.

Lorna now saw that there was a silver napkin dispenser on the table. She hadn't noticed it before and extracted a napkin and dabbed at her eyes. Her sudden anger had dissipated. 'Thank you, Trinity. But none of them are here now, are they?'

No, Lorna.

If they weren't here, there was only one other place where they could be. 'They all went back to Earth, didn't they?'

Yes, young Lorna.

'Please don't call me *young* Lorna. I'm not a child.'

My apologies. I didn't mean to suggest that you were.

'Who else has come here? From Earth, I mean?'

Trinity hummed for a few moments. *To be honest, I'm not good with names. Albert and Florence I only remember because they went on to do something useful. I do like it when God gets things right and picks the right people. Okay, yes, there was someone else quite recently, now that I think about it. Someone called Dorothy. Arrived with a ghastly little dog although it did kill a few hamsters. Widdled everywhere, even on Irene's shoes. I was all for keeping the dog but God wouldn't hear of it. They both went.*

Lorna pressed her hands to her temples, a headache erupting from behind her eyes. 'But God also gave them a choice, didn't he?'

Of course. Everyone who comes here is given a choice.

'Trinity, what did I do that was so wrong?'

I don't understand the question, Lorna.

'I keep remembering a friend of mine,' said Lorna.

Suzie?

'She's angry with me. I don't know why.'

If it's important, perhaps you will remember. If it's not, perhaps you won't. It was your life, Lorna, not mine.

The use of the past tense still unnerved her. Her arm hurt, there was a stabbing throb behind her eyes and she felt sick. If she wasn't in Heaven, where was she?

'Trinity, can I see God?'

Regrettably, Lorna, God is in a meeting.

'In which case, can I see Irene?'

God is in conference with his executive officer. They are discussing a matter of some importance and have asked not to be disturbed.

'A matter of importance?' echoed Lorna.

Yes, sweetie. You.

RAINBOW

The clinic where she aborted Joe's baby was cold and antiseptic. The medics were professional and not over-friendly. The corridor floors were polished to a shine. It didn't take long and nobody offered her much in the way of advice. Perhaps, she hadn't wanted any, already feeling guilt pile in at something done that could not now be undone, and wanting only to be away from the clinic and to smell clean air. When she'd arrived the sky had been blue, but when she left clouds had gathered and a cold wind was blowing.

She didn't want Joe to know; she didn't know how he would react, and she could do without his anger or sympathy. On the morning of her termination Lorna listened in to his radio programme. To her dismay, she thought he was rather good, until he announced that he was playing the next song for a special friend. *If you're listening, you know who you are,* he said. *A special someone whose father was a wizard. So, with all good thoughts for the wizard's daughter, if that doesn't sound too corny, here's the incomparable Eva Cassidy.* Lorna didn't know whether to laugh or cry, particularly when he played 'Somewhere Over The Rainbow', which reminded her of better days and she switched off the radio, wondering if he could somehow have found out about her pregnancy. That thought remained with her for the rest of the day, stayed with her as she was wheeled along clinical white corridors, and nagged at her afterwards as she lay on her back and stared up at a ventilation grille above her bed. They told her that she might experience some turbulent emotions. A bored doctor looked at her chart and barely gave her a second glance. Only to be expected, he said, with a jolly smile, as Lorna began to grapple with the reality of having aborted an unborn someone who would now remain unborn.

For the rest of the week Lorna felt haunted and empty. Only a couple of close friends knew what had happened and they did what they could to offer their support. She couldn't, of course, confide in her parents, although her father would probably have been sympathetic. They didn't need to know. She phoned Mike and told him that she had a virus. Suzie flew up from London and tried to be cheerful. It was for the best, Lorna was told repeatedly. Think what the alternatives would have been, sweetie!

Suzie made an appointment for Lorna at the medical centre, and she sat in the doctor's waiting room, feeling like an impostor among the real sick people. Suzie sat beside her, wearing sunglasses and tapping her foot.

The doctor was podgy, middle-aged and smelled sharply of body odour, reminding her of Mike, but without Mike's enthusiasm. The consulting room's walls had pictures of the human body, neatly stripped down to reveal main arteries and organs. Lorna didn't think that real sick people would want to look at pictures like that. The doctor spoke with a Birmingham accent and although he made sympathetic noises he didn't look very sympathetic. He asked lots of questions, his fingers threaded together, then wrote her a prescription for pills and told her not to mix medication with alcohol.

Later that week Lorna went for a long walk through the city, marvelling at other people's laughter, and across the grassy crags overlooking the Old Town, hearing the wind whisper against her ears. She'd come to this spot with Joe, his hand tight in hers. The sounds in her head were cold and unrelenting. Joe had grown small again, like the tiny figures at the bottom of the hill who were throwing a frisbee to one another. One of them could have been Joe, but she couldn't tell at that distance. Mostly, she stood by her bedroom window, immobile in her dressing-gown, and looked over the city rooftops, until the skyline and her thoughts became blurred.

It was the first week, probably ever, that Lorna did nothing. She had a dissertation to write, tutorials to attend, final exams to study for. She'd also been planning, with waning enthusiasm, to join the G20 demo in Edinburgh, or go to Gleneagles where the world's leaders were meeting, but no longer felt compelled. In any case, Edinburgh seemed to be filling up with a different kind of demonstrator. Lorna could spot them from a mile away: the professional anarchists, who had nothing to say, but were there only for the mayhem. They weren't her kind of demonstrator, and perhaps she was better off just feeling sorry for herself, but it also seemed as if her ambition and compassion had become muddled. How could she think about demonstrating against unfettered capitalism when she was joining a major law practice? How could she stand up for the underdog, when she had killed hers? How could she think of building wells in Africa when she coveted Suzie's car? She no longer knew what she wanted, for herself or for others, and for the first time in her life Lorna felt like a bad witch and rudderless.

* * *

Outwardly she appeared in control. She ate the cheese sandwich that Suzie made for her, the bread tasting of cardboard, the cheese tasting of vomit. She tried to make conversation, asking Suzie questions about her work, but not listening to the answers. Suzie went to the chemist to get her prescription and brought back a bottle of white pills. Under Suzie's stern gaze, Lorna swallowed a couple.

Out of the blue, Toby Redmarsh's wife Tessa phoned. 'Toby's been telling me all about you, dear girl! The star pupil of the university *and* a friend of Graeme Bryce! Toby is *so* hoping you'll join Wilson's. Look, I don't know if you're up for it, but we've got a few people coming round for dinner this Thursday. Do you fancy it? Do say yes!'

It was hardly an invitation that Lorna could turn down.

'Casual, of course,' Tessa commanded, 'so we'll see you at eight. You know our address, don't you?' Lorna didn't, and had to ask.

She watched TV, curled on the sofa, not caring about lectures or tutorials or exams. After speaking to Tessa, she didn't bother answering the phone again and switched off her mobile. There wasn't anybody she wanted to talk to, and couldn't think of anybody who would want to speak to her.

* * *

Towards the end of the week, Suzie emerged from her room with tousled hair and in a bad mood. Lorna was in the kitchen nursing a cup of coffee. Suzie had to go to Glasgow for a long-standing engagement, and wasn't looking forward to it, and now told Lorna that Austin would be arriving later. Lorna narrowed her eyes, not yet entirely sure of Austin, then remembered her pledge to treat him with civility.

'It'll be just for a few days, babe! We've missed each other.' Suzie had put on a little-girl voice to say this, her face scrunched in mock misery.

Suzie's toilet-roll manufacturer had a factory

somewhere in deepest Lanarkshire and was holding a reception for its distributors. Suzie was doing a promotional photo-shoot and, afterwards, as the public face of their product, would be glad-handing supermarket managers.

'What an utterly shit way to spend a day!' was Suzie's upbeat verdict, wrapped in her dressing gown and holding a coffee mug in both hands.

'An appropriate way of describing it, Suze.'

'I mean, if you want to buy a bog roll, you go to a shop and buy one. Buying toiletries isn't exactly difficult. I *really* don't see why I have to swill cocktails with a bunch of middle-aged fuckwits who sell bathroom stuff for a living.'

'Suzie, you can't be a glamour-puss all the time. Just bask in the glow of their adulation, or some such crap. You're becoming public property. Live with it.'

Suzie looked at her sharply. 'I could give you the same advice, Lorna, but I won't. Are you going to be okay?'

'Yeah, yeah.'

After Suzie had left, Lorna drove the Porsche out of Edinburgh. She didn't know where she was going to go, so just drove out of town. In the lee of the Pentland Hills she stopped. She remembered vaguely that on one of the hills was a Stone Age fort. Lorna parked in a lay-by, and crossed a small river on stepping stones, and climbed upwards. She sat on a rock and looked out over the Firth of Forth, the same sea over which her mother had looked when giving birth to her, the same waves rolling in.

Then, when she raised her eyes, she could clearly see the peak of North Berwick Law. Beneath it was the town in which she had grown up. In it would be her parents, many of her friends, and in its streets and stones and sand and water lay her childhood. Lorna thought about this, feeling an unwanted connection to the town she was trying to escape from. It hadn't been a bad childhood, she had to concede. Okay, her dad didn't make much money, but neither did a lot of fathers. Okay, her mum didn't either, but lots of people work in bakeries. Her father had also once been a great wizard before his gift became lubricated and then drowned.

Between her and North Berwick was the giant rectangle of Cockenzie power station. Rising above it were two slender chimneys. A thin stream of smoke was rising from one of the chimneys and immediately she was reminded of 9/11, the horror of it, the toy-like aeroplanes striking home and the way the towers fell downwards, not even a bit sideways like you'd expect, the radio mast on one tower falling perfectly vertically into smoke and dust and oblivion. Lorna hadn't known anybody who died on 9/11 but friends of her dad did, friends who were still successfully employed in financial services. And then Bali: once again, an outrage on the other side of the world. Lorna knew nobody who'd been killed or injured in that atrocity either; but Suzie's agent did: a jobbing actress who had tried her luck in London, failed, returned to New Zealand, and then gone on holiday to Bali with her boyfriend. For every action, Lorna now realised, there are consequences and that, in being tenuously connected to the victims of Bali and 9/11, she was still connected to people that she loved and, through them, to people she had never met, and who she would never meet.

She remembered the day of her brother's death. That evening, their flat filled with friends and relatives, Lorna had taken the torch from her bedroom and gone to the beach. It was a clear night. A light breeze ruffled her hair and small waves hissed ashore. Amid the desolation, Tom's funeral was being planned with, some weeks later, a scattering of his ashes on North Berwick Law. Lorna's mother said that it's what he would have wanted, as if it had ever crossed Tom's mind. It seemed strange to her that such practicalities were being discussed, and that Tom should be involved in the planning, as if he was still alive. She pointed the torch at the sky and clicked it on and off, on and off, on and off until her arm hurt with the effort of holding the torch over her head and her eyes were blinded by tears. She didn't know what to expect, or whether Tom would be watching, or if he was able to reply, but her distress signals went unanswered.

Now Lorna lay on her back in the grass and watched the clouds. She could smell summer, the scent of a storm not long passed, crisp and fresh, and suddenly – she didn't know why – she felt buoyed and no longer alone, finding small connections between her past and future. Then she drove back slowly to Edinburgh, parked the car and climbed the stairs to the flat. She could hear opera from the flat below: Gustav, a young Swedish accountant, who lived with a punk called Martha who had spiky red hair and a bolt through her nose. Lorna only knew them to nod at. Below them was an elderly women called Bo who rarely made it down the stairs. Sometimes Lorna would go and check on her, just to make sure she was okay. Bo always offered her tea and biscuits; once a week Lorna did her shopping: corned beef, mostly, and digestive biscuits. She did have family, Bo would assure her.

A part of her bedroom doubled as a working area, her laptop perched on a glass dining table that she'd pushed against one wall. Most of the table was cluttered with files and notebooks while the rest of the room was filled by a double bed, pine wardrobe, dressing table and another, much smaller, glass coffee table. When she'd moved in, Lorna had thought that working at a smoked-glass table would be cool: she could pretend to be a high-powered lawyer. Now, she realised, it was covered with so much dross that it was impossible to see the glass underneath. It no longer looked cool; it just looked a mess.

She flopped onto the bed. Something had happened to her on the hillside. She felt renewed, absolved. Not happy, but an inner pendulum had swung, hormones coming back into balance. I am alive, she thought, holding tight to a new perspective as she drifted into sleep.

ENGINES

The sun was brighter in Heaven, and the line between sea and sky had become indistinct. Lorna was still standing on the beach, but her eyes were tightly closed. Her memories were returning on fast-forward, almost a blur, and she couldn't stop them. She wanted them to stop, pressing her knuckles to her eyes, her eyelids pressed shut, but they kept coming, faster and faster, making her disorientated and frightened. But she also had a sense that everything was coming to an end: that her memories were almost intact; shards of recollection coming back together like a shattered mirror rearranging itself in reverse. She could now remember her desolation. Joe's loss and then her termination – the overwhelming sense of guilt. And a stranger feeling: that she'd always believed in hard work and that, by work alone, she could shape her life. But it hadn't happened like that. It seemed now that this too had been pulled from under her; that life had crept up on her through undergrowth and jumped out when she least expected it. There were still other shards spinning at the margins, memories she no longer wanted to see, because she could feel the heat of Suzie's anger. Then Lorna felt a hand being placed lightly on her shoulder and, turning, saw that Irene was by her side. Irene's footprints were etched on the sand, a straight line of indentations leading back to the town. Her own footprints, meandering from the table on which the remains of her croissant lay, weaved more aimlessly.

'Okay, sweetie?'

Irene was wearing a dark blue trouser-suit, the same trouser-suit that Lorna had once owned, parading herself to Toby and his associates, with a jumbo bar of chocolate in her briefcase and, just in case, a box of tissues.

Lorna shook her head. The effort of memory was too much, and she felt exhausted. 'I can't take any more of this,' she said.

'You don't have to. God wants to see you.' Irene motioned Lorna to follow her and, legs wobbly, Lorna trailed along behind, the air quickly cooling as they walked towards the town, the hot sun disappearing into scudding clouds. The town looked wet, its pavements slick. 'Why does God want to see me?'

Irene stopped and turned. 'I can't say, Lorna.'

'Can't or won't?' They had reached the High Street, and a clock was chiming the hour. The same clock, or a different clock, had sometimes woken her up. 'For fuck's sake, Irene.'

'There's no need to swear, sweetie.'

'There's every need to swear! My brain feels like it's going to explode.'

'It won't, I assure you.'

'That's not a bloody answer, Irene!'

Lorna's voice had risen and she stood, panting slightly, while Irene smiled. 'Right now, my task is to deliver you into his presence.' She stopped at a transporter stop, beside what had once been the town's bookshop. Now it was given over to rare Persian carpets and Ming dynasty vases.

Doors opening.

'Bridge, please, Trinity.'

Doors closing.

Lorna had never heard Trinity impart such banal information, then remembered that the lift at Wilson's said much the same thing. The holiest of holy offices were on the first floor. The minions toiled on the higher floors, reached either by a dingy staircase or cramped lift. During her visits for interview, she had several times wondered why talking lifts were such bad conversationalists.

They stepped inside and the transporter set off horizontally, then rose vertically, then horizontally once again. Irene, her feet in immaculate court shoes, was tapping one foot impatiently. Lorna held onto the handrail and tried to breathe normally. Inside, she felt as if she was cracking open, like an egg or a piece of porcelain. One minute, on the beach, she knew that Heaven couldn't possibly exist. The next, with a very real Irene, she couldn't be sure of anything.

Fourth floor. Doors opening.

Irene led her into a broad thoroughfare, down the centre of which was a moving escalator. On one side was a wall adorned with advertisements. One was for duty-free whisky, another for electronic equipment, yet another for luxury clothing. In one, incongruously, was Suzie: she was holding up a toilet roll. At her feet was a white puppy. The puppy was looking up with adoring eyes. Suzie was smiling at the camera and ignoring the dog. In real life, Suzie hated dogs.

But it was the other wall that captured Lorna's attention or, rather, the lack of wall. For a distance of some hundred metres, the entire length of the walkway, this side of Heaven consisted simply of glass. For a moment she was terrified, knowing that she was inches away from the vacuum beyond. Then she stilled her fear, and placed both hands on the outer wall, mesmerised once more by the vastness of the universe beyond. They seemed to be on Heaven's topmost level. Looking over to the other hull, Lorna was able to see across its curves and the arrays of communications dishes flashing in sequence down its length.

Irene was smoking and, without saying anything, took Lorna by the arm and onto the moving walkway. Half way along, an ashtray opened up beneath the handrail and Irene deposited her finished cigarette into it. At the end of the moving walkway, Irene led Lorna back to the outer glass wall. She pointed outward and upwards. 'That, Lorna, is what happens when you fly too close to a black hole.'

Lorna followed her finger. She'd seen it as an approaching shadow on the walkway. Now, her face pressed to the glass, its outline loomed large. It was at least two hundred metres tall: an impossibly huge dark structure framed against blazing stars. It consisted of what looked like two pieces of metal, connected at right angles. Lorna's eyes travelled upwards along its length and then reverentially across its arms.

Irene had lit another cigarette. She pointed with its glowing tip. 'Our main engines were once connected to that framework,' she said in a matter-of-fact voice. 'But in the gravitational vortex that we encountered, they sheared off.' The giant crucifix was glowing, as if trapping light and slowly releasing it in diamond pinpricks. It made Lorna feel small, reminding her of childhood, incense in her nostrils.

'Irene, I no longer believe in where I am.' Lorna held up a hand. 'Please don't tell me that I'm in Heaven.'

Irene raised one eyebrow. 'I don't intend to try, sweetie. What you choose to believe is up to you.' Trinity had also said as much. 'However, don't think of Heaven as a place, Lorna. Think of it instead as a *concept*.'

'That makes no sense,' said Lorna, her hands firmly on the outer glass. 'Irene, I don't want to remember any more.'

'But you are *somewhere*, aren't you?' Irene had leaned forwards and was speaking close to her ear. Lorna could feel her words move her hair. 'If you look closely enough,' continued Irene, 'Heaven is full of symbols. Symbols, young Lorna, that may have no significance for you, but will have for someone else. Their imprint lay in the genetic sequence that God used to create you. As the idea of religion took hold on Earth, people started to remember those symbols. In people's minds, as mankind tried to make sense of the infinite, those symbols came to represent how Heaven and Earth could be joined together.' Irene took a puff of her new cigarette, looking upwards at the metal cross. 'To you, the crucifix is a symbol of suffering and redemption. To us, I regret, it merely symbolises eternity.'

At the end of the thoroughfare was a set of metal doors, with a red sign informing them that they were about to enter a restricted zone. As they approached, they swished open. Inside was a windowless square room the size of a tennis court. Around three walls were control consoles with leather chairs sitting askew at random intervals. There were no crew members but, on some of the computer screens, white and blue lights flickered. On one wall was a blue-painted sign. *Environmental Protection.* On another, *Propulsion.* On the third, *Navigation.* The three things to run a spaceship, Lorna recalled, noticing that one of the Propulsion screens was winking words at her.

She went over to look at it. On the screen was one terse phrase. *Finished with engines*, read Lorna, remembering their Norfolk holiday and her father turning the key in the ignition for the last time.

In the centre of the fourth wall, opposite where they had come in, was another door and it had now also swished open. Irene was standing in the doorway, tapping her foot. Lorna swallowed and walked through the doorway.

She had expected the bridge of an immense spaceship, however real or imaginary, to be spacious and luxurious. She had imagined panoramic windows affording views over space, and astronauts in tight uniforms fussing over banks of instruments. Instead, Lorna found herself in a circular room not dissimilar to the bridge of the Starship Enterprise but in which, apart from God, she and Irene were the only occupants.

God was sitting in a large chair in the centre of the room. The chair could also have been Captain Kirk's. However, instead of controls and lights, the walls of the room were covered with TV screens, each image plucked from CCTV cameras. 'It's nice to see you again,' said God, rising chivalrously from his chair and motioning Lorna to a smaller chair by his side. 'Trinity tells me that all your memories have come back. I'm pleased that everything now seems back to normal but I am sorry, Lorna, if that process has been painful.'

'Not everything,' she replied, feeling the onset of another headache. There was still that something else, those last spinning fragments.

'Perhaps not everything,' agreed God, looking momentarily uncertain, 'but most things have, haven't they?'

'I suppose so,' she agreed, although it also seemed that her memories had found a different pattern, fitting together like a jigsaw that could somehow produce more than one picture. God had a folder in his hand, which could have been Mike's or Mr Sullivan's, and was flicking through pages. On its front cover, written in black biro, was her name. 'And I still don't know why I'm here,' she said.

'Everyone who comes to Heaven is here for a reason,' replied God and laid down her file on his armrest.

'I *know* that. But I don't understand equations, and I

already know how to wash my hands.'

Blue light from a hundred TV screens washed across his face. As always he was smiling kindly. 'This is where I come to watch over you,' he said, indicating all the televisions. 'This is where I first saw you. It was dark and you looked sad.'

Lorna looked from screen to screen. The images were fuzzy, and all were in black and white. One image was of the road outside her Edinburgh flat, and she felt a stir of memory, her heart beating faster. 'I think, maybe, that I made a mistake,' she stammered. It wasn't quite a memory, more like a dream hovering out of sight, and she felt slightly sick.

'We all make mistakes,' said God. 'Even me,' he added, placing a fatherly hand on her knee. Lorna saw Irene standing in the background, trim in her sober trouser-suit, nodding vigorously.

She looked from God to Irene and back again. 'God, why am I here?' she asked again. 'I really need to know.'

'To offer you a choice.'

'I know that! But what choice?'

He smiled. 'To do things differently.'

And then Lorna did remember what it was that was frightening her; all those faces in the newspapers and on television, Suzie's anger, and all that faraway anguish in New York and Iraq.

SORRY

Lorna still felt giddy when she woke up, disorientated to find that it was still light outside, and not immediately sure whether it was morning, noon or night. She got up and pulled back the curtains and for a few minutes rested her elbows on the windowsill, the window open, and drank in the outside air. Then she smoothed down her hair and looked at herself in the mirror, studying her reflection from different angles. Her hair was lank and needed a good wash, there were dark shadows under her eyes and her complexion was sallow: the face of someone who had spent too much time indoors. But it was also as if a darkness had been lifted, a creature inside her tamed. She no longer felt like a murderer: someone beyond redemption.

To her surprise she found Austin in the kitchen opening a can of lager. She'd forgotten that he'd be there, and now didn't know how to react. She stood instead at the kitchen door, immobile, trying to think of civil things to say, desperately trying not to say the wrong thing that would end up in an argument or sullen silence. In any case, she felt exhausted. She hadn't slept much for days and still felt frail and weepy, emotions that Lorna had always considered beneath her. She didn't have the energy to do anything but accept the glass of wine that Austin silently handed her.

'Suzie told me what happened,' he said. 'For what it's worth, I'm sorry.'

Lorna could see that, with Suzie away, he also didn't

know what to say to her, or what subjects to avoid.

He scratched his head. 'It can't have been easy.'

Lorna didn't say anything. Instead, she drank back her wine and refilled the glass, feeling tearful again, remembering searching the beach for her underwear and finding only an empty bottle.

'But you'll get over it, Lorna. We all get over things. I got over you, and you'll get over this.' Behind his head hung her castle and her eyes moved between it and Austin. Squaring her shoulders, she walked to the living room, kicked off her shoes and lay down on the battered sofa, balancing her wine glass on her stomach. She could at that moment have gone back to sleep again.

But Austin had followed and was now sitting in the room's only other comfortable chair. 'I'm also sorry about Leo.'

'You've already apologised for that.' She closed her eyes for a moment. 'He said I was weird.'

'You are a bit weird,' he agreed.

'Am I?' She opened her eyes to look at him.

'Well, not *conventionally* odd. Single-minded, maybe.'

'Being single-minded isn't weird.' There was a silence while she thought about this. How many other people thought she was weird? 'Talking of Leo, he emailed me.'

Austin had his feet on the coffee table. He'd also kicked off his shoes. 'He also says that you haven't replied.'

'I might get around to it.'

'Can I tell him that?'

Lorna wriggled backwards and pushed a cushion under her back then, looking into her glass, watched diamonds of light radiating from its surface. 'Yeah, why not.'

'He'd still like to see you again.'

From tearful, she had lurched to sadly tranquil. 'He said that him and his pal are going to buy a boat.'

'The scuba-diving thing? Well, from what he's told me, they're still trying.' Austin put his glass down and knotted his hands together. 'Lorna, I'm sorry if I messed things up between you two. I was just being oafish.'

His voice trailed off. Lorna laid her head back on the cushion and looked at the ceiling. 'I don't want to argue, Austin. Shit happens, end of.'

Austin blew air from his nose. 'That's either being sensible or plain stupid, I'm not sure which.'

Lorna swung her legs to the floor and tipped the glass to her lips. Once more she saw trapped light escape in small incandescent bubbles. 'Well, we are now supposed to be grown-ups, Austin.'

'Technically, I suppose.'

Her glass was empty and then she realised that the bottle was empty. How had that happened? Austin fetched another from the kitchen.

Closing her eyes, feeling drowsy and woozy, she reflected that she'd known Austin for most of her life. During it, he had transformed from one thing to another. He had grown up and given up loving her. But she had also changed, she had to concede, despite being officially weird.

'How long are you going to be here?' she asked.

'A few days, so don't worry. I'm not moving in.'

'Helping to rebuild Edinburgh's slums, is that it? Good for you, Austin … Just don't build any more slums by mistake.'

'It's part of my course,' he said. 'Get to see how it's really done. The company I'm with is knocking down an old warehouse, but keeping the façade, then building flats in the shell.'

'Hopefully *executive* flats,' she suggested. 'Flats for wealthy people … riff-raff not wanted'

He laughed. 'There you go. You're being weird again.'

'I'm not being weird. I'd just like to know where all the poor people are supposed to live.'

'Lorna, I'm just here to learn what being an engineer is really all about.' He looked apologetic.

Lorna was sorry to have jumped down his throat. 'But what I'd *really* like to know,' she asked, feeling that they should be friends again, 'is when you're going to start building bridges?' Lorna looked round at him through half-closed eyes. 'You used to have posters of the bloody things on your bedroom wall.'

He blushed. 'I'd rather hoped you'd forgotten about those.'

'I thought it was quite sweet.'

'I've not given up hope, if that's what you're suggesting.' His hands were clasped behind his head and his feet were back on the coffee table, displaying tatty socks. 'But the fact is that engineering is just the same as any other profession. You start at the bottom and work upwards.'

'That,' said Lorna, finally smiling for the first time in days, 'is a perfect description of Suzie's career.'

* * *

She shouldn't have swallowed another pill or allowed Austin to refill her glass. She was now swinging from elation to the brink of tears, from flat calm to shaking coldness. Austin didn't seem to notice, prattling on about Suzie, telling her that they were getting along just fine, although he sometimes wondered how long it would last. She's an actress, he said, and I'm not even a proper engineer yet. Lorna said that engineers were probably more important than actresses, but found it difficult to explain this. She knew that she'd drunk too much: speaking was becoming an effort and her arms and legs

448

had grown unusually heavy.

Austin was worried that Suzie would eventually go off with someone more in keeping with her image. It's a media thing, he said. She can't very well be seen at a film premiere with a buffoon like me on her arm. Lorna tried to tell him that Suzie was also sensible. A little loud sometimes, but she knew to keep at least one foot on the ground. You're her foundation, Lorna told him. She needs you. You're the engineer, Austin. You know how to build foundations.

She was aware that she was also prattling, which she hardly ever did, always keeping things to herself, and then of her voice becoming slurred and finding it hard to talk. She looked into her glass and saw that the incandescent lights had been extinguished. Her arms and legs now seemed like dead weights, and the glass slipped from her hand. She watched as the stain spread across the carpet, joining other stains from other spilled glasses.

'Lorna, are you okay?'

'Drunk.' Her pill bottle was in her pocket and with difficulty she retrieved it and rattled it at him. 'And I'm not supposed to be drinking.'

'Fuck's sake, Lorna!'

She edged her legs off the settee and found herself kneeling on the floor, unable to move, the room spinning. Everything felt rooted to the floor; she could feel sweat dripping down her face. 'Oh, God, I'm going to be sick.'

In a flash, Austin was off to the kitchen, coming back with the plastic washing-up bowl into which Lorna vomited, feeling wretched and stupid and useless. Then she tried crawling to her bedroom, realising that there was no point in even trying to stand up. How could anybody, drunk or sober, stand up on only two legs?

Austin was kneeling beside her as she inched past like a slow tortoise. 'Do you want me to call a doctor?'

'No doctors,' she said. 'Bastards prescribed me these.' The pill bottle was still in her hand and she threw it against the wall, shearing off its lid and scattering her medication across the floor.

'Christ!' said Austin, not knowing what to do.

'I'll be fine.'

'Lorna, you can't even stand up.'

'I can crawl. Look,' she managed to say, inching forwards again.

Then, without warning, she felt herself being hoisted into the air and for a few moments wondered if she was asleep and dreaming and had regained the power of flight. She allowed herself to be carried to bed and laid down on top of the duvet. Austin returned with the washing-up bowl, cleaned, and laid it down beside the bed.

'What should I do?' he asked.

She couldn't form words.

'Lorna!'

He tried shaking her, but she had already sunk into near-oblivion.

'Christ!' He walked to the window and back again, a hand to his forehead. Lorna was lying on her side, vaguely aware of him looking at her and swearing several more times. He tried propping a pillow and duvet next to her, to prevent her from rolling on to her back. But she felt too hot and with a last effort from her leaden limbs she pushed them away. Austin swore again and walked backwards and forwards, rubbing his face. Eventually, he lay down beside her, propping himself against her. And she fell into a deep sleep.

* * *

Suzie arrived back in the middle of the night. She'd been planning to spend the night in Glasgow, then been concerned for her friend. The next thing that Lorna knew was that her bedroom light had been turned on.

Suzie was standing at the foot of the bed, eyes blazing.

'Lorna, you fucking slut!'

Austin had leaped out of bed. Suzie didn't register that he was fully clothed. Instead, Suzie had marched across the room, nostrils flared.

Lorna raised herself on her elbows, then planted her feet on the bedroom floor. Suzie didn't seem to notice that Lorna was fully clothed as well.

She knew what was coming and closed her eyes. She could have raised her hands to protect herself, but it hardly seemed worth the effort. She was still befuddled and, through Suzie's eyes, she knew what it must look like.

'You fucking, *fucking*, bitch!'

There was an explosion of pain on one side of her face. Lorna just sat there, her mind blank and her eyes closed. When she opened them again, the Porsche was revving in the street and Suzie had left.

* * *

Lorna was sick several more times, and then swallowed aspirin. She couldn't have been asleep for more than three hours, but it felt like three days, because she could now stand on two legs, even walk to the kitchen unaided, despite feeling like death. Neither of them quite knew what to do, or where Suzie had gone. A hotel, probably, or maybe North Berwick. Perhaps she'd come back. They both tried phoning her, but Suzie wasn't taking calls, so they sat in the kitchen, thinking separate thoughts, Lorna shielding her eyes from the overhead light, and suffering from a crashing headache. After a while, there seemed no point in waiting up for her. She'd gone somewhere, and wasn't coming back that night. Austin retreated back to Suzie's room, his mobile pressed to his ear, leaving yet another message.

Lorna sat in the kitchen by herself, the aspirin beginning to work, for some reason remembering a careers talk from Mr Sullivan. It was spring; there were daffodils under her classroom window. It was Mr Sullivan's job to prepare that year's school leavers for the wider world. Some of the class, herself included, already knew what they wanted to do. Suzie, already blurring the lines between school and what lay beyond, had been modelling for years. Kiddie stuff, then adolescent stuff, then beachwear. Others in the class had no idea what they wanted to do, even some who weren't planning to go onto university. It was Mr Sullivan's job to look at strengths and weaknesses and suggest alternatives.

Later on, said Mr Sullivan, I'll want to see you each individually. For now, he said, I'd simply like to know what kind of people you most admire.

Two of the girls in the class said nurses. Under pressure from Mr Sullivan, they explained that nurses cared for people but didn't get paid very much. Another girl said a policewoman. She was planning to go into the police force. You have to care *and* have courage to be a police officer, she said, puffing out her chest. Mr Sullivan didn't bother to ask Suzie who she most admired.

One of the boys also said policeman and a second suggested astronaut. You can't get more courageous than that, he explained. Did he want to go into space? asked Mr Sullivan. The boy shrugged; he was planning to be a plumber, like his dad.

When Mr Sullivan's eyes fell on Lorna, she told him that she admired people who didn't drop litter. A few people in the class stifled giggles. A few didn't bother, and laughed. Mr Sullivan held up a hand, then motioned her to go on. I admire people, said Lorna, who make an effort. I like people who try to do well at things, whatever those *things* are. It doesn't have to be work things, she said. I admire people who try to be good mothers. I admire people who make an effort to be good husbands. I like people who take the trouble to find a rubbish bin.

Lorna wasn't being particularly serious but, with her own future mapped out, she couldn't be bothered playing along with Mr Sullivan. But she didn't know that Mr Sullivan hadn't tried hard enough at being a good husband and that, not meaning to, she'd said something horrible to him.

* * *

That same year, confiding in Suzie about losing her virginity, she'd hurt Austin. Suzie had blabbed to everyone, as Lorna knew she would. Then, at least, it hadn't really been her fault. But in the years that followed, she'd hurt him again and again, deliberately, sending terse messages of rejection.

* * *

Years earlier, pottering on their boat, her mum and dad talking about things that she didn't understand, Tom was sick. They'd eaten lamb cutlets for supper and most of them were now spread across Tom's bed. Instead of sympathy, Lorna gave him a mouthful of abuse. Their small cabin stank. She'd been dreaming about piloting a rebel X-wing, and hadn't wanted to be woken up, and then be forced to endure the stench of his sickness. She'd fetched him a bucket and cloth, but told him to clean it up himself. She'd hissed bad things in his ear, not wanting to shout and wake up their parents. You're always being sick, she accused him. God, I wish you were dead, she said.

* * *

Lorna had always been innocent of bad intentions, but that didn't mean that she couldn't hurt people. Her cheek ached; but it was no more than she deserved.

Towards dawn, drifting in and out of troubled sleep, her phone bleeped. It was an incoming text message, from Suzie.

I'm sorry, it said. *Austn explliened thngs.*

* * *

Relief finally brought sleep. Her dream was of running, with something behind her: she didn't know what it was that was chasing her, except that it seemed only to be a shadow, without substance or form, but that it was close behind. It had reptilian eyes, and it wanted to harm her. Only by running at full tilt could she stay safe, keep ahead of the creature. As she ran, hotter and hotter, bathed in perspiration, she felt the creature slip back, until its shadow was in the far distance and then nowhere to be seen.

In the morning, when she made it to the kitchen, Austin was already dressed, drinking black coffee and wearing a big grin.

'Sorry about last night,' said Lorna, feeling chastened. 'Should've taken the doctor's advice. God, I feel awful.' She searched in a drawer for more painkillers, now shielding her eyes from the low morning sun.

'I've spoken to her, Lorna. She's calmed down. Stupid cow drove to London.'

'She sent me a text.'

'She finally remembered that we weren't both starkers. Once that small detail dawned on her, she began to see sense.'

Lorna had opened a cupboard to fetch down a new jar of coffee. Austin was drinking the remains of the old one. Then she realised that she hadn't been out to the shops for days and days.

'Oops,' said Austin, 'I seem to have finished it.' He was wearing blue jeans and a grey shirt, the same grey as her father's suits. His smile was dazzling.

Lorna was dialling Suzie's number.

'Oh God, I'm really sorry, babe.' Suzie sounded close to tears.

'Suze, I don't blame you.'

'I was tired, that's all. Hours and hours of a bloody photo-shoot and then three fucking hours with the most boring imbeciles I have ever met! Three *fucking* hours of smiling sweetly and being leered at! Lorna, I shouldn't have flown off the handle. I shouldn't have done what I did. But I didn't know what to think.'

'I'm sorry too, Suze. It's just that I'd taken those pills…'

'I should have been there, Lorna. Christ, you're my friend! I shouldn't have left you alone. On top of everything, the fucking puppy peed on my shoes. I couldn't even kick the damnable thing to death, what with everybody looking at me and cheering. What a fucking nightmare! The highlight of their bloody evening! Then, guess what they gave me to clean my shoes with? Actually, babe, no guesses needed! Ultra-absorbent bloody toilet paper, that's what!' Suzie, back at full volume, now paused. 'Still best friends, huh?'

Lorna was standing by the kitchen window, her face

turned to her castle. 'Of course, Suze. The bestest. Always.'

Maybe Suzie heard this, maybe not. The line had gone dead.

* * *

Lorna got dressed and, from behind dark glasses, walked to the corner shop at the end of their street. She'd made a small list of essentials they were running low on. Coffee and painkillers were top of the list. The small grocery was run by a middle-aged Asian man who had been there since she'd moved to Arthuria Road. They were on first name terms, Ali and Lorna, but she'd never asked whether he was Indian, Pakistani, Bangladeshi or Scottish. Or maybe he was from somewhere else entirely. She didn't want to offend him by asking impertinent questions.

In the corner of his shop was a small TV that sat on a bracket suspended from the ceiling. Normally, it was patched into the shop's security camera and Lorna could watch herself shopping. Now, it was showing a news broadcast and a knot of other shoppers were gathered under it.

Lorna handed over money.

'I take it that you haven't heard?' said Ali, handing back change.

'Heard what?' she asked.

FAULT

Lorna had been dreading the Redmarsh dinner party, having only accepted the invitation from a sense of obligation; that Toby was going to be, in all likelihood, her senior partner and that such invitations would only come rarely. This was her chance to shine, to make a first impression. Thinking positively, she'd also concluded that it might do her some good. She'd hardly been out of the flat all week, except to visit a hillside. The dinner party would force her to put on make-up, get dressed up and, perhaps, finally emerge from the dark tunnel in which she'd been sheltering. To be on the safe side, she collected up all the pills that had scattered on the floor, vowing not to drink that evening.

But, despite Suzie's forgiveness, she still felt guilty and tearful. The torpid sadness of the evening before, lying on the sofa and watching the ceiling start to spin, had been replaced by something sharper. She watched the news on TV, her own loss receding as the carnage in London unfolded. All day there were graphic updates and more images of the injured. She phoned Toby to ask if the dinner party was still going ahead. She was told that it was. Things have to go on normally, Lorna was told. Later, applying mascara, she started to cry. The void was still inside her, suddenly sore again, but it was also now visible from the TV. Lorna tried to call Suzie, but her phone was turned off.

Back from the Redmarsh dinner party, Lorna found a note on the kitchen table, written in pencil from Austin.

He'd decided to follow Suzie back to London. *Reclamation can wait!* he'd written in big, bold writing. He'd obviously come back to the flat during the evening, packed a few things, and left.

Lorna poured herself a glass of orange juice and flushed her pills down the loo. She'd never had to rely on chemicals before, and wouldn't do so again. She sat down and switched on the TV. She didn't have to work the next day; she didn't have to do anything all day. The HappyMart could do without her, her coursework was almost complete; an honours degree was as good as hers.

It took her some moments to realise that the phone was ringing.

It was Suzie's mother and she was crying. 'Oh God, Lorna, I'm so sorry.' Lorna listened to sniffles, then the phone was passed to Suzie's dad. 'We thought you should know. You're her closest friend.' He sounded tired and angry. 'We've been trying to get hold of you.'

Lorna didn't say anything.

'She was on the King's Cross tube train.' Her father, presumably at the hospital, was speaking over sirens.

Lorna's heart had stopped. The walls of the flat seemed to sway. There was something awake in her stomach and she could feel it uncurl, pushing against her ribcage so she could hardly breathe. She put out an arm to steady myself. 'She's alive but she might not make it, Lorna,' he said.

She said nothing, couldn't breathe. The thing in her stomach was forcing air from her lungs.

Lifting her eyes, her castle was flying effortlessly above its rock. She couldn't speak.

'She got caught in the blast, that's all we know. She's lost a lot of blood. Lorna? Lorna?'

But by then the phone had slipped from her grasp. The creature inside her stomach was growing larger and more venomous. The dark place it inhabited was closing in around her. She couldn't suck in air and needed to be free.

* * *

Lorna had come up against a brick wall. Her memories had come to a full stop. All she could now remember was the push of wind against her face.

'I told you, Lorna, that we regenerated your body at the precise moment you killed yourself.' Irene was looking at her, a cigarette between her fingers. 'At the time, you didn't believe me.'

Lorna had flown from the flat; she hadn't wanted to be inside. She didn't want to be anywhere, except with Suzie. She looked up and down the street, looking for the Porsche, then remembered that it was now in London. At that time of night, the airport and railway station would be closed. London seemed a universe away. Her thoughts had flown apart; she had made things go wrong.

On the pavement, Lorna saw only darkness; a darkness that she had made for herself, and a darkness she had inadvertently created for her friend. She remembered the approaching car's lights, not caring one way or the other what happened. Its impact would offer a kind of escape: an atonement, if not a very good one. She hadn't meant to step off the pavement. She'd stumbled and lost her balance. Then, watching the approaching car, Lorna had felt a sense of judgement. Being run over made no sense, but it also made perfect sense. Not moving offered a solution. Lorna looked up, seeing stars, the breath of the car touching her face.

'Is she okay?' she asked God.

He spoke in a low voice. 'I really don't know, Lorna. News takes a while to reach us.'

'It was my fault.'

God looked pained. 'The people who set off the bombs were responsible, Lorna. Not you.' He looked up at Irene, who put a hand on Lorna's shoulder. 'I don't know if you meant to step in front of the car,' said God softly, 'but once you had, you didn't get out of its way. You neither chose to live nor to die. I told you, I felt sorry for you.'

Lorna was thinking about Suzie; how she'd gallop her horse through waves, how she could jump around for hours and call it dancing. It took her some moments to force her mind back to the wrinkled old man and his beads. 'Why am I here, God?'

'I brought you to Heaven,' said God, 'so that you can make that choice.'

* * *

In a room full of TVs, Lorna saw her life being played out in fuzzy black-and-white. On one TV, she was lying on a beach. On another, she was walking down an Edinburgh street. Each reflected a part of her life: small fragments caught on camera, meaning nothing. Only if you fitted the fragments together did they make some kind of sense. She saw her father on one screen and saw him again on the bridge of a riverboat. Her mum was sitting on a picnic rug, spreading jam onto bread. Suzie was holding up a toilet roll, a puppy frolicking at her feet, and making it seem important. In another, was the inside of a shop and Mike's bulk filling an aisle; in another, a soldier with an assault rifle. Her life had been a blank canvas, now it was daubed with everything that had happened.

She'd chosen to be a lawyer, but could have chosen to do something else. Mr Sullivan had probably been right. She could have chosen Austin; instead, she had rejected him twice. She could have resisted Joe's attentions, and avoided all unpleasantness. But she hadn't. Her mistakes had all been the result of choice, with Suzie's injury now the worst of them. Lorna's eyes were brimming over.

'Irene, you told me that I was dead. You said that I couldn't go back, remember? You said that the dead can't talk to the living.'

Irene shrugged without apology. 'You are, sweetie, a temporal phenomenon. You are dead in one place and alive in another.'

'But you said that my ashes had been scattered.'

'Time is relative, Lorna. God is merely asking you to choose in which place you'd prefer to be dead.'

'Or alive,' said Lorna, a catch in her throat. Her returned memories, ephemeral yet vivid, had opened new horizons. She now felt dormant wings stir against her spine and, if only she could just open her eyes, she could rejoin the real world and try to make things right again.

'Of course,' said God, looking doubtful, 'you don't need to make your mind up now. If you wish, we can give you more time to consider all the ramifications of your decision.'

He was sitting in his big chair. All around were flickering screens; all were of her past. She glimpsed Tom on the rugby field, but it might have been Austin; her dad bent beneath golf clubs, but that could equally have been Joe. Between the images, other images: a mother's anguish, a child in her arms; a US marine cradling a rifle; a London train station, with hurrying commuters and enveloping dark smoke.

'I choose life,' said Lorna.

'Are you sure you wouldn't prefer eternity?' God had made a steeple of his fingers and was looking at her intently.

A wakeful part of her mind knew that this place couldn't exist. Eternity wasn't therefore a real choice. Lorna shook her head.

'Think carefully, young Lorna.'

'I have done, God.'

'No place like home, eh?'

'Something like that, God.'

'The food's better here,' he offered.

'Maybe, but I'd still like to go home.'

'Here, you can be whoever you want to be.'

'I like being me,' she told him. 'I also have a friend to go back to. I *need* to know if she's okay.'

Irene fixed her with a stern look, then mellowed. 'In which case, there is one bit of bad news.'

'Oh?'

Irene had conjured up a huge glass of white wine and soda that she now presented to Lorna. 'Because, sweetie, you get to ride in a spaceship and I know that you don't much like flying.'

Lorna sipped, hearing ice against ice; it was mostly white wine. She drank some, and almost immediately felt a stab of pain in her arm. Lorna realised that God had placed a hand on her shoulder. Behind his head were jigsaw images from the past: faces she remembered, places she had visited. On one screen, Tom's Chinese T-shirt waved damply. On another, her castle floated above its rock.

'Normally, of course, I give all our visitors a task to perform,' said God. He was frowning, unsure of himself. 'Usually, I provide them with some useful insight to take back to Earth, something to advance your technological or medical thinking. In your case, I can't think of a task to give you. You see, you have no scientific aptitude.' One hand was still on her shoulder, the other on his precious beads. 'So I have decided instead to give you a different kind of task.' He paused, looking thoughtful. 'You only get one life, so your task is to promise me one thing, young Lorna. Do something wonderful with yours.'

462

'That's it?'

'That's it,' said God. 'I could, of course, try to teach you about free-electron lasers, but I doubt you'd understand.'

'I wouldn't,' agreed Lorna. 'I'm a lawyer.'

'A most noble profession, I'm sure,' said God, looking doubtful, 'if not a very useful one.' Behind his head, she now noticed that one TV screen was in full colour and sharp focus. It was an image of her and she was in a bed, her head immobile on a pillow. Her mother was at her side, stroking Lorna's hair, and she wanted to tell her mum that she hadn't meant to kill herself, but then realised that she didn't need to because Lorna could hear voices, familiar voices. She wasn't dead and had never been dead, and she could feel herself waking up.

* * *

From Heaven's bridge she was taken downwards to a grey anteroom off Heaven's flight deck and fitted into a cumbersome pressure suit that zipped down her back. Around the walls hung a variety of space suits, like in an abattoir. Lorna shivered; she hadn't expected this. It seemed like a throwback to technologies that Heaven should have long abandoned, remembering old footage of moon landings and astronauts leaping about on its surface. On her feet were bulky red boots that clipped onto the bottom of her bulbous spacesuit.

'This has all been a dream, hasn't it?'

God was standing behind her. Lorna felt ridiculous in the spacesuit, as if she was back wearing a green dressing gown with a cushion stuck inside and Suzie holding her hand. 'If you say so,' said God.

She sat heavily on a bench that occupied the middle of the room. Around her, like headless corpses, hung other white spacesuits. 'It *has* all been a dream,' she said with more conviction, looking at the floor, looking at anything except the spacesuits.

'The truth is what you choose to believe,' replied God, one hand stroking his strings of beads, the other on one of the pressure suits, feeling down its contours.

'Then that's what I believe,' said Lorna, still looking at the floor. 'I've imagined all of this.'

God was looking at her kindly, like her dad used to look. 'Even me?'

'Even you,' said Lorna. 'You couldn't have brought me to Heaven, because Heaven only exists up here.' She manoeuvred one heavy hand to her head and tapped it.

'In which case, young Lorna, that is the truth in which you must believe.' God didn't seem in any way offended, seemingly content to continue tracing his fingers down the outline of the spacesuit. 'The people who hurt your friend believed in a different kind of truth – for them, a truth that justified killing themselves and other people.' Now God did look pained, and shook his head sadly. 'Between those two truths, yours and theirs, an absence of faith does seem the better option.'

'I'm sorry,' she said. 'I just don't believe in you.'

God smiled a little sadly. 'There's no need to be sorry,' he said. 'I didn't ask you to believe in me in the first place.'

Sixty minutes to transition.

Trinity, her voice seeping from every portion of the room.

'Time for you to say your goodbyes,' said God, motioning her to her feet. Then he put a hand on the small of her back and gently pushed her towards a door that had soundlessly opened, and towards the blaze of light that lay beyond.

464

BEGINNING

God's hand was still on the small of her back, propelling Lorna into a light so unexpected and intense that she raised a gloved hand to her eyes to shield them, feeling at once vulnerable and terrified. The sepulchral cathedral of the flight deck had been transformed. On her previous visit, the huge cavern had seemed desolate, its giant flying machines lined up like museum displays, lights turned down low on a place where few of the crew had reason to venture. Now, artificial daylight burned from a hundred sources high on the flight-deck roof; a white and shadowless light that gave the place new purpose, burning and reflecting off polished metal, flaming like stars on the taut hulls of Heaven's spaceships. But that wasn't the only thing that made her stop and gasp, one bulky hand encased in a heavy glove across her mouth. Assembled in a rough semi-circle, and dressed in their best uniforms, was Heaven's crew, Irene slightly in front. Hundreds of smiling faces now turned towards her; and then spontaneous and deafening applause in the enormous cavern of the flight deck.

Lorna had never seen everyone in their finery before; and she now involuntarily put her other hand to her mouth as the noise lapped over and about her, felt tears prickle behind her eyes. Each in tailored blue uniforms, buttoned down the front and golden epaulettes denoting function and rank. On each lapel, the insignia of Heaven: a golden pair of wings. Behind blast-proof windows on the upper level were more faces, each had an earpiece and they were all dressed in light blue jumpsuits; behind them were serried banks of computer consoles behind which sat operatives keying in data. Lorna waddled forwards to be embraced by Irene.

'We thought that we'd give you a proper send-off,' said Irene, speaking loudly over the cacophony of sound. 'I'm just sorry that there wasn't time for a farewell party.' Irene cast a dark glance at God who was carrying a space helmet in both hands. He shrugged and muttered something indistinct. 'There again,' said Irene, 'you've only just got here.'

Lorna was temporarily beyond words. Irene threaded her arm into Lorna's and led her towards the rest of the ship's crew. 'You could have had immortality. A chance to live among the stars. It's what you wished for when you lay dying. Your last thoughts were of a nursery rhyme. Do you remember?'

Lorna shook her head. She remembered looking up and seeing stars, wondering if her brother was looking down and if Suzie was alive. She could recall a needle's prick, her head being strapped into a brace, a sense of the enormity of what lay above and her own insignificance below. But no, she couldn't recall a nursery rhyme.

'But instead, you've chosen life,' said Irene, offering Lorna a warm smile tinged with sadness. 'Another chance to live out the rest of your life. On balance, I suppose, not a bad choice.' Irene's angel wings gleamed brightly on her tunic.

Lorna now saw the Gemini that was being readied. Mobile arc lights had been rigged around its bulk and various umbilical lines were coiled from its wings and flanks. The first time she'd seen it, inert and immobile, she had thought it beautiful but useless; its graceful lines fluting backwards to giant exhausts that would never again feel the emptiness of space. Now, in a clear circle of white light, with crewmen making final preparations for departure, inspection hatches being closed, it had regained purpose; its hyperspace capability bristling with the power of a thousand suns.

'I also get to ride in a spaceship. Not many earthlings get to do that, you know,' she said. One moment, she seemed on the point of waking up and nothing seemed real; the next moment, wakefulness was beyond reach, and everything seemed real. Until then, Lorna had been thinking only of home and whether Suzie had pulled through. But now she could see the enormity of the journey: this wasn't a bus or train to whisk her across town. The hull of the Gemini towered above her. 'It is safe, isn't it, God? Having come this far, I don't want to be splattered across the universe.'

With his ill-fitting tracksuit and strings of beads, God seemed the person least qualified to have a professional opinion. Among them all, only God had forsaken his dress uniform; or maybe not, she thought: perhaps his cream tracksuit *is* now his uniform. She also remembered his beginnings, ferrying miners between distant worlds. He would once have sat at the controls of a Gemini, seen suns rise across dark galaxies and experienced the space-time jump across lightspeed.

God offered her a wan but reassuring smile, arc lights behind his head lending him a halo of divinity. 'This particular space vehicle has made over two thousand transitions. It may be old and venerable, like the rest of us, but it still functions perfectly well. So, yes, you will be absolutely safe, I assure you.'

'I have God's word on it?'

God smiled and bowed slightly from the waist. 'God has spoken, Lorna. I have commanded it to be safe.'

Slightly behind him, Irene dramatically rolled her eyes, which made Lorna smile. 'I also have something for you,' said Irene, conjuring what looked like a golden brooch from a tunic pocket. She held it up for Lorna's inspection.

It was a pair of golden wings, like a butterfly, with the letters HVN embossed on its central point, the same wings that embellished everyone's uniform. Irene pressed the badge to her flightsuit and stood back to admire it. 'You're now truly one of us, Lorna.' Irene gave her wings a quick polish with her tunic sleeve.

Lorna ran a gloved finger across her new badge of honour, once more feeling like an impostor among those who were its real inhabitants.

'You've been in space longer than virtually anybody on Earth,' said Irene, reading her mind, 'and you're also about to become one of the first human beings to travel faster than light. I'd say you've earned them, don't you?'

'I suppose,' conceded Lorna.

'Don't ever suppose!' commanded Irene. 'Just do! That's what you must remember, Lorna, in your new life. Suppose nothing, just get on with it. Cast your soul to the sea. Isn't that right, God?'

After a thoughtful pause, God nodded.

Although Lorna hadn't been in Heaven long enough to get to know the crew, the next minutes were a blur of farewells. She was photographed with a gang of Brad Pitts from Maintenance and a trio of Kate Mosses from Research. She even kissed a few Hugh Grants, but only on the cheek. Asim, one of the few crewmembers she'd actually talked to, deserved a special hug. Clinton was looking uncomfortable without his cigar. There were also a dozen Kate Winslets to say goodbye to, excluding Irene, and as she was passed through the crew, her progress took her ever closer to the giant flank of the Gemini. Now, she could feel its power, sense its antimatter reactors powering up, its banks of lasers generating the energy of a hundred galaxies. It seemed to shimmer, like a wild animal pulling at its leash, the air crackling with its potency. Lorna looked up at it again, smelling oil and static electricity; frightened yet elated; it alone had the power to take her home.

At the thought of home she grew tearful again. It now seemed so close, despite still being billions of miles away, or just a flicker of her eyelids, and to then find herself in a hospital bed, with her mother stroking her hair. All the while, just behind her, with a sheepish grin on his wrinkled face was God. He hadn't said much since her suiting-up and now seemed content merely to nod benignly at members of his crew and whistle tunelessly. His long white hair, still tied in its ponytail with an elastic band, was oddly out of place among the immaculate coiffures of his crew. He twisted and turned Lorna's helmet in his bony hands, looking wistfully at the Gemini's graceful hull.

She didn't know how long it took to say her goodbyes but one minute she was being kissed, hands clapping her shoulders, the next she was again at Irene's side.

'It's time for you to go home, I guess,' said Irene, 'and time for me to have a fag. Maybe,' she added, 'I should give them up. Damnable habit. Maybe you should as well, Lorna.'

Over her shoulder, Lorna saw that the rest of the crew had fallen silent. A few waved. All stood quietly, perhaps considering that her fate might ultimately be theirs. Others would have made this journey, similarly dressed in bulky pressure-suits, forsaking the stars for the vagaries of uncertain mortality. Perhaps, she thought, they're also remembering other farewells, tearful gatherings on the flight deck in their dress uniforms, angels' wings burnished to gleaming gold. In the silence Lorna could now hear the hum of the spaceship's reactors and feel her scalp crawl with its electrical discharge. Like millions of ants on her skin; she shuddered, again feeling frightened.

God had inscribed the word LOVE on her helmet in thick black lettering. He was now proudly holding the helmet towards her, like a primary child showing off his prowess to teacher. 'All flight crew have their surnames on their helmets. Tradition, I suppose, although I can't really remember why. Anyway, young Lorna,' he smiled, 'it's time to turn around and click your heels together.'

She looked down at her ruby red boots and tried to follow God's commandment, her rubber soles squeaking on the floor. 'They don't click,' she said.

Then, from high in the vaulted space of Heaven's largest cathedral, came a metallic voice announcing the imminent departure of her flight and asking for the flight deck to be cleared. A bell sounded and lights in the further extremities of the flight deck were extinguished. Red warning lights flashed on the outer hull. The ship's crew, with waves and shouted farewells, reluctantly turned away and headed for the blast-doors.

Lorna had only one last question. 'It's not important, really it's not, but it's been bothering me. It's just that, well … why did everyone keep calling me *young* Lorna?'

God handed over her helmet. Despite its bulk, it was surprisingly light, and Lorna traced the letters of her name with one gloved finger. An astronaut, she thought, with my own helmet monogrammed personally by God to prove it.

'It was what your parents called you when you were little,' said God, frowning. 'We thought that's what you'd like to be called, didn't we, Irene?' He looked round to Irene for confirmation, who merely shrugged at God and then winked at Lorna. 'You didn't mind, did you?' God seemed genuinely concerned, as if at the moment of parting, he had committed some giant faux pas.

Young Lorna? But, no, it was something else she had

forgotten, despite remembering so much else. A memory blanked from consciousness, a fact made forgettable by its everyday occurrence. 'No, of course I didn't mind ... I was just wondering, that's all.'

At the foot of Gemini's ramp was another figure in a pressure suit. On his helmet was stencilled the word FLINT. God introduced him as Gary, the best pilot in Heaven's arsenal. 'You're in good hands,' he whispered as Lorna hesitated on the ramp, her feet about to leave Heaven for the last time. 'We'll be watching over you, young Lorna,' he added.

God raised his arms wide, an arc light flaming in his hair: an image of eternity, caught in the blessing of an old man. Then he brought his arms forwards and, grinning, gave her a double thumbs-up. Shaking her head in feigned exasperation, Irene took his arm and led him away like a geriatric in a care home, God looking over his shoulder and grinning broadly.

Lorna ascended the ramp and turned briefly at the ship's door. Most of the flight-deck lights had now been extinguished; only the Gemini was illuminated, so that she felt like an actress at the conclusion of a play. Faces were pressed against windows on the upper levels; Lorna, the lone actor on the stage. She did try to bow, but found it impossible in the pressure-suit. Instead, she raised both arms in farewell, then turned her back on Heaven.

From the ship's doorway, the cramped lift took her upwards from the cargo hold to the flight deck. She knew the ship's layout, having had the guided tour from God but, even so, with all the ship's systems now powering up, it seemed a different place, charged with energy, its awesome power designed to shift time and space and meld them to its whim.

Lorna was to occupy the third seat on the flight deck, just behind the captain and his co-pilot, name unknown, who was already strapped into his seat and running through pre-flight checks. He raised a gloved hand in greeting and returned to his checklist. Gary Flint strapped her securely to her seat, buckling belts over her shoulders and between her legs. Then he plugged her suit with communications and air-supply cables and, lastly, set her helmet over her head. This was what Lorna had been dreading, the moment when she was enclosed. She had always hated small spaces; she had been hopeless at hide-and-seek. Lorna could only hide in large and open places, and was always found first. The helmet clicked into place and the visor was lowered.

Sixteen minutes to transition.

Lorna turned to look out the window at her side. The flight deck had emptied; red warning lights rotated at spaces along its great length. Turning her face forwards, she now saw that both pilots were wearing their helmets and that small lights were starting to creep up the main control panel in front of them. Almost like an aeroplane, she thought, stifling conflicting urges to giggle or cry out in panic.

'Gemini, this is Flight Control. Doors to manual.'

'Roger, Flight.'

Fifteen minutes to transition.

Trinity again, warm and sensual and reassuring.

Lorna became aware of the great ship slowly rotating on the flight-deck floor, umbilical lines popping clear and retracting into the decking; the greyhound slipping its leash, its sleek nose now pointing directly at Heaven's outer hull. On Gemini's control panel, lights continued to cascade upwards in subtle shades of red, blue and green. Lorna took a deep breath, hearing it magnified within the suit's confines. Outside the air was shimmering, Gemini's immense electromagnetic fusion drives venting thermal energy into the flight deck.

'Gemini, this is Flight. Level Two systems are online.'

'Roger, Flight. We have sublight integration.'

Lorna listened to the radio chatter as the control lights ascended while, on the flight deck, huge airlock doors began to open. Beyond the doors lay a vast space, the length of the spaceship. At its far end, another set of blast-proofed doors; the final exit to the emptiness beyond. Down the great length of the airlock walls were lines of lights, each flashing red.

Hyperdrive initiated. Telemetry locked. Containment systems secure, despite rodent attack. God above, the things I have to do! Transition in twelve minutes.

Gemini moved slowly into the airlock, while more lights on the control panel lit up. Like a Christmas tree, the pyramid of the panel rose to a single peak just above the line of the cockpit window. Fascinated, Lorna watched as this one last light, white and pure and clear, shone into the darkened interior of the ship. He'd called it starbright, and it had nagged at her.

'Flight, we have hyperdrive integration.'

It could have been God's voice, his bony frame in the captain's seat, thin fingers running across the cockpit control panel. *The best thing that a space-pilot ever sees, Lorna.*

'Roger, Gemini. You are cleared to go.'

'Thank you, Flight.'

Heaven coming here couldn't have just been coincidence, sweetie. Time and space are too infinitely huge for coincidence. My circuits have the power of many billions of your computers so I positively know that for a fact. It's a spooky thought, isn't it? It rather suggests that there is a God, a real God, and that it was him who brought us here.

Lorna now remembered something else. That birthday on North Berwick Law, her world laid at her feet, scampering on the hill's peak. Another year older, another step towards the strange adult world inhabited by her mother, who sat on a tartan picnic rug and who was spreading margarine onto bread. Lorna frowned; she had always thought of that picnic as being a lunchtime affair. But it couldn't have been, or maybe it had lasted for hours, because she had seen a star, bright and pure and clear in the summer sky. Her mum had motioned Lorna to sit beside her, and then told her to close her eyes. A poem, her mother's voice soft in her ears.

Starlight star bright,
The first star I see tonight,
I wish I may, I wish I might,
Have the wish I wish tonight.

Another memory, bent and broken in the road, her upturned face towards the heavens and starlight in her dying eyes. She'd remembered the poem and with her fading breath had tried to mouth it, the young driver pushing something soft under her head. But what had she wished for, her eyes following the path of a shooting star? For life, she remembered. I wished for life and, if not life, then to live among the stars, where God lived. Her mother had said so, that day on the Law, so it had to be true.

Six minutes to transition.

The outer doors opened and, momentarily, Lorna was blinded by the enormity of the panorama. Before her, a sea of stars and swirling galaxies. She realised that she had been holding her breath, and now exhaled raggedly.

'Gemini, this is Flight. Transferring to orbital internal power.'

'Roger, Flight.'

Gary Flint leaned round his seat. 'Ready, Lorna?'

'Not really, no.'

'Don't worry,' he said and touched a gloved hand to the control panel. 'Gemini, coming up to a go for auto-sequence start.'

With a jolt, Lorna saw that they were now moving slowly away from Heaven and she touched the window with a gloved hand, as if trying to hold onto its sanctuary. Faces were peering from exterior observation windows. In one, she thought she saw Irene, but from that distance all Kate Winslets looked the same. Only God was unique, but she couldn't see him.

God often talks complete bollocks, sweetie, but he was right about one thing. In your new life, just do something wonderful. It's as simple as that. Four minutes to transition.

'Gemini, we have T minus six seconds and main engine start, five, four, three, two, one. Booster ignition...'

Mentally, Lorna had also been counting down, a symphony of discordant terrors jostling, then felt a nudge to her chest as the ship's sub-light systems ignited, the wild animal finally untamed.

'Gemini, you are clear of the tower.'

She could now feel, rather than sense, the ship's great power; the antimatter reactors venting an ion plume at near lightspeed in their wake.

Inside her helmet, Lorna heard nothing more than a distant rumble; like a thunderstorm miles and miles away and although she knew that the ship was now accelerating at an unimaginable rate, she felt only brief discomfort, and then the sensation of being in a fast-moving car. She remembered God trying to explain how environmental protection and artificial gravity systems worked, scratching his head and peering at the Gemini's darkened control panel for inspiration before giving up. *All that matters is that they do work,* he'd said eventually, looking doubtful, as he often did.

A good God, she thought, as Gemini banked left and then settled on a new course. Except for the hamsters or, maybe, because of the hamsters. A better God, certainly, than the ones we've invented for you. A God of Love, she thought, touching her helmet for good luck.

Directly ahead, in the myriad of stars that filled the cockpit window, must be Earth. In hyperspace, you can only travel in a straight line. She knew that, perhaps had always known it, ever since Luke Skywalker had drawn his lightsaber, and Darth Vader had scared the young Lorna witless, water lapping at the hull of their riverboat. It hadn't needed God to explain it.

Two minutes to transition.

On the cockpit console, the bright star of her salvation burned bright, the gloved fingers of the two pilots touching a screen here, or a hidden button there. As the ship's velocity increased, she now saw that stars were moving; Gemini thundering across the galaxy towards a quantum leap to another dimension. Inside her helmet, all was peace, except for the laboured sound of her own breathing. She was approaching a new synthesis, another beginning; starlight burned across her helmet's visor.

'Point nine of lightspeed, Lorna,' the co-pilot said quietly, offering Lorna a small smile over his shoulder. They were now at the limit of realspace velocity, the border country between the third and fourth dimensions.

Transition in one minute.

Trinity sounded unusually soulful, or so it seemed to her. Lorna's eyes had become heavy; she was drifting inexorably into sleep. She tried to keep her eyes open, to focus on that one bright light on the console, to claw back memories of other stars, her mother's arms around her shoulders and the possibility of dreams coming true. *Does God live up there?* she'd asked on the Law, that single

476

star hanging still in the evening sky. *Of course, he does, young Lorna. But a long, long way away where we can't see him.*

And then Trinity again. *It's time for you to sleep, my love, and time for me to say a final goodbye.* Lorna felt another push to her chest as Gemini's hyperdrive initiated and the spaceship inched closer to lightspeed. *I have to go now, petal. I'm way behind on the dusting, and there's always someone wanting filet mignon. But I just wanted to say that it was a pleasure to meet you, sweetie.*

Lorna's breathing was shallow; her eyes unwillingly closing, but aware also of total silence. Gemini's sub-light motors had closed down. The final frontier, she thought sleepily; I am about to go where...

Transferring from one thing to another, she now frowned.

Lorna thought that she'd heard Suzie's voice. For a moment, it seemed as if Suzie was standing over her, but maybe not. On the far wall was a green box with a white cross. There seemed to be other figures. There was also a man in a white coat. On his lapel was a badge with the name Dr Flint. Lorna could feel her mother's hand stroking her hair, smell her mother's perfume, hear the rattle of a trolley.

She knew that everything and everyone would have been changed, herself included, but she reminded herself that she was the daughter of a once-great wizard and, perhaps, she would make good decisions from now on, without the burden of her own expectations. She had changed, as everyone does, but in ways so subtle that she hadn't been aware of them. Waves that knocked her over, those she could feel. Small wavelets, like gossamer wings, were more insubstantial. But they were still able to beat gently against her iron, slowly bending her shape; making her different. She hadn't felt those, or the small indentations that they'd left. The patina of her resolve had changed, but she hadn't felt it. Outwardly, she was who she had always been, so convinced by her future; inwardly, small wings had been hitting soft metal and, over years, changing her from one thing to another.

She blinked but everything was blurred. Then she realised that it wasn't just her vision; constellations of stars were changing from fixed points to streamers of light. Out of the darkness of space was coming a new and blinding light, Gemini crossing the dimensional frontier to hyperspace. Her eyelids flickered, then closed, then opened.

Lorna barely heard Trinity's final parting, like a whisper on the breeze. One word, from a long, long way away.

Transition.

End

One

There have been two moments in my life when everything changed. Moments when things could have gone either way. Moments when I had to make a choice.

The first occurred when, after another disruptive day at school, I stood in front of my head teacher, Mrs De Winter. I'd done the sullen silence thing and waited for expulsion, because I was long past three strikes and you're out. It didn't happen.

Instead she said, with a strange urgency, 'Madeleine, you cannot let your home circumstances define your entire life. You are intelligent – you have abilities of which you are not even aware. This is the only chance you will ever have. I can help you. Will you allow me to do so?'

No one had ever offered to help me before. Something flickered inside me, but distrust and suspicion die hard.

She said softly, 'I can help you. Last chance, Madeleine. Yes or no?'

No words came. I was trapped in a prison of my own making.

'Yes or no?'

I took a huge breath and said yes.

She handed me a book, a notepad, and two pens.

'We'll start with Ancient Egypt. Read the first two chapters and Chapter Six. You must learn to assimilate, edit, and present information. I want 1500 words on the precise nature of ma'at. By Friday.'

'Is this a punishment?'

'No, Madeleine. This is an opportunity.'

'But … you know I can't take this home.'

'You can use the school library and leave your stuff there. Miss Hughes is expecting you.'

That was the first moment.

The second one came ten years later. An email – right out of the blue:

My dear Madeleine,

I am sure you will be surprised to hear from me, but I have to say that, since you left the University of Thirsk, I have followed your career with great interest and some pride. Congratulations on your academic record at Thirsk, Doctor Maxwell. It is always gratifying to see a former pupil do so well, particularly one who laboured under so many difficulties in her early years I am writing now with details of a job opportunity I think you will find extremely interesting.

You will be aware, from your time at Thirsk, of the existence of a sister site – the St Mary's Institute of Historical Research – an organisation I think would appeal to anyone who, like you, prefers a less structured existence. Their work inclines more towards the practical side of historical research. This is all I can say at the moment.

The Institute is located just outside Rushford, where I now reside, and interviews are on the fourth of next month. Do you think you would be interested? I feel it would be just the thing for you, so I do hope you will consider it. Your travels and archaeological experience will stand you in good stead and I really think you are exactly the type of person for whom they are looking.

The pay is terrible and the conditions are worse, but it's a wonderful place to work – they have some talented

people there. If you are interested, please click on the link
below to set up a possible interview.

Please do not reject this opportunity out of hand. I know
you have always preferred to work abroad, but given the
possibility that America may close its borders again and
the fragmentation within the EU, perhaps now is the time
to consider a slightly more settled lifestyle.
    With best regards,
    Sibyl De Winter

I always said my life began properly the day I walked
through the gates of St Mary's. The sign read:

    University of Thirsk.
    Institute of Historical Research.
    St Mary's Priory Campus.
    Director: Dr Edward G. Bairstow BA MA PhD FRHS
    I rang the buzzer and a voice said, 'Can I help you,
miss?'
    'Yes, my name's Maxwell. I have an appointment with
Doctor Bairstow at 2.00 p.m.'
    'Go straight up the drive and through the front door.
You can't miss it.'
    A bit over-optimistic there, I thought. I once got lost
on a staircase.
    At the front door, I signed in and was politely wanded
by a uniformed guard, which was a little unusual for an
educational establishment. I did my best to look harmless
and it must have worked because he escorted me through
the vestibule into the Hall. Waiting for me stood Mrs De
Winter, who looked no different from the last time I saw
her, the day she took me off to Thirsk. The day I got away
from that invention of the devil – family life.
    We smiled and shook hands.

'Would you like a tour before the interview?'

'You work here?'

'I'm loosely attached. I recruit occasionally. This way please.'

The place was huge. The echoing central Hall was part of the original building with medieval narrow windows. At the far end, an ornate oak staircase with ten shallow steps and a broad half landing branched off left and right to a gallery running round all four sides of the hall.

Various rooms opened off this gallery. Through the open doors, I could see an entire suite which seemed to be devoted to costumes and equipment. People trotted busily with armfuls of cloth and mouths full of pins. Garments in varying stages of completion hung from hangers or from tailor's dummies. The rooms were bright, sunny, and full of chatter.

'We do a lot of work for film and television,' explained Mrs Enderby, in charge of Wardrobe. She was small and round, with a sweet smile. 'Sometimes they only want research and we send them details of appropriate costumes and materials, but sometimes we get to make them too. This one, for instance, is for an historical adaptation of the life of Charles II and the Restoration. Lots of bosoms and sex obviously, but I've always thought Charles to be a much underrated monarch. This dress is for Nell Gwynn in her "orange" period and that one for the French strumpet, Louise de Kérouaille.'

'It's lovely,' I said softly, carefully not touching the material. 'The detail is superb. Sadly, it's a bit modern for me.'

'Dr Maxwell is Ancient History,' said Mrs De Winter. Apologetically, I thought.

'Oh dear,' sighed Mrs Enderby. 'Well, it's not all bad news, I suppose. There'll be drapery and togas and tunics, of course, but even so…' She tailed off. I had obviously disappointed her.

From there, we moved next door to Professor Rapson, in charge of Research and Development. He was so typically the eccentric professor that initially I suspected a bit of a wind-up. Super-tall and super-thin, with a shock of Einstein hair, his big beaky nose reminded me of the front end of a destroyer. And he had no eyebrows, which should have been a bit of clue really; but he smiled kindly and invited us in for a closer look at his cluttered kingdom. I caught a tantalising glimpse of a buried desk, books everywhere and, further on, a laboratory-type set up.

'Dr Maxwell hasn't had her interview yet,' said Mrs De Winter in rather a warning tone of voice.

'Oh, oh, right, yes, no, I see,' he said, letting go of my elbow. 'Well, this is what I tend to think of as "practical" history, my dear. The secret of Greek Fire? We're on it. How did a Roman chariot handle? We'll build you one and you can find out for yourself. What range does a trebuchet have? Exactly how far can you fling a dead cow? How long does it take to pull someone's brains out through their nose? Any questions like that then you come to me and we'll find your answers for you! That's what we do!'

One of his expansively waving arms caught a beaker of something murky that could easily have been embalming fluid, the Elixir of Life, or Socrates' hemlock and knocked it off the workbench to shatter on the floor. Everyone stepped back. The liquid bubbled, hissed, and looked as if it was eating through the floor. I could see many other such damp patches.

'Oh, my goodness! Jamie! Jamie! Jamie, my boy, just nip downstairs, will you? My compliments to Dr Dowson and tell him it's coming through his ceiling again!'

A young lad nodded amiably, got up from his

workbench, and threaded his way through the tangle of half-completed models, unidentifiable equipment, tottering piles of books, and smudged whiteboards. He grinned at me as he passed. In fact, they all seemed very friendly. The only slightly odd thing was Mrs De Winter preceding every introduction with the warning that I hadn't had the interview yet. People smiled and shook hands but nowhere did I get to venture beyond the doorway.

I met Mrs Mack who presided over the kitchens. Meals, she informed me, were available twenty-four hours a day. I tried to think why an historical establishment would keep such hours but failed. Not that I was complaining. I can eat twenty-four hours a day, no problem.

The bar and lounge next door were nearly the same size as the dining room, showing an interesting grasp of priorities. Everything was shabby from heavy use and lack of money, but the bar was particularly so.

Further down the same corridor, a small shop sold paperbacks, chocolate, toiletries, and other essential items.

I fell in love with the Library, which, together with the Hall, obviously constituted the heart of the building. High ceilings made it feel spacious and a huge fireplace made it cosy. Comfortable chairs were scattered around and tall windows all along one wall let the sunshine flood in. As well as bays of books they had all the latest electronic information retrieval systems, study areas, and data tables and, through an archway, I glimpsed a huge archive.

'You name it, we've got it somewhere,' said Doctor Dowson, the Librarian and Archivist who appeared to be wearing a kind of sou'wester. 'At least until that old fool upstairs blows us all sky high. Do you know we sometimes have to wear hard hats? I keep telling Edward he should house him and his entire team of madmen on the other side of Hawking if we're to have any chance of survival at all!'

'Dr Maxwell hasn't had the interview yet,' interrupted Mrs De Winter and he subsided into vague muttering. In Latin. I stared somewhat anxiously at the ceiling, which did indeed appear to be blotched and stained, but at least nothing seemed to be eating its way through the fabric of this probably listed building.

'Did they tell you?' he demanded. 'Last year his research team attempted to reproduce the Russian guns at the Charge of the Light Brigade, miscalculated the range, and demolished the Clock Tower?'

'No,' I said, answering what I suspected was a rhetorical question. 'I'm sorry I missed that.'

I was moved firmly along.

We stopped at the entrance to a long corridor, which seemed to lead to a separate, more modern part of the campus. 'What's down there?'

'That's the hangar where we store our technical plant and equipment. There's no time to see it at the moment; we should be heading to Dr Bairstow's office.'

I was still thinking about the Crimean War and the disasters of the Battle of Balaclava when I realised someone was speaking to me. He was a man of medium height, with dark hair and an ordinary face made remarkable by brilliant, light blue-grey eyes. He wore an orange jump suit.

'I'm so sorry,' I said. 'I was thinking about the Crimea.'

He smiled. 'You should fit right in here.'

'Chief, this is Dr Maxwell.'

'I haven't had the interview yet,' I said, just to let them know I'd been paying attention.

His mouth twitched at one corner.

'Dr Maxwell, this is our Chief Technical Officer, Leon

Farrell.'

I stuck out my hand. 'Pleased to meet you, Mr Farrell.'

'Most people just call me Chief, Doctor.' He reached out slowly and we shook hands. His hand felt warm, dry, and hard with calluses. Working man's hands.

'Welcome to St Mary's.'

Mrs De Winter tapped her watch. 'Dr Bairstow will be waiting.'

So, this was Dr Edward Bairstow. His back was to the window as I entered. I saw a tall, bony man, whose fringe of grey hair around his head rather reminded me of the ring of feathers around a vulture's neck. Away off to the side with a scratchpad in front of her sat a formidable-looking woman in a smartly tailored suit. She looked elegant, dignified, and judgmental. Dr Bairstow leaned heavily on a stick and extended a hand as cold as my own.

'Dr Maxwell, welcome. Thank you for coming.' His quiet, clear voice carried immense authority. Clearly he was not a man who had to raise his voice for attention. His sharp eyes assessed me. He gave no clue as to his conclusions. I'm not usually that good with authority, but this was definitely an occasion on which to tread carefully.

'Thank you for inviting me, Dr Bairstow.'

'This is my PA, Mrs Partridge. Shall we sit down?'

We settled ourselves and it began. For the first hour, we talked about me. I got the impression that having no acknowledged next of kin and a lack of personal ties constituted a point in my favour. He already had details of my qualifications and we talked for a while about the post-grad stuff in archaeology and anthropology and my work experience and travels. He was particularly interested in how I found living in other countries and amongst other cultures. How easy was it for me to pick up languages and make myself understood? Did I ever feel isolated amongst other communities? How did I get around? How long did I take to become assimilated?

'Why did you choose history, Dr Maxwell? With all the exciting developments in the space programme over the last ten years and the Mars Project in its final stages, what made you choose to look backwards instead of forwards?'

Pausing, I arranged and edited my thoughts. I was nine. It had been a bad Christmas. I sat in the bottom of my wardrobe. Something unfamiliar dug into my bottom. I wriggled about and pulled out a small book – *Henry V and the Battle of Agincourt*. I read and re-read it until it nearly fell apart. I never found out where it came from. That little book awoke my love of history. I still had it: the one thing I had saved from my childhood. Studying history opened doors to other worlds and other times and this became my escape and my passion. I don't ever talk about my past so I replied with three short, impersonal sentences.

From there we moved on to St Mary's. Dr Bairstow gave the impression of a large, lively, and unconventional organisation. I found myself becoming more and more interested. There wasn't any particular moment I could identify, but as he talked on, I began to feel I was missing something. This was a big campus. They had a Security Section and twenty-four-hour meals and plant and equipment and a Technical Department. He paused for a moment, shuffled a few papers, and asked me if I had any questions.

'Yes,' I said. 'What's Hawking?'

He didn't answer but pushed himself back slightly from his desk and looked across at Mrs Partridge. She put down her scratchpad and left the room. I watched her go and then looked back at him. The atmosphere had changed.

He said, 'How do you know about Hawking?'

'Well,' I said, slowly. 'It's not common knowledge of course, but ...' and let the sentence die away. He stared at me and the silence lengthened. 'It just seems strange that a hangar in an historical research centre is named after the famous physicist.'

Still no response, but now I wasn't going to say anything either. Silence holds no fears for me. I never feel the urge to fill it as so many other people do. We gazed at each other for a while and it could have been interesting, but at this moment, Mrs Partridge re-entered, clutching a file, which she put in front of Dr Bairstow. He opened it and spread the papers across his desk.

'Dr Maxwell, I don't know what you've been told, but perhaps you could tell me what you do know.'

He'd called my bluff.

'Absolutely nothing,' I said. 'I heard the name mentioned and wondered. I'm also curious about the large numbers of staff here. Why do you need security or technicians? And why do people need to know I haven't had "the interview"? What's going on here?'

'I'm quite prepared to tell you everything you want to know, but first I must inform you that unless you sign these papers, I shall be unable to do so. Please be aware these documents are legally binding. The legal jargon may seem obscure, but, make no mistake, if you ever divulge one word of what I am about to tell you now, then you will spend the next fifteen years, at least, in an establishment the existence of which no civil liberties organisation is even aware. Please take a minute to think very carefully before proceeding.'

Thinking carefully is something that happens to other people. 'Do you have a pen?'

The obliging Mrs Partridge produced one and I signed

and initialled an enormous number of documents. She took the pen back off me, which just about summed up our relationship.

'And now,' he said, 'we will have some tea.'

By now, afternoon had become early evening. The interview was taking far longer than a simple research job warranted. Clearly it was not a simple research job. I felt a surge of anticipation. Something exciting was about to happen.

He cleared his throat. 'Since you have not had the sense to run for the hills, you will now have the "other" tour.'

'And this is the "other" interview?'

He smiled and stirred his tea.

'Have you ever thought, instead of relying on archaeology, unreliable accounts and, let's face it, guesswork, how much better it would be if we could actually return to any historical event and witness it for ourselves? To be able to say with authority, "Yes, the Princes in the Tower were alive at the end of Richard's reign. I know because I saw them with my own eyes."'

'Yes,' I agreed. 'It would; although I can think of a few examples where such certainty would not be welcomed.'

He looked up sharply.

'Such as?'

'Well, a certain stable in Bethlehem for instance. Imagine if you pitched up with your Polaroid and the innkeeper flung open the door and said, "Come in. You're my only guests and there's plenty of room at the inn!" That would put the cat amongst the pigeons.'

'An understatement. But you have nevertheless grasped the situation very clearly.'

'So,' I said, eyeing him closely, 'maybe it's good there's no such thing as time travel.'

He raised his eyebrows slightly.

'Or to qualify further, no such thing as public-access time travel.'

'Exactly. Although the phrase "time travel" is so sci-fi. We don't do that. Here at St Mary's we *investigate major historical events in contemporary time.*'

Put like that, of course, it all made perfect sense.

'So tell me, Dr Maxwell, if the whole of history lay before you like a shining ribbon, where would you go? What would you like to witness?'

'The Trojan War,' I said, words tumbling over each other. 'Or the Spartans' stand at Thermopylae. Or Henry at Agincourt. Or Stonehenge. Or the pyramids being built. Or see Persepolis before it burned. Or Hannibal getting his elephants over the Alps. Or go to Ur and find Abraham, the father of everything.' I paused for breath. 'I could do you a wish list.'

He smiled thinly. 'Perhaps one day I shall ask you for one.'

He set down his cup. With hindsight, I can see how he was feeling his way through the interview, summing me up, drip-feeding information, watching my reactions. I must have done something right, because he said, 'As a matter of interest, if you were offered the opportunity to visit one of the exciting events listed, would you take it?'

'Yes.'

'Just like that? Some people feel it incumbent to enquire about safe returns. Some people laugh. Some people express disbelief.'

'No,' I said slowly. 'I don't disbelieve. I think it's perfectly possible. I just didn't know it was possible right now.'

He smiled, but said nothing, so I soldiered on. 'What happens if you can't get back?'

He looked at me pityingly. 'Actually, that's the least of

494

the problems.'

'Oh?'

'The technology has been around for some time. The biggest problem now is History itself.'

Yes, that made everything clear. But as Lisa Simpson once said, 'It is better to remain silent and be thought a fool than to open your mouth and remove all doubt.' So I remained silent.

'Think of History as a living organism, with its own defence mechanisms. History will not permit anything to change events that have already taken place. If History thinks, even for one moment, that that is about to occur, then it will, without hesitation, eliminate the threatening virus. Or historian, as we like to call them.

'And it's easy. How difficult is it to cause a ten-ton block of stone to fall on a potentially threatening historian observing the construction of Stonehenge? Another cup?'

'Yes, please,' I said, impressed with his sangfroid and equally determined not to be outdone.

'So,' he said, handing me a cup. 'Let me ask you again. Suppose you were offered the opportunity to visit sixteenth-century London to witness, say, the coronation parade of Elizabeth I —it's not all battlefields and blood – would you still want to go?'

'Yes.'

'You understand very clearly that this would be on an observation and documentation basis only? Interaction of any kind is not only extremely unwise, it is usually strictly forbidden.'

'If I was to be offered any such opportunity, I would understand that very clearly.'

'Please be honest, Dr Maxwell, is this admirable calm because deep down, very deep down, you think I'm clearly insane and this is going to be one to tell in the pub tonight?'

'Actually, Dr Bairstow, deep down, very deep down, I'm having a shit-hot party.'

He laughed.

Waiting in Mrs Partridge's office sat the quiet, dark man with the startling eyes I'd met on the stairs.

'I'll leave you with the Chief,' Dr Bairstow said, gathering up some papers and data cubes. 'You're in for an interesting evening, Dr Maxwell. Enjoy.'

We left the office and headed down the long corridor I'd noticed before. I experienced the oddest sensation of entering into another world. The windows, set at regular intervals along one side, cast pools of sunlight along the floor and we passed from light to dark, from warm to cool, from this world into another. At the end of the corridor was a key-coded door.

We entered a large foyer area with another set of big doors opposite.

'Blast doors,' he said, casually.

Of course, what was I thinking? Every historical research centre needs blast doors. On my right, a flight of stairs led upwards with a large, hospital-sized lift alongside. 'To Sick Bay,' he said. On the left, a corridor with a few unlabelled doors disappeared into the gloom.

'This way,' he said. Did the man never say more than two or three words together?

The big doors opened into a huge, echoing, hangar-style space. I could see two glassed-in areas at the far end.

'Those are offices. One for IT,' he gestured at the left room. 'And one for us technicians.' He gestured right. An overhead gantry ran down one side with three or four blue jump-suited figures leaning on the rail. They appeared to be waiting for something.

'Historians,' he said, following my stare. 'They wear blue. Technicians wear orange, IT is in black, and

Security wears green. Number Three is due back soon. This is the welcoming committee.'

'That's ... nice,' I said.

He frowned. 'It's a dangerous and difficult job. There's no support structure for what we do. We have to look after each other, hence the welcoming committee; to show support and to talk them down.'

'Down from what?'

'From whatever happened to the crew on this assignment.'

'How do you know something happened?'

He sighed. 'They're historians. Something always happens.'

Ranged down each side of the hangar stood two rows of raised plinths. Huge, thick, black cables snaked around them and coiled off into dim recesses. Some plinths were empty; others had small hut-like structures squatting on them. Each was slightly different in size or shape and each one looked like a small, dingy shack, stone-built, flat-roofed with no windows; the sort of structure that could be at home anywhere from Mesopotamian Ur to a modern urban allotment. Prop a rickety, hand-made ladder against a wall and with a broken wheel by the door and a couple of chickens pecking around, they would be invisible.

'And these are?' I asked, gesturing.

He smiled for the first time. 'These are our base of operations. We call them pods. When on assignment, our historians live and work in these. Numbers One and Two.' He pointed. 'We usually use them as simulators and for training purposes, because they're small and basic. Pod Three is due back anytime now. Pod Five is being prepped to go out. Pod Six is out. Pod Eight is also out.'

'Where are Pods Four and Seven?'

He said quietly, 'Lost.' In the silence, I could almost

hear the dust motes dancing in the shafts of sunlight.

'When you say "lost," do you mean you don't know where they are, or they never came back for some reason?'

'Either. Or both. Four went to twelfth-century Jerusalem as part of an assignment to document the Crusades. They never reported back and all subsequent rescue attempts failed. Seven jumped to early Roman Britain, St Albans, and we never found them either.'

'But you looked?'

'Oh yes, for weeks afterwards. We never leave our people behind. But we never found them, or their pods.'

'How many people did you lose?'

'In those two incidents, five historians altogether. Their names are on the Boards in the chapel.' He saw my look of confusion. 'They're our Roll of Honour for those who don't come back, or die, or both. Our attrition rate is high. Did Dr Bairstow not mention this?'

'He …' I was going to ask how high, but a light began flashing over the plinth marked Three. Orange figures appeared from nowhere it seemed, lugging umbilicals, cables, flatbeds and the tools of their trade. And quietly, with no fuss, no fanfare, Pod Three materialised on its plinth.

Nothing happened.

I looked up at the Chief. 'Um …'

'We don't go in. They come out.'

'Why?'

'They need to decontaminate. You know, plague, smallpox, cholera, that sort of thing. We shouldn't go in until they've done that.'

'But what if they're injured?'

At that moment, the door opened and a voice shouted, 'Medic!'

Orange technicians parted like the Red Sea and two

medics trotted down the hangar. They disappeared into the pod.

'What's happening? Who's in there? Where have they been?'

'That would be Lower and Baverstock, returning from early 20th-century China, the Boxer Rebellion. It looks as if they require medical attention, but not seriously.'

'How do you know?'

'When you've seen as many returns as we have then you get a feel for it. They'll be fine.'

We both stood in silence watching the door until eventually two people, a man and a woman, dressed in oriental clothing, limped out. One had a dressing over one eye and the other's arm was strapped up. They both looked up at the gantry and waved. The blue people waved and shouted insults. They and the medics headed off. Orange technicians swarmed around the pod.

'Would you like to have a look?'

'Yes, please.'

Close up, the pod looked even more anonymous and unimposing than it had from the other end of the hangar.

'Door,' he said and a battered-looking, wooden-looking door swung soundlessly open. After the enormous hangar, the inside of the pod seemed small and cramped.

'The toilet and shower room are in there,' he said, pointing to a partitioned corner. 'Here we have the controls.' A console with an incomprehensible array of read-outs, flashing lights, dials, and switches sat beneath a large, wall-mounted screen. The external cameras now showed only a view of the hangar. Two scuffed and uncomfortable looking swivel seats were fixed to the floor in front of the controls.

'The computer can be operated manually or voice activated if you want someone to talk to. There are lockers around the walls with all the equipment required for your assignment. Sleeping modules here pull out when needed. This pod can sleep up to three reasonably comfortably, four at a push.'

Bunches of cables ran up the walls to disappear into a tiled ceiling.

In amongst this welter of slightly scruffy but undoubtedly high-tech equipment, I was amazed to see a small kettle and two mugs nestling quietly on a shelf under a rather large first aid locker.

'Yes,' he said, resigned. 'Show me a cup of tea and I'll show you at least two historians attached to it.'

The tiny space smelled of stale people, cabbage, chemicals, hot electrics, and damp carpet, with an underlying whiff from the toilet. I would discover all pods smelt the same and that historians joke that techies take the smell then build the pods around it.

'How does it work?'

He just looked at me. OK then, stupid question.

'What now?'

'Is there anything else you would like to see?'

'Yes, everything.'

So I got the 'other' tour. We went to Security where green-clad people were checking weapons and equipment, peering at monitors, drinking tea, running around, and shouting at each other.

'Is there a problem?' I asked.

'No, I'm afraid we're a noisy bunch. I hope you weren't expecting hallowed halls of learning.'

I met Major Guthrie, tall with dark blond hair, busy doing something. He broke off to stare at me.

'Can you shoot? Have you ever fired a weapon? Can you ride? Can you swim? How fit are you?'

'No. No. Yes. Yes. Not at all.'

He paused and looked me up and down. 'Could you

kill a man?'

I looked him up and down. 'Eventually.'

He smiled reluctantly and put out his hand. 'Guthrie.'

'Maxwell.'

'Welcome.'

'Thank you.'

'I shall be watching your progress with great interest.'

That didn't sound good.

We finished with a tour of the grounds, which were very pleasant if you discounted the odd scorch mark on the grass and the blue swans. Even as I opened my mouth to ask, there was a small bang from the second floor and the windows rattled.

'Hold on,' said Chief Farrell. 'I'm duty officer this week and I want to see if the fire alarms go off.'

They didn't.

'That's good, isn't it?' I said.

He sighed. 'No, it just means they've taken the batteries out again.'

This really was my sort of place.

The Chronicles of St Mary's

The Nothing Girl

Known as The Nothing Girl because of her stutter, disregarded by her family, isolated and alone, Jenny Dove's life is magically transformed by the appearance of Thomas, a mystical golden horse only she can see. Under his loving guidance, Jenny acquires a husband – the charming and chaotic Russell Checkland – together with an omnivorous donkey and The Cat From Hell.

Jenny's life will never be the same again, but a series of 'accidents' leads her to wonder for how long she will be allowed to enjoy it.

Hailed as a fairy tale for adults, Jodi Taylor brings all her comic writing skills to a heart-warming and delightful story.

The Sphinx Scrolls

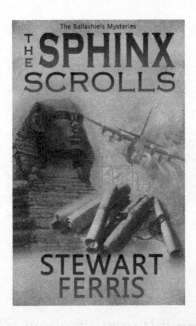

Mayan legends tell of a location where the secret to surviving the end of the world may be found. One part of that legend is recorded on a stone tablet in the dusty attic of Lord 'Ratty' Ballashiels' crumbling manor. The other twin part disappeared from a Berlin museum when the Nazis took power. When Ratty seems about to sell his tablet to the adopted son of Josef Mengele, his friend, the archaeologist Ruby Towers, is appalled.

Soon it is clear that more than archaeology is at stake. The quest to rescue historic Central American artefacts becomes a race to prevent an apocalyptic threatwhen Ruby discovers that the ancients have set in motion something that will threaten the world today.

For more information about **Charlie Laidlaw**

and other **Accent Press** titles

please visit

www.accentpress.co.uk